Waking in Dreamland

Jody Lynn Nye

BAEN

WAKING IN DREAMLAND

A Baen Books Original

Baen Publishing Enterprises
P.O. Box 1403
Riverdale, NY 10471

ISBN: 0-671-87875-1

Cover art by Stephen Hickman

First printing, May 1998

Distributed by Simon & Schuster
1230 Avenue of the Americas
New York, NY 10020

Printed in the United States of America

WHEN YOU DREAM OF FALLING IN DREAMLAND . . . YOU DON'T WAKE UP!

Roan flew high over the Dreamland, his arms outstretched, feeling the cool wind in his face. Thousands of feet below him, the landscape spread out in glorious panorama.

How long this glorious flight would last he didn't know, but he hoped he could get most of the way to the capital before he landed. Flight dreams were a rare treat, but so chancy. He held his arms out on the wind, pleading with the Sleepers to let the influence carry him all the way home. He had only to cross the Nightmare Forest, and he'd be home to tell it.

Roan felt the familiar uneasiness as the green land passing beneath him slowly turned a sickly gray. He shuddered as if the nearly palpable miasma of darkness the forest exuded could reach so high. Roan willed whatever benevolent agency that was carrying him through the air to hurry him over it and away.

As if reading his thoughts, a clawed, skeletal hand made of murky green mist stretched upward a thousand feet from the forest, straining toward him. His heart in his throat, Roan rolled to one side on the air, away from the clasp of the bony fingers—straight into an influence he'd failed to sense in the air just ahead of him. The invisible platform of air that had carried him safely a thousand miles dropped out from beneath him.

Roan sought a solid handhold, but his hands closed on nothingness. The land zoomed up toward him at a distressing rate of speed. The sleeper dreaming him must be looking the other way. If he hit the ground from such a height the fall was bound to be fatal.

"Wake up!" he shouted over the whistling wind, praying for any sleeper to hear him. "Wake up! I'm falling!"

Baen Books by Jody Lynn Nye

The Death of Sleep (with Anne McCaffrey)
The Ship Who Won (with Anne McCaffrey)
The Ship Errant
Don't Forget Your Spacesuit, Dear (editor)

To Maxwell,
from his auntie

Book One of
The Dreamland

Chapter 1

Roan flew high over the Dreamland, his arms outstretched on the wind. He enjoyed the feeling of the cool wind in his face and enveloping his long body like a soft feather pillow. Roan reveled in the ease of high flight. Thousands of feet below him, the landscape spread out in glorious panorama. It made him feel like an angel or a demigod to be able to look down upon the rolling green headlands. He breathed in the clear air, light as light, heady as moonglow.

Streaks of gray-brown woods gave way to the sweet, pale gold of cropland. Roan felt the cold tickle him like a feather as he passed over the Catalept Mountains, second highest massif in the Dreamland after the great Mysteries that ringed the continent. The Catalepts were tricolored from their white snowcaps, down sable slopes that turned brighter and brighter green as they descended toward the protected plain in the central province of Celestia where the capital city of Mnemosyne lay. The Catalepts parted to allow passage of the Lullay River, the imperious stream that refused to permit obstructions in its course. Both sides of the wide, straight, silver band were jeweled with clusters of villages. Fifteen hundred leagues behind him to the south was the border of the nearest province, Somnus. Having slogged that way on foot on the outward journey—indeed, on many outward and inward journeys across the Dreamland on behalf of the king—he was delighted to be able to fly over it as easily as any bird. Roan turned and followed the Lullay, rejoicing when he saw the curved serif foot of the S in Celestia, his home province. He was back at the center of the world. He was nearly home.

The Lullay formed part of the boundary between Celestia

and the provinces that surrounded it. The great river spiraled in from its source in the mountain ridge at the far north border of the Dreamland, making one and one half turns until it wound tightly around Celestia, the central province and capital, entering it along a straight path from the south. In the distance the river pointed toward a bright spot like a diamond in the exact center of the Dreamland. It was the Night Lily Lake, which lay just north of the Castle of Dreams.

On both sides of the Lullay, here and at the border of Somnus, plenty of bridges of every description spanned the deep chasm. They were used daily by travelers, but had been built chiefly as means to escape from province to province in case of natural disaster or Changeover. Such bridges also spanned the deep ravines that marked the borders between each of the other provinces in the Dreamland, where each of the seven individual realms was dreamed by a different Sleeper. The great Collective Unconscious, like the railway bridges, bound them all together.

Of all the Creative Ones whose influences were felt in the Dreamland, the seven Sleepers were the most important. Roan had learned his history lessons in school. The Sleepers' dreams formed the foundation of the Dreamland's seven provinces in which all other dreaming minds interacted. No one knew the Seven's names. All that could be gleaned about the physical world in which They lived their waking lives was through the images and objects reflected and made real in the Dreamland, and even those were colored by each Sleeper's individual perception. Over the centuries, Dreamish philosophers and academicians had speculated about what was real and what hallucination, fantasy, or hope. Conventional wisdom suggested that anything that appeared in all seven provinces probably existed in the Waking World. Bicycles, horses, and trains were real. Clothes and shoes and houses were matters of fact. Television seemed too far unlikely to be real, although Roan saw more aerials sprout from roofs every day. Like all other innovations in the Waking World, such things only became common to the Dreamland when they were common to the Collective Unconscious.

The great Seven had not remained the same throughout history, that he knew. Periodically, an enormous upheaval occurred, known as a Changeover, heralding the departure of one Sleeper and the advent of one who would take its place. Roan didn't know if Changeovers happened because the Sleepers died, or if they awoke, or if they felt it was time to let another influence shape the Dreamland. Even the royal ministries of History and Continuity had not made their minds up about it. In the past, Roan knew, there had been provinces that seemed distorted when compared with others. The current Seven had minds that imbued their dreams with beauty and proportion.

A gust of wind hit him in the face, and his stomach lurched up into his throat as the air supporting him parted and dropped him toward the ground. Roan clutched for a handhold. He shot out spokes of his own influence into the stuff of the air to steady him on its surface. In a breathless moment, he stabilized his flight again, and lay flat, panting. He'd only fallen a few hundred feet. How long this glorious flight would last he didn't know, but he hoped he could get most of the way to the capital before he landed. Flight dreams were a rare treat, but so chancy. He gazed down, determined to enjoy himself while it lasted, and to get his bearings in case he was forced to land.

The broad green plains of Celestia divided below him into forests and fields, hills and marshes, towns and lakes. A network of narrow white roads lay etched upon the terrain, curling lovingly around the foot of hills then dashing boldly up and down rolling green meadows. The twin silver streaks of railway tracks followed the curve of the land at some thirty paces distance from the roads. Roan guessed that he wasn't far from Nod, a small town to the south of Mnemosyne. He held his arms out on the wind, pleading with the Sleepers to let the influence carry him all the way home.

At last, he could see the tall, white spires of the Castle of Dreams, symbol of the collective unconscious of all beings. The palace gleamed in the sun above the sprawling, busy mosaic of color that was Mnemosyne. Roan felt a surge of affection for his city. He loved exploring the wilderness of the Dreamland, but he was always glad to return home to the bustle and business of a million people living side by side. He had good news for the king. He had only to cross the

Nightmare Forest, and he'd be home to tell it. Roan felt the familiar uneasiness as the green land beneath him slowly turned a sickly gray.

Roan overflew scrubby, stunted trees, shuddering a little as if the nearly palpable miasma of darkness the forest exuded could reach so high. He'd been terrified of the Nightmare since he was a child. The forest was as much a state of mind as a physical entity. A Sleeper created the main structure of a province, but the land was affected throughout by the dreams of countless other minds from the Waking World, as if they added embroidery to that vast tapestry. The lesser sleepers created people, animals, and things that interacted with one another in the Collective Unconscious. Their fears seemed to congregate in gray places like this, filling it with dread even for the actual inhabitants of the Dreamland. As children, Roan and his friends had dared one another to enter the Nightmare and face its shadowy menaces. He remembered a long-ago moonless night when he and two equally small friends had made their nervous way in—and how quickly they'd emerged, running with the frights of a million troubled minds howling at their heels. Roan had never looked behind him then. The anticipation of pursuit had been enough to scare the pants off him. Looking down from on high now, the Nightmare Forest seemed as huge and frightening as it ever did when he was small. It might be still larger and more menacing. Roan willed whatever benevolent agency that was carrying him through the air to hurry him over it and away. He didn't want to encounter any of the nightmares of his childhood.

As if reading his thoughts, a clawed, skeletal hand made of murky green mist stretched upward a thousand feet from the forest, straining toward him. His heart in his throat, Roan rolled to one side on the air, away from the clasp of the bony fingers. Who knew what mischief they could cause if they touched him? The swirling plume soared up like a fountain, missing him by a handspan. With a hiss, the empty claw closed in on itself, lost its shape and fell back in dribbles of ugly gray-green steam. Roan let out the breath he had been holding, and flew straight into an influence he'd failed to sense in the air just ahead of him.

In no time at all, he was in the midst of a flock of chattering worry birds. Their shrill calls filled his ears, adding to the doubts he already had about his nebulous mode of transport.

"Ooh, isn't it high up here?" the plump gray birds complained. "We're late!" "It's going to rain, I just know it." "I wonder if we're getting enough air." "The air's so polluted anyhow, it'll kill us for sure." "The water's full of germs." "Oh! Look out!"

The last cry, coming from behind him, startled Roan into breaking his concentration. The invisible platform of air that had carried him safely a thousand miles dropped out from beneath him for good. Roan sought a solid handhold, but his hands closed on nothingness. Worry birds scattered, avoiding him as he fell out of their midst.

Don't panic! he ordered himself as the wind rushed past him. His heart leaped into his throat and he had trouble swallowing as the wind stole his breath. Think! His high hat flew off and his silk necktie flatted upward over his nose and mouth. He clawed the tie away. Roan forced himself to concentrate, but that was difficult with the broad back of the land zooming up toward him at a distressing rate of speed. Lighter than air, he thought desperately, gulping in oxygen. I'm lighter than air. He flattened himself out, parallel to that landscape, and attempted to regain some altitude. Roan possessed considerable natural influence of his own, and he drew on everything he had to save his life.

It was no use. The local cloud of influence prevented him from climbing up again, and the sleeper dreaming him must be looking the other way. If he hit the ground from such a height the fall was bound to be fatal.

"Wake up!" he shouted over the whistling wind, praying for any sleeper to hear him. "Wake up! I'm falling!"

He plummeted down through the clear blue sky, whirling like a leaf, tumbling end over end. This is preventable, Roan thought, gritting his teeth against nausea. Be resourceful. The Sleepers aided those who helped themselves.

He attempted to create a parachute, picturing the white canopy over his head, but no comforting straps appeared around his chest to secure his flapping coat to his body. Think! Rescue by some kind of benevolent winged creatures? Angels, feathered serpents, rocs, even harpies! But the sky remained empty of any winged beast. Even the worry birds had fled into the next province when he had cried out.

Skyhooks? he thought, now desperately. He pulled at nearby influences and felt them resist like steel bands. The toylike buildings of the castle and surrounding city grew larger and larger. Could anyone there see him? But no one was near enough to save him. He'd be splattered all over the landscape.

Roan had only yards left to fall now. He couldn't hope for rescue. The very air felt different close to the ground: heavier, with a smell of earth and stone. Roan concentrated on those sensations, even tried to enjoy them. They'd be the last he'd ever experience.

Suddenly, he felt the resistance give, and the influences rushed in around him in an almost tangible sensation. Wonderingly, he watched as two vast, insubstantial hands of pale gray smoke coalesced and formed a cup beneath him. Less than ten yards above the ground, Roan plummeted into the giant, spongy palms, and braked to a gentle halt. He swallowed to clear his ears, and lay back gasping, staring up at the pillowy mass of fog as the hands lowered him to earth. This was more than a fortunate circumstance. It spoke of intervention by one of the great Sleepers themselves. He was not meant to die after all. He panted, feeling his heart banging inside his chest.

As he landed, the hands set him upright on his feet, patted him on the head, and brushed down his clothes with careful fingertips. One hand picked up his hat delicately between thumb and forefinger and offered it to him.

"Thank you," Roan said sincerely, as the clouds valeted him. He had no idea whether they could hear or understand him. "Thank the Sleepers."

One hand put thumb and forefinger together in an "okay" sign, and the other offered him a very high five. Instead of jumping for the fingertips several feet above his head, Roan bowed deeply. Both hands dislimned.

In years to come, Roan would never be able to decide if the Sleeper had relented, or if he had saved himself by a desperate act of will. His first steps toward the castle were shaky, but he recovered his usual jauntiness quickly. The May air was fresh and full of the scent of flowers. He'd landed in the middle of a green meadow bounded by a white fence. A nearby herd of odd-looking black-and-white cows stared at him dispassionately while they chewed their cud. He looked around for a gate, but there wasn't one. Well, what was a mere fence after the height he'd just fallen? Roan swung himself over the white boards, and headed toward the castle.

Under the warm spring sun, shadow pooled around the base of the high stone curtain wall surrounding the Castle of Dreams. Roan guessed the time to be about noon. Just inside the moat, between a pair of narrow, battlemented towers of the gatehouse was the high, arched entrance. When Roan got a little closer, he could see the sentries standing on either side of the gate, their fierce, toothy, green-scaled faces jutting out over their supple ring-mail shirts. They were crocodiles. They watched dispassionately as Roan advanced over the drawbridge, until he was within spear's reach.

The first crocodile leveled the point of his halberd until it touched the center of Roan's chest. The other guard stood stiffly erect beside the iron portcullis.

"Stand and be recognized," the first guard growled.

"That presents no difficulty," Roan said. He stopped and raised his arms until his hands were level with his shoulders. He knew what the guards saw. Before them was a tall, slenderly-built man with wavy, dark hair. His deep gray eyes wore an untroubled expression, and when he smiled, two lines drew from the corners of his narrow nose down the sides of his well-shaped mouth to his square chin.

"You know me, gentlemen," he said. "I'm Roan."

The scales of the crocodiles' faces melted away until more human characteristics became visible.

"O' course we know it's you, Mr. Roan," the first guard said, lowering the spear until its butt rested on the ground. "But we've got to ask, you know. It's our job. You . . . haven't changed at all since we saw you last, sir." He shook his head in wonder.

"No," Roan said, pleasantly. "I haven't. I never do."

"Are you all right, sir?" the second guard asked, his brow drawing down in concern. "That was quite a drop!"

"I'm fine," Roan said, shivering a little. "I hate falling dreams."

"Same as us, sir," the second guard said. The first one nodded vigorous agreement, then they both looked around with guilty expressions. "Uh, o' course, it's the Sleeper's will."

"Their will and whim," Roan said, with a sympathetic grin. "But it was a handy rescue, wasn't it?" The guards grinned back. Their teeth were still very sharp. "May I go through?"

"Right you are, sir," the second guard agreed. His brown hands, now fully human, set aside the spear and reached for the chain bellpull hanging against the stone wall. The bell clanged loudly inside the castle demesne, battling with squawking, clucking, neighing, clattering, and the hubbub of dozens of voices Roan heard through the portcullis. "Nice weather today, eh? Mighty changeable, it is."

"Always is. Busy morning?" Roan asked pleasantly, as he waited for the iron gate to be raised high enough to accommodate his unusual height.

"Oh, garn, sir, you can't believe it," the first guard said, wiping his forehead with the back of his hand. The air was hot, drying the beads of sweat almost as soon as they appeared on his skin. "Comings and goings! All them scientific types, you can't keep up. All as curious as cats, and twice as bad as cats around doors."

"Some of 'em even look like cats," put in the second guard.

"Right, sir," the first guard said. "They want in, then, they want out. Begging your father's pardon, sir," he added with an expression of shocked embarrassment.

"No offense taken," Roan said, amiably. His father, Thomasen, was a prominent historian of the court, and indeed, rather like a cat around doors. Thomasen was an active man who liked to take a close look at things, and was always on the move. Unlike the "scientific types" of the Ministry of Science, the historians were observers only, not interfering with the events they were meant to record. Quite likely the guards didn't distinguish between one Ministry and another. And the guards might well take Roan for one of the "scientific types," too, since it was his job as the King's Investigator to observe phenomena, but he was passive as he could be in this activity.

"Look out there!" the first guard cried.

Roan spun just in time to see his bicycle, Cruiser, fall out of the sky. He ran to catch it, but long before he could leap over the fence into the pasture, the silver racer hit the ground with a tremendous bang.

"No!" Roan shouted. "Cruiser!"

The frame lay still, and the front wheel spun loosely. Then, as Roan watched with concern, the bicycle heaved itself up unsteadily onto both its wheels. Roan put his fingers in his mouth and whistled. The bicycle turned its handlebars until it was facing him, and wheeled slowly over, its gears squeaking pathetically.

"I wondered where you'd gotten to, old fellow," Roan said, giving him a pat on the frame. "All right?" The handlebars turned slightly under his palm as if responding to the caress. He swung the steed up and over the fence onto the road. The bicycle creaked unsteadily beside him back to the castle.

"Aw, there's lucky, then," the second guard said, eyeing the bike critically. "Barely a scratch or a dent."

"The stablemaster'll see to that squeak," the first guard suggested. "No trouble."

The guards were already beginning to alter again as Roan passed into the courtyard. Their clanking mail unkinked and flowed into long silk robes and head coverings, and their spears became curved swords. The first guard touched his forehead in a polite salaam as his skin and hair darkened, and a mustache sprouted on his upper lip. With the Lullay, fount of the Sleepers' influence, running right through the castle demesne, things changed here almost constantly.

Chapter 2

The heat was the second clue to the Sleeper's changing mood. In the short time it took for Roan to walk between the castle gate and the first row of outbuildings inside the stone walls the weather shifted from temperate summer to sweltering heat. The Sleeper's attention must have turned to a realm of deserts.

The cackle of chickens became the bleating of goats, and the cry of sheep became the impatience of camels. Roan smiled at the herdsmen suddenly being dwarfed by their charges, who added spitting to their usual forms of disobedience. Yet, Dreamlanders were accustomed to constant alteration. Such was the will of the Sleeper of this region who dreamed this realm and everyone in it. Everybody who lived in the Dreamland was used to changing from his or her basic shape, altering looks, sex, even species, when it suited the over-intelligence of their Creator. Everyone, Roan reflected wryly, except himself.

His father, and those of the historians who were of a charitable turn of mind, used to say that Roan was the exception that proved the rule that all things in the Dreamland changed. Roan Faireven was considered to be an oddity, even a freak by some. Where it was natural to shift from paradigm to paradigm like the tumbling clouds in the sky constantly forming new pictures, Roan remained firmly fixed as himself. Oh, he'd changed as he had grown up from tot to child to teen to adult, but what he looked like a year later could have been pretty well predicted from the way he had looked the year before. It was not out of stubbornness, nor of disrespect to the Sleepers that he adhered to one basic form. He simply couldn't help it. He couldn't change himself. Roan was always male, always tall, always gray-eyed and dark-haired and broad-shouldered and long-handed—in other words, always himself. Whoever that was, Roan thought with a sigh. He often felt he'd know more about his inner self if his outer self altered now and again to tell him what was in his subconscious. He was frequently troubled by strange dreams full of portents and weird sights, but then, his dreams were probably no stranger than anyone else's in or out of the Dreamland.

He had the wisdom to know exactly what he could change. Blessed with a decent measure of intelligence and sanity, he had a high degree of control over his surroundings and his possessions. It was his very immutability that made it possible for him to take such a dangerous job as King's Investigator.

He became aware that his good suit of dark wool, tailored silk shirt and necktie were far too hot for this desert. Whereas clothing, like all other inanimate objects, tended to follow the Sleeper's design, anything touching, or indeed immediately near Roan stayed as it had last been put. Roan set his mind to conforming his clothes to a more suitable costume. The fine tailoring shifted and flowed like melting wax, picking up lights from the sun and the heady-scented gardens that blossomed along the pebbled path. Now he was clad in an ankle-length robe of scarlet and blue silk, over silk trousers draping cool around his legs. His formal top hat drooped and became a broad-brimmed sunshade.

Much better. Roan sighed, and worked his shoulders under the smooth cloth. He scuffed in soft boots along the narrow path bounded by round stones. His steed, following on his heels, had remained a bicycle, instead of turning into a destrier or a camel. He wheeled Cruiser to the stables, a welcome oasis of coolness in the noon heat, and turned it over to an ostler, who clucked through his mustache at the dents in the frame.

"Good as new in an hour, by my word of honor," the man said, touching his forehead, lips and heart.

"There's no hurry," Roan said, returning the gesture. "I'm home for a while."

He went out into the sun, and turned toward the main keep. There were a few minor shifts in the landscape, as was normal, while Roan made his way along the crushed stone paths, but the place remained largely fertile-crescentish in flavor. Whatever outward stimulus had prompted the Sleeper to dream of desert kingdoms, He or She had created a place of beauty.

The castle itself looked different than it had when Roan had departed on his last assignment, but then it had surely changed a dozen or a hundred times in his absence. Instead of the drafty, gray stone keep covered with lichens and spiderwebs, with arched cloister windows made up of multiple palm-sized panes of glass, and banshees on the battlements, the great keep was smooth white marble, limned here and there with gold and inlays of multicolored glass and gems. The heavy bronze doors bore deep designs of knots and arabesques. Pillars bearing statuary nestled in recesses at intervals along the walls, and fountains played in the courtyard. All of the window casements were pointed arches, too. He had to admit that this face of the castle was very pleasant. There wasn't a single bat in sight. Obviously, the Sleeper was in good spirits this day. Roan gave thanks. The sun was blazing gold in a clear, blue sky, and green and scarlet birds croaked at him from tree branches. Servers, wearing layer upon layer of diaphanous silk, passed swiftly between the many buildings of the castle's inner courtyard. The individual garments would have been transparent, but the layering lent opacity so that the true forms within could not be seen. Much like the Dreamland itself, Roan thought.

He heard an outburst of noise coming from one side of the central keep. A collection of young men and women hurtled around the perimeter of the building with long measuring tapes slung between them. Oblivious to the heat, they made energetic measurements, jotted down copious notes on pads and slates, or flicked the beads on an abacus. Roan laughed as they disappeared around the other side of the building, djellabahs fluttering importantly behind them. Their quest looked like a cross between a scavenger hunt and a math test.

Those young people looked different than they had before, too, but he knew who they were. The Ministry of Science always assigned its newest apprentices to keep track of the castle's dimensions. Roan thought the task futile, since the basic layout of the keep was always a thousand paces by a thousand, but he never claimed to fully appreciate the analytical mind. If the scientists thought they could learn something fundamental about the Dreamland or the Sleeper by measuring the castle every time it changed, Roan hadn't a clue as to what it might be.

"Roan!" a voice hailed him. He turned from his study of the castle to see a short, stout, scarlet-haired woman, wearing multiple sheaths of crimson silk that fell enticingly over her rolling middle, fall in beside him and take his arm. She beamed up at him, her fat cheeks creasing engagingly.

"My dear fellow, how are you? It's been an age."

"Bergold!" Roan exclaimed, recognizing the pattern of his good friend's speech, if not his current form.

"Indeed," the historian said. He held out a fold of his costume. "Isn't this a fine color? I am partial to red."

"Very nice," Roan said, thinking that it disagreed violently with Bergold's current hair color, but perhaps the historian hadn't seen himself in a mirror. Bergold altered so often and so rapidly it would drive many Dreamlanders mad, but he took it in his breezy stride. Most people had a base shape, and their many changes were variations upon that one. After a lifetime's friendship, Roan was still not certain he had ever seen the historian in his natural form, if indeed he had one.

"Did you come by train?" Bergold asked, guiding him toward the castle entrance.

"Not this time. I just flew in from Somnus, on the wind."

"You lucky soul!" Bergold exclaimed. "Did you fly all the way?"

"Very nearly," Roan said, relishing the memory of his adventure. "I kept hitting fortunate circumstances. My steed Cruiser and I passed through an influence that made him a motorcycle, then another that made him an airplane."

"An airplane!" Bergold said. "Goodness me!"

"Yes, indeed," Roan grinned. "Suddenly I was flying without the plane, flat out on the wind like a bird. Most exhilarating. It took days off my journey."

"This modern air travel is positively astonishing," Bergold said, pulling a notepad and pencil from somewhere in his diaphanous robes. He jotted down a few words. "Someday I hope I can try it, but I'm not sure my noble steed is up to it, nor I. How was the landing?"

"I fell." Roan gulped, remembering the hollow feeling in his middle during that near disaster. Bergold patted him sympathetically on the back.

"Poor old fellow. Falling dreams are always the worst. But you pulled up in time. You landed."

"It took every ounce of sanity I could muster," Roan assured him, bowing to a passing janissary.

"Luckily, you have a generous fund of that. I didn't know you'd gone away. What did you do?" the historian asked, flourishing his pencil.

"Come and hear," Roan said, striding toward the central keep. The guards stationed against the wall saluted the two in turn as they passed through the crowd toward the Privy Gate. The sentries had been right. The courtyard was full of bicycles, horses, carts, and every other kind of minor conveyance in the Dreamland. "I'm here to report to the king. The seventh province has not undergone another Changeover. There was some kind of noisy land disturbance that probably provoked the report. Very few casualties, and no discontinuations. Everything is settling in nicely. If I may be so bold to suggest it, this Sleeper has a peaceful and civilized mind which would be a great loss to the Dreamland should She or He wake."

Bergold nodded. "Never been to Somnus. What's it like?"

"Open savannah, mostly," Roan said, calling up details in his mind. "Dry. Yellow clay soil, too poor to farm. Because of the windstorms there will most likely be emigrations in plenty over earthquakes, and some changes in terrain, so I must warn the king about that, too. They may look forward to good tourist trade: the animals are beautiful. Tall, long-necked giraffes. Elephants! Big cats. Big, yellow-maned lions, lazy, sharp-fanged, beautiful. I watched them rolling under green-leafed trees, washing their cubs."

"Indeed," Bergold asked, listening with a dreamy look on his face. "You're positively poetic." Without meaning to, he started to shift so that gold fur broke out on his broad face and arms. He caught sight of himself in the polished shield of a silk-robed janissary, and changed back to a harem woman. "Sorry, old fellow. You quite took me away."

Roan grinned down at his friend. "You're very suggestible today."

"Bite your tongue," Bergold said, straightening his robes with swiftly fluttering hands. "If anything, I ought to be prickly as cactus, reflecting the turmoil going on in there." He pointed a red-nailed hand toward the keep.

"Ah, yes, the guards at the gate mentioned something of that," Roan said, raising his eyebrows. "Should I stay away and present my report another day?"

"Great night, no!" Bergold said, holding up his hands to forestall such a thought. "The king will be grateful as can be to listen to a little sensible reporting instead of all this speculation nonsense. Carodil, the Minister of Science, has been giving one of her endless speeches again. She's got a bee in her bonnet. It's stung everyone except the people it ought to. The court is full of her supporters, all clamoring to try new things to test reality. Blasphemy. As sure as form follows function, she's going too far this time."

"Now, now, Bergold, there's room in the Dreamland for a whole range of beliefs," Roan said, patiently. His friend's complexion had turned to beet red. Bergold needed to calm down before steam started pouring out of his ears.

"Not in my purview," the historian said.

Bergold and Minister Carodil were old adversaries. So far as the historian was concerned, it was one thing to understand the signs and predict the outcome from previous experience, and quite another to experiment with circumstances and see what resulted. To the historians and the continuitors, who policed the reality that the historians recorded, that was a privilege reserved for the Unseen Imaginations.

Bergold took his job seriously. As one of the most senior of the Ministry of History, he saw it as his duty to keep good records of phenomena observed throughout the Dreamland. Historians were a combination of astrologer-soothsayers and recordkeepers. They gave Dreamlanders a sense of the historical base of an event, so that no change upset them to the point of discontinuation. They noted those things which were determined ubiquitous enough to be real in the Waking World of the Sleepers.

Some people, including the Ministry of Continuity, thought

it was blasphemy that the historians were attempting to reconstruct the culture of the Sleepers, but the historians had the support of the king, who insisted that it was for the survival and well-being of the folk of Dreamland. For, the king reasoned, how much better can one serve the purpose of the Sleepers when possessed of an understanding of their day-to-day life. The historians located trends, so if one saw *this* coming, *that event* may follow.

Historians also publicized signs of upcoming changes that they observed, explaining them with such well-known phrases as Pepperoni Nightmare, Nameless Dreads, Pre-Examination Worries, Anxiety Dreams, Hormonal Maturation, Adrenaline Flashbacks, and the like. The Ministry of History recorded cultural details revealed to them by the Sleepers. Big books detailing the everyday world in which each Sleeper lived, as far as the historians could determine, were maintained in the castle archives, the Akashic Records. The books always remained recognizable as units of information during the Sleeper's changes. "Form follows function" was one of the natural laws of the Dreamland—and a favorite saying of Bergold.

As the two friends reached the high, pointed arch of the castle entrance, the herd of apprentices appeared from around the far corner of the castle and thundered toward them. Their headgear and robes were askew from running, and they were laughing. Since the results of their task never varied, they tended to make a game out of it. Roan grinned at them.

"Too much energy for one hot afternoon, is it not?" Bergold asked, grinning back. His rancor didn't extend to Carodil's staff. The apprentices were nice, harmless young people, no matter what guise they appeared in.

"Yes, indeed," Roan asked, hesitating a moment on the threshold. "By the way, is Princess Leonora at home?"

Bergold slapped him on the back with a plump hand and drew him into the cool shadow of the entry hall.

"Don't ask me, silly lad. Come and find out. Don't fight so hard against love! By the Sleepers, let the events take you forward."

Roan took off his floppy hat and let his hood fall off onto his back as they entered the Great Hall. The first thing to strike him about the vast audience chamber was that even the high ceiling, picked out in gold arabesques and puckered here and there with elaborate carved bosses at the base of each huge brass chandelier, was not high enough to contain all the sound below. It was deafeningly noisy inside. An unctuous young man in sumptuous white brocade met Roan and Bergold at the door and bowed them into the midst of the mob. Men and women of every description, most of them clad in bright, cool silk clothes, stood shouting at one another, waving their arms, and gesturing furiously, as if to convey the import of their message by mime as well as by volume. Adding a soprano counterpoint to the loud babble was the splash and tinkle of fountains of mosaic tile and polished brass, and the cry of bright parrots perched on a high gallery that ran all the way around the walls. At one side of the room, three marble thrones on a dais attracted the eye. The thrones were empty. His Majesty had not yet arrived.

Roan and Bergold stopped short and diverted their path around a woman who abruptly evoked a blackboard on an easel from thin air and began lecturing her companion on some of the formulae written there. Servants darted between them with trays of pitchers and glasses. A messenger in a uniform and a pillbox hat added to the din by banging on a chime and calling out names.

"You came home in time for the annual reports. His Majesty is hearing from each minister," Bergold explained over his shoulder, as they followed the page. "Naturally, everyone has brought between three and fifteen supporters, to prove they really have been productive over the last year." Roan stopped to allow the passage of a small, important-looking man, followed by a trail of young people, all carrying books, scrolls, and reams of accordion-pleated paper.

"I haven't been around for one of these in years," Roan said. "The last one wasn't nearly so well attended."

"The last one wasn't so full of controversy!" Bergold shouted, as he was swallowed up by a group of women pushing a huge map-stand toward the great golden throne at the far end of the room. He emerged on the other side of the crowd, and Roan caught up with him. "You've been away. You haven't heard the rumors?"

"Not a thing," Roan said.

"What?" Bergold shouted.

"Not a thing!" Roan shouted back, into a sudden, embarrassing silence. He was saved by the appearance of a leggy supermodel wearing a tiny red minidress and a puffy coiffure.

A head taller than anyone else in the room, the blonde woman cut between them and strode toward one of the doorways. The crowd parted before her.

"My hat," Bergold said, watching her go by, "who's dreaming her?"

"Wishful thinking," Roan said, with a grin. "Probably province-wide." The girl turned her head, gave him an appraising up-and-down glance, and winked. Roan felt his face flush, but he was flattered.

Bergold touched Roan's sleeve, and pointed to the front of the room. By the dais, a knot of historians huddled, muttering to one another. They no longer resembled the cats the guards had mentioned. Instead, several of them wore camel faces. The lean, drooping snouts added to their expressions of sour discontent.

The two friends elbowed their way over to join them. Most of the men in the crowd stood aside to allow Bergold, in his female guise, to undulate past, and a few leered after him.

"Bergold," one of the historians said, in terse greeting. "Roan."

"Hello, son," his father said in surprise, turning around and embracing Roan. Thomasen's face changed from the visage of a camel to a human face rather resembling his son's. "This is a pleasure. When did you return?"

"Just a short time ago," Roan said. "Bergold met me on the way in."

"Well, well," Thomasen said, pleased, putting an arm around his son. "Your mother will be delighted you're back safely. Come back with me after court and see her."

"I'm not delighted to see him," snapped another of the senior historians. It was Datchell, one of Roan's oldest tormentors. "It's the freak back again, I see." He eyed Roan up and down with open distaste. The long camel's lips moved as if he might spit. Roan held himself ready to jump out of the way. "I thought you'd done us a favor by disappearing.

Why don't you go and discontinue yourself, you abomination against sane dreams?"

"Datchell!" Bergold exclaimed.

"Shame," said Micah, the senior historian, pounding his long cane on the ground. "The boy can't help himself."

Roan's heart sank. No matter how hard he fought not to be stung by such abuse, he always failed. Datchell and others like him always managed to play upon his childhood shame of being constant in an ever-changing world. He was an adult now, Roan reminded himself. His sanity was undoubted, his command over his surroundings above average for any Dreamlander, not far short of that wielded by the king himself. He held a responsible job and was well liked. One man's opinion did not matter, must not matter. Long practice let him keep his carefully bland expression.

"Greetings, Datchell," he said, bowing very slightly, enough to be polite, but not enough to look subservient. Datchell had already turned away, looking disgusted. Some of the other historians offered Roan sympathetic looks.

"Don't start the same argument all over again, Datchell," said one fatherly historian, coming up to put an arm around Roan's shoulders. "You mustn't repeat yourself." Datchell didn't reply. His back showed rigid indignation.

"Tsk!" Micah said to Roan, with a shake of his head. "There are people who simply can't stomach a new idea. Calls himself a member of the intellectual elite, does he?"

"Never mind him," Thomasen said, blandly. "He hates giving reports." He nudged Roan with a playful wrist. "By the way, son, the lass has been asking after you."

Roan felt his breath catch on a warm feeling in his chest as he glanced to the right of the king's seat, at the small throne with the white, marble pedestal as a footrest. It was still empty. He sighed, half with relief. Living as near the Dreamland court as he always had, it was ridiculous for him to feel as shy as he did about the princess Leonora. She had known him all her life. When she was born, he had been six years old. The two of them had made mud pies on the edge of the moat—when there was a moat. He'd helped her pull out her first wiggly tooth. They'd shared secrets, and chased butterflies, and he'd taught her how to make obnoxious whistles out of field grass. When there were minor threats, such as those times she provoked other children in the palace into chasing her, it was to him that she ran, and his pleasure as her devoted defender was to see off the attackers. He had always treated her as a beloved little sister.

But things had changed a few years ago, the month she had turned fifteen. Three days after her birthday, an angry red dragon had attacked the castle. Leonora had been trapped on the roof. The whole court was in an uproar, everyone getting in each other's way to rescue their beloved princess.

Young Roan had managed to thread his way through the chaos and reach her before anyone else. Before he could think what he was doing, he had run straight at the fierce monster, shouting at it to get away from Leonora. It turned away from its intended victim to attack him, and he repelled it with an outpouring of powerful influence that surprised him completely. The dragon was thrown backwards in the sky and exploded in a shower of sparks. Roan couldn't think what had possessed him to attack, alone, bare-headed and empty-handed, until he started to carry the shaking princess down the stairs. She clutched him, but when he wrapped his arms around her, she stopped trembling. He realized at that moment Leonora was no longer a child, but a young woman, one who was precious to him in an entirely new way. Moreover, he knew she loved him, too. But she was the king's heir, the symbol of the future of the Dreamland, and the most beautiful woman in the land. He had been mortified at his audacity, but helplessly in love, and was so to this day.

He was constantly torn between his new knowledge and the long history they had shared as childhood friends. In the great scheme of things, Leonora functioned as that absolute to which everyone in the Dreamland aspired. She was admirable. She was beautiful as a sunrise, remote as the stars, competent, charming, compassionate—Roan's thoughts ran on pleasantly through all the complimentary words he could think of that began with the letter *c*. She ought to be consorting with dukes, presidents and angels, not the boy-next-door-to-the-castle. The king's thoughts must have run along similar lines. He appeared to look favorably upon Roan's friendship with the princess, but whenever the topic of marriage came up, as it increasingly did over the last few years, he had sent the young man on endless remarkable and frustrating errands. Roan thought these tasks might be intended to test his fitness for the princess's hand, but then, they might be delaying tactics, a father's protective maneuvers to keep his daughter from forming an inappropriate liaison. When Leonora appeared in court or on state occasions with her father, she was on a pedestal, too far above for anyone to touch her.

Roan performed his tasks as well as he was able, never shirked an assignment, no matter how dangerous, and he always came back to Mnemosyne. He didn't know if the latter dismayed the king or pleased him. The princess had always appeared to be pleased.

Leonora seemed to be amused by both her father's obduracy and her suitor's willingness to go along with the king's whims. Roan sometimes wondered if she wasn't putting him to some kind of test, too. Roan gave the small throne a final wry look. He hoped he'd know when, if, he passed. He caught Thomasen looking at him with a familiar, fond paternal smile. Reluctantly, he pulled his thoughts back to the present, away from past and future.

"Tell me, what's all today's fuss about?" Roan asked, moving closer to his father. The historians had gone back to muttering and spitting among themselves. Thomasen blew through his lips, a suggestion of the camel returning to his face.

"Pah! The usual doo-dah about improbable nonsense," Thomasen said. "Rumor has it Carodil has the king's ear, leaving the rest of us doing an elaborate kind of mime, so far as His Majesty's concerned. I say the king keeps things well in balance. He's just hearing the other side for a change, but for historians they're remarkably reluctant to understand that facet of perspective."

"No one likes having his ideas ignored," Roan said, tilting his head humorously.

"Mmh!"

They were interrupted by a blare of trumpets. The herald, a stout man resplendent in seafoam green silk velvet and a remarkable hat that wound around and around his head like a snail shell, stalked out before the trumpeters.

"My lords and ladies, all rise! By gracious whim of their Creative Eminences, the Sleepers, His Ephemeral Majesty, Byron, King of Dreams!"

As everyone was already standing, little attention was paid to the herald's command, but everyone turned to face the dais.

Chapter 3

"Silence in the courtroom!" the parrots screamed. They were quelled by a sharp look from the herald. The white silk curtains at the front of the room were swept aside, and the king entered. He wore flowing, white silk robes and a turban with a huge, shining green cabochon on the feathered aigrette at the front. No matter what face he wore, the King of the Dreamland was kingly. The bones of his jaw, cheek, and brow showed the underlying strength of a noble countenance. Beneath distinct, dark brows shone deep blue eyes that moved to meet those of everyone in the room. King Byron smiled at old friends, faithful courtiers, and beloved servants of the court. The bright gaze settled momentarily on Roan, and the brows rose in pleased surprise. Roan, feeling honored by such a friendly reception, bowed deeply. Perhaps the king had been giving some favorable consideration to his suit for Leonora's hand. By the time Roan straightened up with the question in his eyes, the king's attention had shifted to the next man, leaving Roan wondering. Perhaps, since his news was good, Roan would request a brief personal interview later, to see how his fortunes stood.

King Byron settled himself, sitting upright as he could on piled cushions in a throne that had changed from marble to elaborately carved gold.

"I am happy to see everyone here," he said. "Everyone is well, I trust?"

In answer, there were affirmative murmurs and bows. The herald cleared his throat again and bellowed.

"My lords and ladies, Her Benevolent Majesty, the Queen!"

Attended by a host of noblewomen and doctors, the queen made her way to her throne, and sat down in it delicately.

Rumor had had it for many years that Queen Harmonia suffered from a mysterious malady, but not even the most ardent gossips could wrench details from her medical advisors. Roan himself never saw anything wrong with her. She seemed well enough to enjoy most balls and entertainments, and was a firm supporter of the fine arts.

"My lords and ladies, Her Most Admirable Highness, Princess Leonora." There was a more musical blare from the trumpets. From between the silk curtains issued a parade of pages and ladies in waiting. A hum of anticipation arose from the crowd as Drea, the princess's old nurse, came out. She clucked, putting out a hand to offer assistance to her charge, but a soft protest made her withdraw it. Leonora emerged, straight and tall and slender, shaking her head at Drea. Roan caught the quickly hidden expression of rueful but loving amusement in the princess's eyes. The old woman would never believe that Leonora had grown up. Yet, grown up she had.

Leonora looked around the crowd anxiously as she settled onto her small, cushioned throne. She propped tiny feet in white satin slippers with curled toes on her pedestal. As her gaze fell on Roan, she smiled and appeared to relax. He felt his breath catch in his chest, and his cheeks grew warm. Roan did love her, and was rewarded in knowing that she loved him, too. Bergold nudged him hard in the ribs.

"There, and you were worried," Bergold said, teasingly. He wore an indulgent smile that pushed out his rouged cheeks.

"Shh!" Roan brushed his elbow away, but he wasn't really annoyed. The herald stood forward imperiously.

"Silence for the King!" he bellowed, deflating to half his diameter with each shout. The roar of voices dropped to a sullen mutter, and all attention turned to the throne.

"My lords and ladies," King Byron said, his resonant voice filling every corner of the great room, "We have asked you here today for the annual reports. We look forward to hearing from each and every one of you."

The voices rose into excited chattering like the parrots over their heads. Byron raised his hands for silence.

"One at a time," he said, shaking his head with a smile. "My dear Herald, call our first minister."

"Master Kaulb, the Royal Treasurer!"

Kaulb, a bent old man wearing a neat but worn set of robes, tottered forward. Roan knew him as a most frugal man, a worthy warden of the kingdom's wealth.

"Well, Your Majesty," Kaulb began, unfurling a scroll that he took from his sleeve. It unrolled for yards, bounding out of his hands and into the crowd. "The following is a list of the goods and treasures which have been entrusted to my keeping for the period of the last year. . . ."

Roan shifted from foot to foot as the treasurer went through his endless list. The old man's voice drew him into a swaying trance. Only the occasional glances at the princess kept him from falling asleep on his feet. She was also bored, but sitting with a perfectly straight spine. If she could stand it, so could he.

"And that is all," Kaulb said, at last. There was thunderous applause from the assembly as he stepped down. King Byron perked up, shifting his turban back on his head where it had slipped slightly over one eye while he nodded.

"Most complete," the king said, approvingly. "Next, sir Herald?"

"Carodil, Minister of Science!" the green-clad man bellowed.

The Science party was at the far side of the hall from the historians, a cluster of blue-and-white-robed men and women, most of them young. Science had more apprentices than all the other ministries put together. Carodil was a tall, slim woman of middle years. At present, she had a dainty, round face with a milk-white complexion that contrasted with her sharp, dark eyes and dark hair. She offered a shallow bow from where she stood.

"I defer to the next minister, Your Majesty," Carodil said, offering a shallow bow. "My report is of some length and some moment. I would not want to make anyone else wait their minor reports for me to finish. Perhaps I should go last."

"Some length is some moments," Bergold whispered to Roan. "What a pretentious speech!"

"Very well," the king said, flicking his fingers toward the herald. "Call the next minister."

The herald described a magnificent and deferential bow, contrasting deliberately with Carodil's arrogant dip, and the muttering began again. It stilled only faintly when Galman, the Royal Zoologist, strode forward. He was a big, hearty man, with a booming voice. Without waiting for his robes to stop flapping around his ankles, he threw up his hands.

"Good news, Your Majesty, friends! I've just received word from the town of Ephemer that a pegasus has been sighted in Wocabaht!" Joyful hubbub broke out.

"Ooh! What kind?" Princess Leonora demanded, leaning forward on her dainty throne.

"A white one, Your Highness, with gray ticking on the wings and tail," the zoologist proclaimed, with a courteous bow to her.

"Ahhh." The sigh of satisfaction ran throughout the throne room. Of all the remnants from the Collective Unconscious, mystical creatures aroused the most excitement. Even Roan, well traveled though he was, had yet to see most of the fabled beasts that still occasionally turned up in the Dreamland.

"It was first seen grazing the tops of a couple of apple trees in the witness's orchard near the town of Sona," the zoologist continued, excitedly. "It flew off toward the mountains. As soon as the man found he could not follow it on foot, he went immediately to fetch the local officials. A small party has been dispatched to see if they can pick up its trail."

"They won't find it," Datchell said, shaking his camel's head. "They were lucky to see it once in a lifetime. Why, I recall the last time I heard reports of dinosaurs, and that was thirty years ago. The footprints stopped at the edge of a swamp. Not a trace!"

"I saw one of those Neanderthals, once," said Telsander, a Continuity minister, staring at the ornate ceiling with slitted eyes. "A female, she was, wearing shaggy hides and necklaces. Thought I caught a brief glimpse of a male caveman, too. He was sitting on the side of the path beyond her. They both vanished. Hum! It's always astonishing how these things hang on. Cave people have been listed in the historical records for over ten thousand years. They are Real."

"I saw a caveman some years ago," Roan raised his voice.

"Did you, now!" Telsander said, whipping a small book and a pencil out of a pocket in his robe. "I wonder if it was the same one. Being only a race memory, the fellow wouldn't have aged. Give me a description, as detailed as you like."

He licked the end of the pencil, and held it poised. Roan took a deep breath.

"Hush!" Thomasen said, deflating them both. "You can find the details of his observation in the Akashic Records. I want to hear more about the pegasus."

His mellow voice carried far enough for the zoologist to hear. Galman turned toward the historians with a slight bow.

"No more to tell," he said, apologetically. "I agree that it's doubtful our witnesses will see anything more of them. It's impossible to hold onto the older memories for long."

"Mmph!" Carodil snorted, with a significant look toward her entourage, who looked secretly smug. Roan gave her a curious glance.

"Call Micah, Historian Prime!" the herald announced magnificently.

The historians made way as their senior walked forward with his head down, shifting his face from that of a camel to something more human.

"Your Esteemed Majesty," he said, raising a pleasant, wrinkled face to the king. Roan felt his heart sink with dismay. The man's lecture voice was just as Roan remembered it: a monotonous drone that made him tired just to hear it. With any luck, History's report would be short. "I am pleased to report that data are being kept correctly up to date, with no verifiable errors being entered into the permanent record. As this is the beginning of the spring season, we close one volume in which all observations are noted down, and begin the next. This new year makes eighty thousand six hundred and fifty-seven that we have recorded in the archives of the Dreamland since its beginning in one form or another. We are proud of our diligence," Micah had to raise his voice over derisive cries of "ho-hum!" and other catcalls, "but Your Majesty, since we are supposed to keep track of all events of importance happening anywhere in the Dreamland, it would be helpful if we could get more assistants."

"Oh, come now, Micah! We need more help, if anyone does!" Galman protested.

"I say no, Your Majesty," Micah said, raising his voice over complaints from all the other ministries and offices present. "You will of course forgive me mentioning it, Your Majesty, but not only are we expected to keep track of his department's discoveries, but of every other ministry, not to mention maintaining every volume in a readable condition, and the collection in its entirety." He looked hard in the direction of Carodil's people. "Some people do not understand that the historical records may not be checked out. I am stretched to the limit providing copies to those who request them. Assistance is at a premium just now."

"I will take the matter under consideration, good Micah," King Byron said. "Next, please?" Roan fought a yawn down just in time to hear the herald cry out a name not his.

"Call Romney, the Royal Geographer!"

In answer, a single woman pushed through the crowd to stand before the throne. Roan smiled at her, and received a friendly nod. There were murmurs of approval. Romney was the most well liked of all the cabinet ministers. She had a most adaptable nature, which suited the ever-changing face of the Dreamland map in her care. At present, she was short, dark, plump, and vivid, with ruddy cheeks and brilliant blue eyes. No entourage accompanied her, but she had allies and friends everywhere in the room.

She had a small square of crisp, smooth canvas in her hand that Roan recognized as the Great Map of the Dreamland. At the king's signal, Romney began to unfold it. It doubled in size again and again until she was quite hidden behind it. Two footmen ran forward to help her place it on a map-stand near the throne. Once extended, the canvas filled with fine, black lines, dots, and lettering, and gradually brightened with color appropriate to the topography: blue for rivers and lakes, green for lowlands, and gradations of tan and brown for highlands. Romney strolled around to the front of the chart and pointed toward a large patch of brown.

"Currently, I can report an outbreak of mountains in the southwest of Rem," she said. "Subsidence along the Lullay near Hiyume in Elysia over the last few months has replaced meadowland with low-lying jungle terrain. Very swampy and bad-smelling. We're getting reports of some unusual wildlife. Not all of it is welcome. Mosquitoes the size of your fist. They're banding together and carrying off farm animals." People in the crowd gasped, and Romney nodded solemnly.

"That's more up your street," the king said, nodding to the Royal Zoologist, who penciled a swift note on his silk sleeve.

Romney gestured energetically as she indicated change after change in the terrain that had occurred over the previous year. "Tangeray River has moved closer in toward the town of Osier," she said, pushing the air with both palms as if helping the stream along. On the map, the thin blue line appeared to nudge the black dot marked "Osier," which tried to avoid contact with it. "Resulting in the whole Tangeray valley shifting to the southwest. The chances are about sixty percent for flooding in the town." Her hand swept down over the dot. "The citizens are being advised to take precautions. We'd like to scotch this situation before it becomes an emergency. I'm afraid if the Tangeray succeeds in flooding Osier, there may be other bank takeovers elsewhere in the province. More as it develops." She pointed at a pair of high cliffs facing one another over the border of Rem and Wocabaht. "We've got an escalation going on I think we can attribute to rivalry between two villages on either side of the divide. These bluffs started off as low hills, but now there's some substantial headlands on each side, and growing higher every day. They aren't tall enough to interfere with climate. Nothing cloud-high as of yet. I've got an observer staying close to the action." She stepped away from the map and folded her hands. "That's about it, Your Majesty, but I spotted Master Roan over there. I'll just keep the map open, with your permission. After he speaks I may have some updating to do."

"Very well," the king said, beckoning to Roan.

"Oh, my news is of little importance," Roan said, casually, with a glance back toward the clutch of scientists. "It can easily wait until later. I would be happy to defer to Madame Carodil. The Minister of Science seems to have some interesting and, no doubt, vital news to impart." He bowed deeply, both toward the throne and again in the direction of the Minister of Science. "I am most curious to hear what she has to say." Carodil, now fully seven and a half feet tall, glared at him. He smiled at her, trying to look innocent and knowing that his face wouldn't alter and betray him. Bergold, half-hidden behind him, nudged Roan in the ribs with an elbow and let out a chuckle.

"Yes, all right," King Byron said, impatient with the infighting and the delay. "Call Carodil."

"Call Carodil, Minister of Science!" bellowed the herald. Everyone turned to face toward the group at the back of the hall.

Chapter 4

Roan could tell that Carodil was very annoyed. She wanted to be the last to speak, but Roan's polite deferral would have thrown too much emphasis on a second refusal. Instead, she stood her ground, and addressed the court from where she was, projecting her voice so the king could hear her.

"Your Majesty, the historian's son is quite correct," Carodil said, dismissing Roan with a flutter of her hand. "I am pleased to announce an important breakthrough. The statements made by the other department heads simply prove that what I have to say has not been a moment too soon in coming. The sighting of the precious pegasus would not have been so fleeting, nor would we have seen outbreaks of mountains or mosquitoes, if only the world had had access to the newest process that my staff have created."

"This sounds exciting, Carodil," King Byron said, sitting up alertly among his cushions. "What is it?"

Carodil was only too happy to expound. She raised the orb-headed cane in her right hand. The sphere began to glow. "My liege, ladies and gentlemen, we of the Ministry of Science are proud to announce our experiments in cooperative strength have proved successful. We have succeeded in learning how to combine our intellects, and have full control of reality. Using this technique, we are no longer subject to the whims of passing influences, and can, in fact, change reality even to the exclusion of the power of the Sleepers themselves!" She swept the cane down and thumped its iron ferrule on the ground in emphasis.

Her listeners waited precisely one and a half seconds before bursting into hysterical laughter.

"In your dreams," Micah hooted, flapping his white beard at Carodil with his hand.

"It is fact," the minister said, drawing herself up to greater heights until she stood some nine feet tall.

"I wouldn't believe in atoms until you showed me," Micah said, folding his arms and growing to ten feet so he could glare down on her. "I certainly won't believe in such an outrageous claim as this. Prove it."

"I certainly shall," Carodil retorted, jumping to twelve feet in height.

"Enough escalation!" the king thundered. The herald shouted for quiet. "Have you any proof of this astonishing breakthrough?"

"We would be most pleased to give Your Majesty a demonstration," Carodil said, with a slight bow. She let herself shrink back to a mere seven feet. Micah subsided to an average height, and the historians muttered among themselves.

"By all means," the king said, clapping his hands together. "I'm as curious as anyone else. Proceed."

"Anyone can bend reality a little," Thomasen said to Roan and Bergold. "This had better be really spectacular."

Carodil led the way to the front of the hall. She flicked her hand to and fro, and the crowd opened up before her. She towered above them as she passed. A portly man with heavy-lidded blue eyes and rather broad lips fell in behind her. Ten young men and women filed after him. In contrast to their superiors, who were almost aloof, they looked very excited and nervous. Roan confessed to himself that he felt a tickle of anticipation. The faces of the people around him were turned avidly toward the Science party. This was something new.

Describing another of her spare bows to the king, Carodil faced toward to the crowd. "I turn over the floor to my chief researcher, Master Brom, who has supervised this project for me." She stepped aside and the stout man took her place.

"I heard some complaining here today that the great mystical beasts have been too shy in appearing," Brom said, haughtily peering down his beak of a nose, his half-closed eyes gleaming with amusement. He pursed his lips. His mouth seemed made for supercilious smiles. "Allow us to show you how we can fold reality to produce such a sighting."

Brom turned to face the king, and put out his right arm straight from the shoulder. His minions clustered around him in a circle, back to front, with their right arms out and hands piled at the hub of the wheel under his.

"Behold the crucible," Brom intoned. He closed his eyes and started to mutter. The apprentices at once closed theirs and began to chant along with their senior.

Even at a distance, Roan could feel a significance to their actions, a faint eddying in the air, or a slight pull towards the circle. The air above the knot of hands changed. A brass chandelier visible beyond them seemed to twist in on itself, then snap back only to turn into a new pretzel shape. Roan realized that the chandelier wasn't changing, but his sight of it through the air was. The scientists were folding reality. Astonishing.

"Amazing," Bergold whispered. "They are actually combining their strengths! Can you feel the power they're pulling together?" Roan nodded silently, rapt. This was something new, something powerful.

Threadlike streams of matter flowed in toward the roiling air, filling in an amorphous shape. The shape writhed, bucked, turned over twice, and formed into a small green dragon. As Roan watched with his mouth open, it spread its translucent, batlike wings, darted out of the confines of the circle and flew around the room. People near the throne flattened themselves to the floor and screamed as the glowing beast dove toward them. A length of hanging tapestry fluttered as it went by, and the little beast turned in the air on its tail and burned it to ashes with a spate of flame. Roan jumped. The creature was real.

The dragon described another one of its hairpin turns and arrowed downward toward the thrones. Memory driving his legs, Roan hurtled forward, wondering if he could reach them in time. King Byron sat straight and tall on his cushions, staring fearlessly at the beast as it came. The queen, on his right, screamed and fainted into a heap of silks. Her ladies rushed to her. The guards, guessing that the king was the target of the demonstration—maybe attempted assassination—leaped to interpose themselves between their monarch and danger. At the king's other side, Leonora too sat erect, but Roan could see she was terrified. The dragon opened its mouth and breathed out another stream of hot yellow flame. Roan was too far away. She would be burned to death before his eyes.

Just as the flames would have reached the silk banners hanging above Byron's head, the scientists moved their hands, breaking the connection. At once, the dragon and its fire vanished. Roan skidded to a stop, staring at where it had been. The crowd broke into puzzled exclamations. The guards windmilled suspiciously, looking around for the dragon. Captain Spar, a powerfully built man in his fifties, glared daggers at the scientists, and directed a couple of his men to go and stand by them in case they tried any more shenanigans.

"Very impressive!" the king said, applauding enthusiastically. He slapped his satin-covered knee with delight. "By heaven, that's good!" He looked to his queen, who was reviving under the care of her attendants. She nodded faintly at him. Byron turned to Leonora, silent and trembling beside him, and put a hand on hers where it rested on the arm of her throne. "Are you all right, my dear?"

"I am now, Father," Leonora said, and Roan was proud that her voice was strong, without a trace of a quaver. She swallowed. "As you say, it was impressive."

"Yes, indeed," Byron agreed, and turned back to the scientists. "But apart from party tricks, Madame Carodil, what are the practical applications?"

"Infinite!" Carodil said. Her eyes gleamed. "I think it might serve as a lifesaving measure in times of Changeover, for example."

"Meddling with the Sleepers' will," growled Micah. Roan heard that sentiment echoed throughout the crowd.

"Good thing it's not all-powerful," Datchell muttered. "That monster could have killed His Majesty."

"Not at all," Roan said, with a quick glance at his old tormentor. "The king could have wiped out the monster with a wave of his hand."

"So he could," Bergold said, much relieved. "Just because he doesn't often alter reality doesn't mean he can't. He's worth a thousand of the rest of us. I imagine he could summon up dragons on his own, if he chose."

"He wouldn't interfere thusly with the Sleepers' will," piped up Olmus, waving his walking stick querulously. He was the oldest of the historians. He claimed to have lived so long he'd seen Changeovers in every province at least twice.

"Hmmph!" Datchell snorted, blowing out his pendulous camel's lip. He knew the measure of royal power as well as Bergold did, but he had been caught off guard. His fellows wouldn't forget that kind of a slip. He glared at Roan, who quickly turned his attention back towards the dais.

"Is this study much advanced?" Byron asked the scientists.

Carodil bowed slightly and raised a hand to indicate her assistant. "This has been Master Brom's project," she said.

"It is well advanced, Your Majesty," the fat man said ponderously. He stepped past his senior toward the throne and bowed deeply. "We have done many studies. One person has only so much influence, but our investigations are proving that a group's strength is greater than the sum of its individuals."

"Excellent!" the king said. "I am very impressed by the results." Brom's face glowed.

"Thank you, Your Majesty. In fact, we have so much confidence in our new ability as a group to command reality, we feel we are ready to take the greatest challenge ever this year. Our next great experiment: to wake the seven Sleepers!"

"What?" the king asked, producing a tin ear trumpet from thin air and putting it to his ear. "I beg your pardon. I can't believe I have heard you properly."

"Neither can I," Bergold said to Roan, under his breath. "Look at Carodil. She wasn't expecting this." The Minister of Science looked shocked, but was held upright by her dignity in the midst of the crowd roaring their outrage. Some of them levitated over the others to get the king's attention, but Byron was entirely focused upon Brom.

"Perhaps you should repeat what you said."

"I said," the scientist shouted, enunciating the syllables one by one, "that we are going to wake the Sleepers."

"All of them at once?" Telsander asked.

"On purpose?" Micah demanded.

"Of course!"

"Blasphemy!" Micah exploded. "How dare you suggest such a thing?"

"I serve science," Brom said. "It is our job to question."

"Do you have the least idea what your suggestion could mean?" asked Synton, the Minister of Continuity. "Don't you know the Great Theory? The Sleepers maintain the underpinnings of our entire existence! It's bad enough when there's one Changeover transition, when one Sleeper leaves, or dies, or whatever it is They do! Every surrounding province is flooded by terrified refugees coming over the border from the affected area! Fear! Turmoil! Destruction! How can we be expected to maintain continuity for the Sleepers if there is none for us? This could cause mass rioting!"

"Could," Brom said, smugly. "It's only a theory." He snapped his fingers, and one of his personal minions stepped up, holding a sheaf of papers covered with calculations. The youngster looked around at all the eminent personages staring at him, and quickly assumed a beard to make himself look older. "In fact, we have no proof at all that the Great Theory is so."

"You dare?!" Micah sputtered.

Roan felt a terrible knot of fear and uncertainty in his belly. All that he had based his life upon, his personal philosophy of existence—could it be wrong?

"We intend to prove the Theory true," Brom said. "Or false."

"By destroying all the Dreamland!" Micah said, horrified. "Your own existence could be forfeit!"

"Possibly, my lord, possibly," Brom intoned. "But probably not, if our calculations are correct. That is *our* theory. For that reason we have created a device!" He beckoned again.

Two men, obviously twin brothers, with heavy, underslung jaws and shocks of unruly light brown hair, bent in unison, and came up holding a litter on which rested a vast, draped bulk. It was so large Roan couldn't understand why he hadn't noticed it at first. The scientists must have been standing in a protective ring about it. Maybe they had used the crucible to conceal it, even from Carodil. Roan lowered his brows thoughtfully. This surprise had been carefully planned.

Brom, his small eyes glistening, took hold of the drapery. "Behold the Alarm Clock!"

He pulled the cloth away. On the litter was a monstrous machine. It resembled a clock in that it had a round, polished metal body, a white-painted dial, and two huge, brass, domelike bells on the top, but the dial was blank except for the spot at the top center, where the twelve would be. Instead, there was the image of a bright yellow sun. No, not a sun. It looked like the blossoming flame of a terrible explosion.

"We must prove whether or not we exist unequivocally," Brom intoned in a lecturer's drone. "The Sleepers, if they do exist, maintain our reality in a ridiculously tentative manner. Sleeping, we are; waking, we are not. Would it not be better to know if we maintain being all the time? That such a tenuous condition does not stand between us and existence?"

"I do not want such an experiment made!" King Byron exclaimed, and the Great Hall shook at the sound of his voice.

"But that is dishonest, Your Majesty," Brom pressed, not at all intimidated. "Surely, if you care for your realm and your subjects, you would wish to be reassured."

"You are mad," Bergold shouted, his face turning as red as his flimsy costume.

"Anyhow, you couldn't possibly know where the Sleepers are," the Royal Geographer protested.

"That, too, is a theory based upon practical knowledge." Brom smirked. "Observations from the first, third, and fourth millennia, not to mention the eighth millennium, indicate that signs were recorded proving the location of the Hall of the Sleepers. We intend to travel along the most favorable route, avoiding certain geographical features. . . ." He turned to the Royal Geographer and reached for her map.

The map cringed away from his grasp. Romney protectively closed it up with a snap of her wrist. It contracted into a fist-sized ball. She stowed it in her belt pouch. Insulted, Brom turned away, waving his hand in dismissal.

"No matter. I don't actually need your antiquated representation. We have our own charts. The Freedom of Information Act gives me full access to the historical archives, and we have been making use of them. We are ready to leave at once."

"No, you can't!" "You madman, what do you think you're doing?"

A dozen ministers pressed in toward Brom, but he held them back with one hand, his eyes glittering. Roan felt the oppression of many minds attempting to create an influence to change Brom's mind. He didn't know what that would do; the scientist had already made it up.

"Silence!" the king thundered, his face red with anger. "You will not leave at once! You are not going! Put an end to that notion at once, Carodil!"

"Yes, Your Majesty," Carodil said, rounding on Brom. "I order you to abandon this . . . this menace. It doesn't meet with my approval. I forbid you to continue in this research. Destroy this . . . this monstrosity."

Brom looked as if he was going to deflate.

"Your Excellency," the scientist began, raising a hand in appeal. He let it drop. "Well, I should have foreseen this possibility. Of course, I defer to your authority. And yours, Your Majesty," he said, making a deep and respectful bow. "I apologize for any distress I must have caused you."

"You are forgiven," the king said, mollified. "But let's have no more talk about waking the Sleepers. That thing," he pointed at the Alarm Clock, "will be disassembled at once."

"Of course, my liege," Brom said. He signaled to his minions, who veiled the device once again. The hulking shape hovered over their heads like doom. Roan found he didn't even like looking at it that way.

"Roan, my good friend," the king said, beckoning him forward. "We haven't heard from you yet. Pray tell us of your explorations."

"Call Master Roan!" the herald bellowed unnecessarily.

Startled by the blast of sound, the king hastily rid himself of his ear trumpet. Roan stepped forward.

"Your Majesty, august members of this court, I am pleased to report that the threatened Changeover in Somnus was only a rumor."

The king settled back in his cushions with a contented expression. Many of the courtiers pressed forward so they could hear more clearly. Now that the crisis was averted, the room seemed to relax. They were ready to listen to someone else. "Those of you here from Somnus will be pleased to know I made an exhaustive investigation, and there are no signs of mass alteration."

"Excellent, my friend!" the king said. "Then, what caused us to believe that disaster was imminent?"

Roan bowed, and half-turned to address the room. "Earth tremors, my lords and ladies! The earth there seems to shift now and again under its own volition. It would appear that this Creative One believes all things have their own consciousness and motive force. This belief has informed the earth and many other inanimate objects with a certain amount of autonomy."

"Hah!" sputtered Fodsak, one of the scientists huddled around Carodil. "Balderdock. Poppycash."

Roan glanced past the bulk of the chief researcher at the small man, who glared at him.

"Not at all, Master Fodsak," Roan said. "Your own principles demand accurate report—" Something about Brom caught his eye. Roan forgot what he was going to say next, as a sudden thought seized the cuff of his mental pants-leg and worried at it. He turned to the king.

"Forgive me for digressing, Your Majesty, but if I had put so much effort, thought, energy, and heart into a project, I would be loath to let it go."

"What? What is this?" the king asked, frowning.

"The Alarm Project," Roan said, urgently. "My king, after devoting what must have taken years of my life and countless hours of mental effort, I'd hate to have to put the fruits of it aside. When I was so near to proving my theorem I'd do almost anything to continue."

"So would I," Carodil said, shrugging her shoulders magnificently. "What of it?" She turned a cold and fishy eye to Roan.

"I've given my command," King Byron said, lowering his eyebrows. "This fool project is to stop, at once, and it has."

"Of course!" Carodil agreed, bowing to the king. "Brom has given me his promise to cease." She turned to Brom, stretching out a hand to touch his shoulder. "Haven't you, my friend?"

But the friendly gesture had a most unexpected effect. At the point of contact Brom started to waver. Crackly lines appeared on his face and body.

"He's breaking up," Thomasen said, alarmed. "What is this?"

In a twinkling, the broad, tall figure was reduced to thin, glassy shards that dissolved in the air. Carodil lunged for the Alarm Clock, but it, too, was insubstantial. When she touched the edge of the litter, the whole thing burst with a pop like a huge soap bubble. Carodil threw herself backward, covering her eyes. Everyone in the hall began to shout at once.

"They are not really here," Roan shouted over the hubbub. "They're already on their way. What he said about combined intellect is true. Using the crucible they've managed to create fully coherent images of Brom and his device. The real man is gone, and all his people with him! They must have left as soon as they finished their presentation."

"Gone?" the king demanded. "Gone where?"

"Toward the Hall of the Sleepers," Bergold gasped, his eyes huge with dismay.

"But we don't know where that is!" Olmus said, pounding the floor with his stick. "No one does."

"They must think they do," Thomasen said, stroking his chin. "More than just a good guess. He must have foreseen that the king would forbid the endeavor, and we'd try to stop him. He knows he would be stopped as soon as he was found out. Brom wouldn't risk his one chance on failure."

"How about these?" Spar, chief of the guard, stepped forward and grabbed Fodsak's arm. His men-at-arms crowded around the scientists. "They're solid!"

"Only Brom was an illusion," Roan said. "He's the only one important enough to have to be in two places at once. These men and women remained behind probably because they haven't got the stamina for such an undertaking."

"They have defied my command?" Byron snapped, straightening up and staring at Carodil, who had shrunk a foot in height, and was losing stature even as Roan watched. "They intend to destroy our homeland for an experiment?"

"Your Majesty, I had no idea," Carodil said. She was now only four feet high, and her voice was turning shrill. "I allow my people autonomy, so they will give their minds free rein."

"So they could plot the destruction of us all?" the king asked.

The room became suddenly very cold. People huddled together. A sharp wind swirled brown leaves through the air. One whipped against Roan's cheek, and he shivered, breaking the spell of immobility that had fallen over him. The tiny, futile motion of a leaf, helpless to control its own actions in the face of the wind, reminded him that he was not helpless.

"We'll find them, my lord," Roan said. All eyes turned to him, filled with sudden hope. "They can't have gotten far." He spun to hurry out of the audience chamber. The crowd parted before him.

"Stop them now, before any harm can be done!" the king called after him.

Chapter 5

Roan knew even before he passed the great doors that the party of scientists and their burden would be already out of sight. He exploded into the courtyard, looking about for a sight of Brom and his minions. The pigeons scattered, hooting their alarm. The clap of their wings sounded unnaturally loud in the silence.

Roan's pupils contracted painfully in the hot sun as he squinted in every direction. The heat shimmer radiating off the stony ground made everything look as if it was moving. What a time for the courtyard to be deserted! Normally, it was heaving with people on business with the crown or one of the ministers: courtiers, lobbyists, merchants, ostlers, beggars, hangers-on, and servants. Where were they when the very existence of the Dreamland was in danger? Now that he thought about it, where were the sentries? The posts next to the castle doors were empty. He couldn't even see the men who had challenged him on his way into the castle.

Roan dropped to his haunches and searched the ground for any sign that would show which way Brom and his Alarm Clock had gone. The light-gray gravel revealed hundreds of wheel ruts going in every direction. And not a single means of transportation anywhere. Brom's attention to detail, again. Before they had left, the scientists must have scattered all the bicycles. Not one steed, not one carriage, nor any other conveyance remained. Brom had meant to delay pursuit as long as possible.

A slight breeze sprang up, and Roan got to his feet. He spotted a distant glimmer of color in the sky to the north, and strained to make it out. Could that be a hot-air balloon? An airship would be the simplest way to transport a heavy load a long way.

The rumble of an engine alerted Roan just in time. A white sports car screamed into the courtyard, heading straight for the palace doors.

"Hey!" Roan shouted, as the shiny chrome bumper missed him by a hair. At the wheel was a man wearing dark goggles. In the seat beside him was a dog, its face in the wind, its tongue lolling with foolish joy. The car described a tight circle. Roan waved his arms at the driver.

"An emergency, friend! Help, please!"

The car wheeled. Midway through its turn, it became a white charger pawing at the ground, wearing a gold-braided saddlecloth that bore the royal sigil. The man, clad now in shining plate armor, held aloft on his wrist a small hawk that had been the dog. Its tongue was still out.

"How may I be of assistance?" the man asked, raising his pointed visor. "I am a king's messenger and a Night of the Dreamland. My name is Sir Osprey."

Roan crossed to him in a few steps and caught hold of the horse's bridle. "Sir Night, have you seen a group of people leaving the castle in haste in the last few minutes? Carrying a heavy burden? In the king's name, it's urgent. They could be endangering all of the Dreamland. They want to wake the Sleepers!"

"I've seen no one," the Night said, his eyes wide with alarm. "Shall I go and try to find them?"

Roan nodded gratefully. "If you can just find their trail, return here and notify His Majesty. I thought I saw an airship just now, headed northward, but that may have been an illusion. They might be on foot."

"I am on my way," the Night said, and lifted his arm aloft. "My dog will go after this airship. We shall report back as soon as we may. Rely upon us."

"My thanks, friend," Roan said. He had to jump out of the way as the Night turned his steed to thunder out of the castle gate. The hawk bated, beating its wings on the air, and arrowed out of sight to the north. Roan watched after them with gratitude. He couldn't catch Brom alone. He needed help, but time was flitting away. He strode back into the castle.

The great hall was in an uproar. Men and women clutched at Roan's sleeves as he passed, asking anxious questions. He pulled away from them firmly but kindly, making his way to the throne.

King Byron leaned forward, his noble eyes full of concern. Roan shook his head, and the king sighed. Roan explained what he had found.

"They must be stopped, Roan," the king said. "You must go after them."

"I will, Your Majesty," Roan said. "I will follow Brom at once on foot. The steeds will come back soon, but we cannot risk waiting. I'll try and pick up the trail." He started to shift out of his colorful court robes and back into a practical traveling suit. "It's a good thing I didn't unpack yet." He felt in his pocket for his all-purpose knife.

"Go," Byron said, his noble brow creased with worry. "I and the whole of the Dreamland are relying on you!"

Roan bowed. He was honored to be trusted, but his thoughts were troubled. He was already thinking ahead.

"You'll need help," Bergold said gravely, appearing at his elbow. His floating clothes became a sensible tweed suit with a gored skirt, and his silk slippers turned into brown leather brogues. "I'd better get some traveling things together. Bless me! What does one pack to save the world?"

"Everything," said Thomasen, throwing up his hands in a rare show of agitation. "Great Night! I don't know what to do! How many of them were there? Should we send men-at-arms?"

"The radar on the roof shows nothing," a guard panted. "I ran up to look, but they haven't seen a thing."

"They've pulled reality around themselves with the crucible," Roan said. "They're going to make it as hard as possible to find them."

"But where are they going?" demanded Micah, wringing his hands around the head of his staff. "I have no records for the Hall of the Sleepers. Brom has made his assumptions from innuendo, not fact."

"May we see the map?" Roan asked the Royal Geographer. She opened up the huge chart, and they scanned it.

"I see nothing that indicates the location of the Hall," Micah said, elbowing between Roan and Romney. "What is it that Brom thinks he sees here?"

"We must stop them long before they get there," Captain Spar said. "You can ask Brom where it is when I haul him back in chains."

"You, you, and you, prepare food, supplies, tents, and weapons," the king said, pointing at his guards. "This is a serious act of premeditated mayhem. We do not know how far they are prepared to go to defend this unspeakable behavior. I will welcome volunteers to accompany Roan." There was a chorus of voices, and dozens came forward. Princess Leonora stood up, too, towering above the others on her pedestal.

"I want to go, Daddy," she said.

"No!" Roan exclaimed, then realized by the startled look on her face that he had failed in tact. A storm began brewing in her eyes, changing them from hazel to a darkly dangerous gray. Roan had to defuse her temper, and quickly. He had embarrassed her before her parents and her people. He knew she would not stand for that.

"Your Highness," he began, stressing her title and bowing deeply before her, "it's too dangerous for you to abandon the capital. You're the heir to the kingdom."

"One that won't exist for me to inherit if Brom and his idiots destroy it!" Leonora said, dismissing danger with an angry wave of her hand. She appealed to her father. "Daddy, please! I want to help."

"Your Majesty," Roan said, equally insistent, "there's no time."

"My dear, you can't go," the king said, reaching up and taking his daughter's hand. "It's impossible."

Leonora looked from one to the other, disengaged her hand from her father's. The marble pedestal shrank into the floor, and she stalked off it, her face a stiff mask. She threw open the silk curtains and marched through them. Her train of courtiers bustled away behind her. The king and queen exchanged glances, and Her Majesty slipped off her throne to follow her daughter, clucking maternally to herself as she went. Her doctors and ladies streamed away in her wake.

Roan's heart sank. He knew he'd have to face a flood of recrimination and accusations of overprotective chauvinism when he returned, but he couldn't let the one he loved so dearly risk her life on a rash venture. He was expendable, and she was not. She had no experience in tracking, combat, or indeed, sleeping rough. If there had been time, and if he had dared think such an icon would want to acquire rude skills like those, he would have been honored to teach her. In the meantime, the kingdom had to be preserved, even at the cost of his personal happiness. The king met his eyes, and gave him a sympathetic look. He understood his daughter and her suitor's dilemma.

"With your permission, I had better go now," Roan said, grateful for the king's kindness, but his mind was already back on the problem at hand. Inspiration struck him, and he made his way through to the fountain. Scooping up handfuls of the small colored stones that lined the bottom, he filled his pockets.

"I'll leave these as I go," Roan called out. "Anyone who is willing to come along, follow my trail as soon as you are ready."

The crowd closed in on itself behind him, shouting plans to one another. Roan hurried toward the door. He could imagine the land itself urging him forward.

Chapter 6

Roan began to reexamine the courtyard with more care. He doubted Brom and his minions had set off underground, because no one had sensed any seismic disturbance, neither in the midst of the crucible's demonstration, nor in the uproar that followed. Carrying the Alarm Clock, they had to have taken the train, flown, or walked. If they went by train, it would be no trouble to send a message ahead and have the locomotive stopped at once, so Roan knew Brom would never risk that mode of transportation. If the scientists had chosen air, he should be able to find the spot where their trail ended as they boarded their craft. Signs of their departure must be here for him to discover. All he had to do was put the clues together. They had to pull reality around themselves to hide, but he was sure they hadn't thought to hide their footprints. As soon as their clouding influence had passed, such things would emerge. He walked, bent over, scanning the expanse of crushed stone.

Out of the corner of his eye, he noticed a deeper depression than most in the gravel. Roan guessed, by digging his own foot into the gravel beside it, that it must have been made when one of the bearers of the Alarm Clock slipped, twisting his heel. The tracks around that single print were a jumble, but it gave him a direction in which to search. Carefully, he followed the pointing foot outward, toward the palace gardens. He kept the colored stones in his pocket. Within the grounds, he would call for help if he managed to corner the scientists. He was no coward, but the prospect of trying to handle Brom and his crucible alone was daunting. Such seemingly limitless power! Roan was the equal of some of the most powerful minds in the Dreamland, but how could he withstand the combined strength of a group? Such a thing had never been known, in all of history.

The path Roan was following stopped at a chest-high hedge that formed a T-junction to the left and right. The left led to the ornamental rose gardens and to the kitchen garden beyond. The right went only to the Royal Maze. But it was possible they hadn't taken either path at all. Two people bearing a heavy load between them couldn't possibly step over the hedge and keep their balance unless they lengthened their legs accordingly. That was something Roan himself was incapable of doing, but he could alter his surroundings to an extent to achieve the same end. With an act of will, he hardened the top of the hedge so it would bear his weight, and vaulted over.

The ornamental flower beds on the other side showed no other footprints than the ones he made upon landing. Roan had thought it unlikely his quarry had come this way, but it was best to be thorough. He leaped back, and returned the hedge to pliability, although it would have changed back to normal once his influence had passed.

Roan dropped to his hands and knees on the path, hoping the springy grass would have retained some impression from passing feet. Too resilient, alas. Wait—here, in the border of sandy soil along the edge of the walkway was a twisted smear, proof of passage of the bearer with slippery shoes. Roan crawled close for a good look. Yes! There were faint tracks on the grass turning toward the maze. Roan sprang up to follow them. The case for an airship began to look better and better.

As if the scientists had ceased to care about pursuit, the marks of a dozen pairs of feet appeared in the border and printed in sand on the grass within ten yards of the first. At the sculpted archway into the maze, which was clipped out of dark green hedges eight feet high and woven with creepers bearing huge fuchsia flowers, Roan trotted through and found fresh tracks of two pairs of feet, paces identical in length, carrying something heavy. The lighter tracks that followed obliterated parts of the prints, but most of them were intact, and undoubtedly heading inward. Roan followed the trail into the maze, turning where the grass was trampled, until he found himself standing before the fountain and the small marble bench that marked the center.

The grassy sward was free of marks of any kind. The trail had ended. They must have taken to the air here. Their transport had awaited them while they made their presentation to the king, knowing all the time that their experiment would be forbidden. How could no one have noticed such a thing? Roan sat down heavily on the bench in the shade of an alabaster statue with blank eyes, and wiped the sweat from his forehead and neck. Leave it to the scientists to invent a reliable airship and keep the news to themselves. That invention would have been welcomed as being of real use. Now the king would have to scramble a flying beast of some kind to pursue them, and hope that it didn't eat the rescue party on the way.

The sculpted hedges around him, having sensed his presence in the manner of plants used to construct mazes, were busily shifting position and color to confuse the pattern. In a moment, he'd have to figure out afresh how to get out of the maze. That'd be no trouble; he'd done it thousands of times over the years. But as one low-lying, red-leafed bush moved past him and started to change to green, Roan saw something flutter. He sprang up, and chased the shrub until he could seize the fragment from among the thorns on top. It was a thread, of the pale gray-blue that the Ministry of Science favored for formal attire and the party had all been wearing in court. In another moment, the bush's natural chameleonic properties would have hidden the clue forever.

The thread had been on the far side of the shrub from the clearing, outside of the path, as if someone's garment had caught on the thorns when they stepped over it. That meant the scientists hadn't left by air, at least not from here. The entire trip through the maze had been a blind meant to confuse anyone who followed. The shifting bushes would have hidden any evidence in a matter of hours. Roan was lucky that the bush hadn't moved far from its original position when the scientists had been there. Only a stroke of good fortune had prevented the disappearance from the center of the maze from being a unsolved mystery. No, wait, Roan admonished himself. Think! That would have meant that the trail leading into the maze would also have been altered—and it hadn't been. Brom had assumed someone would follow them, and wanted him to believe they had vanished from here. They'd caused the maze itself to hold its place until someone else came, so all the clues would be in place. Roan wondered that Brom could be so profligate with influence. The crucible was a new power in the land, one that had to be reckoned with. Brom and his minions must be stopped until the phenomenon could be studied.

So, where had they gone from here? Roan stepped around the bush, now settling itself in a new hollow at right angles to its old position. A few more paces, and he found what he had been hoping for: another heavy footprint. Roan dodged among mobile box elders and yew hedges shifting to new places, picking up the trail here and there, sometimes having to wait until the maze hedges shifted again. Roan was satisfied that Brom had come this way, to lose his pursuers. But the trick hadn't worked. Roan should be able to catch up with them in no time. Therefore, they couldn't be far ahead. Might they still be in the palace grounds? That would be ironic. The castle stood where it had, wattle and daub or granite and marble, for thousands of years. What if the Sleepers slept right here, beneath it? But, no, Roan thought, the historians would have known that, and Brom wouldn't have needed to sneak away to set off his infernal device. Which way had he gone?

A screen of yew five feet high dodged directly into a passage Roan was about to take, and settled down, sinking its roots into the sandy soil with an air of triumph. Roan shrugged, and sidestepped toward a wide gap that led into a range of juniper bushes. The bushes let him get among them, then playfully closed about him in a ring. The grass under his feet began to conform to the new shape of the enclosure.

"Come, now, this isn't fair!" Roan said, patting the prickly top of a juniper. "It's too hot to play games. I must go on."

The bushes ignored him and began to take root. Roan sighed. He pointed his hand at the base of one bush, and poured influence into the ground, making it buckle, pushing the juniper backward. It protested, waving its branches, and the other shrubs crowded tighter around him. Roan shook his head ruefully as he broke free. "I am sorry. Some day, when we have time, you can confuse me as much as you like, all right?"

This promise did not appease them; the maze liked its little measure of power and hated being ignored, but Roan moved faster than any single component of it did. The trouble was that there were so many of them. It was difficult for him to negotiate his way out. If he appeared impatient, the plants would try harder to thwart him, and he was afraid the scientists were getting farther and farther ahead of him.

Contrarily, the plants figured out that he was trying to follow the trail that lay just inside the high stone wall. The maze closed passages in front of him and opened others, diverting him away from his objective. Lawns altered their shapes in front of him, distorting the footprints into weird configurations. A solid row of holly six feet high stretched itself across the garden from west to east, daring him to force his way between the tight branches full of shiny, scratchy-thorned leaves. He could just see over it, but not walk through. Roan used influence to open a way through that row, and found beyond it a second row, taller and more dense than the first. It loomed over him, threatening to blot out the sun. Roan reached out to push the nearest tree aside, and the leaves raked his skin, drawing blood.

He snatched back his hands, clutching the stinging gouges. If he'd been an ordinary Dreamlander, he could have stretched his own skin over the scratches, closing them instantly. Instead, he plucked a leaf off a nearby tree and formed it into a bandage and plastered it on. The maze was determined to keep him trapped. It would force him to use influence until he was exhausted. It might never let him free. The scientists would reach the Hall of the Sleepers in the Mystery Mountains, and the party that was supposed to be following him would never know what had become of him until the day they found his pitiful skeleton hidden in the maze, if the Dreamland wasn't destroyed in the meanwhile by Brom's heinous experiment. He heard faint voices coming from the direction of the castle. Others were coming out to aid in the search. He cried out for help. Oh, why hadn't he left the trail of stones, as he'd promised?

The hollies, sensing his panic, rustled fearsomely and began to close in on him. Mustering his strength, Roan made the hedge in front of him solidify so that he could climb it. Ignoring the pain in his hands and face where more sharp branches lashed him, he gained the top, and stood swaying on the twigs, trying to see the way out. Another hedge, a foot higher, hemmed in the one he was standing on. Roan leaped onto it, swayed, then jumped down onto the next row of bushes, several feet shorter. It immediately started to grow taller. Roan bounded off and onto the springy twigs of a rectangular-clipped yew that soared upward, flattening him against the sky.

The maze had gone mad, Roan thought, peering down over the edge of the yew. He had been thrust so high up the rest of the garden looked like an embroidery pattern on green linen. Raising his eyes, he gazed out of the castle grounds. The desert motif persisted beyond the gates. The city of Mnemosyne seemed to have vanished. And, among the undulating sand dunes and knots of palm trees to the east, he thought he could see the darker line of a trail, but not close to the castle. He strove to make out more, but the yew continued to push him upward, maybe clean out of the atmosphere. The sky darkened as the air grew thinner. Roan gasped for breath.

"All right!" he rasped. "You win! I offer respect to your . . . to your superior strategic abilities. You've made a puzzle I can't escape from. Now, put me down! Please!"

His last word came out as a squeak. The yew stopped growing so abruptly that inertia almost propelled Roan up and off his precarious perch. He squeezed his eyes shut and dug his fingers into the mass of sharp-smelling needles as the yew began to drop. Roan's stomach turned over twice on the long descent. He'd never known the gardens to behave like this before. He wondered if it was a reaction to the power of the crucible, or another trap left behind by Brom.

Just above ground level, the yew tilted, and Roan tumbled off into the grass, which fluffed itself up to catch him. Brushing himself off, he rose to his feet. The yew was already scampering off toward the other end of the garden to fill in a gap between two others of its kind, and the grass settled back to its normal inch-and-a-half height like a bird flipping its feathers into place. Before Roan, the rest of the hedges opened into a straight aisle, leading directly for the castle gates, which lay open.

"Just like that, eh?" he asked. The grass rustled to itself, seeming pleased.

Without further hesitation, Roan dashed to get out of the maze before it changed its mind.

The riddle of the missing sentries was solved as soon as Roan set foot beyond the walls. Two huge dogs charged toward him, barking furiously. He jumped back and threw up his arms to protect his face. Just before they reached him, each dog seemed to be jerked sharply backward by its neck. They fell to the ground, whimpering. Roan gawked, then realized their collars were fastened to very short, heavy chains attached to bolts in the wall. They had just enough slack to work up speed without being able to reach anyone who walked between them.

Recognizing Roan, the sentry-dogs rose to their haunches and whined for help. Roan tore at the buckles on their collars, but found that they had been welded shut, as had the links of the chains, and the bolts holding them to the walls. No amount of influence seemed to budge either steel or leather. Brom had used crucible power stronger than any one being's strength. Roan could not open them. Time was fleeing before him. He had to go.

"I am sorry, my friends," he said, looking into the dogs' sad brown eyes. He could see their embarrassment and disgrace. "I can't stop to help you. I have to catch the ones who did this to you. The Dreamland itself is at stake."

As one, both dogs sprang up and stretched out noses and forepaws, pointing to the east. Roan stood up and squinted under his hand into the lengthening shadows. The tracks he had seen before were just visible as dark depressions on the sand.

"Thank you!" he said, patting both sentries on the head. "Others will follow me soon to help you."

Roan pulled a handful of colored pebbles from his pocket and dropped one on the threshold. He pitched three back toward the castle door so there'd be something for others to follow when they came out at last. He started walking east.

The soft, fine sand made the going unexpectedly difficult. At each step, Roan's boots sank in to the ankle, making every yard an effort, and every mile an agony. The sun was no longer directly overhead, but the sand and the sky were still hot and dry. His face was hot, and his lips were dry and beginning to crack. Roan's only consolation was that his quarry would find it harder going than he did, burdened as they were with the Alarm Clock. He hoped the Sleeper's mood would pass soon, and leave the landscape a nice open grassland, or something, so he could catch up faster. It was already late afternoon. He had little time to find them before dark.

As if teasing him for his thought, a stray breeze whipped up a small sand cloud. Roan covered his face with his arm and squinted out over the top of his sleeve. A shadow on the crest of a dune to his right caught his eye, and he stumbled forward.

The scientists had managed to eradicate their trail close to the castle, but they had given up disguising their tracks after some ninety paces. Roan had to do some to-ing and fro-ing to find the first trace. Yes, here again was his old friend the Alarm Clock bearer with his slippery shoe. The dust devils were erasing the trail less energetically now, but most of it, leading roughly southward, was still easy to discern. Roan hurried his pace, driving his feet deeper into the sand, until a stitch in his side reminded him that he had a long way to go. Surely, the bicycles would return soon, and the others could catch up with him.

Roan dropped a blue glass pebble to mark his trail, then hurriedly stooped to retrieve it when a passing breeze buried it under a film of sand. That wouldn't do. He molded the glass bead between his hands until it formed an arrow-shaped sign on a post, and set it firmly into the path.

His worried thoughts became a litany as he ran. The whole fabric of life as he knew it could be destroyed. Precious life, sweet as birdsong, as honey-scented as hay and wildflowers, as exciting as wind in the face as he hurtled down a snowy slope on skis. Roan sighed with a desperate feeling in his belly, wondering if he would be too late. What would discontinuation feel like? He'd lived unscathed through regional Changeovers, but what would happen when all of reality was rent asunder? His hands shook a little, and he nearly dropped the arrow he was making.

Brom's audacity still astounded Roan. Was such a thing as he proposed possible? No one had ever dared to find, let alone approach, the Hall of the Sleepers with such a purpose in mind. If, that is, it existed at all. Indeed, the Hall had become a legend. But considering the power of people to shape their own reality, were the scientists merely creating the Hall from sheer will? No, Roan corrected himself. He must not let circumstances lead him to question his faith. He believed in the Sleepers. He'd had plenty of time to think while out on the road by himself, and nothing else he had ever heard would explain the randomness of life. Reality was so strange that it couldn't have happened by accident.

Now past the initial shock of Brom's abrupt disappearance, Roan began to reason logically. Where could he be going? In all of history, no one had ever reported stumbling upon the secret place of the Sleepers. For the sake of their creation, the Sleepers needs must be well sheltered from intrusion. But Roan had heard conflicting learned arguments about their location, and assumed Brom knew the same ones. The Sleepers couldn't be in the midst of the mutability they inflicted upon the landscape. In thousands of years, the Hall had never been revealed by shifting terrain. Therefore, in Roan's opinion, the Hall almost certainly had to be somewhere in the Mystery Mountains, the only thing that had never changed—but where? Whole ranges in the skyscraping massif that circumscribed the Dreamland were still terra incognita. But to outrun pursuit, Brom would have to make as directly for the theoretical location of the Hall as the terrain permitted.

Roan could understand overwhelming curiosity; he himself was afflicted with it. It was more difficult to comprehend always wanting to break something to see what it was made of. Surely there were other ways to test the theory. The lack of regard that Brom and his apprentices had for the lives of others in the Dreamland made Roan's blood chill. They would happily sacrifice everyone else just to satisfy their *own* desire to know what happened.

Roan's feet started to ache. He opted for more comfortable shoes, trading his black boots for sandproof, white running shoes that cradled his feet and gave more support to his arches. These shoes had changed so many times in his travels that he had trouble remembering that they'd been made as riding boots years before. He mentally tied the laces and double-knotted them for security, then glanced down, all the while walking. Much more comfortable. He pitied the people who couldn't form dreamstuff for their convenience. He saw them all the time. They lived in strange, stilted houses made of leftovers that mutated whenever the winds of change blew through. These were the people who came and went when Changeovers occurred. They didn't have influence enough to control what happened to them. In theory, the strong might survive, but would be altered beyond recognition. What would become of them if all the Sleepers were awakened? What would happen to him, the changeless one? Would he float, unaltered, in space, waiting for a new reality solid enough for him to stand on? Could he die of suffocation? Would the very air vanish? It was fascinating to speculate, but it simply must not happen. The Dreamland must be preserved. Roan vowed to use everything in his power to prevent disaster from coming true.

The lengthening shadows actually made it easier to follow the tracks in the sand. It was so quiet he heard a drop of perspiration creep from under his hair and roll down his neck. Roan took off his hat and stretched out the rear and side brim so it shielded the back of his neck and right ear from the sun. How silent the sky was, and how strange that he still hadn't seen another living soul, except the plants and the two dog-sentries. It seemed as if everything had been frightened away by the Alarm Clock.

How long could the bearers keep going under the obvious weight of their burden? Even if they were possessed of new and extraordinary power, they were still human beings. They tired. Was this a weakness in the crucible that Roan could exploit? Sooner or later they would have exhausted all their physical and mental strength, and stop to rest. He would catch them then. Roan stumbled to a halt at the top of a dune and surveyed the rolling desert ahead of him.

In the meanwhile, the scientists were revealing their considerable power. That they had led him along a substantial detour through the maze, walked hidden in plain sight, altered the sentries and attached them by unbreakable bonds to their posts, while all the time maintaining creditable speed overland showed impressive reserves of strength. All this had been accomplished in at most an hour since Brom's startling presentation and pronouncement. Roan felt that he would almost like to try the crucible process once to see how it felt. The younger scientists had looked frightened, exalted, amazed, and proud all at the same time. And they had summoned a dragon, something no single person except possibly the king could have done on his own! Was the sum of the parts that much greater than that of each individual? What a wonder they had discovered! It was a pity that they chose to use it for such an ill purpose.

The trail was more marked on the leeward side of the high, dun slope. Roan took the steep path downward with his weight on his heels. It seemed clear now that the scientists were making south for the Nightmare Forest. Roan felt the familiar uneasiness rise as he contemplated having to pass through the forest, even on a desperate mission. He wanted badly to catch them before they reached it. He could see no one ahead of him, but as they were capable of making themselves invisible, the fact didn't distress him. He would know them by their footprints.

The terrain flattened out into a sculpted, undulating, endless plain made of harder sand that held footprints better. His quarry's steps were growing shorter. They were already tiring in the heat. So was Roan. His mouth was dry, and a crust of light sand had begun to form around his eyes and nostrils. He brushed at his face with a dusty hand.

The air ahead shimmered like the steam over the mouth of a kettle. He couldn't fail to catch up with Brom now, unless—

The end of the thought, ". . . unless they had left guards behind on the trail," was cut off when something heavy dropped upon him from behind. Roan stumbled forward onto his hands and knees. He was too late to see the trap before he fell into it.

Chapter 7

Roan felt a certain measure of admiration for Brom. Once again, the chief scientist had proved he had thought two steps ahead of everyone else. If anyone had managed to see through the subterfuge of the maze, there was a backup plan in place. The scientists had prepared well. They must have been watching Roan come ever since he crested the last dune.

A heavy arm circled Roan's throat and pulled him back onto his feet, and locked his neck against another arm. Roan clawed at his unseen captor, who felt as big as a wall. The sandy ground was unsteady, and Roan ended up strangling himself further as his feet were kicked out from under him. Another huge figure shimmered into existence from the wavering nothingness ahead. How many of them were there? He squinted, trying to see around the edges of the effect. Good, only two.

The second man, slighter and shorter, appeared and aimed a fist for Roan's middle. Roan pulled up his legs, painfully putting all his weight on his arms and his neck, but it had the effect of pulling his captor's face down into the path of the other man's punch. The big man staggered, growling a curse. Roan jerked his head upward and his elbows back, taking his opponent in the chin and the ribs at once. The man let him go as the breath was knocked out of him, and fell on top of Roan into the sand. The second man aimed a kick for Roan's head, but Roan had softened the sand enough to swim through, and burrowed out hastily to a more advantageous position several paces from the mysterious shimmer. He pulled out his red-leafed pocket knife and opened it out into a fighting staff eight feet long. With the staff in his hands, he assumed a defensive stance, waiting for them to come on.

The first man staggered painfully to his feet. The second

sidled quickly, trying to get behind Roan. They seemed to be practiced fighters. He must not underestimate them.

Roan moved to get the high dune at his back. He turned on his heel, maneuvering to keep both of his foes in sight. Could he get past them? He was more lightly built than either of them. He might be able to run up to the top of the dune and signal for help. Roan edged partway up the hill, and ran into a field of influence.

It felt slightly sticky, like waxy steam. The guards hadn't been left behind—they had been traveling *with* the party of scientists. This was part of the fold in reality where the others were hiding. Roan felt with one hand for the edge of the sensation, and followed it farther and farther with a growing sense of panic. There was no edge. The waxiness had closed in all around him. He tried to push through it, and rebounded back, as if he'd hit a giant elastic band.

"Come on, you, take your medicine," the second man said, beckoning with both hands. He had a gravelly voice and a sadistic glint in his small eyes.

"Are you licensed health practitioners in an approved PPO, HMO or other recognized umbrella managed-care entity?" Roan asked, snapping out terms he'd read in an account of a recent hallucination that a citizen of Mnemosyne had had. He sidestepped off the high ground and started moving, keeping his staff ready.

"Huh?" the second man asked, squinting at him, confused. The first looked confused, too, but he controlled his face better.

"You keep your remarks to yourself," he snapped at Roan.

Their guard had dropped momentarily, and Roan learned what he had already assumed. These men weren't part of the charmed circle. None of the influence that held him came from them. They weren't in charge of their own destinies. After many years' experience Roan had developed an instinct for power sources. These two men were brawn, and nothing else. They were the first energy-saving measure that Roan was aware of Brom using, and the first barrier he needed to break down.

The first man lunged for him, and Roan spun the staff in his hands, fetching him a crack over the shoulder. The thug howled and jumped back. The second man took the opportunity to try and get behind Roan, who promptly backed up against the unseen wall. It remained solid, which meant the scientists hidden inside weren't going to come out and help their hired thugs. That protected Roan as well as them, and he took advantage of the shield their cowardice offered him.

The reality inside the sticky circle was free of the waxy feeling. Roan summoned up his own will.

He wouldn't harm his opponents if he could avoid it. He pressed his imagination to come up with a physical form that couldn't attack him, but was still alive and aware. Aha! he thought, triumphantly. The obvious choice!

Matter felt pliable and plastic around him, and he extended the sensation outward until it touched and enfolded the two men. The natural resistance of anything or anyone to alteration not the whim of the Sleepers manifested itself, and the men wailed and writhed as they changed. They rooted into place and grew taller, stretching out thinning arms to the sky. Their skin darkened and coarsened. In a moment, he was alone in the desert with a pair of handsomely leafed-out oak trees. He lowered his staff and gave a relieved sigh. The alteration was painless, but ought to last a while. Now to deal with the cowardly scientists still hidden in the cloud. He prodded the waxy barrier with a tentative forefinger.

A twanging reaction slapped him backward, smack into the opposite wall. Roan stumbled to keep his feet, and raised the staff again. The trees continued to twist, but instead of growing, they began deforming and growing shorter and thicker once again. The ruffians were changing back into human beings. So soon? A face appeared on the trunk. As the stiff bark softened, it saw him and sneered. The other one grew arms, and wrenched footlike roots out of the sand to step slowly and ominously toward him.

Roan ducked a branch that reached for his throat, and dodged behind the other tree-man. Their sanity measure must be fairly high. Even if they weren't capable of controlling the reality around them, they had a good grasp of personal identity, which meant Roan wouldn't be able to change them into anything for long. He wouldn't make that mistake a second time. Once again, he was impressed by the level of planning Brom had put into his mission.

Roan nipped in and out as the two tree-men lumbered in

a clumsy circle, trying to catch him with awkward branch-hands. He needed a diversion to get a chance to examine his prison, and find a way out. He couldn't change himself, and any change he threw on his assailants wouldn't last. But perhaps he could fool them. Roan whipped up a miniature sandstorm until his enemies could no longer see him clearly, then he built himself a disguise. The two other figures continued to shrink and thicken. He formed a tree-shaped shell out of the swirling sand, and pointed a branch into each of the others' faces.

"Hurry," he cried. "Grab him! I'll help!"

In the whirling dust, each of the ruffians could see a tree-shape and a man-shape. Naturally, both lunged for the man-shape he could see, and in a moment were flailing wildly at one another. Roan grinned. They might be turning back to flesh, but their wits were still wooden.

Roan took the opportunity to slip below ground again, darting beyond the confines of the circle. He emerged from the sand behind a number of people in white-and-blue laboratory coats standing with joined hands in a ring around the two combatants and the sand shell he had just left. Most of the apprentices seemed to be under twenty-five years old, but looked so weary they might have been double that.

"No, you idiots!" shouted an apprentice. "He's there. In the tree!"

"Not any more," Roan said.

All the apprentices started when he spoke. The nearest glanced back over his shoulder and saw Roan. His eyes widened and he goggled like a fish.

"Don't hurt me," he begged. He was very thin, with hollow cheekbones and big, staring, red-rimmed eyes.

Roan manifested a quick air pie, which he mashed into the other's face with a deft, practiced twist of the wrist. The gooey cream dissipated in seconds, but the surprise move had the effect of making the man let go of the others' hands to claw at his face. The magical invisibility instantly died away, and the sandstorm abated. The ruffians, standing clutching one another's throat in the middle of the circle, gawked at them. In the cleared air, Roan built up influence, and buried the two men in the sand up to their necks.

"I won't hurt anyone," Roan said, firmly, turning to the apprentices. "Now, back away from the others. All of you, separate!" Using his staff, he gestured them into a line just out of arm's-reach of one another. "Now, we'll wait here until the contingent from the palace arrives."

Most of the men and women went meekly where he sent them, but the skeletally thin one in the most ornate coat stood his ground. It took Roan a moment to recognize Brom. The chief scientist had shed his elegant weight for travel. The placid, submissive expression he had worn in the court was gone. In its place, Roan saw cold ruthlessness and confidence. The very edges of reality trembled where they touched him.

"Oh, no," Brom said, with an easy smile that was frightening combined with the coldness in his blue eyes. "You won't stop us, young man."

Roan hefted the staff. "I must, and I will. Where is the Alarm Clock?"

"Gone." Brom laughed, a brittle sound that chilled the air around them. For a moment, the desert heat abated, and Roan shivered.

"No, you won't stop us." Brom sat down on a golden chair that suddenly materialized behind him. The seat reminded Roan of the king's throne in Mnemosyne, except that this one was bigger and so plain it was clinical. He also noticed that a chunk of the surrounding dunes and plants was suddenly missing, as if something had taken a huge bite out of them. Brom didn't care what he changed or hurt so long as he got what he wanted. The sand oozed to fill in the gaps like blood filling a wound.

"That was clever of you, to confuse my men. I didn't think you had the strength to change them," the chief scientist said, regarding Roan with a wry smile. "Trees. That was merciful. A flaw. Mercy wastes time. I would have left them so they couldn't possibly come after me again. Like this!" He put his fingertips and thumbtips together to form a circle, and pushed it toward Roan.

A lash of energy hit Roan, staggering him backward. He heard buzzing in his ears, and felt a slight tingling all over. Brom was trying to prove his superiority by changing him. At first, Roan was angry, and then wondered if this arrogant man really could do what had never been done before. He wished with all his heart that Brom would succeed. But he didn't, and the astonished look on the other's face told him he didn't expect that.

The failure made Brom stop to think. Roan took that brief moment of inactivity to dissolve Brom's chair under him, making the chief scientist do a pratfall in the sand. As Brom tumbled, Roan jumped for him, changing his staff into a rope as he went. If he could subdue Brom, the others would almost certainly remain docile. Once Bergold and the bicycles arrived, Roan would make one of them lead him to the Alarm Clock, and send the others back under guard to the king. Help couldn't be far away.

To his surprise, Brom's ectomorphic form hid the wiles of a dangerous fighter. Quickly, the chief scientist leaped to his feet. Roan tripped him to the ground again, readying influence to bind his arms and legs. Brom slipped the loop of influence, grabbed up a handful of sand and shoved it into Roan's face. Roan threw up his hand to protect his eyes, and missed the low blow that struck him in a sensitive and unprotected place. As pain shot outward from the center of his body, Roan dropped bonelessly to the ground with a heartfelt moan. Brom laughed, a hollow sound from high above.

Fighting the agony, Roan grabbed upward at Brom, clutching him in a wrestling hold. His grip was weaker than normal, but Brom really wasn't a match for him. He was tough, furious, and knew plenty of very dirty tricks, but he was already panting. He couldn't last very long. He was out of shape, having spent much more of his life on scientific study than on physical education.

"Will you surrender?" Roan asked. "Just wait here, and we'll explai—"

With a fierce, feral look, Brom bent his head and bit him on the wrist. As the tendons in Roan's wrist slackened, Brom kicked out at him, aiming at the crotch again. Roan had to let go to dodge, but he went at Brom again, this time getting a chokehold from the side. Brom struggled, snarling and striking out. Roan held on doggedly. He would have to subdue Brom. Then he could round up the others—no, he couldn't. He had to keep them separated or they'd form the crucible again. Better to tie them to individual trees. He'd have to grow some.

One of an apprentice's flailing fists, by design or accident, struck him in the kidney. Roan gasped in agony and sank slowly to the ground, on fire from the pain in his back. The chief scientist stepped over him, his robe hem slapping Roan in the face.

"You lot," Brom panted, pointing at the two heads poking out of the sand. "Get those men out, and prepare to leave."

"No!" Roan protested, bracing himself weakly on his hands and knees. "In the name of the king—"

Brom turned and kicked him hard in the belly. Roan fell flat. The apprentices hastily dug at the sand. As soon as the bullies' arms were free, they helped pull themselves out, swearing colorfully enough to leave streaks on the air.

Willing himself to ignore the pain, Roan forced himself to kneel, then stand up. Brom was waiting a few paces away, the corner of his mouth curled in a smile.

Roan's rope-staff was on the ground behind Brom. He put his fingers in his mouth and whistled it to him. The rope whisked straight for its master's hand, upsetting Brom, who fell over backward into the sand with a roar.

"Don't stand there like statues!" he shouted at his apprentices as he floundered. "Reform!"

"Stay," Roan commanded them. His voice sounded thin, and he put more force into it. "As of an hour and a half ago, you're in defiance of the will of the king. Any other action you take is a direct contradiction of his orders." The young apprentices looked from one to the other, and so did the two big guardsmen. Both Roan and Brom spoke with authority, and they didn't know which to obey. Roan built on his advantage.

"You probably left the hall too soon to hear that this project has been terminated," he said reasonably. "If you return now, the Minister of Science will hold you harmless in any wrongdoing—"

With a snarl, Brom made a soundproof glass cage form around Roan while he stood up and restored his dignity. Feeling his own influence strong in this place, Roan thinned the glass to air and walked out of it. The real battle of wills was beginning. He studied Brom, wondering how strong-minded he was. While Roan might question Brom's wisdom in creating a monstrosity like the Alarm Clock, he couldn't fault the man's sanity, and in the Dreamland that was where power lay. To control the stuff of dreams, one had to know one's own parameters, not to say limits. With sufficient strength of will, there were no limits, save those of the Sleepers themselves. Roan reached out for pliable matter, and threw armloads of influence at Brom.

Snapping manacles clamped about the chief scientist's legs, feet, arms, torso, and neck. More poured down, burying Brom under a mound of clanking metal, drowning out his angry yells. Roan turned to address the apprentices again, but almost at once, the chains were gone. Brom snarled at him. Roan tried to bring the chains back, but they were gone beyond recall. He felt dismay. Brom had a superior command of influence, as strong as his own. The young apprentices stood nearby, not knowing what to do. They started tentatively toward one another.

"Reform!" Brom ordered them.

"No!" Roan shouted.

None of them had the strength or the talent of their master; they were merely intelligent. The two musclemen started forward, and Roan promptly dropped the ground out from under them, plummeting them again into a steep-sided sandpit with a soft bottom to land on. The momentary lapse of attention gave Brom an uninterrupted move. Machine guns appeared in a ring around Roan. He flung himself down into the sand, and a deafening barrage erupted over him. Were they real bullets? Roan wondered, covering his head with his arms. He was unwilling to lift his head and find out. Would Brom countenance murder to make certain his precious device had a chance to gain ground?

Empty clicking told him the guns were out of ammunition. Before they could reload, Roan stood up and made them vanish with a wave of his arms. There were no holes in the surrounding landscape, or in the bystanders who could not have avoided being hit. So the barrage was a mental ploy. Good. Roan could fight on those terms.

Confusion was the only way to defeat a really sane man

who knows who he is. Roan created several duplicates of himself, and set them to close in on the chief scientist, all wielding different weapons, hoping Brom would wear himself out attacking simulacra. In response, Brom cupped his hands again, and tan clouds of sand blew up. Brom was trying Roan's own trick of mixing up the landscape. It didn't matter how many of him there were, they'd all be lacerated by the whirling sand.

Roan squinted through the blowing storm. He thought he still saw all of the scientists in place, and thought of fixing each one in place like draughts on a checkerboard. He was just drawing the lines in the sand when the ground started to shift under his feet. He felt himself being turned to the right. To keep his prisoners under guard, he pivoted on his left heel. The sand turned him again. He pivoted again. The sand kept spinning. Roan stepped leftward again and again, as if he was dancing on a moving floor. If Brom wanted to disorient him, he was doing a good job, making him dizzy while standing in one place. Roan had to pit every erg of strength he had, every degree of concentration that he could muster to keep his reality his way. Hidden in the cloud Brom could alter small details, and he wouldn't be able to tell.

The tall figure in gray-blue and white tilted his head, and the other, more indistinct figures started closer to him. Alarmed, Roan stopped moving his feet, and allowed the sand to whip him around and around. The scientists must not be allowed to touch. As if seen in a magic-lantern show, Brom's people started to move jerkily toward one another. Roan built with the tools to hand, forming walls out of the sand around each apprentice, willing the panels to transparent, stonelike impermeability. The figures stopped, feeling the confines of their prisons. He heard voices muffled by the roar of the wind, and Brom's shouting over all.

The tall figure turned away from him to feel the translucent walls with the palm of his hands, making him look rather like a pantomime artist. Roan had left no way out of the prison. Brom threw a gesture over his shoulder at Roan. With a backward glance of disgust, Brom had to let go of the influence he was using to break out of Roan's. The King's Investigator stopped spinning so abruptly that he stumbled a few paces and dropped to one knee in the sand, but he kept his concentration fixed on making the walls stay. He had to hold the others in place long enough for help to arrive. How long? he thought. Bergold, where *are* you?

The apprentices tried to climb out of their prisons, and Roan saw hands waving out of the top of cells where the ground was too soft to give them a foot up. He made the glass slipperier, and they fell back in.

"When?" Brom shouted out loud. Roan started. The question was not meant for him. One of the male assistants stopped trying to escape from his prison. He yanked out a gold pocketwatch and opened it.

"Not yet, sir!"

"Wait for it, then!" Brom said. He put his hands together and dissolved the glass walls with a burst of power. The cylinders crumbled, and the apprentices ran toward one another through the shards raining down upon them.

Roan forced the unwilling grains to fountain up and mold back into shape around each of the apprentices. As long as his strength held, the crucible couldn't reform.

He thanked the fate that left him in an immutable body. The chief scientist checked again and again as he almost threw whammies on Roan, then diverted at the last moment to blast Roan's surroundings. Most of the time, he simply tried to knock the ground out from under him. Roan was staggeringly dizzy from his spin, but he couldn't let the feelings of nausea stop him. He rolled when the dunes disappeared from under him, or braced himself when they grew to tower height. He might not have had an adaptable body, but he had a highly developed sense of self-preservation.

Come on, Bergold! he thought desperately. Hurry up!

A dark shadow at his feet made him look up suddenly. He rolled out of the way just in time as a ten-ton weight crashed down into the sand exactly where he had been standing.

Brom seemed to make use of his hand gesture to focus his mental powers. Roan made the glass walls turn into a ribbon of glass that wound around and put a squeeze on him, pinning his arms to his side.

The scientist with the pocket watch shouted, without looking up, "Sir! One of them's coming . . . now!"

Roan wanted to know what "them" was, but he didn't dare break his concentration to look around. Did the little device indicate the arrival of Bergold and the others?

Suddenly, he was surrounded by a crowd of men in white shirts, and black trousers and shoes, and gaudy ties, shouting into small rectangular black boxes held to their heads.

"Sell IBM! No, buy! Sell, sell, sell! Buy IBM! Buy AT&T! No, sell!"

A nuisance! These random neural storms were the product of odd bits of active influence that broke off and swirled through the Dreamland. They almost always appeared at inopportune moments, and interfered with normal activity. Roan flailed at the crowd of investment brokers, trying to see over their shoulders. Someone bumped his elbow. He dropped his staff, and was unable to bend to pick it up in the crush.

In between the confusion of margin calls and buy orders, Roan managed to catch glimpses of the scientists. One by one they were breaking free of his glass cages and running away. Roan tried to apply his will to one apprentice, then another, to get them to stay where they were, but each time, a fragment of the nuisance got in his way and broke the connection.

Roan realized he was letting his attention be drawn in too many directions. Instead of trying to capture the group, he tried focusing directly on the next individual he saw, a thin young man with a plastic half-envelope sticking out of his coat's breast pocket, and gazed at him, making him sink into the sand. Roan would have one captive, at least. Up to his armpits, the apprentice cried out to his fellows for help. Roan filled his mouth with cotton. The nuisance buffeted him up and back, until he lost sight of his prisoner.

Through the crowd of cellular phones and Armani ties, the face of Brom suddenly appeared and leered at him.

"You see, young man? There is no master but science."

Roan saw the end of his own staff shooting down toward his forehead, felt an appalling pain in his skull, then everything went black.

Chapter 8

The sky that had been empty over the desert was full of twittering birds now, swooping down to circle around his head and off again into the sky, in triumphant patterns. Roan stood tall and straight before the throne.

King Byron, dressed in blue silk velvet and rows of snowy ermine, and looking more regal than ever before, congratulated him warmly.

"We shall be proud to have you in the family, my dear young man," he said, shaking Roan's hand in a firm grip. "You're a hero! You have saved the Dreamland!"

Roan smiled, and bowed deeply, feeling his head swim at such compliments. "Your Majesty, I am honored to have been of service, but I have to give credit to those others who helped me by arriving in the nick of time."

Byron smiled back and raised his hands high. "Your modesty ill-defines your courage and abilities. You have swept aside any objections I had to you marrying my daughter. The wedding will proceed at once!" He clapped his hands.

"Her Ephemeral Highness, the Princess Leonora!" the herald bellowed, but even he sounded elegant, and was clad in yards of sea-green velvet and golden lace.

The princess, looking more lovely and remote than ever, dressed in a filmy lace gown that was nearly insubstantial and yet still opaque enough to protect virginal modesty, stepped forward and laid her fingers on Roan's arm. She smiled brilliantly up at him as trumpeters played a slow march. Roan and his chosen lady walked together along an aisle carpeted with white silk and strewn with flowers, to an altar of gold and warm brown wood, backed by a colored window that looked like the intricate branches of a tree with blue sky and green leaves of stained glass between the thick black lines. As the triumphant music rose around them, the princess turned toward him and raised her sheer, white veil; her beautiful brown—no, blue—no, green eyes were full of worry as she looked up into his face.

"Can you hear me, Roan? Darling, are you all right?"

The headache centered behind his forehead throbbed with every single word she spoke. He opened his mouth to reply, and wondered why her wedding dress had turned into a heavy, dark green, roll-neck silk tunic that matched her eyes. Behind her, instead of the stained glass window, was a tracery of branches like black lace. He groaned. He wasn't back in Mnemosyne, getting married. He was lying in the middle of a public footpath within sight of a real forest.

A large fish's head leaned over him, and something wet touched his mouth. Roan tried gratefully to drink. He was very dry.

"He's coming to, my dear." Bergold's voice, thank the Sleepers. He would explain what had happened. Roan turned his head slightly. Behind the Historian were several more shadows, and the outlines of a herd of bicycles, most of them heavily laden with packs. The steeds had come back at last.

"How do you feel?" Leonora asked, gently turning his head back with her fingers. "Can you speak?"

"What are you doing here?" Roan asked at last, his voice sounding far away. Leonora sat back on her heels as Bergold and the others helped Roan sit up.

"I brought your bicycle," she said, with the same bright, intense smile that she had worn in his vision of their wedding—but at the moment he wasn't quite so pleased to see it. "He's very skittish. He wouldn't let anyone ride but me. I had to lead Golden Schwinn. All the steeds are unusually nervous. I don't know what Brom did to them. And we picked up your trail markers. I thought you might want them back." She gestured to one of the men, who brought Roan the bundle of multicolored arrow-shaped signs.

"You shouldn't be here," Roan said urgently, lowering his voice. His head ached mightily, but he managed to touch it gingerly with both hands. It still felt the same size on the outside, but the inside had ballooned with pain enough to fill several provinces.

"Of course I should," Leonora said, the gamine smile taking on a slight edge. "I told you, this is my task as much as yours."

Scenting a private argument, the others tactfully withdrew a few paces. Roan didn't relish what he had to say, but he promised himself he would keep from insulting her this time. He took her hand in both of his.

"You must go home, Leonora," he said sincerely, looking deeply into her eyes. "I thank you for coming now, and I'm happy to see you, because I didn't get to explain my reasons in the court." Roan's head ached as he searched for words. "There are undoubtedly hardships ahead. Brom has proved he will stop little short of murder to carry out his task. We must catch him before he finds the Hall of the Sleepers. Those of us who have experience and training in traveling long, hard distances, sleeping out of doors, and dealing with violence are best suited to this mission. We would find the task that much easier if we didn't have to worry about protecting you at the same time. Please go back to your father, if not tonight, in the morning."

"Certainly not," the princess said, with spirit, dusting her hands together. She manifested a water bottle and held it out to him. "This is my father's kingdom—and someday mine, as you pointed out. It is right that I help save it from those madmen. I'll take care of myself. Are you thirsty? You're covered in sand."

"But they're dangerous! Look at me." Roan felt the bruise in the middle of his forehead. It had swollen into a perceptible lump, and he bet that it was turning purple.

"Yes, but you were alone," Leonora pointed out. "Now, you are not. I brought some of the palace guards. Together, we'll all be safe."

"Does your father know you're here?"

"Of course he does. Roan, I'm not going back," she said, quickly. Roan was aghast. She hadn't told him.

"For your own safety," Roan pleaded. Leonora sat back and folded her arms. Since their childhood, that gesture had meant she had made up her mind, and nothing short of a Changeover would shift her. Perhaps not even that.

"Men!" Roan stood up woozily to beckon to a pair of uniformed guards standing near the bicycles. They had an apprentice scientist between them. His hands were attached at the forefinger-tips by an unbreakable, woven straw tube.

It was Captain Spar himself who answered Roan's call. Spar left the prisoner near the hitching post in the care of Corporal Lum and the two other guards, and came to stand at attention beside Leonora with a crashing salute that made Roan wince for his own forehead.

"Yes, sir!"

"Please escort the princess back to Mnemosyne at once," Roan said. "She's not accompanying us any farther. I think there's enough daylight for you to reach the palace before full dark."

"No," Leonora said, springing up, her eyes sparkling. The soldiers looked from her to Roan, wondering what to do. "Ignore that order. Roan, these men are my father's officers, not yours. They obey me."

Spar gave Roan a look of undiluted sympathy, but he backed away from the princess, who stood with her hands on her hips. Leonora had grown formidable in her beauty, tall, blonde, and sturdy, the green tunic molded to her form as a Valkyrie's armor, and her heart-shaped face thickened at the jaw to show muscle.

"You need to get used to the idea of having me as part of the party," she said, raising a muscular forefinger warningly. "Make the best of that, because that's one thing that is not changing."

Roan opened his mouth, and decided he couldn't trust himself to speak at that moment. He looked around for his hat. The desert whim of the Sleeper had ceased. Sparse trees and bushes dotted the surrounding grassland, which was furnished with a riotous blanket of bright-colored flowers. Roan found his hat half a dozen paces away in a cluster of red blossoms, and slapped it into a wide-brimmed fedora with padding in the crown. What couldn't be cured must be endured. That was one of the old wise sayings that had come down from the Sleepers since time immemorial. Leonora's strongmindedness might actually be an asset to her on the road. She might also tire of the game, if they were lucky, before she got into a dangerous situation. He walked back to her, and she raised an eyebrow at him.

"All right, we'll try it," he said. "But if there's any real trouble . . ."

"I'll stay out of the way," she said, promptly, sensing that she had won. Her breastplate softened again into the tunic that matched her eyes, and her body slimmed to suppleness. She had a playful dimple in her cheek just beside the corner of her mouth when she wanted one. It appeared now. "And if I prove to be a problem, I'll go home at once, without an argument. I promise I won't hold your decision against you. Is it a bargain?"

She held out her hand, and Roan clasped it, feeling more than a little foolish. Her offer was fair enough. She really was perfect. He shook his head, trying to think like a leader, and less like a besotted calf.

"Done and done," he said. She grinned like a child, and he suddenly saw how frightened she was. He immediately had second thoughts. He had to admit he was worried, too.

"We'd better hear all about what happened to you on the road," Bergold said, detecting that the argument was over. He came around to slap Roan on the back. The historian was now in the shape of a man with the head of a fish. His eyes, one on either side of his narrow, flattened face, lacked eyelids, so all their expression was in the expansion or contraction of the pupils. Roan focused on one great, round eye, and told his story. Spar, Lum, and the guards moved close enough to listen, while still keeping an eye on their prisoner, whom they had secured to the hitching post with a bicycle lock. Drea, Leonora's ancient nurse and confidant, fussed over the bandages on Roan's forehead, with Colenna, a retired field observer from the Ministry of History, standing by with a handful of gauze from her amazingly capacious handbag. Felan, also from the Ministry of History, and Misha, from Continuity, were two young men he had seen about court but did not really know. They listened to Roan carefully, as if committing every word to memory for the archives. If this mission was successful, the tale would be an important and popular one throughout the Dreamland. If they failed . . . no one might be around to tell it, or to listen.

"So they've found a way of detecting nuisances, eh?" Bergold said when Roan had finished. He ran a thoughtful finger down the side of one gill. "That would have been a very useful device to the rest of us. Pity Carodil never seems to share the good stuff. And who is this lad?" He beckoned the guards over. The young man between them dragged his feet, swearing colorfully in mathematical formulae and scientific notation.

"One of them," Roan said. "Treat him gently. He never tried to attack me."

"I'm not a physical oaf, if that's what you mean," the youth said. For a moment he tried to duplicate Brom's cold-eyed, intellectual stare, but he couldn't maintain it for long. He shifted back to his own countenance, an amiable, scared, slightly weak-chinned young man. "I'm an intellectual."

"Where are the others going?" Spar asked him, shaking his arm roughly. "Where are they making for?"

"That's classified," the youth said, trying to fold his arms and failing because of the fingertrap. "You won't get me to betray my leader." He and Spar glared at each other.

"I would if I had the time, my lad," the captain of the guard said. "Believe that. You'd best talk while there are teeth left in your head."

"I bet you couldn't trust a word he'd say," Colenna said, peering up into the young man's face. He ignored her.

"We've still got the footprints to follow," Roan said. "He can't hide those. Brom left in too much of a hurry to cover them."

"Shall we take this young buffoon with us?" Spar asked. "Or should we send him back to take his medicine from Carodil?"

At the mention of the minister's name, the young man looked nervous for the first time, but he gritted his teeth.

"Do what you will with me," he said, stoutly. "I'll die in the name of Science."

"You young ass—" Spar began, but Leonora put a fingertip on his arm to arrest him.

"Please, let me," she said, undulating into the young man's line of view. His eyes widened when he saw the princess, but he didn't speak. "You have to help us. Can't you see that what Brom wants to do is wrong? He'll destroy us all."

"What does that matter, if it uncovers the truth?" the young man asked, trying to sound reasonable, but his voice trembled just a little.

Leonora pressed her advantage. She changed subtly a little at a time. Her shining hair unbound itself and unfolded down her back into thick, silky tresses. The heavy, green tunic thinned until it looked more like the gown she had worn in the court, clinging to the curves of her body, then her cloak edged itself in ermine tassels. The small gold locket on the thin chain around her neck became a regal golden pendant with a shining diamond at its heart. Behind Roan, he heard gentle murmurs of approval from the others. The apprentice gulped, but he held his chin high.

"You are a loyal subject of the Dreamland," Leonora said, now more a shining vision than a flesh-and-blood woman. She was the symbol of all good and all beauty. No one, male or female, could behold her and be unaffected. Her voice was persuasive and gentle, permeating Roan's consciousness. He wished he was the subject of her focus. "You want it to continue. We all do. I would consider it a personal service if you would help us. My father would look on you with favor, even offer you a boon, in exchange for your help." She took a half-pace closer to him, and even Roan felt the young man's blood pressure go up. "I would be so grateful. I need your aid. For the sake of the Dreamland."

The apprentice stared at her, red-faced and desperate. "I . . . can't . . . say . . . any . . . more." He turned away and put his hands over his eyes. Leonora stepped back, mortal and vulnerable again, with her mouth open in shock. Roan hurried over to put an arm around her shoulders, and felt her clothes thickening with padding. She was hurt. Never in Roan's experience had such an appeal based on the powerful combination of patriotism and her personal magnetism been turned down. Either Brom must have aroused incorruptible loyalty in his forces or else the normal urges of men were dead in this poor boy. Leonora turned sad, lovely eyes up to Roan, who shook his head. It wasn't her fault. She gave him a bright, brittle smile in a face that looked like a china doll.

"Oh, bother, if the young fanatic's not talking, he'll be a pest on the road. And why should we feed him our travel rations?" Bergold asked, dismissing the apprentice with an annoyed wave. "Take him back to the castle. Here, Misha, would you do it? You look the equal of this young lout."

"Gladly," said Misha, whose natural form was robust and sturdy. He towered over the apprentice. "I might just make Mnemosyne by dark. I'll catch up with you later."

"Just follow the trail," Roan said.

They tied the youth's arms with long grass and put him on the back of one of the pack animals. Misha pedaled off, keeping a good hold on the prisoner's tether. Bergold tilted one large, flat eye while he rummaged through the pouch he carried over his shoulder.

"Aha!" he said, coming up with a pleated bundle of paper and waving it at Roan. "Romney sent a copy of the Great Map with us." Bergold unfolded it part way so everyone could see the leaf that showed where they stood. "You've covered quite a distance on foot, my friend."

"Not enough," Roan said grimly, rubbing his forehead. "I didn't stop them. But I'm grateful to Romney."

"This map will continue to update whenever the Great Map itself is updated. We are to send messages back if we find a feature has altered."

"We will if we can," Roan said.

"Hurry up," Leonora said, urgently. "Dusk is falling. Brom is going to get away from us."

"No, he won't, Your Highness," Captain Spar said.

"They're on foot, and carrying that heavy litter," Roan reminded her as Bergold struggled to fold up the map. "We'll catch up with them before dark. Never fear."

Roan took a moment to compress the arrow signs into small stones again, and put them in his pocket. One never knew when they might be useful again. Lum brought Roan his steed. Cruiser was still nervous. He twitched and curvetted half a dozen times before Roan could get onto the saddle seat.

"Hurry," Leonora pleaded.

"Can you see the trail?" Leonora asked, standing up on her pedals to pump harder. "I can't see it any more."

"It's all right, Your Highness," Lum assured her, riding steadily ahead of the company. He glanced back to nod encouragingly. He was a sinewy man of thirty with an amiable nature. His thick, dark hair was cut close to his head underneath his uniform helmet, and his dark eyes had long lashes in the corners that made them look almond-shaped. The beam of his bicycle lantern made a calico pattern of the path ahead, but he was able to read what signs it had to offer. An expert at orienteering, he had taken over the lead when Roan needed a break to rest his eyes.

Roan felt numb, as if he had been riding in a long, dim tunnel for years and years. The sun had sunk in the west until it was only a glimmer at the horizon. Lum let out a glad cry.

"I've got our lads here. Those heavy footprints are pretty well unmistakable." The young corporal raised one hand to rub his eyes. "It's been a long day. Will we stop soon, captain?"

"We can't!" the princess said, alarmed. "Please go on, please! You're not really tired, are you? I'm not."

"Well, all right, Your Highness," Lum said, obediently, and pulled sharply to one side. He crossed the verge where two footpaths met, and beckoned to the others. "Hup! To the right, please. I almost missed the trail here. They turned."

Roan roused, grateful for the novelty of a change of direction. He shook himself, trying to awaken deadened nerves. "Are you sure?"

"Yessir. Heading east, now, it looks like."

"Are you sure?" Felan echoed, a slim silhouette behind his bicycle lamp. "I thought I saw threshed grass off to the right just now. Still going south."

"Did you?" Roan asked. "Show me. They might have split up. Lum, come with me. Spar, keep on. We'll catch up."

"Yes sir," the captain called. The rest of the party rolled after him, their wheels hissing on the gravel and grass.

"Here, Roan," Felan said. He backpedaled to a stop and extended a long arm to point down at the grass. "See the way it's matted down? It keeps going, too!" He swung his hand outward to indicate the direction. Roan turned his bicycle lamp out that way and squinted.

A strong sensation of influence lay over this part of the land, and receded into the distance. Roan peered out as far as the end of his bicycle's beam reached. The ground had been well-threshed, and recently, too.

"I don't see anything, sir," Lum said, positively.

"Don't you see the way the grass is bent, man?" Felan said, irritably. "Comc on."

Roan heard the sound of bicycle tires hissing on the grass behind him. A guard, Private Hutchings, coasted to a stop, braking with his foot on the ground.

"Captain Spar asks what do you think?" he panted.

"The trail goes this way," Felan said.

"Captain Spar says that the track he's following is inconclusive," the guard said, taking a deep breath. "He says Mistress Colenna got ahead of him in the woods and got lost and started calling for help, and when he found her and she got back in line he couldn't find no trace of the track, not for 360 degrees in any direction, sir, and should the rest of us rejoin you, or halt until daybreak?"

Roan looked at the other two, who were clearly relying upon him for leadership. Felan swung a hand toward the broken ground leading south and raised his eyebrows in a silent question. Lum stood stolidly astride his bicycle waiting for orders.

"Ask him to turn around and join us," Roan said.

More endless riding. The sun had disappeared behind the hills. Even the stars were hidden behind a thick blanket of clouds, leaving only lamplight to guide them farther and farther south. Roan's focus had shrunk to the narrow, bouncing beams. He felt as if the body he inhabited wasn't his own any more. If he stopped pedaling, the bike's wheels would keep spinning anyhow, round and round and round, because the path would pull him along by his eyeballs. Thunder loomed ominously around the edges of his hearing. Suddenly, a blast of lightning split the sky from top to bottom, filling it with a cold, blue glare.

"Look at that!" Spar shouted.

"The trail goes right to it," Felan said.

Roan looked up from the track, and his heart filled with despair. Lightning cracked again, illuminating in a single flash the grotesque face of the Nightmare Forest.

Chapter 9

Everyone braked to a halt, and stood looking up at the twisted, claw-like branches colored the dead gray of ash against the night-dark sky. The trunks were threatening shadows. Among them, the gleam of hundreds of pairs of eyes reflecting the group's lanterns appeared and disappeared before anyone could guess what they belonged to.

"I'm sure they went in there," Felan insisted, putting his foot onto his pedal.

"Oh, no," Roan said, balking. The Nightmare Forest!

"Yes!" Felan said, pointing at the ground. "Look, man."

"If that's the way the trail goes, we have to follow," Bergold said, uneasily.

"Go in there in the dark?" Private Alette asked, her voice rising to a strangled squeak. "We can't . . . I've heard if you . . . go in there after dark . . . you never come out."

"You *can* get out," Roan said, steeling his voice so it wouldn't quiver. All his childhood fears were hammering inside his chest trying to escape. "I did it. It was hard, though."

"Then, let's go," Spar said. But no one moved.

"We must go on," Leonora said, her voice trembling. "If we stay together, we should be all right."

Roan later considered his next act to be the bravest thing he had ever done. Very deliberately, he dismounted his bike, and walked it forward under the looming overhang of the twisted branches. He glanced back over his shoulder at the others.

"Come on, then," he said.

"I'm right behind you," Leonora said, hastily, falling in behind him with Golden Schwinn. Roan could hear the uneasy rattle of spokes as the royal steed twitched with fear. Leonora hushed it and talked to it in a soothing undertone. The sound of her voice calmed him, too. This moment was like many in their childhood, when they had dared the shadows together, although those terrors had been bogeys in one of the castle's many closets and cellars, well-domesticated over the centuries. This was untamed and frightening. He kept her behind him so any peril that threatened her would have to go through him first.

Behind the leaders, the others followed in a cluster, staying as close as possible without running up their heels. Only Spar seemed unmoved by the looming menace.

"It's just trees," he growled scornfully, as the others looked around them white-eyed. "Firewood on the hoof. House parts. Unpulped paper."

The confusing influences Roan and Felan had found leading up to the forest became lost once they were in it. Broken twigs and telltale heavy footprints from the litter bearers were clear evidence something large had passed through. Maybe several large things, in fact, to judge by the condition of the ground. Piles of leaves were kicked up, and the undergrowth was torn. The track ended abruptly in a narrow, impenetrable thicket, at the foot of a huge and menacing tree.

"Where did they go?" Leonora asked, peering ahead over his shoulder. "How did they get out of here?"

"I don't know," Roan asked. He left Cruiser with Golden Schwinn, and leaned around both sides of the great tree with his lamp to see where the trail went. The huge tree shifted slightly against his weight, and Roan jumped back. Another three inches of torn ground appeared under its roots.

"It moved!" Leonora exclaimed.

Uneasily, Roan looked up at the tree. "I think we've been following the prints from this big fellow."

"Don't get it angry," Bergold cautioned him, with an alarmed look on his face. "That's a mad oak. They're slow to react, but they're the strongest things in the world next to an avalanche."

"I won't," Roan said, in a very calm voice, keeping his eyes on the thick branches over his head. He took his hand off the bark, and eased away from it slowly. "Everyone move steadily and slowly until we're off its dripline. Don't disturb any roots."

But it was difficult for a large group of people and bicycles to reverse course in the dark in a strange place without a single accident. Roan steered Cruiser, squeaking with protest, a step at a time. Then, the stinging began. Buzzing no-see-ums alit on his exposed hands and face. Where they touched, painful, itchy welts arose before he could brush the bugs off.

"Ow!" Leonora cried, slapping at her arms. "Something's biting me!"

"Ward yourself, madam," the nurse said, firmly, immediately behind Roan and the princess. "We should have put repellent on before coming outside, shouldn't we?"

Such prosaic advice momentarily calmed the group. Roan drew a veil of influence over himself like a coverall. The no-see-ums withdrew, humming furiously at being thwarted. Roan mentally thumbed his nose at the Forest.

"Keep going," Bergold said, his normally cheerful voice cautious. "We're bound to get out of this in a moment."

"Watch where you're going!" a voice shouted behind him, and Roan heard a loud crash. He looked back over his shoulder. Felan's steed and that of one of the guards had locked handlebars. Both bikes bucked and jumped to free themselves, with their owners trying vainly to pull them apart.

"Here, you!" Spar shouted at his guard. "Private Alette! Put your beast under control!"

"I'm trying, sir!" the husky young woman said, yanking at the frame of her fighting steed. She glanced up at her captain, and her eyes widened into saucers at something beyond him.

Roan looked up. Two enormous, twisted branches were reaching down towards the battling bicycles. Leonora shrieked a warning. Felan let go of his steed, and pointed at the tree, aiming all the influence at his command, but the Nightmare Forest was stronger than any single being. The branches brushed him and Alette aside, snatched up the two bicycles, and flung them far off into the darkness.

Squeaking with fear, the other steeds jerked loose from their riders' grasps and retreated along the narrow path, rolling right over their owners' feet in their panic. Roan grabbed for Cruiser and missed. The silver bike crashed into the undergrowth, with Golden Schwinn right behind, creaking for help. In a moment, they were all gone.

"Stop them!" Leonora cried.

"Stay here with Spar!" Roan shouted to her.

He plunged into the forest after the frightened bicycles. Their high-pitched squealing receded in several directions. Roan cast about, then followed the loudest sound.

Within a few paces, he realized he had made a mistake. What lamps the party was carrying were attached to the bicycles or in the packs. None of them were in his possession. He was alone in the dark in the middle of the Nightmare Forest. He turned to go back, and realized he didn't know which way he had come from.

A deep rumble stirred the ground under his feet, and sinister whispers began in the treetops above him. In a heartbeat, Roan was back in time twenty years, and the shouts he heard were the voices of his two small friends. They had dared each other to go into the haunted woods. He was a fool for letting himself be convinced to come. The trees all seemed so much bigger in the dark, and he could no longer see the sky. Roan hoped he wasn't making any of this happen to him. He wrapped his arms around himself and concentrated, trying to contain his own influence. He was an adult, surrounded only by shadows and trees. The noise came from the wind in the boughs. There was nothing to fear.

The laughter got louder and more raucous. No, the Forest had all the power it needed from the fears of millions of dreaming minds, and it made light work of any barriers he put up.

"All right," he shouted, wildly. "I'm still a scared little boy. But I'm leaving!"

He felt blindly around him for the way back to the others. They would have to wait until daybreak for the bicycles to come back. Another delay; he hoped Brom couldn't be too far ahead.

His questing hands brushed against one tree bole after another, but failed to find a gap between them. The trunks stood in a solid ring around him. How had he made his way into this glade if there was no space between the trees large enough for his body to fit? But, no, he had forgotten they could move.

His eyes were becoming accustomed to the dark, which

only made things worse. He could half-see the pointed branches waving around him. One clawlike cluster reached for his eyes, and he dashed it away. Shadowy axes waved over his head; arms brandished swords; clubs whisked dangerously close; evil, glowing, green goo dripped from mysterious beakers and hissed where it fell; tax forms rattled in his face. Roan staved them all off, but there were always more threats beyond them.

Then, something dropped on his hand, and Roan jumped. With myriad crawly legs, the something ran off before he could brush at it. Another fell on top of his head. He looked up, and two more fell on his face, and scurried off. More and more dropped from the trees. There were thousands of them, pouring down the tree boles, filling the space around his feet. In moments, he'd be drowning in vermin.

"Help!" he shouted. "Can anyone hear me?"

Low, creaking laughter rose around him in the blackness, and Roan went on guard. He reached for his pocket knife, remembering that there was an emergency lamp attachment in it. He fumbled with the blade, and had one fleeting glimpse of red, malevolent eyes, before another branch knocked the knife from his hands. He dropped to his knees to search for it, but a knobby root slipped over it. Roan scrabbled at the rough bark, and the laughter mocked him.

"Are you there, sir?" asked a man's voice.

Roan stood up. "Yes! Come help me!"

"Roan?" cried Leonora's voice. "Where are you?"

"Here!" he called into the blackness, pounding on the nearest tree. "I'm trapped! I can't get out! Bring an ax!"

A thin beam of light pierced the dark, shining between two trunks. Roan thrust an arm out and waved to show the searchers where he was.

"Here!"

"Right you are, sir!" Captain Spar's voice said, and the reassuring silhouette rushed up to him, with the slender shadow of the princess behind. "Never fear, we'll scare these wooden boys off. I've got a big, sharp ax just waiting for one of them." He shone his lamp through the gap past Roan.

In the spillover from the light, Roan saw his eyebrows go up.

"Sir," he said, in an entirely different voice. "Why didn't you just go out that way?" His other hand came through and pointed. Roan turned his head to look.

The way was open. There were no large trees behind him. A few shaggy saplings clung together in the light looking like terrified deer.

"They had me surrounded," Roan protested. "They were huge. They knocked my knife out of my hand and stood on it with a root. I was trapped. Really!"

Spar's head tilted. "Things go funny in the dark," he said, and his voice suggested it was more than moving trees. "Come on, then, Master Roan. Isn't that your knife down there?" The beam angled downward and picked up a finger of red and silver. Roan bent to pick it up and brushed at its case. It was covered with a thick coat of moss, a parting jeer from the trees. He turned to show it to Spar, but the captain was already leading the way back to the narrow clearing. Feeling sheepish, Roan ducked around the few trees that remained of the ring, and fell in behind.

"Are you all right?" Leonora whispered, dropping back to slip her arm through Roan's.

"Apart from a wounded dignity, I'm fine," Roan assured her. "Did the bicycles come back?"

"No," she said. "Isn't that funny? It's the second time today they've been scared off. At least those trees didn't throw a pair of people."

For a gently reared noble lady for whom the greatest terror was having to dance with visiting dignitaries and taking final exams from private tutors, she was coping remarkably well.

"We'll have to walk out of here," Spar said. "The steeds will come out in the daylight, if they can. Otherwise, we'll double up until we can get replacements. Form up!"

"Sir!" Lum said, appearing beside him and throwing a crisp salute. "We found 'em!"

"The bicycles?" Roan asked.

"No, sir, the scientists," Lum said, highly excited. Alette and Hutchings were behind him, nodding agreement. They had altered to be slightly taller and more fit, and their uniforms were tailored, deep olive camouflage shirts and trousers, with round steel helmets encased in netting. "I heard their voices, off to the west, sir. We all heard them. Voices, and machine sounds. It had to be them, sir."

"Good," Leonora said. "I'll have something to say to Master Brom about making us bungle around in the woods after him. I have *never* liked it here."

Spar frowned while his uniform changed to match those of his troops. "Can you find it again, Corporal? The path keeps moving."

"Sure of it, sir," Lum said. "We followed my compass back here. That's stayed true, at least."

The captain rubbed his hands together and flexed his knuckles. "That'd make this worthwhile, then. What do you say, Master Roan?"

"We'll do it," Roan said. "Lead the way, Corporal."

"Yessir!" Lum said. He pointed his lantern off to the right toward where the trees were more widely spaced. "This way to start."

One pace behind, Roan found it easier to maneuver in the dark. Leonora fell in beside him, and put her arm through his. In the light of the lantern they had borrowed from one of the guards, he could see her eyes, huge and wary.

The trees cast fearsome shadows on their path, but Roan kept turning the lantern toward them and reducing them to twigs and leaves. A sharp hooting from a night-bird made them both jump, and then laugh nervously. Leonora maintained a tight clutch on his arm.

"How far is it, Corporal?" Roan asked, after a while.

"Not much farther," Lum said. "If you're quiet you can sort of hear their voices now."

"Can't hear much of anything with all the threshing we're doing," Spar grumbled from his position at the rear.

"Shh!" Leonora hissed impatiently. "Listen."

Roan strained to understand the low susurrus coming from ahead of them. Gradually, words surfaced. "Turn back. It's a trap. Lost. You'll die here. Die." Was it a warning, or just the natural malice of the forest?

"Did you hear that?" Roan asked.

"Hear what?" Spar asked. "Just the wind in the branches. Sir."

"I hear it," Hutchings said. "Sounds like threats. The Forest doesn't want us here. It'll kill us."

The female guard was sobbing quietly to herself. "I was lost here once when I was a child. The voices almost drove me mad. The words!"

"It's all right," Roan said, soothingly, reaching out to grasp her shoulder. "We're together. Stay close."

Mustering lanterns, pocketknife lights, torches, even bright ideas to light their way, the small group marched onward. The needle in the miniature compass that was attached to the side of Roan's pocketknife pointed toward the Castle of Dreams off toward the right, so he knew he was headed west. The ground underfoot was dry and relatively even.

Something with dozens of cold, tickly legs landed with a plop on the back of Roan's hand, almost making him drop the knife. Not again! he thought. He jumped in surprise and slapped at his hand, but hit only his own flesh. There was nothing there. Another illusion.

Something else tickled the nape of his neck under his left ear. He jumped and turned. A glowing face leered at him. Roan gasped, and the face vanished. Some of the guards shouted. Roan turned, and another face loomed ahead of them, with vacant eye sockets and a grinning mouth. Lum raised his quarterstaff and struck out at the face, but hit nothing except more tree branches. The glowing mask vanished with a chilling laugh. A gargoyle face with horns, pointed ears, and a forked tongue, more horrible than the first two, appeared right in front of Roan, who jumped, startled. Leonora screamed.

"Nightmares," a familiar voice said, cheerfully. "Harmless."

Roan let out a relieved breath. "Bergold. You've changed again."

"Hmm," Bergold said, scratching his ear, and frowning when he discovered the point at the top. "Bad?"

"Horrendous," Leonora said, firmly. "You glow in the dark."

"Interesting," Bergold said, unperturbed. "Then I ought to go first, and lend my countenance to this expedition." He pushed forward, and walked beside Lum.

"Easy does it," Bergold said. "Wait, whoa, *hold*!"

In between the "wait" and the "whoa," the ground rolled

under Roan's feet and heaved itself up into a hummock. By the time Bergold got to "hold," he had fallen backwards onto his friend, knocking Roan into Drea, who toppled into the file of guards, and they all collapsed on one another into a hollow full of scratchy tree roots.

"This wasn't here just now!" Lum exclaimed. "We just walked over that spot, and it was flat as a pancake. I do most earnestly beg your pardon, Your Highness," he added, moving off the princess's legs in extreme embarrassment.

"Is it alive?" Leonora asked, scrambling to her feet. She hadn't really noticed the imposition in the confusion. Her nurse was beside her, helping her up. They clambered out of the hollow as quickly as they could.

"If the trees can move, so can the ground," Bergold explained, grimacing and showing about eighty pointed teeth. "It's not alive as we know it, but it's got a kind of consciousness, and a sense of malicious mischief. Not very nice, is it? Is anyone hurt?"

"No, sir," Spar said, counting heads and noses, and finding an equal number of each.

"Look!" Felan said, behind him. "A light! They're here!"

"That's it, sir," Lum exclaimed. "That's what we saw!"

"Shh," Roan whispered. "Brom's people will hear you."

"They won't hear a thing," Leonora murmured from beside him. "Listen to all the noise they're making."

Roan stood silent. He heard numerous voices talking in low tones, plus many other sounds that were unfamiliar: liquid burbling, mechanical chuckling, and odd, tinny music. But there was no sensation of alarm or urgency.

"They've made themselves right at home," Spar whispered.

Roan put his hand in front of his borrowed lamp so it would be visible to the others, and cocked a finger to beckon them close.

"They don't know we're here," he whispered. "We'll make ready, then charge into their encampment. Remember, we want to destroy or disable the Alarm Clock. And don't let the group get close together. Their influence is surprisingly strong when they touch."

"I remember," Spar hissed. "A dragon, out of thin air." He drew his sword, and motioned for his soldiers to do the same. Roan opened his red pocket knife, this time selecting a heavy cudgel studded with steel knobs. The princess moved back in the ranks to stay with Bergold who, as a winged gargoyle, could protect her if necessary.

"Now, don't charge until you see where everyone is," Roan warned them. "Don't let anyone sneak around us."

The clearing ahead of them glowed with a blue-white light so bright it was difficult for Roan to make out details from where he crouched. Figures, looking oddly attenuated, moved back and forth before the light source. The machine sounds were unfamiliar, but that was unsurprising. Only the Sleepers knew what other machinations Brom had come up with. Roan made himself a wager that the scientists had more technical advancements in hand than they would ever show the king.

As his eyes adjusted, he squinted through the harsh light looking for the Alarm Clock. A light touch on his arm from Lum made him glance to his right. Some of the figures were moving around a humped shadow. It looked large enough. Roan nodded to the corporal, who tiptoed silently back into the undergrowth. In a moment, Roan felt three taps between his shoulder blades.

In a move calculated to startle, Roan burst out of the woods into the clearing. Slack-limbed with surprise, the shadowed figures turned to stare at him. He saw their eyes, looking huge and dark in their faces.

"Ladies and gentlemen, you are under arrest in the name of the king!" Roan announced, hefting his staff. "Please do not attempt to escape. If you cooperate and come quietly, it will be better for you."

"Stop them!" Felan cried, a silhouette to Roan's left. "They're running away!"

"Get them!" Spar roared, charging into the clearing. "In the name of the king!" He set off in pursuit of the shapes scampering across the open glen. Roan joined in the chase. Brom's minions had a head start, but on his long legs he should catch up with them in no time.

"There's a cave up there!" Lum shouted, pointing at a low hemisphere of shadow many yards ahead. The scientists were pouring into it. For a moment, in the gleam of the light, Roan got the impression that they weren't wearing any clothes. Had he interrupted some weird scientific ritual?

"We have them now," Spar said, gleefully, waving his sword. He gestured to his guards. "You two, stay out here and guard the door. Lum, inside with me!"

"No!" Leonora cried, her voice rising above their war cries. "Don't go in! Look!"

Roan, only steps away from the cave mouth, windmilled his arms to bring himself to a stop. At last, he was close enough to see one of the figures he had been chasing. It turned a startled, ash-white face toward him. The enormous eyes didn't belong to any minion of the Ministry of Science he had ever seen. The creature had thin lips and no nose, and the cave it was running for was not dark inside. There were jewel-colored lights everywhere, and a flat, altar-like table in the center floodlit by a hot, white beam. Four of the white-faced beings stood around it, beckoning to him ominously. Roan backed away in haste.

Suddenly, he was the quarry, and they the hunters. A handful of the odd beings grabbed for his arms and legs, seeking to drag him into the cave. Roan threw himself to the ground and rolled away, feeling the drag of their long fingers on his shoulders, his cloak, his hair. Leonora shouted as the soldiers reached him and pulled him free. The last of the beings dove into the strange cave as Roan scrambled back to his feet.

A door slid across the cave mouth, sealing it, and the whole hill vibrated with a deafening hum. Red and white beams of light chased themselves around its surface, and the whole hill and surrounding ground, including the place where Roan had just been standing, shot up into the air. Roan and the others stood gawking upward at it. The saucer-shaped mass stopped a thousand feet above them, emitted a five-tone musical burst of sound, then arrowed away toward the south.

"Bless my soul," Bergold said, breaking the silence. Roan blinked and came back to earth. His friend's gargoyle face was wreathed with a happy smile that was positively terrifying with his current features. "Where are my notebooks? I must get that down on paper before I forget a single detail."

"Take mine," Colenna said, rummaging in her capacious bag. She beckoned one of the guards over with his little lantern. The yellow beam seemed suddenly inadequate and insignificant after that blinding white glare, but it was much friendlier. Bergold took the proffered notebook and began to scratch away, talking to himself all the while.

"Well, that wasn't them," Felan said. "What now?"

"It appears to me," Roan began, "that Brom and his people never did come into the forest. We would have found at least a trace of them by now if they had. They might even have joined forces with . . ." he gestured upward, "with whatever that was. We should count ourselves lucky. Let's get out of the forest, and set up camp for the night."

"Right you are," Captain Spar said, briskly, slapping his sword into its sheath. "I for one am hungry and thirsty, and I could use a solid night's sleep. Corporal!"

"Sir!" Lum said, coming to his side and saluting.

"Lead us out of here, lad." Spar lined everyone up in a double file behind his corporal, and took the rear himself.

The forest once again tried to block their way and confuse them, but its efforts were half-hearted. It seemed to have given its best shot with the attempted abduction. Everyone stayed close together, refusing to be separated out for individual terrors. Roan found he was less frightened by the invisible spiders that dropped down on him, by the phantom auditors that whispered in his ears, by pop-quizzes flapped in front of him, by the monsters that paced the party threateningly. He realized he had to run for them to chase him, so he did not run. He was too tired to be scared. In a very short time, the party was alone.

"Shh!" Bergold said, tilting a sharp ear to the left. "I hear rustling!"

"Check it out," Lum directed his soldiers. They squeezed between the bushes, but the others kept their lamps trained on their backs. In a moment, Roan heard glad cries, and Alette returned, smiling.

"It's the steeds!" she said.

"Really?" Leonora asked, at once solicitous. "Are they all right?"

"Yes, Your Highness. This way!"

Leonora and Roan followed their guide into a small hollow where the four missing bicycles were clustered in a frightened mass. Leonora knelt between Cruiser and Golden Schwinn, and soothed, petted, and complimented them both until they huddled around her shoulders.

"There," Leonora said, pleased. "They'll be fine, now."

Roan checked the packs. "Everything is still in the panniers," he said. He patted Cruiser, glad to have his silver friend back with him. They followed the lights back to the path. Corporal Lum again took the lead.

A hundred yards later, Roan could see murky starlight through the tree branches.

Suddenly, a log ten feet thick crashed to the ground in front of Lum, strewing spiky branches everywhere. The bark was thickly coated with thorns as long as fingers. The bicycles reared and squeaked. Roan put a hand on Cruiser and Golden Schwinn, to keep them from bolting again. He threw his head back.

"All right!" he shouted at the forest. "You win! You've driven us away! We're leaving. We can't take your horrors any more. All we want is to go!"

The rocking log paused, appearing to consider his words. Then, just as abruptly as it fell, it broke in half. Each half, hollow as an eggshell, rocked on its spiky exterior, and collapsed into several sections no thicker than bark, spraying decayed wood-dust in every direction. Lum caught the full cloud in the face, and choked until Colenna pounded him on the back.

"It's dead and dust!" Spar shouted in surprise.

"Let's go before something else falls on us," Leonora said.

"Right you are, Your Highness."

The group tiptoed warily over the remains of the tree, looking around for more booby traps, but Roan knew there would be none. The Forest had released them at last.

"Whew!" Bergold said, brushing himself off as they passed the last overhanging tree branch. The phosphorescent quality of his face began to fade, until he was merely grotesque. Gradually, he became an ordinary man again, though this time with a mass of curly dark hair going gray and a sharp nose. "Roan, how did you do that?"

"I learned a lesson earlier," Roan said, humbly. "Show respect, and menace loses all its power over you. I wish I'd known that twenty years ago." He hadn't completely banished the bogey of his childhood, but he'd beaten it back, for once.

"Well, we're exactly where we went in," Spar said, in disgust, looking around at the night-bound land. "Waste of time. They never came this way. Brom must have skirted the woods, never passing through."

"No, but we had to check," Roan said.

"I'm truly sorry," Felan said, humbly, striking himself in the side of the head with his hand. "The trail seemed so very clear."

"We could have been following the path that tree made," Roan said. "I believed it, too."

"Well, so long as you forgive me," Felan said, with a shamefaced grin.

"What seems so incredible to me," Roan said, thoughtfully, "is that after escaping from me, Brom and his minions made it as far as the Nightmare Forest, and turned back again."

Bergold pursed his lips together and emitted a long whistle. "Goodness," he exclaimed. "I hadn't thought of the difficulty of such a journey. Theirs is a very considerable power."

"Unique," Felan said, in a low, respectful voice.

"Well, we've lost them for tonight," Bergold said, throwing his hands up. "I'm ready to drop. We'll have to stop for tonight, and backtrack to where we lost them tomorrow morning."

"I agree," Roan said.

"Oh, no!" the princess protested. She had seemed to perk up once they'd left the forest, but she looked alarmed again. "We can't stop! They'll keep going. We can find the trail, now that we're out here."

"My dear, we have to get some sleep to be of any use tomorrow," Bergold said reasonably, taking her hand. Dismayed, Leonora looked from one person to the next for support. The others shook their heads apologetically.

"Brom will stop, too," Roan said, gently. "They have even more need for rest than we do. They're running ahead of us, carrying heavy and delicate equipment through dangerous terrain, and they're maintaining that link among themselves. They also must disguise themselves so we won't spot them. All of that at once must be exhausting. They will sleep, I promise you. We need rest and food, or we won't have the strength to pedal tomorrow."

"What if they've caught a train somewhere?" she protested, helplessly. Roan could see now how frightened she was, and just tired enough not to be thinking rationally. "What if this crucible of theirs can carry them all night long?"

"Even if it does, they can't reach the Sleepers tonight," Roan said firmly. "I believe they're going to the mountains, and it's a long way from here, no matter which range they're headed for. We can't go any farther. The bicycles will dissolve if we don't rest them," he added, patting his steed. Cruiser slumped against his legs as if thankful for the break.

Leonora's own shiny gold bike collapsed suddenly to the ground and lay there, its front wheel spinning wearily. She looked at it, and a small, rueful smile touched the corner of her lips.

"All right," Leonora said. "They can't take any more. I'm tired, too. But we go on at first light."

"Of course, Your Highness," Roan said, offering her a smile and a very deep bow. "Uh . . . shall we camp a little farther away from the forest's edge?"

Chapter 10

"Glinn! Glinn!" Brom's voice came sharply through the twilight.

"Here, sir!" Glinn said. He halted the small procession, and clambered onto a hummock in the field next to the road so his light-colored coat was visible in every direction.

Taboret squinted down the hill, and unhooked a thumb from her backpack harness to point at the sticklike figure hurrying towards them, elbows jutting outward at every step. "Here he comes," she said, unnecessarily, because anybody could see him. He must have been visible for miles, glowing like a living flame.

"Feeding on the anticipation of our success," Glinn muttered, as if he was reading her mind. "Must have gone well back there." Several shapeless shadows trailed behind him less energetically.

"*They* don't look happy," Dowkin said, shifting from foot to foot to ease the weight of the litter on his shoulders.

"Not a bit," echoed his brother, at the other end of the Alarm Clock's platform. Brom closed the rest of the distance on his long spindly legs, and Glinn jumped down to meet him.

"Report," Brom barked at Glinn. "Is all well?"

"Yes, sir," the young man said. He was earnest and handsome, and sometimes a tedious bore when he got going on the Theory of Root Causes, his pet topic, but on the whole, Taboret liked him. She had always admired his ability to compartmentalize his thinking so that it seemed he was concentrating fully on more than one thing at a time.

Such a skill was an asset in the lab. He was always decent and friendly, unlike some others she'd known. "No undue influences or nuisances. We ran into a weather pattern, but we pointed it off to the southwest."

"Four of you?" Brom gave him a sharp look. "With no loss of speed?"

"None," Glinn said, with pride. Yes, Taboret thought. They hadn't slackened, and she'd had to run alongside the litter holding hands with Dowkin and Doolin as they carried it. Taboret had felt so drained when the crucible's energy was pulled in two directions at once she had been close to resigning her position on the spot and running back to Mnemosyne alone. Luckily, she had made her traveling form sturdy, with splendid calf muscles. She had a long mane of dark blond hair braided behind her and keen hazel eyes in a heart-shaped face. Not beautiful, she thought, but not unpleasant to look at.

"Good," Brom said, flicking a glance over the rest of them. "We are progressing well toward remote control. We've lost Dalton. The palace investigator followed us, and captured Dalton during a nuisance that we were using as cover to get away from him."

"Roan did?" Glinn asked, surprised. "How did he find our trail? We swept those footprints for a hundred yards beyond the castle gates."

"I don't know," Brom said, tersely. "But we're rid of him now."

Taboret swallowed nervously at the finality in Brom's tone. She hoped nothing horrible had happened to Roan. She liked the historian's son. He was a nice man, although strange in a . . . changeless sort of way. She wanted the project to succeed, but not at the cost of other people's lives.

Suddenly, Brom spun on his heel and stared down at her, his eyes glowing from within. She gasped, hoping he hadn't picked up what she had been thinking. His finger stabbed at her, then at some of the others.

"We will stop just over the crest of this hill for the night. You, and you, will help the men unload the device. *Carefully.*"

"Yes, sir," Taboret said, her heart pounding like a trip-hammer. He hadn't caught her being negative. Thank . . . thank something. She trudged down the hill behind the litter, through the small stand of woods to a glade that smelled pleasantly of flowers and sweet grass. Brom signaled them to a stop, and pointed at the clearing.

"Here," he said.

Taboret halted well behind him. She had to be more careful to keep her mental tone light. The chief had already proved that he could sometimes read the thoughts of the others through the link. She was more than a little afraid of him. At twenty-three, Taboret felt lucky to have a job that she loved. She loved the exhilaration of knowing the very rightness of scientific discovery, and the tingle that went down her spine when a theory was proved a fact. Reading the old books and seeing how the great scientists of the past had come to their conclusions was the greatest adventure she could think of. With Brom dedication went deeper than that. He seemed to have a tap into the ways of Fate itself. His vision consumed him from within, and he felt that everyone should be as enthusiastic about his project as he was all the time. Thank the Seven that his telepathy was intermittent and not very accurate.

Brom seemed to pick out feelings better than words, so she kept up a shell of pleasurable excitement when she was around him. Most of it was genuine now. She'd never been so far out of Mnemosyne before, and the land around her was strange and new. It was becoming such a good mental disguise that she occasionally caught Brom beaming at her with his mad eyes.

Taboret flinched as she noticed the chief studying her now. She went to help Glinn unbuckle the yoke from the two men bearing it. Dowkin and Doolin were twin brothers, as stubborn as pigs. Whenever fate hit them and they changed, they always stayed identical. Among the apprentices, largely a gregarious lot, the Countingsheep brothers kept to themselves, as if the other sibling was all the company either one ever needed. They were so unpleasant Taboret was glad to let them be, whenever she could. Brom only kept them around because they were brilliant scholars and strong as oxen.

"Watch it, you clipped my shoulder," Doolin complained, as she unfastened one of the heavy clips on his harness.

"Watch what you do to my brother, careless," Dowkin snapped at her, while Glinn freed him.

"She hasn't done anything to him," Glinn assured him, lifting the harness up so Dowkin could slip out of it. The brothers glared at her anyway, and Taboret retreated to the side of the framework.

"Thank you," Taboret said, peeking at him under the litter where the brothers couldn't see her.

"It's nothing," Glinn said. "Everyone's touchy because they're tired."

Taboret let out a long sigh. "Me, too."

"Together now," Glinn said, and the group took the litter and set the Alarm Clock on the ground. Brom clucked henlike around them, grimacing when the huge swaddled mass settled onto the grass. The big bells on top of the unit swayed slightly on their posts, and touched delicately against the hammer between them, creating a faint humming. They made Taboret nervous. Once in a while they chimed together under the canvas. The resonance of the metal domes rang on and on in her head until it felt as if it would split. Taboret wanted to run away, dissolve her part in the link. She forced the thought out of her mind as the chief's gaze upon her turned coldly speculative, and bent to tuck the canvas farther under the framework. She had agreed, as had the rest of the apprentices and the two mercenaries, to carry on all the way to the end of this mission. Once it had concluded they could continue in the service of the Ministry of Science, or move on, as they chose, with a testimonial in hand, but there were to be no quitters during the project.

If someone had given her the choice this moment, Taboret might have turned back. She had never been so exhausted in her life. Her duties as a trainee member of staff were ordinarily light. Measuring, recording data, running errands for Brom and the other senior staff, minding the apparatus of an experiment in progress—nothing strenuous. Carodil always told them that one day their time to use their superior faculties, for which they had been chosen from the thousands of applicants, would arrive. Then Brom came forward with his proposition: increased creative power now for a select group of apprentices, a process they could use forever, if they would help him with a complex and intriguing investigation. Taboret couldn't resist the combination. A Dreamlander might be capable of wielding only so much influence, but she knew she hadn't as much as some people. To increase her personal strength was irresistible. She volunteered at once.

The way Brom had explained his proposition brought to light the doubts Taboret had always harbored about the Sleepers. She wasn't sure she really believed in them. They were part of a tale her parents told in an awed hush. Taboret didn't respect tales. She believed in what she could see and touch and prove. The power of the link was perceptible and tangible. She heard people's minds. She saw things come out of the ether that were too complex and large for a single mind, no matter how powerful, to create. As a result, she had been eager to go along with the chief's theory about the Sleepers, if only on a hypothetical basis. Proposition: If the Sleepers existed, then the chances were calculable that they behaved much as the legends consistently described them. They slept. If a living being slept, logic dictated that it could almost certainly be awakened. Therefore, the Sleepers, if real, could probably be awakened. Therefore, someone should seek them out and try, and see what happened.

Taboret had been surprised by the shock on the faces in the audience chamber when Brom put forward his proposal. It hadn't really occurred to her how much the unknown frightened people. Why weren't they fascinated by the possibility? Didn't they want to know the truth of their most overarching legend?

She hadn't been on the team that built the Alarm Clock. The machine had already been under way in the most secret and best insulated of the laboratories in Mnemosyne. The Clock was a completely new thing in the Dreamland, something that had been purpose-built, not found, not molded by will, not dreamed by the Sleepers, and did not appear anywhere in the records of previous inventions. The chief's design was revolutionary. The insides had been cut laboriously gear by gear out of metal forged for the project from ore someone had actually dug out of a mountain. To make the clockworks, the chief had copied the mechanical workings of a pocket watch he had taken apart. The Alarm Clock had to be absolutely reliable, because it couldn't be tested complete until it was used. It might change shape, like all other things in the

Dreamland did, but form followed function. It would still do its job no matter what it looked like.

Brom waved them away from the litter so he could be alone with his great invention. Taboret went to help set up camp. The first night was more unstructured than the following nights would be, to give the apprentices a chance to work with crucible energies and learn how they felt. Brom had encouraged them to make use of their resources and design abilities.

The grassy hollow was broad and gently sloping down toward a shallow stream. The cook had taken the flattest part of the clearing near the stream as his impromptu kitchen. Basil, a plump, dark apprentice with a knack for food preparation, had assumed the cooking duties. With the help of a few of the other apprentices, he set up a full-sized four-burner stove, and re-formed a huge boulder and two fallen logs into a stone refectory table with benches on either side. Basil had made a pegboard for his utensils out of a net of vines hanging from a nearby tree. He looked up from chopping onions to smile at Taboret. Technically, crucible power could have made one thing to eat into something else to eat without all that effort, but Basil liked cooking. To him it wasn't work.

Taboret's camp task was personal hygiene. From her pack, she took a ceramic washbowl and a zinc bucket with a lid, and put them both on the ground half a dozen paces from the stream. She took a glance around to see who could come and help her. The twins, Dowkin and Doolin, sat on one of the benches, watching Basil. As if they could guess what she was thinking, they gave her identical twisted-lip sneers, and turned their backs. Basil shook his head and pointed his knife blade toward Carina and Gano, who had just finished making camp beds and were heading towards the table.

"Sure, we'll help," Gano said, impishly. She had red hair and full cheeks that creased when she smiled. Carina was older and shorter, with thick brown hair and very black eyebrows. "This way, we get first crack at the facilities. Will this have a shower?"

"That's the most efficient form of bath," Taboret said, "but I hope we can do better things. Here's my plan." Unrolling her blueprint, she and the other two women joined hands around it.

In less time than she had ever dreamed possible, the bathroom was finished. The transformation of one similar item into another with the same purpose was far easier than changing its nature even within the boundaries of normal influence. The washbowl became a carved marble tub and a pedestal sink with chrome shower head and taps. The zinc pail grew a tank with a chain and an elaborate seat that made it look, well, like a throne. The whole process was as close to being magic as a rational mind would allow. Crucible power was astonishingly efficient. Taboret drew down a curtain of moss hanging off the tree over their heads to make a handsome privacy drape as Gano and Carina finished making the walls from a cardboard box. They grinned companionably at her when she met their eyes, always seeming to look up at the same moment she did. There was a tangible joy in the cooperative process. If Brom accomplished nothing else, he had created an environment in which teamwork was stressed and supported. Only the twins were horrid and uncooperative.

"It's beautiful," Carina said, standing in the center of the room to admire her handiwork.

"It certainly is," Taboret said. "I can't wait to crawl in that tub."

"Me first," said Gano, taking fluffy towels out of the linen closet next to the mirror.

"Second dibs," said Carina, raising a hand before Taboret could speak.

"I'm third, then," Taboret said goodnaturedly, stepping out of the door and closing it behind her. "Come and get me when you're done."

Outside, Taboret felt suddenly sick, and had to shut her eyes to stop the roller-coaster sensation in her midsection. She took a pace away from the bath, and the sensation stopped. She stepped back again, and her belly rolled the other way. For some reason the influences felt funny in the vicinity of the bath. She wondered if something had gone wrong with the construction, but the sink ran hot and cold water perfectly, the toilet flushed, and the shower was producing beautiful hot steam. She decided she was just tired.

"Nice job," Glinn called to her. He knelt on the ground in

the homey red glow of thirty shaded lanterns hanging in the trees around the perimeter.

Taboret forgot about the nausea as she took in the transformation of the camp. For all their lack of social graces, the Countingsheep brothers were hard workers. They had set up the dozen camp beds, each with a mosquito curtain suspended above it. Lurry, a scrawny, big-nosed apprentice, whose latent pyromania always a subject for reprimand in the laboratory, straddled a tree branch as he put up the last of the lanterns. Bolmer and Mamovas, a man and woman both slim and dark, were putting the finishing touches on a thin curtain wall that circled the camp to discourage animals and other pests, and to hide the light from outsiders. Glinn grinned up at her as she came over to see what he was doing.

"I'll be glad of a bath," he said. "I'm sore from my heels up to my ears. Today was rough going. And Basil's a slave driver. I helped him set up his kitchen. You'd think from the fuss that he was making a sterile facility."

"Today was miserable," Taboret said emphatically. "We can't slog along on forever on foot. We're moving so slowly because of . . . the *thing*. We can't make good time. Someone will catch up with us."

"We're not going to be so easy to catch," he said cheerfully, dumping his pack on the ground. "And we're not going on foot. Voila! Transportation!" Taboret bent to look at the heap of small sacks.

"Paperclips?" she asked, letting handfuls sift through her fingers. "You're mad. Those'll take forever to mature." One of the scientific principles about metal that she'd learned way back in grade school was that bicycles were the adult form of paperclips. "The process will take months!"

A sensible person never stored too many paperclips together, because when the day came that you needed one, there wouldn't be any around, but there'd be a tangle of coat hangers hanging in the closet. The larval form liked that kind of dark, dry place to mature. Then, one day, the coat hangers would disappear, and you'd trip over a knot of bicycles the second you stepped outdoors. Taboret's first bike had come from a litter at the house next door. She wondered why Glinn was grinning.

"Aha," he said, tapping his own temple. "You're thinking in pre-crucible terms. We can do this overnight."

Taboret raised her eyebrows. They could. He was right. That was why he was Brom's second in command and she was rank and file.

"Okay," she said, shaking her head at her own failure to adapt. "But I want a blue one."

"Frivolity?" Brom demanded, walking up to stand between them. "This is a serious scientific expedition, young woman."

"Yes, sir," she said, making herself meet his eyes. "I continue to observe, sir. I am merely trying to ease the stress of travel by controlled levity." It sounded like a load of philosophical codswallop to Taboret's own ears, but it seemed to satisfy the chief.

"As long as you know what you are doing," Brom said, in his ponderous lecturer's fashion. "Do not allow the . . . levity to get out of hand."

"No, sir."

"It's my fault, sir," Glinn said, gallantly, standing up between Taboret and their superior. "I encouraged it. I enjoy comradely badinage, particularly Taboret's. You could consider her a candidate for morale officer."

"This is not a military organization," Brom said magisterially, but the crisis had passed. He beckoned over the others who were nearby to form the gestalt around the sacks of paperclips. The metal twists were well on their way to report-binder size by the time the circle broke. Taboret was grateful when Basil rang a triangle with his cooking spoon to summon them to supper.

During the meal and the cleanup that followed before bedtime, Taboret kept feeling eyes following her. Every time she turned around, Brom was watching her. When she turned her table scraps into compost, when she came out of the bath, even when she glanced up from turning down her camp bunk, he was there, standing under one of the hanging lanterns, staring.

What have I done? she wondered.

"I heard you," Glinn said, in an undertone, appearing unexpectedly at her shoulder. She jumped when he spoke. "Don't think like that if you can help it. The link is getting stronger. Can't you feel it?"

"Yes, I can," Taboret said, thinking of her experience with Carina and Gano. "But why is he watching me that way?"

"He's watching everyone. Making sure that there aren't any king's spies among us."

"What? Who would want to jeopardize the project?"

Glinn shrugged apologetically. "Well, it could happen. You saw what went on in court. We were told to cease and desist, right?"

"Shortsighted," Taboret snorted, feeling the knot of tension ease. She sat down on the camp bed and undid her boots. If that was Brom's problem, she could disabuse him at once. "The Sleepers could . . . roll over in bed one day, and wake each other up. Then we'd all be gone—maybe—and no one would know why. We want to do it under controlled conditions, so everyone knows what actually happens."

"Exactly," Glinn said, letting out a sigh. More people were coming into the sleeping area, so he lowered his voice again. "But, Brom is worried. You'd be, too."

"No one would betray him," Taboret said, confidently, remembering the way the chief's eyes bored into her. "They'd be too frightened."

Chapter 11

The sun tiptoed silently up over the horizon, blushing pink with mischief, and stuck a finger of light in Roan's eye. He started in his sleep, and came awake all at once, turning his face away from the glare with a groan. The tendril of light recoiled, and crept off to look for another sleeper to pester.

Roan stretched to unknot the kink in his back. The nice flat piece of ground where he'd unrolled his sleeping bag seemed to have taken undulation lessons from the Nightmare Forest. He'd had smoother rides on lame camels.

From the look of those of his fellow travelers still huddled in their covers, they were sleeping no better. The twitching bundle next to him was Bergold. Roan watched with fascination as his friend's nose and ears changed size or bent upward to avoid contact with the stony ground.

On his other side Roan could see a square, white pavilion which had been set up to shelter the princess and her servant, Drea, from the night. The slight figure on the pallet beyond the translucent, hanging gauze seemed hunched up and miserable. The modest shelter was far less than Leonora was accustomed to, but the party had been dangerously tired by that time. They had given every element of the tent their best attention, but it was makeshift, at best. In the early sunlight it looked like faded, hanging rags.

Forced by the lateness of the hour to choose the first likely campsite they came to, the party had concentrated less on comfort than on safety. Using what strength they had left to gather influence, Roan and the others had built an invisible but protective wall around the place where they intended to sleep. Two guards were posted on the perimeter for a very short first shift while the others bedded down as quickly as possible. Roan didn't remember anything after that until the dawn woke him up. Even as he gazed at the lightening sky, a large obstruction interposed itself between Roan and the landscape, and grinned down at him.

"Good morning," Misha said.

"You're here sooner than I expected you," Roan said, squinting up at the large young man. His hair was the color of sunshine, his eyes a clear and untroubled blue, and his cheeks were pink. He looked disgustingly hale for someone who had made the round trip to and from Mnemosyne in the time it took Roan and the others to get lost in the Nightmare Forest and have a miserable night's sleep.

"It is a terrific day for a ride," the young continuitor said, offering Roan a hand up. "I'm not sore on the bottom because the steeds are horses today." He gestured toward the stand of trees where the bicycles had been tied up the night before. Instead of two wheels, all of them stood on four legs. "I slept the night in the palace on a bed, and I've been riding since about false dawn, but I didn't have to pedal a yard."

"Thank the Sleepers for small mercies," Roan said, yawning. "My calves wish they'd been cast out of iron, and I'm accustomed to long, forced rides. The others are no doubt in worse shape. What can you tell me about the man you brought back to the palace with you?"

"When I left they still hadn't managed to get anything out of him," Misha said, shaking his head. "Nothing of use, anyhow. He would only repeat what we already know: Brom's going to wake up the Sleepers. The interrogators are having to resort to drastic tactics. The acting head of security sent for his *mother*."

"Brr!" Roan said, shivering in sympathy for the prisoner. "Is anyone else up?"

"Almost everyone. Spar and the guards are drilling down that way, by a stream," Misha said, pointing. "Felan is on the other side of the steeds, writing furiously. I surprised him when I rode up."

"Writing?" Roan asked, pausing again for another good stretch.

"Yes, writing," Felan said, when Roan stumped down the hill to ask him. Felan wore gold-rimmed half-spectacles over myopic blue eyes. He held up a scroll of parchment half covered with minute script. "I'm composing a message for Micah. Someone has to keep the court apprised of our progress. I'd send a message in by grapevine, but there are none near here." He gestured backwards over his shoulder with his quill pen toward the edge of the clump of trees. "You can wash up first if you want to. I'll just finish this and get it sent off."

"Can I help add anything, Master Felan?" Roan asked, leaning over the historian's shoulder to read the document.

"Not really." Felan glanced up at Roan, and his brows drew together, puzzled. He readjusted his glasses to full-frame lenses. "Don't you get tired of shaving the same face day after day?"

"Not really," Roan said, uncomfortably. He moved away, and Felan turned to concentrate on his writing, almost certainly unaware of the sting his question had raised. Roan hated feeling like a freak among ordinary Dreamlanders. Usually, when he traveled, he wasn't around anyone long enough for them to notice that he never changed. He felt as if he had brought the court with him. I'm functional, responsible and respected, he thought, gritting his teeth as he stumped back up the hill. The king himself entrusted this mission to me. Why does my sameness rob me of respect I have honestly earned?

Hanging from the trees just out of reach of the horses was a draped enclosure that appeared to have been made out of someone's cloak. Roan pushed the cloth aside and found a pitcher and bowl balanced on a tree stump. From the soggy place next to the cloaked area, Roan guessed that the water had been changed several times already. Behind the stump was a makeshift seat suspended over a hole in the ground. Beside the crude facilities was a large, thin-leafed book with several of the front pages torn off.

"All the amenities of home," Misha said cheerfully. "Think I'll scare up something to drink. I brought some pastries from the palace cook."

"I'll look forward to them," Roan said, heading back to his sleeping place for his razor and sponge bag. "Anything to help me wake up. We need to be on our way as soon as possible."

Washing out of a small basin was something Roan never enjoyed while he was on the road, finding it uncomfortable and inefficient. Instead, he took the water pitcher and extended it so that it formed a makeshift shower, perpetually refilling itself from the basin, which he widened enough to stand in. The water was cold, and the cloak-curtain kept blowing against his body, but it refreshed him to be clean again. He hung the mirror on the edge of the pitcher handle, now an elongated ear of porcelain attached to the shower pipe, and shaved while the water cascaded over his head.

He opened the curtain to dump out the dirty water as Misha was coming back down the hill. The young historian's eyes widened with interest at the pitcher arrangement.

"Very clever," he said, picking up the basin to fill. "Please leave it this way for me."

"All the comforts of home," Roan said.

Roan found Spar and the others in conference around the map on a flat rock beside the stream. Colenna smiled sweetly up at him, her gray eyes bright in a weather-worn face leaner and sharper in outline than the one she wore at court. She was an old friend, and an ally against such detractors as Datchell. Her gray hair was longer today, tied back in a braid with a leather thong. Felan raised an eyebrow at Roan in greeting.

"Good morning," Roan said, pleasantly. "Did everyone sleep well?"

"My back's killing me," Colenna said, gruffly. "It's been a long time since I slept on the ground. Too many rocks."

"You could have softened them up," Felan pointed out.

She shot him a shocked glance. "Young man, you'd never make a field observer. Touch, but don't alter. I've had to make a general distribution of painkillers for sore legs and seats," she said, turning back to Roan. "Lucky I had some with me."

"You're always prepared, Colenna," Roan said. Colenna threw him a friendly grimace.

"Lum's just come back from scouting, sir," Spar said. He turned the map toward Roan, who knelt down to see it. "We clean missed the trail last night. They turned off miles back. Just about here." He put a thumbnail on the paper where the road left a small wood two thirds of the way from Mnemosyne to the Nightmare Forest.

"We must've been following that tree all this way," Lum said apologetically.

"My fault, Captain," Roan said. "I insisted we try the southern route."

"My guards are not supposed to make mistakes," Spar said, tightly. "This is a serious matter."

"Indeed it is," Roan agreed. "But we've got a long way to go together. Let's just solve the problems that lie ahead of us, without reliving what is past."

"As you say, sir," Spar said, without expression.

"Are you in charge of this expedition?" Misha asked.

"He is," Spar said, nodding his head toward Roan. "The king himself gave him the assignment."

"Oh, I just wanted to know," Misha said. "I wasn't there."

"I hope you have no objection to that," Roan said.

"None at all," Misha said, pleasantly. "By the way, the Royal Geographer said things are expected to be very changeable today in this region, and we should be careful."

"We'll keep that in mind," Roan said. "We ought to get on the road as soon as we can."

"I left Hutchings at the place where the two paths intersect, in case the road tries to shift," Lum said, keeping his usually cheerful face serious. "Alette's followed the second path a ways to make sure. It won't get away from us this time, sir."

"Good man," Roan said. "Thank you for your diligence in making up for my errors."

Lum reddened under Spar's glare, and said stiffly, "Nice of you, sir."

Leonora's nurse, Drea, stalked into view, and nodded at them with great dignity. From her knapsack, the old woman produced a large leather bottle, and stooped to fill it at the stream.

"Is Her Highness awake?" Roan asked.

"My lady isn't ready to receive callers yet," the nurse said, frostily. She turned her back on Roan and carried the bottle away. In her hands, it looked like an ethereal crystal ewer. Only for the princess would Drea bother with such a transformation. Where Roan only loved and adored her, the old nurse was her votary, idolizing her as a goddess incarnate. Small wonder that if Leonora had come away from Mnemosyne with only one servant, instead of the host that usually accompanied her, it should be Drea. She had dandled Leonora as a child, and coddled her ever since. Almost a living security blanket.

"Shouldn't be long, now," Colenna said.

"How many of them are there?" Felan asked Lum.

"About ten or twelve, I should say," said the corporal. "Hard to tell, because I think they kept switching the load between themselves. The footprints change a bit when they do that, as they alter to bear the weight. But I think we're outnumbered. Should we send for reinforcements?"

"We're not going to meet them in combat," Roan said. "All we need to do is to destroy that device of theirs. They can do what they like when that's been disabled."

"But they'll just make another one!"

"I doubt it," Roan said. "If they could make another so easily, they wouldn't need to carry the one they have cross-country. They'd just have gone to the Hall of Sleepers, and built an Alarm Clock when they arrived."

"Good morning, all," Bergold said, stumping down the slope toward them. He'd added a short beard to his ensemble this morning, saving himself the trouble of having to shave under primitive conditions. "I'm last, eh?"

"Not quite," Misha said. "Her Highness is still getting ready."

"What a night! My fingers are still cramped from writing my notes."

"So are mine," Felan said, shaking out his wrist. "I'm just about ready to send my report." He felt in his pouch, and came up with a book of stamps. He took one, licked the reverse side, and stuck it firmly to the corner of his folded parchment.

At once, the stamp expanded, took on bulk and feathers, and became a bald eagle. The white-headed bird crushed the envelope in its talons, and, with a fierce look at the humans, opened its great wings and took off. Above them, it wheeled and made northward. In just moments, it was out of sight.

"Nothing like airmail," Bergold said. "We must be under a popular route. I saw another airmail fly overhead only a little while ago."

"Wouldn't it be nice if we could just stick stamps on ourselves and mail us to Brom?" Lum asked wistfully.

Felan gave him a rueful grin. "I didn't bring enough postage."

Roan glanced uphill but caught no glimpse of the princess yet. While waiting for Leonora to finish getting ready, they had a light breakfast and broke camp. The guards disassembled the invisible defensive wall, taking down each section with great care and exaggerated movements. Captain Spar had explained the danger of accidentally wandering into the wall during the night, and had carefully marked the exits for the others to see. Roan wondered briefly what would happen if a soldier dropped one of the invisible blocks. There'd probably be an explosion like they'd never seen. But since the bricks were invisible, would the blast be, too?

He rolled up his sleeping gear and mess supplies, folding them small so they would fit into his saddlebags. Bergold helpfully shook out the campfire, and folded it up in a rustle of red and silver foil. He tossed it to the soldier who was loading the pack animals.

Colenna had the most interesting outdoor gear. In her pack, she had one of everything that could be used as a base to transform into anything she might conceivably need on the road. Roan had seen the handsome pottery cup she was now putting away used as a bowl, a cooking pot, and a footbath. The item Roan envied most was a clever little stove that could be used in turn as a nightlight, torch, fire-starter, or bedwarmer. Some very clever craftsman must have fashioned it for her. Its base shape had to have been fire in its purest form.

When Roan went around the small stand of trees to stow his property in Cruiser's saddlebags, he saw that the wash area had been transformed for the princess's use. The curtain which had served as a privacy barrier for the others had become a solid and impenetrable wall with the cloak clasp reformed into the handle of a narrow but serviceable door. Roan heard Leonora humming over the sound of trickling water.

He went over to tap on the door. Before he could reach it, the nurse headed him off.

"Where do you think you're going?" she demanded, staring up at him defiantly. She had a bundle of clothes over her arm, and hastily tucked some fine, filmy garments out of sight among the others when she noticed Roan looking.

"I wanted to tell Her Highness that the rest of us will be ready to depart at her pleasure," Roan said, pleasantly.

Drea looked mortified. "My lady hasn't had her breakfast yet," the old woman said. She tipped a hand to show Roan where a small table and chair had been set up. "This may be an emergency venture, but some things do take priority! You can't ask her to take to horse without a decent meal inside her."

"Well, no," Roan began, uneasily. He glanced back at the others, aware of their impatience to be off, and his own. "Will it be . . . may we expect her soon?"

"One can't just bolt down food and expect it to sit," Drea said, with a touch of the old nursery manner. Roan felt chastised, but he noticed then that the humming had stopped. Leonora had fallen silent inside the washroom to listen to their conversation.

"Will you ask Her Highness to let us know when she is ready to depart?" Roan asked, keeping all traces of annoyance out of his voice.

"It's already ten o'clock," Hutchings muttered behind him. "She's taking an amazing long time to get cleaned up."

Roan turned and glared a warning, but it was too late. They heard a rustle from the washroom.

"How dare you talk about my lady like that?" Drea demanded, rounding on the guard. Instead of a dumpling, she looked like a dragon. Hutchings backed up a hasty pace.

"Drea!" the princess called. The claws and wings subsided at once. Drea hurried over and slipped in the door with the armload of clothes. It closed firmly behind her. Roan signed to the others to be about their business of loading the horses. To their credit, they looked abashed, particularly Hutchings, who went about his tasks with downcast gaze.

Within a few moments, Leonora emerged, fastening the blue cloak around her shoulders. The others tried not to stare, but she was aware they were aware of her. She met all their eyes in turn, wearing a fixed little smile, but her cheeks were red.

"My chicken, they can't treat you this way. You're a princess, beyond reproach. They ought to know that," Drea said, trailing behind the princess bearing her night things.

"Be quiet," Leonora snapped. "Please."

"Oh, all right, my lady, but you know it's true."

Roan smiled and held out a hand to Leonora, but surprise at her abrupt appearance had made him pause, and he knew she had noticed the hesitation. She was near tears from shame. She held her head up proudly, chin out and shoulders back.

"It won't happen again," she said, and stalked past Roan without touching him.

"Here, someone, take this," Bergold said, irritably, the tangle of accordion-pleated paper in his hands festooning him and his horse. "I can't do a thing with it." He pushed the map away. Lum took it. The young guard flipped it open, and folded it over and over again into a neat bundle. He beamed as Bergold snatched it back from him. "By the Seven, I hope that's not your only talent," the historian said. Roan, watching this byplay over his shoulder, hid a smile from his old friend. "Are we lost?"

"We're on the right path," Lum said, pulling his steed to the side of the dirt road to point northward. His horse danced and curvetted at yet another break in the pace. "It's still a ways that direction, sir."

"We came a long way in the dark," Roan said, trying to make peace. "Don't blame Lum for it. It was my fault."

"Well, we're going in circles," Spar snapped, from the front of the file, where he was riding beside Colenna.

"No, we're not, sir," Lum insisted.

But, indeed, they seemed to be. Roan was certain he had seen that handful of blue-green spruce trees off to the left before, several times. There was a ring of toadstools on the bank of the stream to his right, and a broad field of daisies with rabbits running through it, just like one they had left miles behind them. Yet, they had ridden north for an hour with the sun on their right. It was now straight overhead in the clear blue sky, and the heat was making everyone irritable.

"Now, stop it, everyone," Colenna said, holding out her hands. "We've run into a spot of Déjà Vu, that's all."

"No, we haven't," Spar said. "This young fool's just lost."

"I'm not lost, sir. It's right here on the map."

"It's Déjà Vu," Colenna said. "You'll see."

Roan rubbed his eyes. "We'll get out of it. Just keep on."

Beside him, Golden Schwinn's hoof pecked at a stone, and

the horse shied off the path into a patch of marshy grass. The princess, an excellent horsewoman, managed to control her mount, and steered it back onto the road. Schwinn trod on a toadstool. Roan was sure it was the same one the steed had crushed three times before. The road curved to the left and went uphill, away from the stream.

The group rode in silence. In spite of the dangers, Roan would almost have been willing to take the risk of traveling alone to get away from all the bickering. Colenna's back was hurting her. It was a long time since the senior historian had been on so long a journey. Drea kept breaking out of line to go forward and fuss over her mistress. Leonora, who felt delicate about being coddled after her embarrassment of the morning, kept shooing the nurse away, which made the old woman cross.

The princess herself shot furtive glances toward Roan, but every time he tried to meet her eyes, she would jerk her head forward and stare haughtily ahead of her. Today, she looked like the image in a centuries-old church missal: slim and almost sexless. Her face was long, narrow, and pale, with a high, bald forehead, thin eyebrows, heavily lidded eyes, and a small, folded mouth. There was hardly any color in her face, except her eyes, which were brown and watchful. To Roan, who had known her from childhood, this was the mark of an intensely bad mood. She'd had to bolt her breakfast, her mount was misbehaving, and she had been shamed in front of the whole party, whom she knew didn't want her along. She had also curtly refused Colenna's offer of a muscle-ache remedy, though she rode as if she needed one. Roan didn't dare approach her to offer small talk.

Even the usually cheerful Bergold was in a pet; the map the Geographer had given them resisted being folded the same way by the same person twice. He was lost again behind a mass of accordion-pleated paper, while his horse wandered back and forth across the trail, occasionally bumping into Lum's patient mount.

"Well, we're going in circles," Spar said, pointing ahead. "Look, there's those trees again."

"It's perfectly possible that a feature of the landscape repeats itself," Bergold said, without coming out from behind the map.

"Such things have not been unknown in history. Why, remember the Building Booms fifty years ago?"

"These children are all too young," Colenna said peevishly, shifting her hip to look behind her at Roan. "After the Second Mud Battles, the Dreamland started to fill up with plots and plots of identical houses. Even mine fell into the scheme, right there in Mnemosyne. Any night, you didn't know if you were coming home or housebreaking. I was glad when that ended, and we went back to some individuality of construction."

"Yes, but who'd make identical rings of toadstools?" Alette asked, as Golden Schwinn backed over the same one for the fourth or fifth time.

"This isn't just alike. This is the same," Spar insisted.

"Just wait it out," Colenna said.

"Where exactly are we?" Roan asked, reining in to ride beside Bergold. The historian poked his head out from under the map folds, and pointed at a middle panel of the document that was inside the tent over his head.

"We are here. If I could get this dratted thing folded . . ."

Roan took it away from him, and by dint of fate, the map obediently collapsed into a neat pleat.

"Cheek!" Bergold exclaimed. "Wait until I see Romney!"

Roan smiled, and studied the map. If he could believe the geographical features he saw around him, they had come only ten miles from where they had camped. He traced the line of the stream that ran parallel to the road, and found the place where it almost touched.

"Is this Déjà Vu a surprise Brom planted for us to walk into?" Roan asked, handing the map back to Bergold. "A booby trap?"

"Not at all," the historian said. "This has the feel of a natural phenomenon." Bergold pulled a small volume from his saddlebag and thumbed through it. "Yes. Déjà Vu. Yes, Colenna's right. Hmm. Could be tricky."

"Yes, indeed. We're winding ourselves up in reality," Colenna commented, her chin on her shoulder. "As we keep heading north—and we are—we build up a tremendous forward energy that's trapped like the potential in a stretched bowstring. Physically, we are riding through the same terrain, but in linear time, we're quite far from here. Prepare yourselves. When it lets go, the reaction might be powerful."

"Ah!" Misha said, at the back of the line. "So the collateral force is building up around us. How do we release it?"

"We won't have to. The Dreamland itself will trigger it, or a nuisance, or an influence, or one of the Sleepers changing his or her mind. You don't know. Just be prepared."

"The tension's appalling," Felan said, in his bored voice. "Look, we're a lot of strong, influential minds. Let's break the bond ourselves."

"Young man! And you call yourself a historian?" Colenna was outraged. She turned full around in her saddle and glared until her eyes became fire red. "This is the Sleepers' will! You must take what comes, when it comes."

Unmoved, Felan clicked his tongue. "Tsk, tsk, tsk. All this heat over nothing." Colenna glared at him. Roan believed Felan enjoyed baiting her. It was his way of passing the time.

They rode by the stream, and Golden Schwinn crushed another toadstool, or the same one. As the road curved and turned uphill, the horses turned into bicycles.

"And at the most inconvenient moment, too!" Felan said, irritably, standing up on his pedals to ride up the slope.

"That was a fundamental change," Colenna said, sitting up taller on her saddle. Roan felt forces brush past his cheeks like warm wind.

"There's a strong influence around here," Roan said, alarmed. "A very strange one. Do you sense that?" he asked.

"Yes! We're coming to the edge of it," Colenna said, as they crested the hill. "Hold tight to your handlebars, and *try not to fall oo-off!*"

Colenna's last words were drawn out into a wail as her steed was yanked forward by an invisible hand. It vanished down the road at incredible speed.

"Well, will you look at thaaa . . ." Spar began, when he, too, was captured by the influence. The others looked at one another in alarm, watching the captain disappear after Colenna.

"Help, it's got meee," Leonora cried, alarmed. She clutched Golden Schwinn's handlebars as she was swept away. Roan grabbed for her and missed.

"Just hold ti—" was all he had time to say before the breath he was exhaling was knocked back into him by the wind in his face. He planted his hands on the handlebars, and squeezed the brake levers with all his might.

The landscape streamed past him in a smeared, ribbonlike tapestry. He had brief impressions of trees, hills, rivers, and animals. Small mud and thatch huts in the distance seemed elongated into whole terraces of houses. Roan ordered his hat brim to descend over his eyes to protect them, because he didn't dare lift his hands. He hurtled forward faster and faster, until the landscape around him was a thousand-color jumble with no identifiable features. Then everything went dark green, and the air filled with a heady fragrance that made him gasp. Just when he thought he might pass out from the force, he felt the brake levers close under the pressure of his hands, and he slowed to an abrupt halt. His hat dropped forward over his eyes. He pushed it back.

He found himself in the middle of an evergreen wood, which explained the color of the landscape. His feet and tires rested on a thick bed of yellowed pine needles yielding their deep, resiny odor. The riders who had been carried away before him were waiting for him, safe and well, except that the princess's hair was blown into a wild aureole about her head, and Spar looked even more disapproving than usual.

Drea came screaming towards them. As soon as she stopped, her mouth snapped shut. She jumped off her steed and hurried over to fuss over the princess. Though her own hair was windblown into a fluffy bird's nest, she tidied Leonora's hair and patted her veil back into place.

"Leave me alone, Drea," Leonora said, impatiently.

"You can't go along looking a sight, Your Highness," the nurse said. Roan saw Leonora glance at the others, who quickly turned their eyes away so they wouldn't be staring at her, and her cheeks turned even pinker than the wind had made them.

"Wooo-hoo-hooo!" Bergold hurtled into view, his face flattened by the g-forces. "What a ride!" He was followed closely by Lum and the other guards, their knuckles white on their brake handles. Felan appeared a few moments later, more sour-faced than ever.

"There," Colenna said, with satisfaction, smoothing her long gray queue. "We've snapped out of it. And there's the trail."

"All that for nothing," Spar said.

"No," Bergold explained, smiling literally from ear to ear. He produced the map and opened it to the appropriate panel. "This is where we would have been if we had kept riding straight." He indicated a place on the map along the main southern road out of the capital. "And this, unless I've lost all my skills with this wretched atlas, is where we are now." He put his finger on a spot much farther north.

"Remarkable," Roan said. "I've traveled all over the Dreamland, and I've never been propelled in that manner before."

"You're usually on your own," Misha pointed out. "Collective mass equals more energy. The more of us there are, the greater the power of a Déjà Vu."

Roan raised his eyebrows, interested. "Can you duplicate the effect artificially?"

"Ask Brom when you see him next," Felan said, with a leer. "That's clean out of either of our departments, isn't it, Colenna?"

"You are disrespectful, you wretched youngster," the older woman said. "If I get big enough at any time on this journey, I'm putting you over my knee."

"We must make a note of the event," Bergold said. "Micah will be very interested in a Déjà Vu. Felan, you ought to put it into your next report home."

"I certainly will," the younger man said, pulling his sleeve cuff out over the back of his hand until there was enough surface to write on. He reached behind his ear for a pencil, and made a few jottings.

"We're past the place where we turned off," Lum said, after leaning over Bergold's shoulder for a moment's inspection of the map.

"We have to turn back? Into that—that effect?" Leonora asked, her eyes huge. She had forgotten her temper in her curiosity.

"It has passed," Colenna assured her. "It's a time effect; very unstable. We've nothing to fear from it."

"We could go around the area," Roan suggested, glancing at the princess to see if the suggestion made her feel better.

As soon as she caught him looking at her, she turned up her nose. Roan sighed.

"That's the road, though, sir," Lum said, glancing up with a puzzled look on his mild face.

"Never mind," Roan said, embarrassed. "It was just a thought. We turn back."

They found the turnoff for the eastern road without trouble. Roan immediately recognized the heavy tread of the Alarm Clock bearers, and wondered how he had ever mistaken tree roots for those footprints. Spar didn't say a word. He just pedaled stolidly at the head of the line. Colenna, bad back and all, was more gracious. Her eyes traveled over every feature they passed, observing everything. Occasionally, when she looked back over her shoulder at Roan, she gave him a comradely smile. He was grateful to her. Her philosophy of accepting what couldn't be changed was much easier on his nerves than the guard captain's blanket disapproval.

"Do you smell that?" Lum asked, as they left a deep valley and began their way up a long, low hill. "Something burning. Something big."

Roan sniffed the air, and a sharp odor curled the hair in his nostrils. It didn't quite smell like firewood or cooking. It had a metallic heaviness that made him uneasy. The tang grew stronger as they crested the hill and rode into a small glade, where it was gaggingly strong. They had found the scientists' camp.

"Not five miles off from where we lost them!" Spar growled resentfully, and coughed. "We could've been done with this last night."

"They're long gone, sir," Alette said, gazing about her as they rode into the clearing.

"Nightmares!" Misha said, staring about the glade.

Roan, too, was shocked at the condition of the grounds. The grass had been thoroughly trampled, and there were burned patches on dozens of trees around the center where lanterns must have been slung. He found two more scorched places, both of substantial size. One, near a long, clinical-looking stone table, was surrounded by spatters of fat and charred particles of food, in the center of a pile of stones that must have been used as a makeshift cookstove. The other, rectangular in shape, lay at the opposite end of the clearing. Fumes still rose from both sites.

Beside the stream which ran near the table, the ground was churned up into a stiff ring of dirt that looked as if a cylinder of earth had melted down. A curtain of dead and rotting moss lay draped over all.

"They had to have camped here last night, but it feels as though it has been abandoned for years," Roan said. "It's like a ghost town."

"All the vitality has been sucked out of this place," Bergold said, his round nose twitching. "It's rotting away."

"Conservation of energy," Misha said, shaking his head. "They use a lot of power for their tricks, don't they? It has to come from somewhere. What they do pulls the life right out of the land."

Colenna was looking at the boulder table and shaking her head. "They built this for one night's use. Wasteful!"

"Others can make use of it," Felan said, coming over to look at it. "Very nice design."

"It's cold," Leonora said, in a small voice, standing by herself in the center of the ruined clearing.

"Now, all of you stop trying to scare my lady," the nurse said, bursting in between them like an angry pigeon. "She can't take this kind of fright. She won't sleep. Stop it at once."

"Drea, don't," Leonora said. The nurse put her arm around her charge.

"I'm just trying to protect you, my sweet." Leonora pulled away.

"I don't need protection!" she said, a little wildly. "It's the Dreamland that needs protection, not me!"

"You're not thinking of yourself," Drea said.

"I'm not supposed to be! Leave me alone." Leonora set her chin and hugged her arms around her more tightly. She turned her back on Drea. "Yes, leave me. Go away." The nurse shook her head and made as if to hug her.

"You don't want me to leave you now, pet. Not in all this desolation." Leonora shook loose.

"Yes! Yes, I do. Now, go away. Don't come back," the princess said. There were tears in her eyes. Roan took a step towards her, wanting to hold her, but the stiffness of her posture kept him from coming close. "I don't want you any more, Drea. I don't *need* you."

"Well, my kitten, if that's what you say. . . ."

"It *is* what I say," Leonora snapped. "I mean it. I can get along on my own. And don't call me baby names."

The old nurse looked sad, but there was a kind of satisfaction in her wrinkled eyes. "All right, Your Highness. You know best. You're all grown up now, aren't you?"

"Yes!" Leonora snapped, without really listening. "Now, go away!"

Shaking her head fondly, Drea vanished in a puff of steam that smelled of fresh ironing and cinnamon oatmeal. Leonora's eyes spilled over, and tears ran down her face.

She stood beside her bicycle in the midst of the ruin, looking stricken and lost. The air seemed colder than ever. The spell broken, Roan and Bergold hurried to her side to reassure her. She leaned into Bergold's arms, shivering, not a remote symbol, but a frightened young woman.

"Oh, Bergold, they've destroyed this glen," she said, forlornly.

"It will be all right again in no time," the historian said, encouragingly, patting her back. "The Sleeper will clean it up just as soon as his mood shifts again."

"Or an influence will come through," Roan suggested. "You know how quickly things change. It won't take long."

"But it's so desolate," Leonora said, with her face buried in Bergold's jacket shoulder. Roan put a comforting hand on her arm. He understood what she meant. It wasn't only that the scientists had left a mess. There was something wrong with the area. The colors were dulled. The leaves and flowers were thin, paperlike, artificial in feel. Like the desert in the first hours Roan had pursued Brom and his minions, the camp lacked life. He didn't even hear insects buzzing. Leonora must have felt the destruction even more keenly than he did. The king was the heart of the Dreamland, and she was the king's daughter.

The Sleeper must have felt a twinge of discomfort in this area of his dream, because a light wind began to blow, stirring the grass around their feet.

"There, do you see that?" Roan said. "He heard you." The

princess looked up. Her face was tragic, with eyes larger than before and colored a deep, mournful blue, but she watched where he pointed.

As the wind passed slowly, the mossy glade shifted into an open field full of daisies, like a curtain being pulled over the scene of an accident. The sun broke through the clouds, and brightened the grass to an astonishing emerald green. A trill of birdsong startled them with its clear beauty, and the singers wafted above them on open wings. The horrid stench thinned away. In its place, Roan smelled wildflowers and the rich scent of earth after a rain.

The people were not unaffected by the winds of change. The palace guards' uniforms changed to bright scarlet tunics and black trousers, their hats became flat-brimmed and high-crowned, and their faces grew more noble. The rest of the party transmuted slightly to become more beautiful or handsome, and their bicycles took on a polished gleam. Roan, as always, remained the same, but he felt cleaner for the blessing of the wind. The sorrow in the princess's eyes lifted a little.

"That's better, isn't it?" Roan asked her anxiously.

A good deal of the damage had disappeared, but some of the daisies still had a fundamental wrongness about them: too many petals or the wrong color eye. It would take more than one healing touch by the Sleepers to correct what had been done here. Over the princess's head, he and Bergold exchanged glances. They ought to get her away before she saw that the blight had not been cured.

"We must go on," Roan said, putting his hand under Leonora's elbow and escorting her quickly back to Golden Schwinn. Once out of sight of the blight, Leonora recovered her dignity, and pulled away from Roan's grasp.

"Thank you for your courtesy," she said coldly. "Schwinnie!"

The golden steed withdrew its front tire from where it had been nuzzling up against Cruiser's, and rolled over to her hand. Leonora put the bicycle between her and Roan and wheeled it away.

Roan gawked at Leonora's back in dismay, and Bergold pulled him away.

"She's still not talking to me?" Roan said. "It's been hours since this morning. What can I do? What should I have done?"

"Oh, come, come, boy," Bergold said, patiently, hands folded on his round belly. His hair had faded to red and lay slicked back on his head, and his cheeks were pink and plump. "She's used to better treatment from you. You should have defended her."

"But she did hold us all up," Roan said, helplessly. "She made us a promise."

"And you a man in love," Bergold said, shaking his head, ambling over to look at the ring of mud, now covered with leggy grass seedlings. Felan sidled up to them.

"What do you suppose this was?" he asked.

"Some kind of privy would be my guess," Roan said. "It's handy to the sleeping area—at least, I would guess this is the sleeping area—and downstream from the cooking."

"Do you suppose they destroyed it to keep us from seeing it, or did it self-destruct on its own?"

"I think that when the energy is used up, their constructions will collapse in on themselves," Colenna said, standing in the middle of the clearing with her arms wrapped around herself. "Beware the arrogance of waste."

"And what do you think about all this?" Felan asked Roan, indicating the area around them with a very small gesture, so as not to alarm the princess further. Leonora was by herself at the end of the glade. Very casually, Captain Spar had gestured to Alette to stay behind the princess and keep an eye on her. Roan approved.

"Something Brom is doing is perverting the landscape wherever they go," Roan said, keeping his voice low. One of the daisies near his feet abruptly dropped all its petals. Roan and Felan exchanged a glance, and Roan exerted a modicum of influence to reattach them. "I observed it when I was following him before," he said. "Things twist where they have passed."

"But will this mess ever go away?" Felan asked. "You saw the wind of change. It erased very little of this desecration! I'm afraid of something that can cause damage even the Sleepers can't undo."

"It'll take a while for it to heal," Bergold said, placidly. "If not today, then one day."

"Most alarming," Felan commented. "What if they do this to the rest of the Dreamland, Mistress Colenna? They're natural beings, too. Isn't what they do part of the Sleepers' plan?

"If we are meant to stop them, we will," Colenna said, heavily, with a lecturer's air. "If we do not, then that is also the Sleepers' intention. But I believe that if we do not meddle, we will see the Sleepers' design more perfectly."

"It must be very comforting to have everything set out so clearly for you," Felan said, disgustedly. "Brom doesn't seem to buy into your view of the world. What if they make the Sleepers wake up?"

"That, too," Colenna said, sadly. "It's not our choice, nor our right to change things."

"But it is Brom's?"

"I didn't say that! We will try to stop him. If we can't, that is fate."

Roan had been brought up by a strictly traditional historian, but he was encouraged to think his own way. He did not agree with Colenna, but now was not the time to say so.

"Look!" Bergold said, uncovering a small nest in the grass.

Hidden under a broadleafed weed, it resembled a small, gray, folded box formed of chewed fibers. Inside it were scores of tiny paperclips the length of Roan's fingernail. Bergold picked a few out of the box and squinted closely at them. The others, hearing the outcry, clustered around Bergold and his discovery.

"What is it?" Lum asked.

"Paperclips!" Roan said. "Brom picked up bicycles here. Look for a trail. Not footprints—tire prints. They aren't on foot any more." Bergold peered at the box closely, then opened his pocket gazetteer.

"What's curious is that these aren't native to this area," the historian said. "They're not mountain bikes at all. See?" He showed them colored plates of comparable species. "These are all-terrain clips. They've been newly laid."

"Couldn't some passing bird or a picnicker have dropped a single clip in the grass . . . ?" Leonora began, but let her voice die away. She knew better.

"There has to be a significant mass of clips," Misha reminded her, gravely, "otherwise, nothing will happen. One is not enough to engender others."

"They brought the progenitors with them from Mnemosyne," Roan said, his heart sinking. "Matured in a single night." The advantage of speed he hoped to have over the group of scientists was lost.

"My respect for Brom grows," Bergold said, tucking the tiny wires back into the box and shutting it. "I hope that he's not as good at waking people up as he is at planning an expedition, or we're doomed."

Without another word, Spar, Lum, Felan, and Misha ran for their bicycles, and pedaled hastily off in opposite directions to seek out the trail. But it was Colenna who found the way, leading away northeast behind the table rock.

"Wasteful," she said, shaking her head, as she looked back at the clearing. "They destroy so much, and for so little reason."

"They want to wake up the Sleepers just to answer a question," Roan said, pedaling after her.

"I didn't want to go on a cross-country journey," Felan said, once the party was well on its way. This new road was bound on both sides by eight-foot-high hedges, rendering invisible anyone who passed. "We should have caught up with them by now. Where in the Seven's names are they going?"

"The Hall of the Sleepers," shouted Spar. "Or so they said."

"But where is that? It isn't on any map we have."

"I've been thinking that over for the past twenty-four hours," Roan said, pedaling hard. "I have a theory. We have to think as Brom did where the Hall must lie. What do we know about the Sleepers?"

"There are seven of 'em," Lum said helpfully. "Not the same ones all the time. Each of them dreams a province."

"Yes," Bergold said. "From the earliest records we have, once humans began to differentiate between the provinces, they discovered that there were seven overminds. That has never been disputed. Seven is an important number in the Dreamland. Er . . . observers found that the provinces suffered Changeover independently, that those who fled over the ravines and rivers from a changing land to a stable one remained as they had been. In a Changeover transition, the whole character of a province alters. All the provinces are different from one another except where they are the same, generally indicating similar experiences."

"The Sleepers, their number and their character, if not the individuals themselves, have remained unchanged in all of history, correct?" Roan asked.

"Correct."

"So we are looking for something that hasn't changed," Roan said.

Felan blew out his lip derisively.

"But everything in the Dreamland alters over time. Gold mines become sandstone caves; houses, palaces, and hovels interchange freely; birds and bees can mate because they're both airborne creatures."

"But what doesn't change?" Roan urged him.

"Nothing," Felan said, flatly.

"What?" Misha asked, becoming interested in the story.

"The borders," Roan said. "But most significantly of those, the mountains. I would bet that the Mysteries haven't altered substantially since the beginning of time. The Dreamland, for all its mutability, has a fixed, natural boundary."

"We have visitors all the time from the other realms," Felan pointed out.

"Yes, one can cross the Mysteries, but I'd bet you can't change them," Roan said. "They're as eternal as . . ."

". . . As your face," Felan said, offensively. "So what?"

"Brom is going to the mountains," Roan said, ignoring the man's supercilious grin to address the others. "The Hall of the Sleepers must be beneath them."

"The mountains!" Leonora exclaimed, surprised into speaking. She gave Roan a withering glance, and looked away hastily, her lips pressed together.

"Yes, but which ones?" Colenna asked. "Toward which range are they headed?"

"Surely the ancient names hold some significance," Bergold said. "Those, too, have remained constant in the historical records since the beginning of recorded time. Let me see, there are the Deep Mysteries, the High Mysteries, the Sacred Mysteries, the Dark Mysteries—"

"—The Great Mysteries, the Lesser Mysteries, and the

Forbidden Mysteries," Misha interrupted, eagerly. "They're all as different as the Seven themselves." He glanced back and ahead at the others. "Right?"

"Yes, of course. We all took geography in school. So which one is the Hall in?" Felan asked.

"I haven't a clue," Bergold said, simply, raising his palms. "They're all equal and equally different."

"I don't know, either," Roan said. "I was hoping some of you could offer suggestions."

"Oh, that's fine," Felan said, in disgust, dropping back in the file. "I'm none the wiser." At the head of the line, Colenna snorted.

"Did no one ever observe a difference in the amount of influence issuing from a particular mountain range?" Roan asked.

"There's nothing like that in the history books at all," Bergold said, consulting his book. "No records. That's why I was surprised you suggested such a thing, but it makes good sense."

"Think, everyone," Roan said. He brooded over Cruiser's handlebars, trying to recall all the things he'd learned in school. Bergold paged through his small book, muttering to himself.

"Look, sir," Lum said, his brows drawn down in thought, "no matter what, if you ride outward from the center, you'll hit some mountains. What if they're all alike, like that Déjà Vu we went through? Can't we just head for the perimeter of the Dreamland, and it won't matter where we arrive?"

"The mountains *aren't* all alike," Spar put in, speaking for the first time. "I was brought up near the Ancient Mysteries, in Elysia province. My dad took us to see the Dark Mysteries, and the big Sea there. You couldn't mistake one for the other."

"But form only follows function," Misha argued, pedaling up beside the guard captain. "There are many influences on a geographic feature, including the mood of the Sleepers themselves. Inside, they might be all the same as each other."

"The mountains *don't* change," Spar said. "They are as they are, and always have been."

"That brings me to a most unfortunate conclusion," Roan said, glumly, staring at the nut that fastened Cruiser's handlebars. "It won't be possible to beat Brom to his destination, because we have no way of guessing where he's going. We simply have to keep following him. I hope we never find out where they intend to go, because I mean to stop them before they get there."

"Seconded," Captain Spar said. "*That's* something I can understand."

"Hear, hear," the others chimed in.

"But I don't want to go on another wild-goose chase," Felan said. "Are we absolutely sure they went this way?"

A small creature flashed across the road and into the underbrush as the bicycles approached it. Before it disappeared, Roan caught a glimpse of a cardinal's red crest and belly and yellow beak, and the brown paws and fluffy tail of a squirrel.

"Yes," he said. "I'm sure."

As they rode on, Roan tried to make small talk with the princess. She may have been riding beside him, but she occupied the precise middle of her lane as if the road was only that wide and nothing existed to her right but the hedgerow. Even Golden Schwinn stayed aloof from Cruiser, and the two of them had been fast friends since they were coat-hangers. Leonora continued to make vivacious conversation with the others—but she sounded *too* bright and cheery. She was still angry with him, and wanted him to know it.

Roan felt sorry for himself, but he began to wonder if he was the most at fault. Considering they had vowed eternal devotion to one another, she had a right to be angry that he didn't defend her in front of the others. He wished she would give him a chance to earn her forgiveness. Though the day was sunny, it was a cold ride for him. He felt the temperature of the air drop farther every time she glanced his way.

This behavior of hers was odd. He knew Leonora had suffered worse snubs over the years. Her lessons in diplomacy had forced her into situations with visiting dignitaries that were outright insulting, and yet she carried herself with friendly aplomb. He knew she knew he hadn't meant to hurt her feelings. There had to be more to her mood than one tiny, inadvertent pause.

With a mental slap to his forehead, he understood. The princess was scared. She was frightened and overwhelmed by Brom's threat, and must have been terrified at leaving the safety of her home for the unknown. He'd agreed to allow her to come along, but hadn't been any help to her in adjusting. Roan felt even worse than when he'd only believed she was angry. For many years he had traveled all over the Dreamland, encountering perils and relying upon his wits to escape them. She never had gone anywhere with fewer than ten servants and a whole train of baggage animals. She had willingly brought only her nurse with her—almost more of a security blanket than a host to care for her. This was the first night out from under a roof she had ever spent without her own pavilion, a beautiful tent as well-appointed as the palace, and without being surrounded by her father's courtiers. And now, she had dispensed even with her nurse. It was an act of the utmost faith in his leadership.

Roan realized, and appreciated, the real sacrifices the princess had made to accompany them on this perilous journey. It was courageous of her to come down off her pedestal. All her comforts had been left behind, even the last. It was hard for her to ride hours without end, into who knew what hazards, when she knew they didn't want her with them. Yet he also understood why she felt she had to come. Her father the king had almost certainly felt the same way. He would have wanted to defend his country in person, but knowing he couldn't abandon the rest of his responsibilities to go, King Byron delegated the task to others, leaving them to succeed—or fail—as they could. Here was Leonora, vulnerable as a newborn, without training or experience, wanting to help and knowing how much of a hindrance her presence was among them. She had never faced trouble before, let alone the possibility of a world-shattering disaster. Her powers to affect matter would be an asset to them in case of disaster, though she feared the unknown. Roan was ashamed. She was much braver than he. She deserved his wholehearted support, and he hadn't offered it. What a dolt he was! He vowed she would never fall into danger while in his care.

He turned in his saddle and waited until he caught her eye, then offered a tender smile with his whole heart in his eyes. Tentatively, timidly, she returned it. The hedges opened out suddenly into open fields full of grapevines, which started buzzing at once with the wonder of it all. Roan was in love, and he wanted the whole world to know it. He reached out his left hand, and felt her slender fingers slip into his. The warmth in his heart spread throughout his whole body, and he sighed with joy. They rode side by side for a while in silence. Roan was happier than he could ever remember being.

Colenna caught the glance that passed between the two young people, and cleared her throat.

"This will be the first long trip for you, won't it, my dear?" she asked Leonora. "It's been a harrowing ride so far, hasn't it? I do enjoy some parts of travel far more than others, let me tell you. Why, I remember my first venture on behalf of the Ministry, and a thankless lot they were, too."

"Oh, no, they wouldn't be," Leonora said, politely.

"Hah! You don't know bureaucrats!" Colenna launched into a spirited narrative about a trip to the sixth province, Oneiros, on behalf of the Ministry of History, to pick up documents discovered there that were believed to date from five thousand years before. "I was just a young thing, thinking I was going to be traveling around the Dreamland as easy as riding a flying carpet. I was full of ambition to see things no one else had ever seen, be the one whose name was on those stone tablets and in those palimpsests. But it wasn't all as nice as the first few minutes when I first rode away from the castle, oh, no!" Cheerfully, she described herself getting into and out of various nasty situations, and rather neatly, Roan thought.

"And after that," Colenna concluded, triumphantly, "I never go anywhere without an eggbeater and a multipurpose knife. I bring everything with me, whether I know I'll need it or not! I like to be prepared, Your Highness. You can find anything you want in a town, but there's a lot of empty space between population centers."

"Sometimes," Bergold reminded her.

"Yes, I know, you old stickler," Colenna said, impatiently, and returned to Leonora. "Find what you can't do without, and bring it. Never travel with more than you can carry yourself." Then she looked a little dismayed, but Leonora didn't notice. She was nodding.

"I would consider it to be an honor to convey Her Highness's belongings," Misha put in, courteously rescuing Colenna.

"And I," Roan said, regretting he had not been the first to speak. "It'll be good for you."

"You are very kind," Leonora said, glancing at all of them, but most warmly at Roan. He felt his hopes come tiptoeing timidly back. "I am very sorry for my behavior this morning."

"Inexperience, that's all, if you'll forgive me, Your Highness," Colenna said. "Why, by the time we get home to Mnemosyne, you'll be an old pro."

Leonora smiled, showing the dimple at the corner of her mouth, and let her face relax from the waxen medieval image into something far more human and lovely. Her lips reddened and became full, and her eyes widened so that the long lashes surrounding them were a frame instead of a cage. Roan caught Misha watching the transformation, and saw the moment in the young man's face when he fell helplessly in love with her. Every man did, Roan thought, shaking his head. He was just the most fortunate, since she returned his affection.

"What's the most important thing I have to do to be a good traveler?" Leonora asked, earnestly.

"Keep your eyes open," Colenna said. "Be sensible. You're not at home now, you know."

"I know."

"And leave things be! Don't leave a mess. Don't take anything more away than a memory or a photograph, and don't leave more behind you than your footprints."

"I've always preferred taking footprints and leaving photographs," Roan said, feeling more like his old self, before the present crisis began. "I have a large collection."

"You," Bergold said, with the corners of his wide mouth turning up, "would."

Thereafter, things passed far more merrily. They were able to make excellent time on the road. Misha devoted himself to Leonora, telling her jokes and making her elaborate courtly compliments that made her laugh as much as the jokes. When the party stopped for refreshments on the banks of the stream near a handsome old wooden bridge and cool berry bushes covered with knobby buds, the others told stories.

"I was only a tot at the time of the last Changeover in Rem. Lucky there was lots of notice," Lum said, scratching his ear to jog his memory. "My dad got us into a wagon, and hustled us over the bridge. I wanted to stay out and watch, but he paid no attention. Told me I was a foolish kid. Now I'd be too scared to get near one."

"So would I," Misha said, waiting on Leonora. He poured fruit nectar into her goblet. The bicycle left behind by Drea still held all the princess's luggage, including her tableware.

"Sounds like you grew some sense," Spar said.

"Did you ever see a Changeover?" Leonora asked Colenna.

"No, I never have," Colenna said. "I stayed well away from that sort of thing. It's only sense. I like me as I tend to be, thank you. I understand your beau has, though."

"You?" Felan asked.

"Yes," Roan admitted, looking away.

"It was before your time in Mnemosyne, Felan," Bergold said. "Two Changeovers ago, in fact. I may say that the event, and the following event, were the most amazing story I have ever heard and the most disgraceful thing I have ever witnessed."

"We were in Somnus when I was a boy," Roan explained, putting down the chunk of bread he was buttering. "My father let me run around on my own while he was conducting business for the Ministry. There were rumors that a Changeover was imminent, rumblings and so on, but since the disturbances were local, conventional wisdom put all the disturbances down to a Personal Crisis Dream. That Sleeper had been prone to that kind of problem, and my father was hoping to see the Crisis Point break out."

"I remember that from continuity class at school," Misha said, nodding. "An interesting phenomenon, although personally I've always wanted to see the hallucinations of a Pepperoni Nightmare instead."

Roan grinned. "Hang about the northwestern end of Celestia for any length of time, and you'll get your wish. There seems to be a regular eruption in that area. At any rate, Father was observing the manifestations. A few of the local continuitors and historians had taken him to meet people affected by the circumstances of Personal Crisis. Very interesting. Mistaken identities, rampant denial, and so on. Married couples were coming home after a day's work, and being unable to recognize their partners, even though you know you can almost always tell who is who, even after an alteration. I'd read some of the historical documentation of Personal Crisis Dreams on the trip down there—not much for a boy to do on a long train ride, after all—but to me, there was something not quite right. There were other manifestations that didn't correspond to descriptions in the old books."

"Every Sleeper's personality is different," Alette pointed out.

"But the historians only record those characteristics which appear every time a circumstance occurs," Roan said. "That's their science, if you like. There were earthshakes and thunderstorms—you may say both of those are typical of a lot of dream events," he said, holding up a hand when the guard started to speak. "These weren't normal. They seemed somehow . . . fundamental to me. I tried to find my father to tell him, when the ground split in front of me.

"People started screaming and running around. A man noticed me just standing there watching, and warned me to get over the border, or I'd discontinue. He was sure, as I suddenly was, that a Changeover was on the way." The others caught their breath, and Roan nodded. "To me, it meant the next worst thing to death, losing all my identity, so I stopped looking for my father, and ran for my life. I was sure he would have recognized the signs—at least, I hoped so—and would meet me safely on the other side, in Oneiros.

"Everyone was panicking. Some of them were disoriented; they were running away from the bridge. I turned them around. Before I knew it, I was directing a flow of refugees. The crowd got larger and larger. Everyone was shouting. The ground began to rumble under my feet, so I started running, too. Then, there was a bright flash, and the sound of explosions that went on and on like an echo."

Roan felt his insides twist at the memory. Years had passed since it had happened, and he still experienced it afresh every time he thought about it. "I always thought later that I was imagining it, but I knew I was feeling the pain of thousands of men, women, children, animals, plants—the land itself! And then," Roan said, recalling it with relief, "a dreamy peace. It was almost deafeningly quiet. I was in the midst of a crowd of people on the far side of the bridge, with no idea how I had gotten there. They had been watching the Changeover from a safe distance. They said I had walked straight over the bridge in the middle of the explosions."

"I don't believe you," Felan said, frowning. "You read all of this out of a book."

Roan met his eyes. "I couldn't concoct such a story, Felan. I . . . I remember looking at my hands. They seemed familiar, but I wasn't sure."

"You were in shock," Colenna said wisely.

"In a way," Roan said, thoughtfully, leaning against one of the bridge's uprights and moving fully into its shadow so the sun wasn't on the back of his head, "it was a moment of great serenity. I've never felt such peace. People started straggling across the bridge toward us. I didn't recognize one of them. The Changeover had caught them. They soon went back into Somnus. They belonged there now. They had been made to fit the new Sleeper's visions."

"But not you," Misha said. "Did you change at all?"

"No." Roan sighed. "Not a bit."

"I don't believe you," Felan repeated.

"Well, no one else did," Roan said. "My father had escaped in plenty of time. When Thomasen found me again, he brought me back to the Ministry so they could question me about my experience. A number of them, like you, accused us of fraud, claiming that because I hadn't changed I couldn't have been in the middle of a Changeover. Never in all the records had anyone passed through what I had without becoming different in some way. A few of the chief historians, Micah included, were inclined to believe I'd only been caught in the backwash and knocked out."

"So what did they do?" Felan asked.

Roan grimaced, and Bergold gave him a sympathetic glance.

"The next time a Changeover was imminent in Rem," the historian said, "Roan was made part of the delegation to observe it, and a few of my colleagues, who shall remain nameless, in spite of their pusillanimous cowardice, trapped him there in the midst of it all. And then, the land went crazy. This time, when he walked out of it unchanged, they had to believe him. In fact, they were dumbfounded, and ashamed of themselves for actively trying to alter the fate of a being created by the Sleepers, but they never apologized to you for it, did they?"

"It's not important now," Roan said, embarrassed. He ate the piece of bread and reached for another.

"That'd be the one we ran away from, sir," Lum said, nodding.

"What was it like?" Misha asked.

"Terrifying," Roan said, simply. "But very exciting. The world melted away—no, that's not right. It was as if it shed a skin and put on a new one. And I was able to watch the whole thing."

"So you're some kind of freak, then?" Felan said, lying back on the grass and putting his hands behind his head. "Stuck in place, eh?" Roan gawked at him, unable to think of a retort. Felan had hit him in his most sensitive spot.

"He's not a freak," Leonora said, jumping to her feet. She looked at Roan, her eyes shining with pride. "We are all being dreamed by different sleepers, after all. Roan's just more . . . durable than most, that's all."

Felan snorted.

"*What* was that?" Leonora asked, hardening her voice. The marble pedestal appeared under her feet, and raised her three feet in the air. She looked lovely, cool, remote, and very powerful standing silhouetted against the sky. Felan sat up at once, and rose onto one knee in respect. "*What* did you say?"

"Er . . . You are right, Your Highness." Felan's manner had lost all trace of casual insolence, and he bowed his head. He'd forgotten with whom he was talking, and Roan almost felt sorry for him.

"I know," Leonora said, sweetly. The pedestal shrank into the grass. The princess offered her hand to Roan to assist her down from her plinth. "Occasionally, this thing is convenient. I think we ought to go on now, don't you?"

"Thank you," Roan whispered to her.

Leonora glanced at Roan under her eyelashes, then away, still watching him out of the corner of her eye.

"*I'm* proud of you," she said. "I love you just the way you are."

The declaration should have filled him with delight, but it

just reminded him that he was different. Leonora must have guessed his thoughts. She shook her head with a rueful little smile. Roan hung his head, honored beyond words. She looked so lovely that he sighed, and the bushes near him burst into bloom. Birds swooped out of the sky to circle them, twittering. She blushed, trying to keep the smile off her face, then gave up. Her cheeks turned pink, and Roan could tell she was pleased.

"Help me onto my bike, won't you?" she asked.

Roan heard romantic music swell up in the distance.

"With all my heart," he said.

Chapter 12

"Look at that!" Bolmer, riding ahead of Taboret, pointed to the side of the road in great excitement. "A *Camellia nutrans*! Absolutely one of the rarest plants in the world! Unmistakable. My hat! I haven't seen one in ten years, and that was in the marshes of the fourth province." He craned his head around to get a second look at the plant.

Taboret had half a second to glimpse the weird, vase-shaped flower among the reeds before she, too, had passed it.

"Incredible!" she said, but in the back of her mind she felt boredom. It told her "I've already seen that. And in a marsh, too." But Taboret knew she never had seen a flower with four pointed blue petals spotted with pink. She had never been that enamored of botany. Among the apprentices, only Bolmer was such a plant freak.

Another twinge in her mind told her not to be so negative about other people's interests.

It wasn't fair. She was being nagged by Carina, without ever opening her mouth! Such things had been happening more and more frequently over the course of the day, at first subtly, so she hardly noticed it, then more insistently obvious, as now. Her memories, and even her conscious mind, were becoming combined with the others'.

Taboret felt a surge of fear, which she quickly suppressed. When a discovery was no longer new, if information could be immediately shared, or learned without one even knowing it, where was the joy? Where was the excitement? Was she losing her identity? Not even Brom's promise of power was enough to make up for that!

Glinn noticed her inattention and nudged her bicycle from behind with his. Startled, she came out of her reverie and concentrated on riding in unison with the others. Right foot down, left foot down, right foot down. She glanced behind her and mouthed a "thank you" to him. He nodded back, and lowered his shell-shaped helmet so she couldn't see his eyes. Right, left, right, left, right. The chief insisted on their maintaining identical paces. Why wouldn't he allow them to explore the trail or run ahead of the group from time to time? Where was the harm? On her bike she could be back in the formation in seconds. But the chief insisted that this exercise would also make the apprentices more of a unit. When they moved in rhythm, it was only the next step until they *thought* in rhythm. Then they would be the most powerful single gestalt being in the insubstantial realm. Unless they ended said realm by accomplishing their experiment. Taboret shuddered. Right, left, right, left. . . .

"Time to change!" Brom announced. Basil and Carina gratefully brought their bicycles to a halt, and waited patiently while the others helped them unbuckle the Alarm Clock's frame from their shoulders. Glinn and Taboret moved into place, and assumed the heavy burden between them. It was Taboret's turn to ride at the back, which suited her because it meant that Brom couldn't see her face. She wanted to think, while she still could, without having him suspect her of independence.

A sound like an everlasting raspberry began as a whine in the distance, and grew into a sky-filling roar.

Maniune, one of the hired musclemen, came racing up, and skidded to a stop, throwing up a cloud of debris. His steed had been adapted into one of Brom's new inventions, a motor-bicycle, making it ten times faster and a dozen times more aggressive than unaltered and unpowered transportation. Such things existed in the archives, and were becoming more common every day, but Brom's motorcycles were guaranteed not to be affected by influence. They would stay permanently in that shape.

As if aware of its inalterable status, the motorbike danced and curvetted, intimidating the apprentices' steeds. Gano's green bike spooked and dumped her into the thornbushes that lined the road. Maniune grinned, teeth showing white through the black stubble on his chin.

"Stop that!" Brom ordered, and Maniune made his beast retreat to a decent distance. Carina swung off to help Gano up. The shorter woman had scratches on her hands and one side of her face, and was looking bloody murder at the mercenary. So were the rest of the apprentices. To Taboret, having mercenaries along did not seem appropriate to the task. And they behaved as crudely as the Countingsheep brothers, without being taciturn. They were openly offensive.

"Report!" Brom demanded.

"They're still following us, sir," Maniune said, pitching his voice over the roar of his mount. "Got a message. The diversion worked like a charm—took them all the way to the Forest—but they're turned around."

"How many?" Brom asked, raising one eyebrow.

"Ten. Four soldiers from the palace guards, including Captain Spar himself. Three historians."

"Too many!" Brom scoffed. "They'll tie themselves up in knots of protocol and indecision. Roan would have done better to follow us on his own. I have some respect for his tenacity. We will have to enact Plan B: speed up and deter pursuit."

"And another thing," Maniune said. "Princess Leonora is with them."

"What?" Brom asked, his gaunt face going hollow-cheeked. "This is . . . unexpected." He put his chin into his hand, and lowered his eyebrows until Taboret thought they'd brush his nose. "She did not figure in my calculations of risk. . . . However," he raised his head defiantly, "we cannot let her presence stop us. Carry on with the plan. Deter pursuit. Everyone has their instructions. Where's Acton?"

"Still guarding the road, sir," Maniune said.

"Good! How far behind us is Roan?"

"Hours. They're clear on the other side of Hark."

"Excellent. Do not let them close the distance. Use what means you deem necessary, but only the minimum required. Lurry, you go with him."

"Yes, sir." The apprentice looked down at his bicycle, and up with a question at Brom, who nodded.

"Form the crucible," the senior scientist ordered. "We will make another motorcycle, and then move on."

Nobody said anything, but Taboret felt a collective groan

go through the group. Brom certainly felt that; he sent a glare around at all of them. Obediently, everyone but Taboret and Glinn dismounted and put their right hands together.

"Gano, we will transform your steed," Brom said. "Everyone is to focus upon the green animal. You all know the design parameters. Take your time. This is crucial work. We do not want the beast to die. There isn't time to replace it. Slowly and carefully, now. We have no time to waste."

"Wasn't it a mistake to stop for supplies, then, sir?" Bolmer asked. "It slowed us down, and we left witnesses behind us."

"Nonsense," Brom said. "We confused their minds sufficiently. It will be difficult for anyone who saw us to describe us. We can use part of the crucible's energy to slow Roan down." He smiled, and that faraway light showed in his eyes. "We will see if we can create our own nuisance. Yes, we will do that first. Glinn, you will monitor."

"Yes, sir," Glinn said. The front of the litter shifted on Taboret's shoulders as her partner reached into his pocket for the detector he carried.

Taboret felt her blue mount bounce impatiently under her, making a ratcheting noise. The combined weight of a human being and half a philosophical device was a lot to ask a new bike to carry. She looked wistfully in Maniune's direction, wishing she had a motorcycle, too. Maniune, a dark-haired, coarse-featured ruffian, misunderstood her expression, and made a kissy-mouth toward her. She snarled and retired behind the Alarm Clock. If she wasn't contributing every extra erg of influence, she'd bury him ankle deep in biting ants.

Brom snapped his fingers for attention. "Together, now!"

The young people closed their eyes and concentrated. Taboret felt the mental link form that joined her to the others. Being unable to touch them physically, she had no control over how her influence would be used, but she concentrated anyhow on creating a nuisance. What did a nuisance look like?

Fuzzy pictures began to form in her mind. A nuisance was a large, smelly person who kept poking one on the bus. A nuisance was a can tab whose key broke off in your fingers. A nuisance was a flat tire, a sudden gust of wind, a lost slip of directions, a bang over the funnybone. In short, and here Taboret sensed Brom's more precise mind, a nuisance was a measure of annoyingly wasted time, and that was what was at stake here: time.

She peeked out of one eye at the crucible forming above the joined hands. Something formed there, all cloudy colors and indistinguishable, raucous noises, and flew off toward the south.

Without opening his eyes, Brom snapped his fingers again. "Glinn! Report!"

Her fellow apprentice's voice was hushed. "It is a nuisance, sir. I don't know how stable it is, or if it will go where we send it, because it is. It really is a nuisance," Glinn finished, with a gulp.

"Very good," Brom said, not stopping for self-congratulations. He opened his eyes. "Now the motorcycle! Concentrate!"

For this transformation they did not need to use their imaginations. In Taboret's mind the green bicycle went through precise step-by-step alterations, down to the bright lamp that replaced the removable lantern at the front of the head tube. The new motorcycle gave an excited roar, and revved its engine. Taboret opened her eyes at that sound.

The others had, too. Gano went over to touch her green steed with an expression of awe. It roared again, enjoying its new voice.

"Mechanical check," Brom barked. Gano swung up on her mount, and rode it in a wide circle, followed by a series of maneuvers to test its reactions. She was grinning widely when she came back alongside the others.

"Now, if we can do that so well, why not an airship?" Taboret asked, forgetting to be tired in her envy. "Air travel to . . . to our destination would take only hours."

"No!" Brom said, wheeling to aim a long, skinny finger at her. "Too risky. We would have to make one that could not fail. That would take too much time to design. I will not guess. I will not risk my precious Device in *mid-air*. Bicycles are reliable. They exist everywhere, a true design. Motorcycles are an improvement on bicycles. We shall all have them very soon."

"Hope so," Carina said, rubbing her shoulders. "My legs are getting worn out from pedaling. I sure hope we hit a change where this thing grows its own motive power."

"You have to feed horses," Basil reminded her. "And rest them."

"You have to feed and rest me, too," she said acerbically.

"I knew you were going to say that," Taboret said, in surprise.

"And I knew you were going to say *that*," Carina snapped. "Mind your own business. Stay out of my head!"

"Wish I could," Taboret said. She was now aware of an undertone of a hum that were the thoughts of her fellow apprentices. Brom's mind was a loud booming over them all, not clearly distinguishable as words or thoughts yet. She hunched unhappily behind the Alarm Clock.

"The bickering will cease!" Brom announced, waving a hand over the handlebars of his elegant conveyance. His was more than a bicycle, but still less than a motorbike, and yet he did not seem to have to pedal it very often. Probably, Taboret thought, it was a design in process he would tell them about when the time came. "Lurry, bring your beast forward!"

Under Brom's direction, they formed his bicycle into a sidecar to fit against Maniune's motorcycle. Taboret cringed inwardly when the steed cried out as it was squished and squeezed into its new shape.

"We must increase our pace," Brom said when the crucible broke. "That is all for now. We will make more motorcycles when we can. For the moment, we must move on. Maniune, you will report back at our next stop. You have your instructions. Keep them from closing the distance. Lurry is empowered with a certain amount of influence for you to use. I will not be disturbed."

"But his rotten dirty tricks could hurt the princess!" Taboret protested, and knew that her concerns were shared by the others. "Or . . . or kill her."

Brom turned an unconcerned face to her. "If they do not wish to be hurt, they will turn back."

Chapter 13

"Did you see that?" Lum demanded, goggling.

"Yes," Bergold said, very pleased, watching the big, square vehicle vanish into the middle distance. "A streetcar just went by. We must be getting closer to civilization."

"But there's no tracks."

"Doesn't need any," Bergold said, cheerfully. "Just a street, and that we have." He unfolded the map on his handlebars as he rode. "Now, let me see. Unless I am quite wrong, we must be near Hark."

"I've never heard of it," Colenna said.

"Not a big place," Misha said, peering over Bergold's shoulder at the map. "Looks like it's about the size of its name. Wha— Whoa!"

The young man rose high into the air on his bicycle's saddle. Wobbling madly, he flailed at the air for a moment, then desperately clutched at the handlebars, trying not to fall off. For a moment, it seemed as if Misha's placid mount was about to buck him off. Instead, the front wheel grew until it was double its normal diameter, and the rear wheel shrank down to the size of a dinner plate. Misha kept his grip, and wiggled forward with his feet on the pedals, now placed at the front wheel's axle, while the bicycle's shape struggled to stabilize.

"Stop, everyone!" Roan commanded. "Dismount, quickly!"

Roan's warning was just in time. Within moments, all of the other steeds were transforming into pennyfarthing bicycles. Spar stared up at his mount in dismay. The saddle was on a level with his head.

"Someone change this thing back," he complained. "I can't ride it. It's undignified."

"Gladly," said Bergold, who now wore his hair sleeked back

on his head and sported a handsome handlebar mustache with waxed and curled ends. He left his own beast in Lum's care and laid hands on Spar's bike. Roan felt the waves of influence pouring out of his friend's aura, enough to divert the course of a stream, but they had no effect upon the bicycle. Instead, some of the plants and rocks beyond the bicycle grew shorter and more symmetrical.

"Sorry, my friend," the historian said, ruefully, twirling one spiraled mustachio. "Sleeper's will. I would have to say that the design must be in keeping with the mood of whomever is dreaming Hark today."

"Oooh!" Leonora squeaked with surprise. Roan spun on his heel, ready to defend her from any menace. The princess had both hands on her middle, which seemed unnaturally slender even for her. "Corset," she gasped. "They're tighter than I thought. Great Illusions!" Her hands flew to her head.

Her plait of hair had unwound and was plumping itself on top of her head in a mass the shape of a cottage loaf. The comfortable outer traveling garments she wore started to alter, too. Her riding trousers became a long, full skirt, and her tunic a tight shirtwaist and jacket. A bustle popped out behind, making Alette's pennyfarthing shy. The hood hanging at her back became a banded straw hat on a ribbon. Instead of the jewel colors she favored, this outfit was a dull plum.

"Oh, how heavy this is," Leonora said, looking down at herself in dismay. "And how boring!" She spread out her hands, and between them the self-effacing purple began to brighten to a more cheerful shade of red.

"No, don't," Roan said, hastily. "We want to blend in with the townsfolk, if we can. We need to pass through here as quickly as possible. Find the trail, and go on."

"All right, but I'm not going to like it," Leonora said. She brought her hands together, and the warm color faded to dullness, but she left the elaborate embroidery at wrists and waist.

"As long as we're going through Hark," Colenna said, "we ought to pick up supplies. I hope they have coffee, but any stimulant will do for the pot."

"Good idea! I can get some more stamps," Felan exclaimed, looking to Roan for approval.

"Since we are uncertain when we will catch up with Brom, it is best to be prepared," Colenna added. "I for one only packed three days' worth of rations."

"An excellent suggestion," Roan said, with a polite nod and a bow for the older woman. "This is the last town of any size for some distance, on this road at least."

Colenna's outfit was much like Leonora's but with more lace at the neck and wrists. The garments of the men had changed, too. Spar looked uncomfortable in a blue-black wool uniform with a double file of bright brass buttons down the front. The handsome flat-brimmed hat he'd worn since the transformation in the scientists' campground became a cap with a bill. Lum looked as if he liked the costume. His headgear was now a helmet. Alette, also in uniform, had become a man with a magnificent mustache under his nose. Bergold, Felan, and Misha found themselves kitted out in charcoal-gray knee-length coats, and trousers that tapered to the ankle. Roan changed his clothing to match their attire, and noted that it was not too different than what he usually wore for formal occasions. He popped his traveling hat back into a topper.

"Now that we're dressed for it," Roan said, swinging up onto Cruiser, "let's go on to Hark."

"Uncomfortable, unsteady monstrosity," Spar said, scrambling up into the seat. "Feel like I'm on display."

They bumped over the railroad tracks, and around the corner of the train station, a large, handsome red brick building with white-painted shutters and window boxes. No one was waiting on the platform, and Roan noticed a red-striped hand signal that was to be pulled down if the train was to stop for a passenger. The town of Hark must be quite small.

Nevertheless, it was a bustlingly busy place. The narrow streets were packed with handcarts and horse-drawn wagons, plus a few daring and noisy motorcars that were steered with a stick.

Plenty of neat little shops lined the high street. It must be market day, and probably a school half-holiday. The sidewalks were full of graceful women gliding along in long skirts and carrying baskets, and crowds of children like flocks of birds. Roan noticed one woman shopping with two small, hairy beasts lurching along behind her. One of them scooped up in its fearsome claw a hunk of pavement, tasted it, then flung it at the other beast, narrowly missing it. The other grabbed an orange off a handcart as it went past, and smashed it into its sibling's face. The two little monsters squabbled until their long-suffering mother turned around to break up the fight.

Another woman emerged from a pastry shop and passed by, nodding at the first woman. She was followed by a little angel, complete with white robe, wings, and halo, who simpered at the other mother and her offspring and floated past, not quite touching the ground. The two little monsters glanced at each other, and as soon as the mothers were both looking the other way, they grabbed flowerpots off a grocer's display and lobbed handfuls of mud with deadly accuracy at the back of the little angel. She let out a shrill squeal, and turned into a miniature fury, with bat wings and nail-sharp claws and teeth as she rushed at her assailants. Roan didn't stop to see the outcome.

"How do women stand these clothes?" Leonora hissed, as they rode toward the main marketplace. "I'm going to faint from the heat!"

"Bear up, Your Highness," Colenna said, wearing her tight shirtwaist and blue suit with grace. "Look, we can leave the bicycles and sit down a moment."

"The rest of us will get the supplies," Roan said. He looked about him. "Find a place to rest yourselves while you can."

"Good heavens," Bergold said. "This place is like a time capsule. These clothes were in fashion a century ago. And I see no signs of modern technology."

"Things change slower in small towns than in cities," Roan said.

"Look," Felan said, pointing to an open square at the end of the block, "a farmer's market. I'll be happy to do the bargaining, if you like. Do you have money?"

"I'll keep on the trail," Misha suggested. "We don't want to lose our way."

"Take a couple of the guards," Roan suggested. "That way you can send a messenger back to us if there is need."

"Right, sir," Spar said. "Hutchings and I will stay here with the steeds."

The captain pointed at Alette and Lum, who turned their tall, wobbly bicycles to follow Misha back toward where they had entered town. The others followed Felan to the edge of the market, where stall-holders made their tents larger or pushed them in front of others to get the attention of shoppers.

"Go on, now," Felan said, heading toward the first covered stall of vegetables. "I'd prefer it if you don't hang over my back while I'm striking a bargain. Kibbitzers always bring me bad luck. Go somewhere else."

"Don't forget the coffee," Colenna said. "And something to eat with it. Biscuits, perhaps."

"Scat!" Felan said, shooing her away. "Discontinue!"

"Humph!" Colenna snorted.

Felan collected cash from the others. He jingled the coins together and put them in his pocket. "Give me half an hour to get everything," he said. He set off with purpose toward the vendors.

Roan looked around the edge of the square, and noticed a hand-lettered sign that said "Sundries." In the shop window was a big display of fresh flowers in glowing colors. He glanced toward Leonora, and saw that she hadn't yet noticed it. Roan tapped Bergold on the shoulder.

"I'll be right back. I need to pick up a couple of things."

The historian let his eyes drift in the direction Roan was looking, and smiled. "I would consider it an honor to escort the ladies around until you return."

"All I want to do is sit down on something that isn't moving," said Colenna, fanning her face with her hand. "And a cool drink would be a pleasure."

"That's a good idea," Leonora said.

Roan bowed, trying not to meet the twinkle in Bergold's eye. "Then, if you'll excuse me. . . ."

The small shop turned out to be as well-stocked as a bazaar. After choosing a handsome posy of pink roses for the princess, he kept browsing the tall wooden shelves while the plump shopkeeper wrapped the flowers in green paper.

"I'm folding some water in here, too," the man said, "so they don't dry out. Nice day, eh?"

"A fine day," Roan said. Not wanting to abandon the others

for long, he quickly selected some sweets, several boxes of firelighters, and salve for sore muscles on which the label boasted "So good you won't know you've got a body." He dropped his selections off on the counter whenever he passed it.

"Been to Hark before?" the shopkeeper asked, companionably. He was able to maintain eye contact with his customer in spite of the displays by means of a series of mirrors. Roan was surprised almost every time he looked up to find the man's bright eyes on him.

"No, indeed," Roan said to the little round mirror above the shaving impedimenta.

"It's a nice place. Small, of course. The train station's the biggest building in town. But there's a kind of humanity in a small town you don't find in a city."

"Mm-hm," Roan said, noncommittally, as he scanned the merchandise. Following Colenna's dictum, he wanted to make certain he didn't lack any truly important equipment for the mission. He saw nothing that made him clap a self-admonitory hand to his forehead. They were reasonably well prepared.

At the end of one row of tall shelves, he came to a tray full of all-purpose pocket knives like the one he carried. A delightful pen-and-ink illustration showed all the attachments for the top-of-the-line model: knife blade, can opener, corkscrew, saw, walking stick, umbrella, et cetera, et amazingly cetera.

"Ah," said the distant voice of the owner, and his eyes gleamed out of a square mirror to Roan's left. "Can you believe everything they've thought of stuffing into one of those little things? Quite fantastic."

Roan reached for a dainty knife whose outer leaves were of the princess's favorite color, periwinkle blue. He counted the blades, and his eyebrows went up.

"Yes, sir," the shopkeeper said, in answer to his silent question. "It has all the attachments. The very best quality, sir."

"How much?" Roan asked.

"Fifteen chickens, sir."

Not too much for a peacemaking gift, Roan thought. And with it she'll feel more as if she's part of the group even if she never so much as unfolded a blade.

"I'll take it," he said. He brought the blue knife to the counter under the multiple eyes of the owner, who had Roan's other purchases wrapped neatly in brown paper and tied with string.

"Thank you, sir," and the deft hands twitched the little tool into white tissue paper. "Is it a gift, sir?"

"Yes. For a lady," Roan said, fascinated by the hands, which went at once to a display of boxes at the edge of the counter and chose a small, narrow one. "Have you had any other visitors today? Strangers, I mean. They'd all be wearing blue and white, and with pocket protectors?"

"Pocket protectors?" The shopkeeper looked up curiously as he tied the last knot in a ribbon and handed Roan the wrapped box. "Now you mention it, sir, I did have a few like that come in. Very fussy they were." He glanced past Roan, and his eyes widened.

"Uh-oh, two minutes to twelve. I am out of here at noon. Would you mind?" Roan started digging into his pocket for money. The shopkeeper looked up at the ceiling. "Let's see, that's two biros one pencil for the candy, one newspaper and a pencil for the flowers—they're on special today—loaf of bread one biro for the salve, and the firelighters are a pencil apiece, sir. Plus the knife, is fifteen chickens two loaves one newspaper one biro."

"Can you change a Sunday edition?" Roan asked, producing three five-chicken coins and a handful of small silver change from his pocket. "No, wait, there's another chicken." He held out the large gold coin. The man handed him three pencils change. "Now, about those other customers?"

"Thank you, sir. We are delighted to have your business, and hope you will come back again when you're next in Hark," the shopkeeper said, hustling him toward the door. He put the parcels, now in a clean flour sack, into Roan's arms, and set the bouquet of roses on top of it. "You'd better step out, now. Thank you for coming, sir." He shut the door and clapped a CLOSED sign on the inside of the plate glass.

"But . . ." Roan turned on the doorstep, but the shop dissolved into thin air, leaving a gap in the line of stores like a missing tooth.

"Great heavens, it discontinued!" Bergold exclaimed behind him.

"I asked him about Brom," Roan said with concern. "I hope I didn't frighten him into nonexistence."

"Him? Not a chance."

A woman, dressed much as Leonora was, with her white straw hat clamped firmly onto the top of her pumpkin-shaped hairdo, slowed her pace at the edge of the empty lot.

"Not him," she said. "He only exists half-days on Wednesdays. Bother. I wanted to buy some magazines and wicks for my gaslights."

"He doesn't exist all the time?" Colenna asked.

"No," the woman said, with a disgusted twist to the corner of her mouth. "Not worth his while, I suppose. He's always been lazy. Good day."

"Good day," Roan said, tipping his hat politely as she walked away. "It is too bad. The shopkeeper actually waited on Brom. By the way, this is for you," he said, handing the roses to Leonora with a bow.

"How thoughtful of you," she said, looking up with shining eyes. She stood on tiptoes in her pointed shoes to kiss him.

"Anything for me?" Bergold asked, playfully.

"Firelighters," Roan said, shoving the bag into his friend's arms. He put the small wrapped box into his pocket to present later, at a more private moment.

"Your Highness, Your Highness!" A well-dressed man in a top hat bustled toward them, hastily transforming his fussy tie into a chain of office. He had obviously been roused from his place of business at a moment's notice. Several men and women followed him, also wearing their decorations. "Your Highness! Great heavens, we thought it was you. There were rumors all over town. Forgive me," he said, pausing breathlessly before the princess. He bowed deeply, whisking his hat past his knees. "I am Mayor Georgeton of the fair town of Hark. Honored to meet you, madam. May I present the town council? What brings your grace to our humble precincts?"

The crowd with him bowed or curtseyed to the princess. Leonora smiled at them all, and offered her hand, which the mayor took with a kind of astonished delight. An amiable man with white hair and curling eyebrows, and kind, light blue eyes, Roan liked him on sight. So did Bergold, who began to change until he resembled the man.

"Well, I am . . . traveling," Leonora said, looking over the mayor's head at Roan, who mouthed the word to her. "Incognito, your honor."

"Incognito! Surely not," the mayor said gallantly. "How could one disguise such a regal beauty as yourself—if I do not offend by saying so?"

"Why, no, you don't offend at all," Leonora assured him, with a sly look toward Roan, who kept his face politely blank. "Thank you."

"Ah, well, since we have penetrated your disguise, we can't let such an opportunity as this one be missed. You must come to lunch. It won't be as fancy as we'd like," the mayor said, with a touch of understandable chagrin. His face brightened. "Perhaps one day you will return to us, and we can give you the banquet you do deserve. . . ."

Leonora seemed on the edge of accepting, but she was mindful of the embarrassment of the morning. Roan saw her disappointment as she shook her head.

"I am so sorry. We can't stay."

"Oh, but, please, Your Highness!" Georgeton protested, and the councillors added their prayers. "Tea? Champagne? Anything? *Please* allow us this honor."

Roan caught her eye, and gave a nod and a rueful shrug. He knew that maintaining good public relations with her subjects was just as important a function as any they might fulfill, such as saving the world from destruction. Leonora smiled like the sun coming up, and turned to the mayor.

"Very well, your honor. My friends and I would be most delighted to have tea with the kind citizens of Hark," she said. Georgeton was elated.

"Thank you, Your Highness! This way! This way!" Georgeton said, with sweeping gestures toward the north end of the square. "Preparations have already begun!"

Roan joined Leonora and offered an elbow to her. She put her hand through it, and leaned close, still smiling at the rejoicing townsfolk who romped around them like a crowd of puppies.

"Can't we tell them why we're here?" she asked in a low voice. "Don't they have a right to know they may be in danger?"

"Do we have a right to tell them, and disrupt their lives?"

Roan looked around him. For all the careful Victorian character of the town, the houses were made of oddments. "These people aren't in charge of their destinies. They are the ones to whom things happen. If we tell them, the warning will do nothing but worry them, and nothing at all might happen."

"Only frighten them," Bergold added. His mayorlike face appeared beside them and made Leonora jump. "And if we fail—they'll never know, that's all."

"These are the ones we have to save," Roan said.

"We will," Leonora vowed, setting her chin. "I swear it."

In the next square a table had been set up. It was long enough, Roan guessed, to accommodate the entire population of the town. On a long white cloth huge bouquets of blue periwinkle flowers were piled around the place setting in the center of the table at one side, where beaming townsfolk in their best clothes were waiting to seat the princess. Her tastes were well known throughout her father's kingdom. The immaculate china didn't match, but some effort had been made to disguise the fact with a sprig of blue flowers on each plate.

"Your Highness, pray sit here," the mayor urged, gesturing her toward the place of honor. He put out an arm for her to take, judged himself too bold, and jumped away again before her fingertips touched him. With a backwards smile to Roan, Leonora allowed the silly straw hat to become a genteel tiara, which looked wonderful on her inflated hairstyle.

Roan was ushered to a far end of the table by a uniformed maid, as the townsfolk sought to sit as close to the princess as protocol allowed. The scrimmage left the traveling party all together. Felan, parcels in a huge shopping bag at his side, was herded down the queue. He grabbed Roan's arm.

"What is going on?" he asked.

"Her Highness has graciously allowed Hark to have her to tea," Roan said.

"But we've got to be on our way," Felan said.

"I know," Roan said, "but this should not take too long." Their companions found them, and sat down. Colenna settled between Bergold and Roan, and enjoyed herself as waiters in short white coats poured tea, coffee, and lemonade from silver pitchers, and dispensed sandwiches and pastries with silver tongs.

"Look!" she said. "They're serving Her Highness with gold. How dear of them. It's nice to see these old customs haven't died out everywhere." She nodded as the server's tongs hovered above a cream cake, a chocolate cylinder filled with raspberries, and a snowy white meringue. "Glorious! Look at these!"

Roan accepted a plate of delicacies and a cup of tea, then he and the others waited. From where he sat he couldn't see the town officials, who would consider it a breach of manners if anyone took a bite before the guest of honor. Gradually, like a wave, diners in turn raised forkfuls of food to their mouths. Roan gratefully cut into the wedge of cheesecake on his plate, and took a hearty bite. He looked at Bergold out of the corner of his eye. The historian swallowed his portion of lemon sabayon.

"Interesting, isn't it?" Bergold said, carefully.

"Most unusual," Roan said. The cheesecake had tasted like mashed potatoes. He broke off a portion of croissant and ate it. It looked like butter pastry, but it had the distinct flavor of soda bread. Roan and the others exchanged glances. In order to honor their guests, the citizens of Hark had changed whatever they had to look like fine foods, but they lacked the strength to add the flavors, too. Colenna shrugged.

"It's a fine spread, and nice of them, don't you think?" she said, taking another sandwich from the hovering waiter's platter. "Food's food, after all."

"Yes, of course," Roan said. After the first shock, the mashed-potato cheesecake wasn't at all bad to eat; the hasty cook had used plenty of butter and milk in the recipe. The soda-croissant was a trifle dry, and required lashings of jam from the china bowls on the table. The jam did taste like jam, although it was ordinary grape and apple rather than the exotic fruits the bright colors suggested. Roan was reminded again that this was not a rich or powerful community, yet they had gone to a great deal of trouble to do their best for unexpected guests. He felt a twinge of guilt for not appreciating the food, and a deep affection for these people. They tried. It was for their sake that he was making his effort to stop Brom.

All at once, he was impatient to resume his journey. Brom and the Alarm Clock were getting farther ahead with every second's tick. The others must have felt the same, because they finished their meals as quickly as they could, and signed that they were ready to rise when Roan gave the word. He started to push back his chair.

Then the toasting began.

"Ladies and gentlemen!" the mayor shouted, rising to his feet with a glass in his hand. "Ladies and gentlemen, raise your glasses! To His Ephemeral Majesty!"

"To the King!" everyone chorused. Roan joined in, and drank the toast. The wine, at least, was real.

"To Her Luminescent Majesty!"

"To the Queen!" came the roar from three hundred throats.

"And to our illustrious guest, Her Highness, the Princess Leonora!"

"To Princess Leonora!" Everyone drained their glasses and set them down on the white tablecloth. The mayor, his goblet empty, snapped his fingers, and three servers hurried towards him with pitchers. Now members of the council rose to offer their toasts, echoed by the townsfolk. When a toaster couldn't think of something to say, he or she would roar out, "To the King!"

While the glasses were being refilled for the second time, Roan slipped out of his chair and made his way down the long table to the princess's side. The mayor and the councillors were making small talk with her. Roan could see Leonora smiling and nodding politely, although he couldn't hear her replies. The townsfolk nearest them stayed silent and wide-eyed, breathing in excited short gasps, at their proximity to the heir to the throne.

Or perhaps it was lack of oxygen. As Roan approached the place of honor, the air did seem to grow thinner and more rarefied until by the time he reached the princess's side, he could hardly breathe. The mayor turned to look at him as he knelt down beside Leonora's chair.

"Oh, my lord mayor, may I present Master Roan? He is the King's Investigator," Leonora said. Roan nodded, concentrating on taking in enough oxygen without gasping openly.

"How very interesting," Mayor Georgeton said, not caring

much at all for the interloper's presence. "Your Highness, som prenoply venre dimal simcot lomp ital."

Leonora laughed. "Venitre dimal midgal nomig silomp. Roan moktu benek op lur."

"Som poplu vog, dewep?" Georgeton turned to his council, who nodded wisely.

"I beg your pardon?" Roan asked. He was dismayed to realize he couldn't understand a word they were saying. Georgeton was deliberately speaking too loftily for anyone not of his echelon or higher to comprehend. Leonora glanced at him apologetically.

"Don't you agree that it is more pleasant to travel so you can really experience the Dreamland, instead of simply taking the train?" she said, rather slowly and carefully, trying to draw him into the conversation. "I said that you had traveled widely over the last several years, and used many different means of transport."

"Yes, indeed, I have," Roan said, struggling for air.

"You could tell them scov batiluh sminit combulon da ena, virdo?" Leonora had lost him again, as she turned to include the others. "Vobla bam dininat moper waga."

"Somibuno," Georgeton agreed politely.

"Well," Roan began, trying to think of a tale that would amuse them.

"Pofi nipt jabal!" a blonde female councillor in her middle years interrupted him, and launched vivaciously into an anecdote of her own. What she was saying sounded interesting, and Roan struggled to understand. He felt as if all he had to do was turn his perception sideways, and the jumble of words would become clear. Also, every time he took a breath, he got a stitch in his side from lack of oxygen. He was afraid if he had to reply at length to anyone, he might black out. He stood up to go away. The princess laid a hand on his arm.

"Sami peh," she said, imploringly. He didn't know the words, but the meaning was clear. *Don't go*. With a sigh, Roan sank to his haunches again.

"Roan!"

He heard a shout from the edge of the square, and stood up. Misha and his two escorts came pedaling out of the narrow lane. The young man, breathless and red-faced, leaped off his bicycle and ran it to a stop beside the table. Roan pulled him aside and gestured him to keep his voice down.

"We've found where they left town," Misha gasped, his long legs almost collapsing under him. Leonora watched them from her place at the table, her eyebrows telegraphing a question. Roan put up one finger, asking her to wait a moment. "We ought to hurry and get on the trail before it moves again. It's a very busy road. It goes all over the place. Heading north."

"Are you sure it's their trail?"

"Yes, sir," Lum said, definitely. "They crossed the railroad tracks, sir."

"How can you tell?" Roan asked, curiously.

"We mean they *crossed* them," Misha said. "One's lying over the other like 'X marks the spot.' "

"The Alarm Clock's perverting nature more and more as it goes," Roan said. "I'll get the others."

But their companions at the end of the table had already seen the advance party return, and hurried to join them. Spar, too, had seen the scouts from his end of the high street, and led the steeds down to meet them. Roan took a deep breath and went back into the airfree zone around the princess.

"I beg your pardon," he said, bowing deeply to the mayor and his councillors. "Your Highness, at your pleasure?"

Leonora telegraphed a question with her eyebrows, and Roan nodded, tilting his head back towards Misha and the others. She looked over at them, then turned to the Mayor and extended her fingers to him.

"My lord, it has been an honor to receive this gift of hospitality and kindness from you. The break to our journey was most welcome. I feel renewed. I do hope I may return someday soon."

The mayor and the others scrambled to their feet as Leonora arose from her place. The rest of the townsfolk rose from their seats in an outward moving wave.

"Your Highness, we are the ones who are honored," Georgeton said, beaming at her, but not before looking ruefully at Roan. He bowed over her hand. "Thank you for giving us this chance to show our appreciation of you and your most royal father. Are you sure you can't stay longer? We have some more toasting we'd like to do."

"No!" Leonora said, withdrawing her hand. "Thank you so much. Goodbye."

"And may I say," Roan said, shaking hands with the mayor, "it has been schmati gobbledigook binreeta."

"What?" asked one of the councillors. "What did he say?"

With a regal smile, Leonora allowed Roan to escort her to Golden Schwinn and assist her in mounting to the saddle.

"Farewell!" Georgeton said, waving a handkerchief after them as they rode out of the square.

"Goodbye!" the townspeople called. "Sweet dreams!" "Be careful!" "Don't let the bedbugs bite!"

"Would it was only bedbugs," said Bergold.

"What was Misha so excited about?" Leonora asked Roan in a low voice, pedaling alongside him through the deserted streets. As soon as she was out of sight of the Harkians, she parted the irritating dress into long, light trousers of bright white silk, and dismissed the bustle. The tiara she kept as it was, and she added a wristband to Roan's posy so she could wear it on her sleeve.

"You'll see in a moment, Your Highness," Misha said, behind them. "There, look!"

Flags and raised bars marked the place where the level crossing passed over the road that led out of town. The stationmaster, a thin, old man in a dark blue uniform tunic, stood amidst the weeds with his cap off, scratching his head as he stared at the tracks at his feet.

"I've put the red signal up," he said, as Roan and the others braked to a stop near him. "This'll make a terrible mess of the schedule. That will never do."

Roan got off for a good look. As Misha had said, one enormous silver band lay over the other. The metal was smooth and bright and unmarked. Everything looked perfectly normal except that the tracks were crossed, without a clue to show how the trick had been done.

"The Alarm Clock," Bergold said, in a whisper to Roan. "Incredible."

"Is there another twist farther up the line?" Roan asked.

"Just the one, lad," the stationmaster said. "I've walked a mile in either direction. Lucky thing it is only the one. My men can help fix it as soon as they stop lollygagging in town. They ran off to have tea with the others in honor of the princess—Oh, hello, Your Highness," he said, offering her a half-bow. "Royalty and fancy meals are all very well, you know, but the trains have got to run on time."

"Are the grapevines still intact?" Leonora asked, frowning at the tracks. "Please send a message to my father the king. He'll dispatch engineers to help you."

"We'll do it ourselves, lass," the man said. "We do cope with change. It's the nature of things, after all."

"So it is," Colenna said, with an approving nod.

"So there's nothing you need do, Your Highness," the stationmaster said, smiling at her paternally. "But it's nice of you to take an interest."

"It is our duty," Leonora said. "But if you require assistance, please do ask."

"I've . . . already heard from Your Highness's father," the stationmaster said, with an inquiring look at Leonora. "We got a message with all sorts of details, last night already. Shall I tell him I saw you, Your Highness?"

"Just tell him I'm all right," she said, turning away hastily, and sent a meaningful look to Spar. The guard captain took his place as head of the party. "Thank you for your service." The stationmaster bowed deeply to her back.

"You didn't tell your father you were going, did you?" Roan asked, as they rode over the tracks.

"He knows now," Leonora said, rather flatly. "What's important is that I'm helping to bring a menace to justice and saving our homeland."

And that's that, Roan thought.

The moment marked a decision for him, too. If he was going to send her home, this would have been the time. He could have made her wait safely here in Hark for the next train, whenever that would be. All the train lines led back to Mnemosyne. But he knew he couldn't force her to go. Yet, he still worried he was risking her unnecessarily. His conscience troubled him. If he had any sense he should have begged her to wait here for the next train home. Georgeton would have been delighted to take care of her in the grandest style of which his little town was capable. And yet, Roan agreed that Leonora had as much at stake as anyone else. His dilemma remained unresolved.

She rode quietly on the tall, awkward bicycle, staring straight ahead of her as Spar led them out of town. She didn't blink for so long Roan finally interrupted her reverie.

"Did you have a nice time in Hark?" he asked.

She blinked and started. "Oh, yes. Yes, I did. They were kind, weren't they?"

"They were thrilled to meet you," Roan said. She turned wide, worried eyes to him.

"We must protect them, Roan. I was just thinking how awful it would be if they all . . . went away. We have to stop Brom."

"We're trying," Roan assured her. "We are doing all we can."

Chapter 14

Just outside of Hark, the road was a generous two lanes wide. After the narrow forest paths and lanes in town, Roan and the others were glad to spread out across it and give one another space. Within a hundred paces, the pennyfarthings changed again. Roan stopped pedaling mid-push when Cruiser manifested as a fine horse and protested having his sides scraped by Roan's boots.

"Ah!" Bergold said, settling himself happily on his pink and gray palomino. "Now we can make up some speed!"

The horses were eager to stretch their legs after the constricted ride through town. Misha's playful beast let its legs go very long, propelling itself far out in front of the others with two spiderlike jumps. Its strange gait spooked Colenna's mare, which broke into a wild canter and ran off with her, past the young continuitor, and away.

"Whoa-aa!" she cried, hauling back on the reins.

"Wait! Stop!" Misha shouted. He turned his beast to follow her, but it evidently decided it had stretched its legs enough, and turned into a wooden sawhorse. Misha grabbed for a handhold, but pure momentum took hold and propelled him forward over the horse's head onto the road. The horse laughed a long, braying whinny. As Spar and Roan passed him, Misha stood up and dusted off his rump with a look that boded no good for his steed.

The two men hurried their mounts to catch up with Colenna, who was disappearing ahead of them in a cloud of dust. Beyond her, Roan could see a bend in the road. Trees blocked the view of the terrain ahead. It could be stones, or mire, or a cliff where no one was dreaming anything beyond it.

The older woman lost her flat straw hat, and her long hair flew out behind her, bouncing at every gallop. With a burst of speed, Roan urged Cruiser into the race, running until he was a neck ahead of Colenna, and reached for the mare's reins. He pulled back, slowing Cruiser at the same time. The runaway trotted to a walk, blowing through its lips. The older woman was crouching over the mane and laughing, her face now decades younger than her silvering hair.

"My dreams, but that felt good!" Colenna said, sitting up as the mare checked her pace.

"You could have broken your neck," Spar growled, and Roan realized he seemed personally concerned for Colenna's safety.

"Oh, I'm fine," she said, playfully slapping the guard captain's arm. He grunted, and looked away hastily. Colenna shook her head, and patted her hair back into its plait.

Roan, relieved that she wasn't in danger, surveyed the highway. It was well made, with a bed of stones covered by a layer of screened gravel, and went on for miles through an arcade of widely spaced trees. Ahead, another similar avenue intersected their road at right angles. The other riders caught up with them. Misha had retrieved Colenna's hat, and restored it to her with a flourish.

"Thank you, my dear," Colenna said, putting it on again. "I'm sorry to frighten you all, but you must admit this is an excellent road for a run."

"I thought you'd be killed," Leonora said.

"Not her," Felan said, darkly. "She'd rather have us die of fright."

"It's nice that you care," Colenna said, without a trace of sarcasm.

Felan looked startled, then hastily turned his mount to the back of the file. Colenna smiled after him and trotted placidly alongside Spar to the crossroads.

"Corporal! Which way?" Spar bellowed.

Cautiously, Lum spurred his horse to the front of the line, and swung off to examine the road. Roan admired his orienteering skills; there wasn't a hope of footprints or tire prints on the stony surface. Lum's bay horse danced nervously at the end of his reins. The guard corporal squinted in both directions down the intersecting road, and shook his head.

"I still say it's the same way, sir," he said. "The weirding only goes ahead."

"The weirding is all over the place, if you ask me," Felan said, under his breath.

"They didn't go off on a path to one side?" Roan asked, peering down the avenue.

"No, sir! We've got a nice clear trail to follow," Lum insisted. "They're on this, sir. They need a good road, what with that heavy load of theirs."

"On we go, then," Roan said. Spar clicked his tongue, and his horse led the way.

More confidently, they pressed on, admiring the pleasant grassy downs and hillsides. The avenue opened outward and began to wind, until they could no longer see very far ahead of them. The trees became shorter and more scanty.

"Hooonnnk!"

The horses danced and shied as a huge black automobile swung around the bend ahead and bore down on them. Roan grabbed for Golden Schwinn's reins and pulled Leonora off the road just as the car hurtled past, spewing black smoke.

"Someone's in a hurry," Alette said, sourly. She had resumed female form as soon as they had left Hark though she had retained her uniform. The double-breasted wool coat with its silver buttons was rather becoming to her. "If there's too many of those about, we should get off, Captain."

"Let's go on," Bergold said, guiding his horse back onto the road surface, now paved with black asphalt, "or we haven't a chance of catching up with Brom before dark."

"Don't worry," Lum said. "This should be easy going."

The clop-clop-clopping of the horses' hooves was a peaceful sound under the clear, bird-filled sky. The road not only remained paved, but widened out still more. A white stripe dashed down the center of each side, dividing the two lanes into four. Instead of riding two abreast, the party was able to move freely up and back. When Misha thought of a joke to tell the princess, he'd urge his steed into a trot beside her without edging Roan into the ditch. Only Spar and Colenna continued to trot along side by side at the head of the party, not paying much attention to anyone else. Roan felt no need to disturb them. They were making good time.

"Hooonnnk!"

At the sound of another car behind them, Roan signaled to everyone to move onto the shoulder of the road. A small gray automobile shot past them, and vanished over the hill.

"Aayyyrrrruuunnnggg," its horn whined as it went by.

Just as Roan was about to gesture them back onto the tarmac, a red car zoomed by in the gray's wake, beeping a shrill, staccato protest. Then three vehicles, a blue, a red, and a green, roared towards them side by side on the opposite half of the road, which obligingly opened out to six lanes. Cars began to come from both directions, at first a few at a time, then in tens, then in hundreds, filling the lanes, crowding Roan and his party off the road. The horses huddled together, twitching, on the graveled shoulder as thousands of cars and trucks sped by in both directions.

A sharp honk startled Roan. Cruiser bucked under him, and Roan controlled the steed with difficulty. Golden Schwinn had fled off the road entirely, and had to be coaxed back up from the shallow ditch beside the shoulder. Roan made Leonora ride on the outer edge, and put himself and his mount between her and the speeding steel boxes. Spar and his guards spread out to protect the others.

"Is it a nuisance?" Roan shouted over the roar of the engines to Bergold.

"No," the historian shouted back. He lifted the protective goggles that now covered his eyes. His coat had changed to a long, white duster, and he had a cap with a wide bill on the front and a veil on the back. "This is a vision from the Waking World. It's real. It's called traffic. It appears to be a growing phenomenon everywhere!"

"Horrible!" the princess exclaimed.

Roan stared at the dismaying spectacle of endless streams of cars, all belching smoke and revving their engines. Spar ordered the panicking horses into a double file, and led them northwards, staying to the far side of the shoulder. Cars snarled and honked at them. The horses shied and showed the whites of their eyes. Roan thought that their riders looked just as wary.

They traveled uneasily beside the perilous river of steel. Roan witnessed hundreds of near-collisions where the bad-tempered vehicles accelerated, tires screeching, to get past one another in a single narrow lane. A low-slung red vehicle with its windows so darkly tinted they couldn't see inside howled past, knocked into another car, and spun out of control, right off the road, coming to a rest facing Spar. Its headlights glared insanely at them, and steam hissed sideways out of the front wheel-wells. It revved its engine, once, twice. It was going to run them down! Roan rushed forward, unfolding his quarterstaff from his red knife, to put himself between the metal monster and the princess.

"Get back!" he cried.

The soldiers and their captain went on guard beside him with swords drawn as the car accelerated toward them, its grille grinning a death's-head smile. From nowhere, Roan heard a trumpet playing the staccato challenge to single combat. He braced himself for the impact, ready to smash the monster right in the hood ornament. He knew the beast could crush his staff into splinters. He wished he had some more fearsome weapon, but he was not accustomed to having to carry one.

Only seconds before it would have struck them, the red car veered sharply right, and shoved its way back into traffic.

"Whew!" Lum whistled, blowing out the flames on his sword and resheathing it. "I thought we were going to have to fight it back."

"Too bad we don't have cars, too," Felan said, glancing at the endless stream to his left with envy. "Then we could really eat up the miles. Can't we do that?"

"Excellent notion!" Bergold said. "We can try."

Roan thought of the white sports car that the king's messenger had driven to the Castle of Dreams, and tried to will Cruiser into a similar shape. He concentrated hard, thinking of wide mag tires and a five-gear transmission instead of horseshoes and muscles. The horse's shape wavered and shifted between animal and mechanical. Roan actually dropped into a driver's seat for one moment, before Cruiser snapped firmly back into animal shape. He looked over his shoulder at his master with reproachful eyes.

"I can't do it," Roan called. "The paradigm is beyond me. Has anyone else had any success?" The others shook their heads. The most that had happened was that the guards' uniforms changed to khaki jackets and trousers, and their sword belts became heavy and laden with all sorts of mysterious small pouches of leather and fabric. Roan was fascinated by the round blue dome that replaced their saddlehorns.

"We'll just have to endure going slowly," Bergold said. "Just keep your eyes open, everyone."

Roan did keep his eyes open. In the lines of traffic, he observed fourteen more near-misses, a dozen or so minor impacts, and one more spinout that resulted in the vehicle landing upside down in the ditch. Still, there were rules to the road. He saw that the lane farther away was moving faster than the one nearest them. What if they could get into the fast lane? If they were very careful, it might boost their speed, and help them catch up with Brom.

He explained his reasoning to the others, who reacted with open horror.

"You're mad," Felan said, watching sports cars whizz by. "We'd all be killed."

"I'll try it, Captain Spar, sir," Hutchings offered. When his captain gave him a wave of permission, the guard wheeled his horse, and, blue saddle light rotating, began to trot alongside the stream of cars. With care, Hutchings watched until another pair of speeders had another near collision. Then he spurred his horse out into the resulting gap. The horse began to gallop. The cars seemed to respect the blue light, and hung back the split seconds it took for the horse to gain speed. Miraculously, it seemed to keep pace with the line of traffic, which was moving several times faster than a swift steed could canter.

"It works!" Hutchings shouted.

"Come on, then!" Roan said. He kicked Cruiser into a run, and galloped until he was side by side with Hutchings. The guard pulled up his horse slightly to let Cruiser in front of him. Horns honked furiously, but stayed behind Hutchings's official light. One by one, the others joined the queue. Leonora spurred Golden Schwinn into the lane ahead of all the others, leaving an appreciable gap between her and the car ahead. A large automobile at once veered in front of them, nearly clipping the shining golden horse's hooves. Schwinn shied and neighed with terror.

"Show no fear," Roan insisted, spurring his way to her side.

Narrower than cars, the horses had more maneuverability on the road. "Show no fear. Don't look them in the lamps, and they won't challenge you. Keep close! Watch out for Brom!"

They cantered on. Roan was pleased that his hypothesis was correct. The landscape seemed to roll by with amazing speed. He allowed the others a short time to get used to the noise and the jarring of the road under the horses' hooves.

"Now for the fast lane!" he cried, signaling to Hutchings to lead the way leftwards.

Using the same tactics, they managed to move through the middle and into the inner lane. Now they were passing car after car on their right, moving amazingly fast but only riding at a normal trot.

"Whhhooonnnkkk!"

A louder noise than any of the car engines erupted behind them as the road opened into four lanes on each side. A huge, multiwheeled vehicle joined the fray. It came up on their right, towering above their heads, and merged in front of Cruiser and Golden Schwinn without hesitation. The truck spewed black fumes out of a tall smokestack affixed next to the cabin, and the contrail enveloped the riders in clouds of greasy, reeking ash. Everyone coughed, squinting through tears. Spar swore a blue oath, leaving smoke trailing behind him.

More trucks appeared, filling the lane nearest Roan, and started to edge over into the fastest lane, threatening the speeding horses, even those adorned with blue lights. Roan felt they faced a new danger now. The ditch beside the road was too steep for them to ride down, and the shoulder was hard concrete. If they left the lane, they would have to keep running to keep the animals from stumbling, perhaps fatally. The noise was overwhelming, and the smog stupefied him.

"Can't . . . keep . . . going," Leonora said, coughing. She had put a veil over her face to keep out some of the smog, but the air was full of it.

"We must," Roan said, coughing, too. "We'll get off as soon as it's safe." He made himself a gas mask, which bumped uncomfortably on his chest, but filtered out the noxious fumes from the air.

Just ahead of them, the land beside the road crested, then started to drop away precipitously on both sides, and the surface under the horses' hooves changed from thudding asphalt to clanking metal grillwork. Roan could only spare a moment's glance at a time to see, but he realized they had moved onto a bridge. He glanced down through the metal mesh under Cruiser's feet, and felt his stomach fall a thousand feet. A river, a tiny, blue thread, wound its way along the bottom of the deep gorge. It was the giant Lullay on its first spiral turn around the Dreamland. It looked deceptively narrow at this height. They were leaving Celestia, and heading into the northeast province of Wocabaht.

They had come a long distance on this fast highway. Hark had been only two-thirds of the way from Mnemosyne to the border. Looking down gave Roan the horrible feeling that he might fall. The more he thought about it, the more spongy the mesh became under Cruiser's hooves. The wiggly wire netting could give way at any moment! Roan willed himself to stop being afraid of falling. The others could fall through the hole he created. He must not let his fear cause an accident. The bridge is solid, he insisted to himself. Solid! He stared straight ahead of him, refusing to look down.

He was relieved when the ground started upwards, and the grillwork gave way to hard road surface.

As soon as they were over the headlands, plants and trees reappeared along the roadway. The leaves were turning red and brown, in sharp contrast to the green they had just left behind. Roan thickened his coat against the sudden chill in the air, and noticed that the others' gear did the same as soon as they had crossed the bridge.

He hadn't been in Wocabaht in years. The temperature was lower here because the seasons were on a reversed schedule to the other six provinces, which meant that here it was nearly winter. The historians didn't have an explanation on which they agreed for the phenomenon, except to reiterate that every Sleeper was an individual. This Sleeper was just more individualistic than the others. The exhaust belching from the roaring cars' tailpipes turned into gray clouds in the chilly air.

Suddenly, behind them, there was a louder roar than ever before. Alarmed, Roan glanced back over his shoulder, and gawked. A single vehicle was hurtling towards them, but what a vehicle! Its enormous, black wheels were each over a lane wide, and the silver-grilled front covered the rest of the road. It bore down on them at astonishing speed.

Instead of getting out of its way, the other cars and trucks ignored it. They continued to jockey for position, honking and revving their engines. The monster rolled right over them, and where it passed, it left nothing in its wake.

"Get over!" Roan called, pointing toward the slow lanes. "Hurry! Get off the road!"

Lum, Hutchings, Alette, and Spar threw themselves into the near lane, forming a barrier of flashing blue lights to provide safe passage for the others. The road machine loomed closer and closer. Roan made sure Colenna, Bergold, Misha, Felan, and Leonora all got into the middle lane before he abandoned the innermost lane to the thundering trucks. One by one, they crossed the road, narrowly avoiding accidents, all the time glancing behind them at the approaching monster. He urged the princess off onto the hard shoulder. She fell behind, and Roan lost sight of her. One by one, the others leaped out of traffic, leaving only Roan and Spar.

"You'd better jump!" the captain roared, just barely holding back a surging pickup truck. "Here it comes!"

"Together!" Roan shouted. "One, two . . . !"

The monster road machine was nearly upon them. With a wild neigh, Cruiser leaped off the road and cantered down into the ditch. Roan, lying bent over the horse's mane, held on with both knees and hands, plunging through stones and slippery grass, and finally sandy mud, until they bumped to a stop at the bottom of the trench. He sat hunched in the saddle for a moment, until his head stopped ringing. Cruiser stood, head hanging down between his forelegs. Roan swung out of the saddle on wobbly legs to examine him. The horse seemed fine: no broken legs, no flat tires. His coat was muddy and grass-stained, but so was Roan's. He patted Cruiser's neck, and the beast leaned against him, panting. Roan didn't feel too steady himself.

"Roan! Are you all right?" Bergold's voice called from high above him. Roan looked up, and saw the plump figure of the historian peering down over the edge at him. "I can't believe you survived that! This pit is sixty feet deep!"

"We're fine!" Roan called back. Cruiser raised his head and gave a faint but affirmative neigh. "Is everyone else all right?"

"Yes, we're all safe," Bergold shouted down. "Can you get up here? You must see what happened."

Roan looked around him. He was at the deepest point of the drainage ditch. Ahead of him, the ground sloped upward until it was almost level with the road. He pointed forward, and Bergold's head nodded before it was withdrawn from view.

Something *was* different, Roan thought, as he rode to join the others. Something was missing. Suddenly he knew: the noise. All the cars and trucks had fallen silent.

Cruiser found footing in between the rocks, and propelled himself along gradually toward where the others were waiting. Roan let his feet hang slack in the stirrups, and stared at the roadbed in disbelief.

The monster machine had literally eaten up the miles. Nothing remained of the vast paved surface as far as Roan could see. His companions stood in the midst of an unbroken sward of grass.

"Now, that, *that* was a nuisance," Misha said, pointing in the direction the vehicle had last been seen.

"Well, thank the Sleepers for it," Colenna said. "I thought a hundred times that we'd be killed by those unspeakable cars. Now we're rid of the honking, smelly pests. And those trucks! Good riddance!"

"Yes, but now we have nothing to go upon," Felan said, his narrow face full of disapproval. "Literally and figuratively! We were making good time, too."

"Too dangerous," the princess said, shuddering. She changed her veil and tiara into a warm hood and tied the strings under her chin. "Brr! I hate traffic."

Roan sniffed. The smell of the cold air improved by the moment, and another wind of change came toward them, bearing the smell of wet grass. It began to drizzle.

"With change comes its perils," Bergold said lightly. "The Sleepers often give and take away with the same hand."

"Must have amazingly broad palms," Felan said in an undertone, earning him another sour look from Colenna, and, to his evident surprise, one from Spar as well.

"You must have been at the bottom of your class, sonny,"

Colenna said. "How did you become attached to the Ministry?"

"We've no trail now," Spar said. "Blast this meadow! We'll have to go back and figure out where we lost them."

"There is a good side," Roan said. "The steeds were uncomfortable on a paved road, but they're perfectly suited to riding over smooth grassland, better than any other mode of conveyance. And we have less fear of skidding on an asphalt surface in the rain."

"Cold comfort," Felan said, darkly, making a rainproof hood out of his hat and clapping it on his head. He, the historians, Roan, Misha and the princess had no trouble in waterproofing their garments against the mist, but the guards lacked transformation ability, and needed some assistance in providing themselves with rain gear. Roan helped fit them out with regulation slickers and hats.

"Which way do we go, then, on this perfectly suitable surface?" Bergold asked, as his steed pawed the grass.

"I would hazard that we should continue to head northwards," Roan said, carefully. "Otherwise, Brom would not have bothered to cross the river here."

Lum searched the terrain for indicators, and came back to the group with his amiable face puzzled. "It looks like the trail got swept up with the rest of the road. I don't know where to start."

"Stands to reason that we'll find traces farther on," Spar said. "But how far?"

Roan squinted around them. It was as if they had been sealed into a box with the key on the outside. The others looked at him hopefully. They expected him to make a decision. He felt under the dual pressures of being in charge and knowing that at least some of them thought he was inferior because he was different. If he'd been alone, he wouldn't be so worried about making a mistake. There was nothing here to go upon. He'd led them this far, only to come to a dead end.

No, wait, he thought, staring at one of the clumps of trees a hundred yards or so distant. Signing to the others to stay where they were, he rode toward it to confirm his hopes. There was a mark on one of them, a white arrow as long as his little finger. Then he thought for a moment. Was it mere chance that provided this clue, an impulse of the Sleepers? The mark was not well drawn. It could be a random smudge shaped vaguely like an arrow, that meant nothing at all. Or did they—could they?—have a friend ahead? If it was chance, then thank the Sleepers. But if it was deliberate, he had an advantage he never had counted on. He glanced back at the others. He mustn't tell anyone until he was certain. It would be wrong to give them false hope. As Roan bent down to rub dirt into the mark, he saw what he was hoping for and stood up to wave.

"This is it," he called. "Come on!" He knew he was beaming all over his face.

Spar and Lum came at a trot, and the rest followed.

"What have you found, sir?" Lum asked.

"The way, I think," Roan said, gesturing to the left of the clump of trees. Lum rode to where he was pointing, and let out a wordless cry of joy.

"You're right, sir! Look at this back here, tire prints! Clear as anything. But aren't they odd ones?"

Veering off at a westward angle were the familiar cluster of tire prints. Roan examined them with care. He recognized the tread patterns from the blighted glade where Brom and his minions had picked up their bicycles. Lum was correct. There was a difference: many of the tracks were several inches wide, but if he accounted for the heavier cast, they were the same as others he had noted before. Brom had increased those bicycles' nature in some way. The gestalt was powerful. Roan had no idea what else they might be capable of.

"And it's weird here, sir," Lum added, happily. "Just like the other warping and strangeness. We're on the trail again."

"How do we know they haven't left another false track?" Spar demanded, looking from his corporal to Roan. "I don't want to spend another unnecessary night in the open, like last night. This was supposed to be a rapid pursuit and apprehension."

"But that changed. We simply must go on following," Bergold said. "His Majesty has put out bulletins all over the Dreamland to stop Brom if he is spotted, but I believe we are still the ones with the best chance to apprehend him."

"Bergold is right," Roan said. "We'd best be on our way. There's no way to tell how far ahead of us they are."

"If they're still together," Felan said, sourly. "Who says they haven't divided the party as they did before. What if we're after the wrong half?"

"We *don't* know," Roan said, a little more sharply than he intended. "Have you had any reply to your airmail?"

"Not a word," Felan said, looking worried. "I'd better send another note at our next stop."

The guard captain wheeled his mount, and took his place at the head of the line.

"We're going into Cloud-Cuckooland, if you ask me," he said. Far away to the west, they all heard a crack of thunder, followed at a distance by the bright flash of lightning. Clouds rushed to fill the sky above them. The sun darkened to a grayish blot. Rain poured down in a torrent.

"Wonderful," Spar growled. "That's all it lacked."

Colenna pulled rain gear out of her bag, and changed Spar's regulation slicker to a completely waterproof tunic and hat.

"There, it's not so bad," she said, beaming.

"Look on the bright side," Bergold said, heartily. "It rains on the just and unjust alike."

Roan followed Spar's answering stream of blue smoke into the worsening downpour.

Chapter 15

Taboret started counting when the clap of thunder came. One one thousand, two one thousand, three one thousand, then the sky to the north was peppered with small white zigzags indicating lightning strokes. Twenty one thousand. Flash! Lightning burned the sky overhead bright white, and left it a dark ash. It had been raining for hours, and Taboret's cold hands were starting to slip on her handlebars.

Overhead was a massive capital L surrounded by an irregularly circular isobar that stretched out almost from horizon to horizon. Numerous isobars ringed the central one, and off to the west Taboret caught glimpses of a long, blue, low pressure front studded with blue semicircles. This was one of the largest rainstorms she had ever seen. Where was the high pressure H that would bring them dry weather? Taboret got a stream of water in her left eye from her hood brim when she tilted her head to look. She ducked her head to avoid a branch that bent and showered her with its load of raindrops.

She was fatigued. The extra influence she and the others had provided Lurry to plant traps for Princess Leonora's party, as well as continuing to ride and occasionally transforming their surroundings to ease their passage, left them drained and silent. Brom had had them halt a short while for a high-calorie meal, but did not allow them much time to rest. The break had done some good for their bodies, but couldn't help Taboret's feelings of guilt. She was trying to hide her distaste for her forced complicity in possible regifilicide. And the Alarm Clock dug into her shoulders like an attack of bad conscience.

Several times since they'd crossed over into Wocabaht, Brom

had had them create holes in reality, to be filled by chance-met who-knew-what that was attracted to the vacuum. Instead of erasing their trail, they had purposely left it in plain view to lure the King's Investigator into it. Sooner or later, Brom reasoned, the pursuers would be discouraged by the dangers, and give up. Taboret was afraid of the holes. She felt as if they sucked creative force out of whatever came near them. Roan would never give up, so he and everyone with him could be killed.

The roar of an engine surprised Taboret by its enormous volume. Brom signaled them to a stop as a huge vehicle came over the horizon and rushed toward them with the menace of a charging bull. Taboret squinted. It was one of the mercenaries' motorcycles. The bike had been enhanced again until it was twenty feet high, with wheels the size of houses. At the machine's peak was a wheelhouse that looked tiny in perspective. Lurry, now bearded and wild-haired, was visible behind the windshield, waving. He gave them a happy thumbs-up. Maniune, just as bearded, but looking grimly satisfied, hunched over the steering mechanism.

As they approached Brom, the vehicle shrank rapidly until it was reduced to the motorcycle and sidecar. Lurry's steed detached itself from the host bike, and reasserted its own form as they rolled to a stop before the chief scientist.

"Report!" Brom ordered. "Did you find Roan?"

"We've been having some fun," Maniune said, showing his teeth in a feral smile. "We tore up the road he was on."

As if in confirmation, the motorcycle let out a tremendous belch. Maniune patted it. Lurry grinned, and Taboret got a sudden mental picture of the road rolling up like a carpet.

"Did they get away?" she asked, anxiously, and flinched as Brom's gimlet eye turned to her. "If not, we won't have to worry about pursuit any more."

"True," Brom said. "Well?"

"He jumped in time," Lurry said, gleefully. "You should have seen them. Wheee-ew," he whistled, describing an arc with his hand that traveled up and then down. "Right off into the weeds." Brom raised an eyebrow.

"Is that all?"

"No," Maniune said. "We put some traps down. We left

the trail alone, like you wanted, up to where we planted some misdirections. If they manage to find the way again, they'll have some other surprises waiting for them." The feral grin reappeared, and the mercenary's canines sharpened to little points. Taboret gulped.

"Any messages from our *friend*?"

"Acton is finding out," Maniune said, jerking a thumb behind him. "Here he comes."

The other motorcycle, fearsome albeit unenhanced, roared up, and ground to a halt on its side in the mud.

"Report!" Brom said. "What news?"

"They still don't suspect a thing," Acton said, hauling his beast to its wheels. He brushed at the mire clinging to his legs and chest. His steed shook itself clean, spraying filthy drops all over the apprentices.

"Is this your assessment?" Brom asked, coldly.

"Nah, we got a message from your mole," Acton said, with admiration. "It was stone clever of you to leave somebody behind who'd spy on anyone chasing us."

"*Clever*." Brom mused upon the compliment and found it within the low range of acceptability. "Thank you. What became of the message?"

Acton grinned. "I ate it."

"Good," Brom said. "Perhaps some of the writer's subtlety will infuse you from within. However, we must not depend solely upon what we have left behind. We must make some headway. Staff! Form the gestalt! We will create a ridge of high pressure directly over this road, and ride in dry weather."

"But the road might shift," Basil pointed out.

Brom dismissed the objection with a flick of his long fingers. "Then we will change the pressure zone to keep us dry. Would you rather talk about the weather, or do something about it?"

Tired as they were, the apprentices hopped off their bikes and joined the circle gratefully. Strapped to the Alarm Clock, Taboret couldn't take a direct part in the procedure, but she was glad to lend her energies to them. If there was a chance to be dry and warm again, they wanted it. It was amazing, Taboret thought, that when they left Mnemosyne they had all been dreaming of power. Now all she wanted was clothes that didn't chafe anywhere.

Brom gathered in the apprentices, and laid his heavy, cold hands atop theirs. Taboret watched with interest as the beings of the apprentices shifted just a bit, taking on characteristics of one another, and everyone looking a little like Brom. She felt the warmth flow from her, funneled together with the others, which flowed endlessly outward, until she was part of the landscape. Her hands—not her physical hands, but *metaphysical* ones—pushed up and out against the clouds and wind. Taking the substance of air, they created a solid egg-shaped shell on one small place in the road. Suddenly, the pit-a-pat of raindrops on her upturned face ceased. Her hands relaxed.

The boundaries receded, leaving her in her own body again. She looked down at her hands and saw a different color of skin, and new texture. All the others had changed, too. It was odd experiencing the effects of the crucible from outside. This was a new function, that her energies could be used without having to touch the others. Before they had set out, Brom had given them a list of potential stages of development. He'd said that later on in the journey each of them should be able to tap into the crucible energy from a distance without being able to see one another.

Taboret looked up. It seemed miraculous the way the blue lines turned their arrows away from the road ahead, and the huge H-balloon wiggled its way into the center. She could feel her clothes drying out already, and used a mite of personal influence to make sure they stayed soft. The Alarm Clock felt a little lighter now that Taboret wasn't coping with other miseries.

At Brom's signal the group took to the road again, Taboret looking right and left through a glasslike wall of water, while she pedaled in the dry air. They passed a farmer herding his cows from one field into another in the rain. The man gaped at them curiously, water running off the brim of his peaked felt hat.

"Let him stare," Brom said, triumphantly. "We are the future."

"If we've got one," Gano muttered.

Taboret glanced behind at her, but the older woman was huddled into her collar, concentrating on the road.

Now that she was more comfortable, Taboret's conscience began to nag at her again. She started to worry about those holes in reality Lurry and the mercenaries had been strewing behind them. They might kill someone, maybe even the princess! Taboret had always envied Leonora her wardrobe, her beauty, and the adulation of the masses, but never, never wished her any harm. There had to be something she could do to help save her future sovereign's life.

The road curved ahead, leading through a grove of narrow saplings. With an imperious gesture, Brom pointed upward, and the high pressure center actually began to turn with them. Everyone was watching with wonder on their faces. Taboret had an idea. At the last minute, as she passed a clump of trees closest to the road, she skidded her rear wheel sideways, ramming the axle with a bang into the bole of a sapling. Glinn let out an exclamation.

At once the Alarm Clock reacted to a shift in its center of gravity. The bells under the tarpaulin warbled a low warning sound, ringing on and on in her head. Taboret gritted her teeth. Brom wheeled his nonpedaling bike around to confront her.

"What happened?" Brom demanded, his eyes flaring red from within. "What did you do?"

"I'm sorry, sir," Taboret said, shrinking under the yoke. "I'm just tired. I'm sorry. I was careless. I'm sure the Alarm Clock is all right, sir. I'm so sorry. I apologize, truly I do."

She babbled contritely on until Brom got disgusted and went away. He hated emotional displays, and she knew it. Taboret was satisfied. She had managed to leave a solid, intentional mark on that tree, and function would affect form. The pursuers would know the true road now, in spite of Maniune's machine and machinations.

Taboret pedaled on in grim determination, keeping her thoughts firmly on the road and the rhythm of her knees. She jerked her mind away from the contrived accident, flooding the scene with remorse for almost damaging the Alarm Clock. Brom left her alone, and no one else had energy left to talk.

"Whoa," Glinn's voice said softly from the other side of the draped litter. Taboret coasted to a stop and craned her neck to see over the edge. Brom had come to a halt in a rocky niche just off the road. Above him, a cliff face soared high into clouds of mist. A line of wet, dark stone showed where runnels from a spring coursed gently down into a pool behind the senior scientist. It was so pretty it didn't look quite real.

"This is where we stop for the night," Brom proclaimed. "We have reached this point sooner than I thought." He folded back his chart, took a pen from his breast pocket, and made a note on it. "Good. We are making excellent time. We can stop early."

"And not a moment too soon," Gano muttered to Taboret. She ordered the green motorbike to stand still as she helped to lift the yoke off Taboret's shoulders. Together, they set it on the ground at the edge of the cliff face. Brom stood rubbing his hands together over his precious device.

"May we begin, sir?" Glinn asked. He cleared his throat loudly. "Sir?"

Brom seemed to wake up when Glinn addressed him, as if he was coming back from a place far away. He looked up, straight at Taboret. The expression in his eyes was positively inhuman. Taboret thought she was looking at a being that was part man, part . . . thinking machine. She reddened, but held on to her awareness of how tired she was, projecting that as hard as she could. The machine acknowledged her, and whirred on to the question it had been asked.

"Proceed," Brom said, waving them away. "Follow the plan. You have it, Glinn."

It was a statement, not a question. Taboret couldn't help lifting an eyebrow at the cold tone. Glinn just nodded and turned away, gesturing to the others to come with him, away from their chief, who had already retreated into deep contemplation of his plan.

The first night the apprentices had been allowed to use individual plans they had created for assigned parts of the campground in order to get them used to working together on small programs in gestalt. This night was to be a trial run of complete domicile-building according to a single master blueprint.

Glinn studied the chart, and pointed out a natural sheltered corral where the apprentices could wheel their bikes.

According to the print, which Taboret read over Glinn's shoulder, a stable with natural-seeming camouflage would build up around it when the plans were carried out. Brom had either made use of some very detailed research about this specific locale, or the plans changed themselves to suit. Whichever was the truth, Taboret found it impressive.

"Form up, everyone," Glinn said, holding out his hand. No one moved. After a moment's hesitation, Taboret put her hand on top of his, and positioned herself so there would be plenty of room for the next person to stand behind her. Glinn gave her a grateful look, and bent his thumb upward to give her hand a little squeeze. She gave him a half-grin, and thought hard at projecting support for his effort. With an impatient grunt, Gano joined them, followed by Carina. Gradually, grudgingly, the others fell into line. Taboret could feel through the link a tinge of resentment towards Glinn for acting as supervisor, even though any fool could tell that Brom wasn't paying any attention to them, and no one would sleep in a bed tonight if they didn't get cracking.

"All together now, the way we studied it," Glinn said, flipping the paper out flat over their fists so they could all see it. "This is Housing Plan Two. Do you recall the images? Then, let's begin."

Taboret closed her eyes and concentrated on bending reality. The plans were in her mind, reinforced by the minds of all the others. They recalled details that she did not, and her memory provided information to fill in gaps in theirs. Well done, so far. She was enjoying this part, in spite of the Countingsheep brothers, whose irritating presence was ever more palpable through the link.

Her thoughts reached out to touch the cliff face, and stopped against the surface. It felt solid, cool, and moist. With a gasp, Taboret opened her eyes. It was *real stone*. She couldn't believe that the chief expected them to be able to sculpt that. She had thought when she had seen his grandiose plans back in the castle, that he meant them to be working with nebulosity, a substance that felt mushy, like marshmallow fluff at the bare end of tactility, but was easily molded into temporary structures. She never dreamed he'd try something so ambitious, so *impossible* as forming stone.

"Go on," Glinn's voice said in her mind. She turned her head to meet his eyes, and he gave her an encouraging nod. Taboret looked up at the cliff-face. All right, she'd try. It was only the impossible, after all. She shut her eyes once again.

She saw the blueprints in her mind's eye. Angle the stone walls upward until they closed together in a seam like a peaked roof. Above her, a vaulted ceiling hung with glittering glass lamps shut out the sky. Natural gaps in the rock became baffles for ventilation, wide so they could breathe easily but narrow enough to prevent them from being observed from outside. All the time, the apprentices were also making the walls grow outward to envelop their circle.

Those walls in her mind's eye smoothed over, and sprouted red nodules that lit up: Brom's patented security system. Near the original cliff, a small door was to be formed through which only one person could pass at a time. Stone melted down over it in a concealing curtain only a millimeter thick. This was a secret escape hatch, meant to act as a last hope if enemies invaded during the night. Other walls grew out to form rooms. One of them enclosed Brom and the Alarm Clock. A pit in the ground opened up, and fire belched out from the middle of the earth, and a fireplace-stove combination formed over it, with a chimney reaching for the ceiling flowing upward like a wax taper melting in reverse motion.

When Taboret realized that she was shifting stone as easily as changing her mind, she thought of bursting through the hidden door and leaving a her-shaped hole behind her as she ran home. She was astonished, frightened, and exultant all at the same time. She had always had a reasonable command of her surroundings, but it would have taken months for her to accomplish what the gestalt did in moments. The wonder and awe felt by the others coursed through her body, and a surge of giddiness made her sway on her feet. When at last they were finished with all the details of the plan they stopped. Taboret looked around. She was impressed, and exhausted.

"Well done, all," Glinn said. His voice sounded tired, too. He took his hand away from under hers, breaking the spell of the gestalt, and the feeling of camaraderie died away. Quickly, all the others withdrew, too. Taboret felt forlorn as she was left alone in her own head. "Now, let's eat, and we can get some sleep."

"Right you are," Basil said, immediately buoyed up by the prospect of cooking, his greatest passion after scientific research. "Give me five minutes." He bustled away. Taboret grinned indulgently after the plump apprentice. She hadn't liked him much when they'd started their journey, but he was growing on her.

The apprentices sat down to dinner as soon as the food was ready, without changing their traveling clothes, or even brushing off road dust. Taboret's only accession to etiquette was to take off her outer tunic, damp with sweat, and carefully remove the pen protector to her undertunic's pocket. The next level of construction plans would call for an automatic cleaning system that would tidy and launder them without physical effort. In the meantime, they had to wash themselves and their clothes in the old-fashioned way, by influence or elbow grease. Without wanting to appear rude, she sprang up as soon as the meal was finished, to be first in line at the bath. Her legs were long in this particular body, and she took advantage of their extended stride. Carina looked a little perturbed, evidently having similar plans, but the older woman arrived at the door a fraction too late.

"Second," she said, giving Taboret a speaking look.

"Sorry," Taboret said. And she *was* sorry, but to be clean and dry suddenly felt like a matter of life and death.

She bathed as quickly as she could. She put on her night clothes while her day things slapped against one another in the tumble dryer, and slipped out to let Carina take over the facility.

Her camp bed lay on the new stone floor within arm's length of the tiny waterfall. The cataract trickled down the stone face into a minute pool that emptied into an equally small rivulet. Downstream, the flow had been channeled into the sanitary facilities, but here it was virtually unchanged. Taboret was grateful that the chief's plans included the bathroom, so she didn't have to make them up by herself. She was tired. There was no oomph left in her to do anything.

Stretching out on her belly along the cot, she reached out and dabbled her fingers in the water. About fifty-nine degrees, she thought. Clarity, ninety-seven percent, color brownish, probably due to a combination of lichens and mineral content. Almost certainly drinkable.

"Does that feel good?" Glinn asked suddenly. She looked up and found him standing nearby, watching her.

"Good?" Taboret asked, surprised, curling her legs around and sitting up. "I suppose so. Can't you tell?" she added, with more force than she intended.

Glinn looked away, a little embarrassed. "I . . . felt coolness over my fingers, and I wanted to know where it was coming from."

"I'm sorry," Taboret said, at once apologetic. "You must know that, too. Sorry. I don't mean to be rude. Doesn't it bother you that everyone knows everything you feel or think when you're in the gestalt?"

"Well," Glinn said, sitting down on the nearest bunk to hers. "Not everything." His cheeks reddened. "I mean . . . there are some things. . . ." He smiled at her, and his soft brown eyes wore a hopeful expression.

"I know what you mean," Taboret said, hastily. She was aware again how much she was beginning to like him. With the growing strength of the link she could no longer could hide it from him, or anyone else in the group. And it felt, it almost felt as if he liked her, too. Did he? "Glinn, I've . . ."

"Are we settled?" Brom asked. He appeared at their side, looming over them. Taboret stared up at his glittering eye like a mouse caught in the gaze of a bird of prey.

"Yes, sir," Glinn said, springing to his feet.

"Good! Let us finish making up our little comforts, then seal this place up so we will not be disturbed." Brom stared down at Taboret. "It will not take everyone's influence. These are small tasks. You may rest."

Taboret settled gratefully on her bunk to watch. She was sorry for Glinn, who looked as tired as she felt. He and the chief closed the great stone doors, and locked them with a huge key that Glinn took out of the keyhole to wear around his neck.

"Aren't you going to set the Clock? Haw haw haw!" Lurry called from his corner of the sleeping area, and the Countingsheep brothers laughed. Brom gave them an icy look that quelled them, and Taboret climbed into her bunk, pulling up the cover to deliberately shut out the sight of them. In spite of the early hour, she was ready to go to sleep.

The chief had spoiled that lovely warm mood. He had a knack for appearing just as she and Glinn were starting to have a real conversation. Taboret regretted that she'd never know what either she or Glinn had been going to say before Brom interrupted. She had known what Glinn was thinking, to a certain extent. Could he read her thoughts? Did he have an inkling that she had betrayed the mission? Taboret knew she ought to feel remorse, fear, or justification, but it just didn't seem very important at that moment. She hoped no one would read her dreams.

Chapter 16

Lightning crashed overhead, illuminating decrepit old houses on the top of the surrounding hills. In the barren fields amid blackened, wasted crops, Roan caught the occasional glimpse of skeletons hanging on crossbars. Bare trees creaked in the wind. Roan peered out from under the stiff brim of his hat at the road. It had been raining for hours, yet the tracks they were following barely imprinted the soggy ground, as if they had skimmed lightly over the surface. Lum was puzzled by the anomaly, but Roan suspected another of Brom's machinations. The steeds had become bicycles when the rain turned cold. Roan wished he could deaden his nerve endings at will and still remain functional.

His clothing was soaked through, in spite of a quick waterproofing and the wide brim of his hat, which deflected much of the rain. Beside him, the princess pedaled gamely onward on Golden Schwinn. Her hair under her hood was dampened down, curling into dark ringlets at the sides of her face. It looked perfectly charming, although it was as much as Roan's life was worth to mention it. He would have been enjoying riding out with her through the countryside if it wasn't for several factors: the rain, their mission, and the discomfort of riding for so far and so long.

Leonora noticed him looking at her, and blinked water off her lashes.

"We have to get in out of this gale," she said. "At this moment, I wouldn't care if Brom dropped a bomb on our heads."

Roan nodded, and started peering ahead through the downpour for likely shelter. At the top of the next rise, he thought he caught a glimpse of red lines in the sky.

"I think I see dry weather up ahead," he called to Spar. "Let's step up the pace if we can."

"Hah! Gladly!" the guard captain shouted back. He raised his hand to signal to the others.

The rain whipped into Roan's face as his tires spun downhill. Now and again, images of trucks from the dreams of minor sleepers appeared on the narrow path, crowding the riders to one side. The party formed a single-file line with Colenna and Leonora riding between Spar and Roan, then Bergold and Lum. Roan kept an eye on the clouds, searching for that trace of red he'd seen. It had been there a moment ago, near the horizon to the northeast. Weather was so unpredictable. If they didn't run into that high pressure system soon, he'd have the group take shelter somewhere and continue on when the rain ended.

"Whiiinnnggg," a small truck whined reproachfully, zipping past them. Another one followed in its wake. "Whoiiinnnggg."

"Traffic's getting heavier," Felan complained, shouting over the wind. "And I think the road is narrowing!"

The junior historian was right. The sides of the road were closing in under their tires. Soon it seemed no wider than a tightrope. The steeds clung to the narrow pavement. Another vehicle came straight at them. Spar let out a hoarse cry. The truck swung wide at the last second. The gray road bed expanded like a rubber band under its wheels so it just missed them.

"Hang on," Roan said, encouragingly, though his own heart was pounding in his chest. "The dry weather's just ahead. We can pull off in a moment."

"Hard right!" Spar shouted. A pair of glowing yellow globes appeared in their path, taking up the entire roadbed. It was a big truck, its engine roaring. "Jump for it, men!" He started to veer toward the right, into the red band that Roan thought was a high-pressure zone, but where an H should have been was a roiling, greasy-looking glaze of white.

"What's that?" Leonora screamed.

"It's a hole!" Bergold shouted. "Don't go into it."

Roan gasped, and grabbed for the rear fender of Leonora's bike. He misjudged his aim, and Schwinn's rear tire scraped his hand. He urged Cruiser to go faster so he was beside her, and shoved the frightened steed over and away from the hazard, but the red border stretched outward like an open mouth. The truck roared nearer, forcing them over into it. The bicycles squeaked with fear as their tires skimmed the edge. Roan hauled hard on the handlebars, forcing both steeds backwards, away from the red band, but it reached out to envelop them. They were blinded by a mad swirl.

The glow died away, and they found themselves on a road that looked the same as the one they had just left, except that it was no longer raining. Roan coasted to a halt and looked around them.

"What was that?" he asked Bergold.

"A hole in reality," the senior historian said. "We were lucky. This one was very mild. Nothing happened to us."

"But where are we?" Leonora asked.

"Right where we were before," Bergold said. "But things changed around us."

"That's not possible," Lum said, wrinkling his forehead.

"Soldier, all things are possible," Spar said. "What in the Nightmare are those?"

He pointed to clump of trees surrounded by a wide band that stretched from a foot off the ground to as high as Roan could reach.

"I've no idea," Roan said. Bergold opened his small book and leafed through it.

"Is it there to protect the trees?" Hutchings asked. He put out a hand. The moment he touched the belt, there was a huge CLANG! He was flung through the air, steed and all, right across the road into another banded clump of trees. That one, too, let out a mighty jangle, and propelled him away. He flew toward a third clump, but fell just short of making contact. Roan and the others rushed over to help him up. There was a loud clicking noise in the air, but Roan could not see the source of the sound.

"Fascinating!" Bergold said, standing and looking around him with interest. "I've heard of the Bally effect, but I've never seen it before."

"That could kill you," Hutchings said, staggering to his feet. He was pale with shock, and his light brown hair stood out from his head. His steed, a little dented, squealed wildly as Misha helped it up.

"Avoid touching any more of them," Bergold ordered. "We have to find our way out of this effect. Look for anything that says 'Game Over.' "

Avoiding the trees was not easy. The forest was thickly overgrown. The party had a tight squeeze to pass between two clumps that flanked the road. Lum led the way, crouching over his handlebars, and looking warily from side to side, as if fearing the bands would reach out and kick him. Roan pedaled cautiously, keeping his knees in as much as possible. Bergold forced his usual comfortable bulk into a tall, narrow form, until they eased out into a wide meadow, where the path ran safely out of the reach of any trees.

"Well done, everyone," Roan said, turning in his saddle. But he had spoken too soon. Felan, the last to pass through the gap, brushed a tree band with the edge of his sleeve. Roan only half-heard the clang, as he and all the others were repelled hard enough to send them tumbling off the road toward another group of trees. Head over heels they rolled, caroming into protruding rocks and each other, causing meadow flowers to light up like candles. Roan scrambled to his feet, then turned at the princess's scream just in time to see an object like a triangular gate swinging down toward them. It caught them hard on the backsides, tumbled them helter-skelter into a very complicated tree clump, which scattered them in several directions. Rocks, hillocks, and even bushes were surrounded by the bands of force. Anything they touched shot them across the meadow again. Helplessly, they ricocheted around like marbles.

"Stop moving," Bergold panted. "Grab anything. Stop. Hold on."

Roan managed to clamber to his knees as Leonora was catapulted toward another of the triangular gates. It opened back, preparing to deal her a mighty swat that would send her flying. He sprang, making a tackle just in time, and landed half on her, half on Golden Schwinn. He helped her up, and they stood clinging to one another for a moment. Schwinn leaned against their legs, emitting a creaking whimper. The gate screeched forward into its original position, as if disappointed.

"Are you all right?" Roan asked. Leonora nodded, clutching the bicycle handles. She was quaking. As soon as he was sure she could stand alone, he ran to help the others.

Bergold and Misha had managed to catch hold of one another's legs like a live hoop. As they rolled past Roan, he stood ready, then pushed them over so the hoop fell on its side, bringing it to a halt. The two men sprang to their feet, and Bergold reasserted his normal, rounded body type.

"Whew!" he said, patting his belly. "There's no advantage to being a beanpole like you."

Misha grinned, and the three of them split up to save the rest. Spar was caught between two clumps of trees. They threw him back and forth, like a giant tossing a bag from hand to hand, accompanied by deafening jingling and clattering. Roan rushed at him while the guard captain was in mid-air, and brought him to the ground beyond the reach of either copse. Together, they rescued Colenna, trapped in the exact center of a triangle of ringing bands. She stood with her arms wrapped around her body, afraid to move. With Roan's help, Spar extended long arms into the enclosure, and plucked her out. She clung to him for stability.

"What are we looking for?" Roan asked, when the party had reassembled at a safe distance from the nearest band.

"The gates," Bergold said, casting around. "If this is a true Arcade Pinball dream, we have to pass through a pair of gates to get out of here. From the data I've read in the Akashic Records, the ground tends to slope downward toward them. That's a clue."

"There's a downslope that way," Lum said, nodding toward the southwest. "And along that way, too. I got tossed about there a bit, so I know."

"Which way, then?" Spar asked Roan.

Roan studied the land. The ground was packed hard under the light sward of grass. There'd be no trace of Brom in this fold in reality. They would simply have to find the trail again once they got out of here.

"That way looks most likely," he said, pointing down the long axis of the meadow.

"Now, don't you touch anything else," Spar told Felan. The young man glared.

"Do you think I did that on purpose?" he demanded. Spar just looked at him.

"Success!" Bergold cried, pointing ahead. Before them, at the bottom of a long, gentle slope, were two triangular constructions, banded like the trees, and studded with glowing flowers. Roan eyed them. As he approached, the gates started to move closer together.

"We won't make it," he said. "The gap will be too narrow to slip through."

Just as he said that, the gates reversed their motion and drew outward again, but colored rocks with lit flowers rose from the earth in their path, preventing a clear run.

"It's rhythmic," Misha said. "See that? If we time our dash properly, they won't touch us."

"Everyone be careful," Bergold said. "I don't want to go careening into any more trees."

The noise near the paddles was almost overwhelmingly loud. Whenever one of the party stepped on a new patch of ground, more flowers and trees lit up, accompanied by jangling, clicking, whistling and the now familiar clanging. All these factors were meant to confuse intruders. Roan was concerned that they would distract him from dashing safely between the gates. It also worried him that he couldn't see what lay beyond them.

"Shall I go first, sir?" Hutchings said, squaring his shoulders until he looked more of a mathematical construct than a man.

"No," Roan said. "I will." He stepped astride Cruiser, who was dancing at the noise. Roan observed that there was a moment when it was possible to get all the way to the gates without hitting a single band. It would take very careful timing. Steadying the steed with the pressure of his knees, Roan took a deep breath, and started pedaling.

As soon as he began to move, the gates started to edge towards one another again. The gap narrowed more and more until it was less than six feet wide. Roan pumped harder. If his observations were correct, then it would reach its perigee moments before he reached it, and would be increasing again when he passed through. If they were wrong, and it kept closing, he'd be trapped between the paddles. An impact at that short a range might easily break his back.

All seemed to be well, until he rode over a shallow depression in the turf. Cruiser bumped right out of it, but the pressure appeared to have triggered some kind of reaction in this strange forest. A round pillar as wide as a house sprang up from the ground between him and the gates. Cruiser squeaked in alarm and reared high on his back tire. Roan struggled to control the steed, wheeling him in a circle to avoid falling off. They veered around the banded pillar, which jangled loudly at him. The gates had opened as wide as they would go, and were closing again. Roan put on a burst of speed, wove between the glittering rocks and hummocks, and hurtled between the gates into the darkness.

At once, the ground dropped away from under them. Cruiser let out a shrill squeal. Roan hung on tightly to the handlebars. They dropped several feet, where Cruiser bumped to a stop on a smooth floor. Roan looked up, and realized the mouth of the pit was perfectly round. He hadn't been hurt at all, although the fall almost made his heart stop. He opened his mouth to shout a warning, when Felan fell in almost on top of him.

"Phantasms!" Felan swore, clutching his steed's frame. He landed upright, and the surprised bicycle bounded to a halt.

"Look out," Roan shouted, pushing Felan off the spot where they'd been standing. The rest of the party slapped down one by one into the pit, heralded by more jangling, sounding like music played so loud it distorted the very atmosphere in the pit.

"My stars!" Bergold said, as soon as his steed stopped bouncing.

When the last person arrived, there was a fusillade of clicking, and the ceiling lit up with enormous red and yellow letters: "revO emaG." Roan couldn't read them. Then he realized that they were backwards.

"It says 'Game Over'!" he said.

"Good!" Bergold said, pleased. "We're free." The sound of clicking continued on, and the senior historian listened with dismay. "Oh, dear. That sounds ominous." More letters appeared. Roan read "emaG eerF" on the ceiling.

"Run, everyone," Bergold shouted. "We've triggered a free game!"

"Oh, no," Colenna said, hopping onto her steed. "I'm not going through all that again. Which way?"

Now that Roan's eyes were accustomed to the dark pit, he could see the shadow of two tunnels that led off the main chamber. He shone his bicycle lamp down them. They looked equally uninviting, but a loud rumbling started to come from the tunnel on the left.

"Come on," he said. "I don't want to find out what that is."

He led the party through the tunnel on the right, another perfectly smooth, perfectly round passage, until they came to a slotlike opening in the earth. At the top, Roan heard the sound of falling rain.

"I knew it was too good to be true," Spar said, pulling his hat brim down to his eyebrows. "That Arcade thing took us right out of our way, didn't it? The only question is, did we fall, or were we pushed?"

"Brom, do you mean?" Colenna asked. Bergold frowned.

"That would mean a huge amount of power," he said. "The Arcade is a natural phenomenon. It comes and goes throughout the Dreamland. Could he harness something like that?"

"I think it's possible," Roan said. "Or if he couldn't before, he can now. It may be that the influence of the crucible is increasing."

"That's terrifying," Leonora said, her eyes wide and blue. "We have to catch him before they get so powerful we can't stop them if we tried."

"On, then," Spar said, grimly, leading them out into the rain. "Where to?"

The only prospect that offered itself was a single-lane track that wound its way up into the hills above the pinball valley. It ended at a road that led back the way they had come. They followed it.

The first turning they took, on a slight downhill slope, led them to a dead end at a rockfall on a jutting lip of land that overlooked unbroken forest below. Neither Roan nor Lum was satisfied that they going the right way, though there was enough distortion in the countryside to justify the attempt. They dismounted beside a blank cliff-face with a pool pouring out of a small crack at its base. It appeared as if at one time wheeled transport with the right kind of tire patterns had passed by here, but left no clear trace of where it had gone after that. The trail stopped near the cliff as if it had been turned off. There was even half a footprint. Roan tested the gravel beside it with a toe. His mark filled at once with rainwater. Nothing had passed here in the last several hours.

"Could they have flown from here?" Colenna asked.

"I doubt it," Roan said, peering this way and that from under his hatbrim. "If they didn't fly before, they must have some good reason for continuing to travel on the surface. But where did they go?"

"The land could have shifted," Misha said, examining the tracks. "I've seen something like this in property settlements, where each partner gets half of everything."

"I don't think Brom negotiated a divorce right here in the middle of Wocabaht in the rain," Felan said, scornfully.

"I don't like it around here," Leonora said, huddled in her cape. "It feels . . . spooky. There's something wrong with the land."

"That's the distortion," Lum said. "It seemed stronger up there, before we turned off." He pointed up the last rise.

"Then they stayed on the road," Felan said impatiently. "We went the wrong way. What about it?"

Roan was puzzled. "I would swear that we did come the right way," he said.

Bergold lifted the edges of his big poncho cape, and unfolded the map. Water slicked off it in sheets as he held it up for them to see.

"Well, this is the only big road for several miles east or west. They have to take it to continue northward. If we stay on it we can catch them."

"My corporal isn't stupid, as you're all implying," Spar said, with an impatient gesture. "They might be here somewhere." He wiped rain off his face. "Guards! Start looking for clues."

"Chief!" Maniune shouted. The yell woke Taboret woke out of a sound sleep. She sat up in alarm. Everyone else had turned to look at the big mercenary, who was standing sentry at the door. "They're outside! They've found us!"

"Roan? Here?" Brom's long lab coat fluttered behind him as he hurried over to see. He put an eye to the peephole in the right-hand door. "Tenacious man. They've managed to get by the first puzzles we set them."

"They'll try to get in," Acton said. He drew his sword.

"Put that thing away," Brom said, with his face against the door panel. Acton resheathed the sword, but not without an expression of resentment. "They don't know we're here. This stronghold looks like a mountain on the outside. It's pure chance that they're here."

"Yeah, but they're *looking*."

"We ought to take 'em out," Maniune said. "Finish them now."

Taboret stared at the mercenary, horrified. Finish off the princess? All those innocent people?

"Nonsense," Brom said, to her relief. He pulled away from his observations to glare at his henchman. "An inappropriate use of force? How then will we continue with our little game?"

"Yeah, but look at them," Acton said, staring through the left-hand peephole.

"What about them?" Brom said.

"What if they sniff us out? We ought to, like, dissuade them."

"Well, then," Brom said, with amusement in his voice if not in his face, "let us use subtlety. Why use a Buick when a flyswatter will do?"

"What's a Buick?" Acton asked.

Brom waved the question away impatiently. "We'll make minor use of the gestalt. That should be adequate to drive them away before they discover our creche. Dowkin, Doolin, you'll do. Come here."

The Countingsheep brothers, in the middle of another one of their private grievance sessions, looked up.

"Why us?" Doolin asked. "How come we have to do extra work? Why not everyone else?"

"Because you have sufficient strength to carry out a minor task. Come here! Now!"

The brothers, looking more like a pair of donkeys than usual, shuffled over to Brom. The two mercenary soldiers moved well out of reach. They were learning respect for the power of the gestalt, as they saw it demonstrated again and again. Taboret had begun to understand the two men better. Where she had been terrified of them as bullies before, in a remote part of her mind—which she guessed belonged to Brom—she knew that they could be mastered by a show of confidence.

Reluctantly, Dowkin and Doolin offered their joined right fists. Brom covered their hands with his own, and the white cloud appeared overhead. Taboret felt a drawing upon her own energy, and concentrated on giving instead of resenting the interruption to her sleep. She did think hard about making the effort a benign one that wouldn't hurt the princess or anyone with her, and hoped her will would have an effect on the results.

The process didn't take long. Within moments, Brom broke the connection, and sent the brothers back to their cots.

"There," he said. "That will give them the equivalent of a psychic hotfoot. We want them to go on their way at once. We have also given them some red herrings to follow, so they will waste energy following a confused path."

Maniune was unimpressed. He crossed his arms. "We can still snuff 'em, chief," he said, hopefully. Acton added a vigorous nod, and put his hand to his sidearm.

Brom's eyelids lowered halfway over his glittering eyes. "No need. It's a game, a contest, and we are winning. They have lost our trail, almost certainly irrevocably. They're ahead of us now. We can carry on freely to our destination," Brom said. "Go to sleep. We have much work ahead of us tomorrow. We are making an early start."

"Nothing," Spar said, disgustedly, returning to Roan. The princess and Colenna huddled in the shelter of a small overhang at the edge of the path a dozen yards from the end, sharing a single umbrella. Ivy and other plentiful plant life on the mountainside gave them a windbreak as thick as a bower on the southwest side of the road. "They've got clean away."

"It's this rain," Misha said. "We might be able to find them again when it stops."

"We need to find a place to camp for the night," Roan said. He looked around.

"Why not here?" Felan asked, sweeping a hand out. "It's flat. And, look, there are grapevines. I can send a message back to the palace."

"The flat part, as you point it out," Bergold said, very patiently, "is a public thoroughfare, my friend."

"It's a dead end," Felan said. "No one will come this way."

"I'd rather not stay," Leonora said, clutching the umbrella handle with both hands. "I don't like the atmosphere. Something feels wrong. The steeds sense it, too."

"I don't like it much myself," Spar said. Roan nodded, spattering raindrops. "Something evilish happened here, it feels like. I don't like not being able to see all the way around. Let's go."

"Then we'd better move on," Bergold said. "I'm wet through, and I'd welcome a chance to rest, but not here."

Roan suddenly found that he couldn't wait to continue. "Agreed," he said, hopping onto Cruiser. "It's uphill, but it's fairly gradual."

"But, the grapevines?" Felan asked, pointing back toward the curtain of leafy trailers.

"Send your message and catch up with us," Roan said impatiently. "We should be easy to find. There's only one road. Hutchings, you stay with him."

"Yessir," the guard said, looking miserable.

The party had no choice but to turn around into the teeth of the rain, and begin pedaling uphill again. The downpour had lessened for a time, but it had resumed in full force. Cruiser's tires slipped again and again on the gravel path.

At the first crossroads, Roan turned them toward the right. According to the map they were heading roughly north by northeast. The leaden sky was no help to orienteering, showing neither sun nor compass points among the blue isobars. Both right and left paths seemed to lead further up. It felt as if the upward angle got sharper the moment he started climbing. The next turn offered only more rising slopes.

"I don't remember mountains this high on the map," Bergold said, panting.

"I think I'm right," Misha said, after a while. "These hills are moving. We should be hitting downslopes, but we're always pedaling uphill."

"The landscape is playing with us," Colenna said, stoically. "Press on. That's all we can do."

By this time, Roan didn't know if he was soaked with rain

or sweat. The others were tiring quickly, and the sky grew darker. Leonora held out heroically, but at last she ran out of strength to pedal her golden steed. Roan tied a rope to Schwinn's frame and helped pull them up a steep stretch of road, until he couldn't ride any farther, either. Everyone dismounted and walked their weary steeds upward. Above him, Roan caught a glimpse of flat hilltop sheltered by trees with rain-heavy crowns.

"What about that?" Bergold said, poking him in the ribs from behind.

"It'll do," Roan said. "It had better. I hope it clears up before morning."

At the crest of the hill, Roan turned to look back at the ground they had just covered. The countryside looked rather pretty in the rain, like a watercolor painting. The slopes that they had struggled to climb had subsided into green and gold meadows and downs. He hoped it didn't mean the Dreamland itself was conspiring to allow Brom to reach his goal. Could even the Sleepers be curious about the scientist's theory?

Though it was still raining hard, Roan and the guards took great care to make up the princess's pavilion. Together, Roan, Misha and Bergold used their influence to join all of their cloaks into one big waterproof sheet to protect the rest of them. They attached it with a rope to the trees, creating a makeshift roof. There wasn't quite enough room under it for the steeds, who clustered together out in the rain.

"I hope they won't rust before morning," Felan said, giving his steed a final pat.

"It shouldn't hurt them," Lum said. "They're supposed to be all-weather beasts. Mine's been through worse."

With her all-purpose firelighter, Colenna made up a huge bonfire and lit the brazier inside the princess's pavilion. Leonora thanked them all, and disappeared into her small tent. The others sprawled before the fire, grateful for the warmth. They let their outer clothes dry out somewhat before changing to crawl into their bedrolls to sleep.

Roan's muscles ached. He thought of the tub of salve in his bag, but he was too tired to get up and use it. He listened to the pattering on the top of the tent and the murmuring of the wind in the trees.

"I may never move again," Felan said, slipping into his cot with a sigh. "I don't know how Brom got so far ahead of us, carrying that heavy load."

"We've got to catch up with them tomorrow," Spar said, from his regulation bag a few feet away. "I want a word with that Brom. A personal word."

Chapter 17

A delicate clinking sound woke Roan. He was glad to escape from the troubling dream he was having. It was the same as the night before. He had been juggling dozens of eggs to constant applause. He knew that if he dropped one it would destroy the world. At the same time, he felt that he was an impostor, substituting for the real juggler. At any moment, he feared the audience would discover the imposture and walk out on him.

He listened. The rain had stopped falling. It was almost perfectly silent on the hilltop. He heard just the lightest tinkle of birdsong sound in a tree over his head, but that hadn't been the sound that roused him. The air was dry and fragrant with flowers—and something else. He drew in a deep breath. It was the tantalizing smell of hot toast and scrambled eggs that tickled his nose. The warm scent came closer, mixed with an indefinable and exotic perfume. He opened his eyes. Leonora was standing over him, wearing her traveling clothes. She knelt beside him and put a finger to her lips.

"Would you like to have breakfast with me?" she asked in a whisper. Roan nodded. He flicked aside the cover of his sleeping bag and rolled to his feet.

It was just before false dawn. By the dim, rosy light, Roan could see the shadows that were the others asleep in their bunks. He walked carefully so he wouldn't wake them. The princess, going soft-footed and silent, led him toward her pavilion.

Inside the little tent, a delicate little table was set for two. On it burned a pair of candles whose warm glow illumined silver chafing dishes, a china bowl heaped full of berries beside a matching pitcher, rows of gleaming silver utensils, a crystal jam pot and spoon, china, napkins edged with lace, a bud vase containing a single rose, and even a cut crystal water pitcher.

Roan helped Leonora to sit down, and waited for her nod to seat himself. He realized that there was soft music playing, quiet enough that the morning birdsong trilled louder.

"Now," said the princess, flicking out a napkin with pleased satisfaction, "we can have a nice, leisurely breakfast without delaying anyone else. May I help you to some berries?"

"Allow me," Roan said, reaching for the slotted silver spoon. He was full of admiration for her. After two days of hard travel, she had arisen early to make her toilet and prepare this regal setting with all the accouterments that she was accustomed to at home. Leonora was going to keep her promise, on her own terms. She might be having to live in a tent in the middle of nowhere, but she would do so in gracious, royal style. "It's the very least I can do."

"I'll do it," Leonora said, plucking the server out of his hands. She spooned berries into two shallow bowls and poured a liberal dollop of cream over each.

"How long must you have been awake to accomplish all this?" Roan asked, watching her slim hands move. "Hours?"

"I'm sure it isn't quite that long. Will you have sugar?"

"Just a bit. And I'm sure it must be hours," Roan said. "It's as if a whole army of serv—" He stopped.

"No," Leonora said, appearing not to notice his slip. "Just me." She picked up a silver pot. Fragrant steam drifted out of its spout.

"Coffee, tea, or cocoa?" she asked.

"Coffee," Roan said. She poured coffee for him, and, after a pause during which the silver pot thickened slightly and grew a broader spout, cocoa for herself. Both smelled ambrosial. Roan took a sip, and let out a sigh of pleasure. "Delicious." Leonora beamed at him between the tapers.

"You do look beautiful in candlelight, my dear," he said.

The dimple appeared in her cheek. "Thank you. You're very gallant for such an early hour."

"You inspire me," Roan said. Hastily, he took a spoonful of berries.

"Don't you wish you could fly after Brom, like you did when

you came into Mnemosyne this last time?" Leonora asked, looking at him playfully over her cocoa cup.

"No," Roan said, savoring the intimate, affectionate tone of her voice as much as he did the flavor of the berries. Their argument of the day before was forgiven, forgotten and gone. He was happy. "I can't possibly picture anything I would have enjoyed more than this."

"In spite of all the danger, in spite of the fear that this could be the end of the Dreamland?"

"I would sacrifice all comfort for a moment like this one, to be here with you," Roan said, with all his heart in his words. "If the world ended now, I would have few regrets." Leonora shook her head impatiently, disturbed by a thought of her own.

Roan reached for a morsel of bread and rolled it between thumb and forefinger into a penny. He offered it to Leonora. She took it, smiling at the childhood custom, but still looked worried. Roan waited patiently. Soon, she broke the silence.

"Roan, I'm scared."

"So am I, my love," he said. "All we can do is try."

"We have to do more than that," Leonora insisted. "We must succeed."

Roan nodded resolutely. "Then, we will. If I live to catch up with Brom, there's nothing he can do that will prevent me stopping him from carrying out his terrible plan."

"And me," Leonora said, with a tentative look.

"Yes," Roan said, definitely. "You're a part of this team. By the way, I have a present for you."

Leonora cooed with delight as he handed over the little white box. She undid the ribbon, and he admired the smooth skin of her cheek and the sweep of her eyelashes in the candle's glow.

"Gracious, what's this?" She looked up at Roan with a twinkle in her eye as she freed the penknife from its cotton nest. She pulled open the blade attachment that happened to be a fifteen-inch crosscut saw, and delicately touched one of the sharp teeth. "Not the usual gift for a lady."

"But very appropriate for a companion and partner," Roan said. Leonora's cheeks flushed with pleasure.

"I must have a serious talk with my father," she said, suddenly.

"It's absurd of him to be so obstinate about letting you ask for my hand. He's not holding out any hope at all. I just won't have it. After all, where am I going to find a prince to marry who has all the same good qualities you do? The Waking World?" She laughed.

At the sound of her laughter, the rest of the party began to stir outside.

"A joke?" Bergold's voice asked sleepily.

"A private one," Roan said, smiling across the table at Leonora.

"Oh. *Oh!* Well, that's a good sort, too," Bergold said. He peered in the flap of the pavilion. His smooth, round face, curly hair, and long striped nightshirt and cap made him look like an enormous baby. "You enjoy it for me."

"Thank you, my friend," Roan said. He gazed at Leonora, whose eyes were large and dark with emotion, and beautiful. "I shall."

The historian found his personal bag and picked his way across the encampment toward the cleaning area. Roan looked back at Leonora. Her eyes, a thoughtful dark blue, were fixed on him.

"Poor Roan," she said. "Not only are you having to lead us, but you have to handle our hopes and fears and doubts and bouts of bad temper."

"And I must deal with mine, too," he said. "I'm almost afraid I'm leading you all on a fool's errand. Some of the others think so, too. I can see it in Felan's eyes every time I make a decision which way to turn. He thinks I'm a fraud as well as a freak. I'm the only one of us who has seen Brom anywhere but Mnemosyne. For all anyone knows, I could be his agent, keeping you out of the way until he manages to ring the Alarm Clock, for better or worse."

"Nonsense," Leonora said. "I know you're honest. I see you worrying. You're a good leader, better than you know. Thank you for this," she said, holding up the blue penknife. "I'll keep it in a very special place."

She drew the tiny gold locket bearing an engraved capital *L* out of the neck of her silk tunic, and opened it. Roan peered over. The locket was special, given to her by her only aunt, the Duchess of Elysia, and a woman he admired very much, even though she had thwocked him over the wrist with a key or a ladle or whatever was handy many times during his childhood. Leonora cached her particular personal treasures in the little jewel.

"Do you remember this?" she asked, drawing out of it a crumpled and almost dry daisy chain. "You made this for me on my sixteenth birthday. I never told you, but I think I liked it more than any of the other presents I was given that day."

Roan, remembering a summer day full of strawberries and whipped cream, ribbons and balloons, a glorious sunset and a first kiss, shook his head in wonder. "What else is in there?"

She drew out a folded piece of paper, and Roan recognized it as a love letter he had written to her during his first long trip on his own as the King's Investigator. Leonora unfolded the creased bit of paper and read the few lines to herself, her lips parted in a gentle smile. Roan didn't have to look at it to remember what he'd written. She folded it up and put it to one side with a gentle pat.

"I was worried you'd never come back," she said.

"*I* was worried I wouldn't make it back," Roan admitted. "I think that's why I dared to say so much. Was I too presumptuous?"

"Not presumptuous enough, I thought," Leonora said, an eyebrow cocked humorously at him.

The tiny gold box also contained a handsome portrait of her parents, a minute jeweled brooch, a roll of breath mints, a thin glass flask of perfume, and one diamond earring.

"So that's where it was!" she exclaimed, picking up the last. "I've been looking for this for months! It was in my locket all the time!"

"Thank the Sleepers," Roan said. He finished the last bite of his toast. "We'd best be stirring. The sun is coming up. I must get the others up." He watched her pack the treasures back into the locket, putting the knife in last. "I am astonished by what you can fit into that."

"Heavens, this is nothing," Leonora said. "You ought to look in Colenna's purse."

"I did once, thanks," Roan said, with a grin. "There's a rumor that she was married once, and her husband fell in looking for a handkerchief and he's still down there somewhere."

Leonora looked sentimental for a moment. "Do you think she and Spar might marry? He's a good man, and she is so very kind."

"I hope so," Roan said, taking her hand and kissing it. "In my experience, she's always been prepared for every eventuality before anyone else. She has probably already planned the wedding. He just doesn't know it yet."

Leonora laughed, and Roan stood up, still holding her hand. There was much to do, but he hated to leave her. He felt fortified, and well supported by her esteem, and totally gratified by the extraordinary effort she had made to fit in with the party. He loved her so very much. She continued to inspire him. The very least he could do was follow her example. He wanted to go and prepare for the day, then do some reconnaissance of the area before everyone else was ready to go. He bent to kiss her fingers again. They were warm and soft, and one bore a minute dot of raspberry jam. He straightened and looked deep into her eyes.

"I . . . I hope they'll be as happy as you make me."

Leonora stood up into his arms, and he bent to touch his lips to hers. Her hair was silken under his hand, and the curves of her back fit in his arms as though they were one piece of warm, loving flesh. Roan felt fireworks zooming and exploding and heard thunderous band music as they kissed.

"All right! All right!" Felan protested, sitting up with his hands clapped over his ears. "Stop it! I'm awake! Sleeping Gods, it's still before sunrise!"

"Where now?" Spar said, when everyone was packed shortly after sunrise. Lum started casting about for the trail.

"We're setting out northeast again," Roan said. He did not feel very confident about the decision, and it must have shown in his face. "Our road should be downhill all the way, after last night."

"How do you know?" Lum asked, his honest face puzzled. "There's no weirdness to follow. Nor any tracks."

"Well, it is the only main road in these parts," Roan said, reluctant to explain his reasoning. "Brom did come in this direction, and he'll have to carry on going that way, unless he plans to turn right around and go almost all the way back to the bridge. I doubt he wants to take the time to backtrack again."

"And how do you know that," Felan asked suspiciously, "without any markings to guide you?

"Look at the map," Roan said. Bergold obligingly offered it, but Felan waved it away.

"I'm not continuing this wild-goose chase unless you show me at least one feather."

Leonora stood by, offering silent encouragement with her eyes. Her traveling cloak was fastened under her chin, and all of her parcels were ready on the back of her steed. She couldn't help him, and he knew it. If he relied solely upon her support, the others would never respect him. Still, he felt unhappy to have his leadership doubted. He disliked being under the spotlight. It would have been so much easier to travel on his own. He was always at his best on a private investigation for the king, for if he made a wrong turning or a wrong decision, it wouldn't inconvenience others. Besides, alone, he could both know a secret and keep it, something that couldn't happen if he told them how he knew what he did.

"Trust me, Master Felan," he said, displaying as much confidence as he could. "It's only logical. He knows we are following him. He must hurry on to his destination, without any sidetracking."

But Felan wasn't satisfied. He continued to stare with gimletlike hazel eyes at Roan as if he was thinking the word "freak." Colenna and Bergold were simply waiting, nonjudgmentally. It was hard to remember that only two days had passed, and he clearly had yet to earn his party's trust as leader.

"We've been going on traces and tracks all this time," Felan pointed out. "Why strike out blindly now?"

"We aren't going blindly," Roan finally admitted. To reveal the truth might jeopardize the source of his clues. He started to speak, stopped again to bite his lip, uncertain, then in the face of the doubt in Spar's and Felan's eyes, he made his decision. He beckoned everyone away from all visible grapevines, and made sure there were no little birdies nearby to carry the tale.

"Well," Roan began, "I've been receiving information from

ahead of us. I haven't heard from . . . that person this morning yet, but I've been finding clear and deliberate indications. I haven't got any physical evidence at this moment, but I do know in which general direction they're traveling. We're sure to find the trail again soon. There's only a limited number of roads in this region capable of carrying them. If necessary, we can split up to cover them later."

"Ahead?" Felan asked. The rest of the party stared, openmouthed. "You mean from Brom's group?"

"A spy?" Spar demanded. "You've got a spy in Brom's camp?"

"A friend," Roan said.

Spar started laughing. "You canny brat, you."

"Captain Spar!" Leonora exclaimed, shocked.

"So sorry, Your Highness. I beg pardon," the guard captain said, still wearing a grin on his craggy face. "And you didn't tell a one of us. All right. Follow my leader, then. Guards! Mount up!"

Chapter 18

Midday. Taboret felt the sun beating down on her from an implacable sky. After her long shift of the day before she wasn't required to carry the Clock for at least another couple of days. That liberty meant she was free to act as a construction worker. She hadn't known when she was well off. Luckily, her body was well suited to hard work, being lean and strong. Her tanned arms, bared to the shoulder, were well muscled. Quite a difference from the pasty, soft academic body she usually had back in Mnemosyne.

She kept pushing the thought out of her open mind that it was shortsighted of Brom to let Roan get ahead of them in a place where there was only one road. Now they had to build their own road through rough terrain to regain their lead. Forming their campground overnight had used up a lot of crucible power; this was draining the gestalt to its dregs and reaching down through the bottom of the vat for more. But no use in annoying Brom. He had plenty to irritate him without any additional grief from her.

The ground here was rocky and unstable, almost barren of vegetation. Bolmer had discovered a deposit of nebulosity in the narrow canyon. The apprentices excavated it and used it to patch together a decent roadway over the high points of the rocks. Nebulosity felt nice and soft underfoot, or rather, underwheel. As part of the highway most of it looked like black tarmac, but it felt like sponge rubber. With huge overinflated tires on their modified bicycles and motorbikes, those apprentices who did not have to carry the Alarm Clock went around behind the litter over the waist-high boulders and yawning chasms to pick up the sections of nebulosity and bring them around to form the next section of road as the bearers cycled over it. Taboret guessed that she'd handled each featherlight paving stone at least a thousand times already. It wasn't the carrying so much as the bending and lifting and bending again. This was slow going, and she was getting very bored.

"Watch it!" Glinn's voice barked out.

Taboret felt the Alarm Clock jangle before she actually heard it, and yanked her protesting steed off the pavement and onto the nearest real rock. There was a wild cry and a terrible squeal. She felt terror, not her own. Wheeling her steed around, she hurried to see what had happened.

Bolmer lay on the valley floor a dozen feet below them. His steed had fallen with him, and lay broken into two pieces over the back of a sharp-edged boulder. She revved her bike's engine to hurry down to him. Basil flung the stone he was carrying to one side, and clambered over the boulders.

"What happened?" she called.

"He was bending over to lay a section of pavement, when the bells rang," Glinn said grimly. He swung off his motorcycle, and climbed down to help Bolmer. "It dissolved, and he overbalanced."

Bolmer was sitting up, gingerly feeling his head with his fingertips. He had a ferocious headache and a host of other hurts that spread out along the link. Taboret let out a hiss, as much from alarm as referred pain. Nebulosity was sensitive to the sound of the bells, and reacted in strange ways. Sometimes it changed, but most of the time it simply vanished like smoke.

"It's not our fault," Doolin said, angrily, sticking out his prominent jaw. He was strapped to the front of the litter. "We bumped on a crooked stone. This road's not smooth enough."

"No," Dowkin agreed. "Everyone's trying to make us trip up."

Shock could be felt all the way through the link. The brothers sensed it, and sat with folded arms and shut lips as everyone stared at them.

"How dare you sit there and try to defend yourself when he could have been killed?" Taboret shouted at them. They tried to look indifferent, but she could tell they were scared.

"Enough!" Brom said, rising up from his machine. He

appeared more annoyed than concerned, and they all felt his displeasure. Taboret subsided.

"You, you, and you," he ordered her and the two apprentices nearest her, "help Glinn pick him up and bring his steed back up here. We will form the crucible and effect repairs."

They used the remaining nebulosity to form ladders and slings down to the valley floor, and carefully raised Bolmer up to one of the intact paving stones. Glinn helped him to lie flat, and went over him to discover the extent of his injuries. Besides bruising on his head, Bolmer's leg was broken. He was moaning with pain, and shifting in appearance with every twinge.

"Stop that," Carina said, laying her hands on him to hold him still. She had the most extensive knowledge of first aid. "I can't set your leg if you keep moving."

"It hurts, curse it!" he complained. "Everything hurts."

Taboret knelt down beside him and offered a little of her personal strength to ease the pain, and he gave her a grateful look.

"There, that's better," Carina said. She directed Taboret to sit down on Bolmer's chest, and together, she and Glinn pulled the leg out until the bone popped back into place. She used some nebulosity to mold a cast around it.

"Can't we use some gestalt energy to mend the bone?" she asked Brom, who was standing overlooking them from the next stone span.

"Of course. And we must put his cycle back together as well," Brom replied. He held out his hand, and the others joined him. Taboret glanced back at him over her shoulder when she stood in her place in the pattern. His eyes were half-lidded. He wasn't thinking of poor Bolmer at all. His mind was off somewhere devising devious traps. She shuddered.

Afterwards, Bolmer's steed whimpered a lot and stayed near its owner, suspicious of everything that moved. It clattered at the other mounts when they came too close. Bolmer himself looked as if he was bearing a solid grudge. Taboret knew that it was aimed at the brothers, but because of the link, they all shared the blame.

"Bolmer, you will stay beside the litter and guide Dowkin and Doolin so they do not hit any more bumps," Brom ordered.

"I'll make sure of it," Bolmer said grimly.

"Everyone! It is time to get back to work. We have a long way to go today to remain on schedule."

Taboret, lifting a nebulous paving stone as large as she was, had a brief mental flash of a map. It showed their position as a point marked "X" in the middle of nowhere. The distance behind them to where they had left the main road was greater than it was to the point where they would rejoin it again. She was relieved, until her mind's eye read the key to the distances involved, and gritted her teeth. Their goal was still quite far away, especially if they had to create every single yard of the road.

Because some of the paving stones had vanished when the bells rang, the apprentices had to find more nebulosity and shape it. Lurry discovered some not too far off to their left. This particular deposit was obstinate, wanting to stay in the form of turf with flowers. The apprentices were able to shape it into rectangular sections, but it became more bedraggled and crumbly every time they moved it.

Acton and Maniune sat guard at either side, watching them work. After dropping off her burden, Taboret looked up as she swung back onto her motorized cycle. Maniune noticed, and cracked a huge, exaggerated wink the next time he caught her eye. Taboret turned away, annoyed with herself for even looking at them.

"Why can't those bruisers help us?" Gano asked, passing Taboret as she went back for another stone.

"They're bigger than any of us," Basil agreed, going by in his turn with a slab in each hand.

"They have their own job to do," Brom said. ("Slacking off," Basil muttered.) "When we are a little closer to the road, they will go and stop Roan from passing us until we're on it. It will be an exercise in distractions."

"If they can get to the main highway," Glinn said, glancing back the way they had come. Since they had been carrying the road with them, no surface remained behind on which to drive. It would be slow slogging, although not as slow as the road crew were moving. Brom caught the edge of the frustration, and scanned them all. Everybody bent energetically to their tasks, avoiding his eye. Not for the first time, Taboret wished she was back in Mnemosyne, measuring the Castle of Dreams.

"Mamovas," Brom called, "I want you to accompany Maniune and Acton. We require delaying tactics so that Roan is prevented from coming up on that part of the main road until we have reached it. You will have the ability to draw upon us for power. Use your ingenuity."

Mamovas grinned, lifting her thin black eyebrows. Taboret knew she would enjoy herself setting traps for the unwary followers. She had a wicked sense of humor that bordered on the sadistic, and would see the situation as an elaborate game.

"Why not me, sir?" Taboret asked, suddenly, raising her hand.

"You?" Brom said.

"Yes, sir. I'd make good roadblocks. I have lots of ideas." She tried to look businesslike and think precise and logical thoughts. Brom looked upon her almost kindly.

"Your ambition does you credit, but perhaps another time," he said. "I want to use Mamovas's particular talents in this instance."

"Thank you, sir," Taboret said, accelerating away to go get another block. She didn't want anyone else to see the worry on her face. How could she warn the princess of danger if she wouldn't even be there? She hoped Roan was as good a survivor as rumor around the palace had it. She hoped he used all his skills to keep the princess from getting hurt.

Many more blocks later, Taboret again saw the mental picture of the map. The "X" was much closer to intersecting with the road.

"Time to go," Brom instructed the mercenaries. He beckoned to Mamovas, who placed her last section of nebulosity and spurred her mechanical beast to the chief's side. "By the time you do your tasks and return to us, we will be within a very short distance of the main highway. I need to be assured that we have plenty of time, plus an additional factor for error."

"Yes, sir," Mamovas said. She openly enjoyed the importance the assignment gave her, and the tingle of anticipation tickled Taboret as well. Mamovas would be the first one to try remote control of the crucible.

The feeling lessened slightly as the three steeds bumped away over the rocks. In a way Taboret was relieved to have Acton and Maniune no longer looking over her shoulder, but it meant that the remaining apprentices had that much more work to do without Mamovas. The chart showed plenty of hard going between them and the main road.

"Time to change," Doolin announced suddenly. Brom glanced up from his perusal of the map.

"It isn't time yet."

"Yes, it is," Doolin said. He took his hands off the handlebars and folded his arms.

"That's right," Dowkin said. "We put in extra time in the gestalt last night, and no one else had to do it."

"We calculate that the discrepancy in effort means that our shift ought to be shortened by an hour and twenty minutes," Doolin said. He pulled a watch out of his pocket and consulted it. "That was five minutes ago, so we worked overtime for a while without complaining."

Brom's strange steed bore him in a loop back to the brothers. Its tires grew taller or shrank in the extended fork so that the chief scientist was always riding at eye level to the brothers. Taboret thought it was so he could glare at them more effectively. His eyes were rubies lit from behind.

"Gentlemen," he said, in a dangerously even voice. "You are not being cooperative. Think of your fellow apprentices, and how hard they are laboring."

"No one thinks good of us," Dowkin said. "I can hear 'em. So can you."

"That's right," Doolin agreed. "Now, don't you stare at us that way, chief!" He squared up his shoulders to Brom, making the litter on his shoulders shift. "We don't like having everybody looking into our minds like that."

"It is part of the project," Brom said, still looking calm and sounding reasonable, but there was a storm raging through the link. Taboret felt her nerve endings withering. "Gentlemen, you agreed to the terms long ago. You had plenty of time to consider all the details. In fact, you were enthusiastic about the concept."

"Well, that was before we experienced the advanced form," Doolin said, drawing down his brows. "There's no privacy anymore! You're all listening to every single thing we think!"

"It's not true," Glinn said. "We receive emotional impressions and the very occasional visual image, but that is all."

"Hah! We bet you're reading our personal ether," Dowkin said. He blushed and turned his head into a drape of canvas. Taboret *didn't* get any images, but she guessed it had something to do with his love life. Of all the tedious prigs . . . As if they had the interest in snooping out that kind of details!

Glinn's eyebrows went up. "Are the two of you experiencing a more advanced form of thought transfer?"

He'd hit the nail on the head, to judge by the shade of red Doolin turned.

"None of your business!"

"How very interesting. Isn't it, sir?" Glinn asked.

"Yes, it is. The ramifications, hmm . . ." Brom stroked his chin, momentarily distracted. Then his face turned beet red and steam poured out of his ears. "Nonsense! We don't have this time to waste!"

"Don't care, do we?" Doolin asked, tilting his head back toward his brother.

"Nope," Dowkin said, emerging as belligerent as ever. "Fair's fair. Someone else takes over, or send us home."

"Gentlemen," Brom said, once again under iron control. The emission of steam seemed to have done him some good. He was back to his persuasive old self. "We can't send you away now. You're part of the gestalt. You're a part of this group. We need you."

"Then show us you value our efforts," Doolin said. "As of now, we're on strike." He didn't budge. Taboret could tell that if Brom wanted to move them, he'd have to give in. A twitch of agreement down the link told her everyone else thought so, too. The brothers, sensing the same thing, grinned obnoxiously.

"And we don't want to ride bicycles," Dowkin added. "We want ours made into motorcycles like the rest. It's too much work to pedal and carry this thing at the same time. Meaning on our next shift, that is."

Taboret felt the justice in their request. By now all of the steeds had been motorized except for the brothers'. But she doubted the gestalt had any extra power to spare, between the dirty tricks Mamovas had gone to plant on the princess's path and making their own road.

"We will relieve you of your burden," Brom said, at last. "The next pair in the rotation will take your place."

Gano and Lurry groaned. Brom merely raised his eyebrows, and the two subsided at once. They spurred their cycles onto the paving stone beside the brothers, who carefully edged their steeds over to make way. There was little room on the stone for the others to help transfer the litter. Taboret made the mistake of glancing over her shoulder at the ravine far beneath. The lurch in her stomach broadcast at once to all the others.

"Don't do that!" Carina pleaded, gripping her handlebars with white knuckles. "It's bad enough doing this on a tightrope."

Once free, the brothers stood working their shoulders and necks to get the blood circulating again. Their backs and arms narrowed to more normal proportions.

"Okay," Doolin said, clapping his hands. "Now for motorcycles."

"That won't be possible at this moment," Brom said. "Please mount so we can continue on."

"We don't like being treated like second-class technicians," Dowkin said, frowning until his eyebrows thickened and met over his nose. "Come on, we have reserves of power."

"May I explain, sir?" Glinn said, with a nod to Brom, who gave a magisterial wave. Glinn addressed the brothers with sincere focus. "We are stretched to our limit at this moment. If a nuisance or a change in a Sleeper's mood came along, we would need those reserves. Why, look," he said, pointing at their feet. "In the time it's taken us to have this . . . conversation, the nebulosity has started to shift again."

Taboret hadn't even noticed, but Glinn was right. The paving stone on which they were standing had begun to grow grass right under their feet. Some of the others had warped completely out of shape. One had become the statue of a woman with her arms cut off, one looked like the prow of a wooden ship, and two of them formed golden arches.

One had vanished from its place completely. Taboret looked down at the valley floor. The nebulous stone had broken apart into a hundred dozen doughnuts.

"Oh, no," Basil groaned, surveying the litter. "We're going to have to form these all over again."

"We have lost hours because of this ridiculous argument," Brom said. His face filled out wider than his usual death's-head gauntness so that the jowls could sag. He swept an arm at the sections of nebulosity. "This could set us back another day! Start flattening those out at once."

"Yes, sir," Glinn said. Always the good example, he dismounted, descended to the valley floor, and started to pick up pieces and reassemble them. Taboret gave him a fond look before following him. They started placing the paving stones again, and the procession moved forward.

There was nothing enjoyable about laying road in the hot sun, but Taboret suddenly experienced a sensation of wild glee. Just as abruptly, her cycle's engine sputtered and cut out, then vanished. In the space of moments, the bike went from powered to unpowered to powered again.

"Oh!" Gano exclaimed, although it sounded more like a groan. "What's happening?"

They spun to look at Brom, who had a look of inner bliss on his face. "Mamovas has just laid her first trap."

Taboret felt her heart constrict. She tried hard to picture what Mamovas had done, but the other woman must not be as strong a visual projector as Brom. Her mind was a disheartening blank. She shifted guiltily on her saddle. Brom turned his heavy gaze on her, taking her discomfort for impatience.

"You will have your chance soon," he promised.

Taboret smiled at him uneasily.

Chapter 19

The crowd of animals bounded up out of the ochre-yellow ravines almost underneath the hooves of Spar's steed. The guard captain threw up a hand and hauled back on the reins until his mount reared up and danced on the dusty road, barely in time to avoid a collision. The other riders skidded to a halt behind him, staring at the oval-eared, tan-coated beasts hopping across the road.

"What are they?" the princess wanted to know. "I've never seen giant rats on pogo sticks carrying handbags!"

"Looks like yours," Felan said to Colenna, pointing to the brown leather clasp bag one animal was clutching in its paw. "Somewhere around here there's an illusionary rat looking for his purse. You ought to give it back."

"Impudent boy, those are natural creatures," Colenna said. "I've been here in Wocabaht before. They carry their young in those cases."

"Natural! Surely not," Misha asked hopefully. "They must be a sign of the distortion. Aren't they?"

"There's none here," Lum said, definitely, looking over the ground. He stiffened, as if aware he had unintentionally insulted Roan. "It's been a long time, now, sir. Everything looks too natural."

"I know, Corporal," Roan said, confidently, refusing to take offense. "We'll pick up the trail again soon."

"Well, all right, sir," Lum said, uncertainly. Roan liked the young man. Lum was honest and thorough, and he had the gift of loyalty. He'd done Roan the honor of offering that loyalty to him, though Roan hardly thought he deserved it. Privately, he was getting worried. There hadn't been a trace of Brom or the Alarm Clock for miles. Had the scientists learned how to mask its passage? Or was Roan going the wrong way, as Spar and Felan kept insisting? He had only vague indications given him by that mysterious contact ahead of them. Had he been wrong to trust? Roan hated to think he was disappointing one of his most fervent supporters, but what could he offer in return but hope and a handful of air?

"Ride on, sir?" Spar asked, impatiently.

"Yes," Roan said. "It's too cold here to let the horses stand." He kicked Cruiser to a trot, and the others followed suit. It might look like a savannah or a desert plain here, but the season was late autumn or early winter. The wind was chilly. His steed liked warm weather, and so did he.

"Oh, no," Leonora said. She veered close and tugged Roan's elbow. "Look at that!"

Roan turned to see, and his eyes widened. Off the left side of the road, a cloud of gray dust rolling towards them resolved into a whirling cluster of furry animals like small bears with very large black noses. Weren't they . . . ? No, they couldn't be. . . . But they were waltzing, in pairs, and in time to music only they could hear.

"It's another nuisance," Bergold said. "It'll intersect the path ahead of us in a moment, and hold us up for who knows how long. Ride faster, and we can avoid it."

"Hurry!" Leonora said. She kicked Golden Schwinn to a trot, then a fast canter. Roan and Cruiser kept pace with them. Colenna and Spar galloped ahead. The cloud of spinning animals gained on them rapidly.

"Look out!" Spar called hoarsely. Roan gawked at an advancing mass of yellow. "Sandstorm!"

The storm came on too quickly for them to avoid it. The swirling dust engulfed Spar and Colenna. Three paces later, Roan's vision was blocked out by a blank yellow wall. He held up his arm to shield his eyes from the stinging grains but he felt only the cold wind beating against him that seemed to pierce right through his thick coat and riding trousers. He shivered mightily, and held tight to Cruiser's reins.

The storm was not very dense. In a few moments, he had passed through it. He was glad to see that the others were safe, too. Spar and Colenna appeared unharmed, with one notable alteration. They were riding . . . bareback. All of their clothes were gone. Colenna looked down at herself, squawked, and clutched her handbag to her large bosom like a shield. Spar pulled his horse up, and spun to stare indignantly at the others, as if they were responsible for this outrage.

"Oh" Leonora cried out. Roan turned to her, then jerked his eyes away so quickly he twisted his neck. She was nude, her delicate skin pink with cold. Her face had flushed red, from embarrassment as much as exposure. She quickly reasserted her own influence, and a thick mist arose about her. Felan reined in his horse and sat in the saddle, seeming impervious to the cold or his own nudity, and stared openly at Leonora. The princess regarded him with royal disdain, and thickened her cloud cover to almost total opacity. She rummaged through the panniers on Golden Schwinn's saddle, ignoring the historian. Felan looked disappointed.

"Every single bit of clothing is gone!" Leonora exclaimed.

"I'll lend you something, dear," Colenna said. After a brief search in her saddlebags and purse, she looked up. "I haven't got a thing, either."

"We must find her more garments at once," Roan said. The sharp wind was picking up. He was cold, too, but Leonora's comfort came first. He reached for the clasp to unfasten his cloak and sweep it around her, but felt only bare skin. How strange. He patted his chest to make sure. Roan looked down, then at each of his arms and legs, more and more astonished at each revealed limb. He couldn't be. But he, too, was stark naked. His pocket watch and chain, without buttonhole or pocket to hold it, lay across his thighs. His purse was on the ground a few paces behind him. He couldn't dismount and pick it up, not like that, not in front of *everyone*. This was a mortifyingly embarrassing dream. It had never happened to him before. What had Leonora seen? Was she offended? She wasn't looking at him, deliberately, he thought. He hunched over to cover his private parts, then was afraid he was calling more attention to them that way. He put one hand down, and gingerly sat up straight.

"Bergold," he called hoarsely. The senior historian had ascertained his own condition, and was rummaging in his horse's pack for covering. He glanced up, and his round face became oval as his mouth dropped open.

"You, too?" Bergold asked, running his gaze up and down as if he couldn't believe his own eyes. Roan blushed. He knew everyone was staring at him. "I'd have thought it was impossible. That was one powerful patch of influence!"

"Sir!" A strange man on the side of the road stepped out of the brush and waved them down. "I say, sir! Please!" Then his eyes went wide as he took in the sight of ten naked people on horseback. "Coo-ee!"

Spar pushed his horse close to him, making him look up at his face. Roan admired his self-control. He knew he was blushing. The guard captain had wiped all expression from his face.

"What's *your* trouble, sir?" he asked, putting a strong emphasis on the word "your." The man looked very distressed.

"Ah, yes. Do you have the time, sir?" the man asked.

"Do I what?" Spar demanded, jutting out his jaw. "Of all the useless—"

"Please!" The stranger held up a gold pocket watch. The hands were circling crazily in opposite directions around the face. "Please! I need to know."

Spar covered his private parts with an arm and dipped his hand into a small pocket on his pack. He withdrew the regulation timepiece he always carried and held it out so the man could see it. "Half past four, sir."

"Are you certain?" the man asked, spinning the stem of his watch between his fingers. The hands slowed down for a moment, then began revolving the other way.

"The weirdness, sir!" Lum said. He had a strawberry mark in the middle of his chest that glowed red when the stranger glanced curiously at him. "We're in a big patch of it!"

"Are you sure, Corporal?" Roan asked. When he spoke, the stranger turned to gaze at him. Roan concentrated on Lum's eyes, looking nowhere else.

"Oh, yes, sir," Lum said. He started to pick up his hand, turned scarlet, and nodded his head toward one side of the road. "There's variation in the stones over there, and the plants, too." Roan looked. The landscape did seem to be wrong in patches, but only in patches. He nodded eagerly.

"The crucible!" Spar exclaimed. "Are we close to Brom?"

"No idea," Bergold said, still going through his steed's packs.

The first thing that came to his hand was his bedroll's groundsheet, so he wrapped himself in that. "There's no way to judge the time of their passage."

"Yes, the time! Tell me!" the man wailed. Roan picked up his watch, feeling as if he was exposed on a stage, and looked at the dial. "I have four-thirty-two, sir."

"That can't be right, either!" The stranger was becoming very distressed, and Roan worried what kind of dreamer was suffering through a nightmare of being unable to find the correct time.

"This could just be an ordinary Public Nudity Dream," Misha said. He'd pulled an armload of odd things out of his pack to cover himself, and had a book open upside down on his lap. Alette had taken down her hair, and arranged it across her chest to conceal her bosom.

"Too strong," Bergold said, with a shake of his head. "Roan has been through Changeover unaltered. That storm must have had the full weight of Brom's group behind it. They are getting more powerful and dangerous. We've reached a kind of breaking point. This is a very subtle and powerful kind of influence, if Brom can do what the Sleepers couldn't."

"Dear lady," the man appealed to the princess, "surely you can tell me what time it is?"

"It's just about half past four," Leonora said. Her watch was a dainty affair on a diamond-studded chain that she drew up out of her cloud covering to examine. The man shook his head sadly, and went to Felan.

"Do you . . ." he began.

Felan snarled, and started to raise a hand to him. "Would you get out of here? We're on an important mission."

"This is important, too!"

"Push off!" Felan looked as if he was on the edge of striking out.

"Smile!" a cheerful woman said, stepping out into the middle of the road. She held put a large camera to her eye, and pushed the shutter release. The flashbulb exploded under the nose of Colenna's horse, making it buck. She aimed her lens at Roan, who raised his hand to forestall her, then dropped it again to cover himself. The flashbulb went off in his face. "Page one!"

Blinded and embarrassed, Roan turned away.

"Excuse me," a little boy said, appearing at Roan's stirrup. "How do I get to the store?"

"Where's the bathroom?" a little girl on Roan's other side asked him.

"I'm sorry, I don't know," Roan said, looking from one to the other. Was he decent? Would the shock of seeing grownups naked affect them all their lives?

"I beg your pardon," said an elegant woman wearing a huge red hat like a boat under full sail, "but where is the ladies' lingerie section? Goodness, look at you! You should be ashamed!"

Dozens of people appeared out of nowhere, getting in the way of the horses and each other. They went from one person to another, asking for directions, or for help with simple tasks, or pleading for spare change. All of them stopped to stare or comment on Roan's lack of clothes. Instead of behaving nonchalantly, like Felan, Roan felt more ridiculous every time someone pointed at him.

"Come along," Bergold said, firmly, coming to the rescue, his book at the ready. "This is not just a Public Nudity Dream. It has an Unanswerable Questions Variation." He picked up his reins, and clicked his tongue to urge his horse forward. "Behind me, Roan! Everyone! Excuse me, please! We're coming through. Thank you. Excuse me. Pardon me. I beg your pardon. . . ." The crowd continued to get underfoot and block their way, but slowly Bergold led them out of the throng behind his pink and gray horse. Roan forced himself to ignore the comments he heard.

"Smile!" said the photographer cheerily, letting off another blinding flash in their faces. Cruiser whinnied and jerked his head, but Bergold's imperturbable steed just kept walking. "Thank you! This will be in the paper tomorrow! And just one more. . . ."

"Sorry," Bergold said, politely but firmly. "This is a picture of us leaving."

"Look," Colenna said, pointing off to the side of the road. "There's a fig tree. Quick, someone."

"I will," Misha said, gallantly. He walked his horse carefully towards it, avoiding unnecessary jouncing in the saddle.

"I'm so co-co-cold!" Leonora said. Roan glanced at her again. He was almost unable to help himself; she had such a perfect figure, and his subconscious wanted to make sure he got another look. Fortunately, the opaque veil hid everything—almost. She gave him a playful sidelong glance and shook her head.

"Here's something, ma'am," Alette said, spurring to Leonora's side. She was scarlet-faced, but thinking of her liege before her own comfort. She held out a handful of woolly caterpillars to Leonora. "It's bound to be a bad winter, with all of these in the trees."

"Thank you, Private," Leonora said. "Won't you keep some for yourself?"

"Not regulation, ma'am," the guard said, shortly. Alette's spine was very stiff, as though she was wondering if it was all right to feel modest while on duty.

Roan kept his eyes fixed on her hands as Leonora spun them out to form a lacy but warm shawl, which she threw over her shoulders. It fitted itself around her, and she nestled into it gratefully.

Misha returned. He edged to the princess's side, holding out a handful of fig leaves, with his head turned gallantly away. Leonora gave Roan a meaning-filled look before stretching out her hand for them. He and she might be old friends, but they weren't affianced yet. Roan turned his back, and shot a glance at Felan to suggest he'd better do the same at once. The skinny historian might have no respect for Roan's normalcy, but he knew better than to risk his influence.

Misha offered fig leaves to everyone else, who separated to a decent distance to don these makeshift undergarments. Roan put the leaves in place on his person, and changed them quickly into a singlet and shorts. As soon as he was decently covered, the tension and mortification fled. It was so good to have clothes on again. His brain seemed to unlock. He could think again.

How vulnerable he was, when a simple state of undress could undo him so thoroughly. Why hadn't he done what Leonora had done, and made himself an opaque covering, or made clothes out of air molecules? He had the control to do it, but it hadn't occurred to him to try. Brom's power had put him off his guard. Roan wasn't used to having to think about the randomness everyone else suffered at the whims of the Sleepers and passing wisps of influence. He must contemplate that when he had a chance. In the meantime, there were tasks he could do, and do well.

"Captain Spar, may I be of assistance to you and your soldiers?" he asked, raising his voice.

The guards sat at attention on their horses in a row facing away from the rest of the party, not looking at one another. They'd all covered their personal parts, front and back, with the leaves, but were unable to alter them to suit.

"We'd be grateful, sir," Spar said, staring straight ahead of him. "Can't do anything with this damned vegetation. Regulation suits, if you please."

"Right you are," Roan said, rubbing his hands together. "You'll have to instruct me as I go."

" 'A full length body covering with arms to the wrist bone and legs to just below the ankle bone with nine buttons from neck to junction of legs in front and two buttons securing regulation flap of not less than fifty-four square inches in rear,' " Spar barked, as if reciting a paragraph from a manual. Without actually touching the leaves, Roan used influence to stretch out their substance until they covered the guard captain's whole body from the neck down. Fig leaves were marvelously elastic. Their nature was such that they would completely cover whatever parts one required in order to preserve modesty. " 'The material shall be of a good grade of red cloth, wool in winter, flannel in spring and autumn, and cotton in summer. . . .' "

"This'd be at least autumn, sir," Lum put in hopefully, also staring straight ahead. Roan made the necessary alterations, specifying a smooth, itchproof wool flannel.

" '. . . The buttons to be of wood or horn or plastic, depending upon materials available, but able to pass army stress tests, see regulation number 245.a, subheading 34-UW.' Thank you, sir," Spar finished in the same rapid-fire voice, but he looked relieved. Once covered, the guards' backs relaxed. Roan thought the standard issue design looked warm and even comfortable. He changed his singlet and shorts for a similar union suit.

Colenna returned to the road clad in an all-over undergarment that covered her from shoulders to knees. It was formfitting from her shoulders, over her large bust and down to her waist. The skirting draped loosely over her hips and knees. Spar kept turning away so as not to stare at her, but she was as unconcerned as if she was wearing a suit of armor.

"What now?" she asked the others. "Grass skirts? Barkskin suits?"

"This land is nearly bare of vegetation," Bergold said, checking about him. "It'll have to be mudcloth."

"Good enough! It's been years since I tried that," Colenna said, pleased.

"Will it be comfortable enough for the princess?" Roan asked, concerned at the sound of it.

"Oh, Roan," Leonora said. Under her cloud-covering, Roan glimpsed the outline of scanty underthings in periwinkle blue. A garment like Colenna's would have been practical, but he admitted that those were far more attractive. "We're all in this together. I'll do what everyone else has to do."

Colenna eyed her. "I can make you a dress out of your tent."

"Good," Roan said. "Please do that."

"No, no special privileges, please!" Leonora protested.

"It'd be my pleasure, dear," Colenna fluttered a hand at Roan. "You go on. We'll stay right here."

The mud alongside the road proved to be malleable, and was easily rolled out into a heavy fabric that appeared to have been block-printed in earth-toned colors. Roan was grateful for his new clothes, and made his cloak and cap double-thick against the steadily increasing wind. When he returned, he had to stifle his smile. Leonora glared at him between folds and folds of white fabric that lay draped over her shoulders and head. Colenna's talents in dressmaking were limited, to say the least. The draperies looked warm, albeit clumsy. He opened his mouth to say so.

"Don't!" Leonora said, lifting a warning finger out of the midst of her all-enveloping garment. "Not one word!"

Chapter 20

They took to the road again. The delay had been annoying, but Roan was relieved to have found a further sign of the gestalt, although not enough to be satisfactory to all. Spar was perturbed about the loss of his guards' uniforms, muttering darkly about a lack of discipline, and laughingstocks. Roan missed his old boots most of all. He had had them for years, through numerous adventures, including the second Changeover. Those boots conformed to every arch and curve of his feet. The substitutes he had made out of slips of fig bark and mudcloth were simply not the same, although, Roan thought, looking down at them, they could grow on him after a while. Their clay origin enabled them to model themselves to a maker's design. They were already taking on the appearance of formal shoes, more suited to his personality. Soon, they might be black leather, with comfortable insoles and extra wide toe boxes.

Suddenly, another pair of feet, in identical makeshift shoes, appeared on top of Cruiser's stirrups. Roan found himself riding pillion behind another man, who glanced back over a shoulder. It was him—Roan! There were two of him on the horse's back, both clad in printed cloaks and trousers. Roan flinched in surprise. He hopped backwards off the saddle.

The second man pulled the horse over to the side of the road. Roan walked around to stare up at him. The other man looked down at him solemnly.

"I could be looking in a mirror," said the man on the horse.

"How strange," Leonora said, reining Golden Schwinn to a halt beside them. She looked from one to the other. "Which of you is the real Roan?"

Roan felt a moment of doubt. Was he in his own body, or

not? It was strange seeing himself doing something, and not feeling his muscles move.

"I think he is," Roan said, pointing.

"He is the real one, I'm sure of it," the double said, at the same time. And his motions were identical to those Roan had seen himself make reflected in mirrors and windows, but from this man, they looked more deliberate.

"How would we know?" Roan asked, still staring in bewilderment. "I've lived all my life thinking I was an original person."

The double peered at him closely and touched his own cheek, then reached out and almost touched Roan's. He hesitated, drawing his hand back. "You do look more real than I do," he said.

"I was going to say that to you," Roan said. He felt a strange sense of disorientation, as if he was floating in space. If he faced the genuine Roan, who was he? And where did he come from? Perhaps the changeless person he had always been was a distant shadow of this man. It was possible. There was a historian's theory that every person had a doppelgänger somewhere in the world who exactly resembled him. And this man certainly did. Chance had simply dictated that they had never met until now. The legend also said that you had to kill your doppelgänger, or he would kill you. He felt a thrill of terror. Roan knew he couldn't kill himself. Was he about to die?

"Are you sure?" It was Leonora's voice, but it came from another young woman of stunning beauty riding up on a twin to Golden Schwinn. This Leonora had red hair, high cheekbones and long, almost slanted eyes. When he looked for his princess, she had just acquired the same characteristics.

"I . . . I think so." Roan studied his twin. "You're the real one. You must be. But then, who am I?"

"No, you are real," the other said, just as earnestly. He dismounted and threw the reins to Roan. "I'm not. I couldn't be. We shouldn't have met. I . . . I'll go away. Please don't harm any of the others."

Roan looked at him, puzzled. "So the legend isn't true?"

"I hope not," the other said, so sincerely Roan had to believe him. They breathed identical sighs of relief.

The second Leonora took a moment to study the first one's

costume critically, even though she was robed in the same billowing white. The first princess straightened her skirts with a surreptitious use of influence so it resembled a gown instead of a tent dress. They exchanged nods, royalty to royalty. Roan sensed a little influence was exerted on each side, to make sure each looked her most beautiful while under scrutiny from a discerning eye. Roan knew that Leonora—his Leonora—was frightened, but her training kept her from showing it. Meanwhile, other duplicates were appearing. Two Mishas, long and lanky, gazed at each other in bemusement. Two Alettes gawked.

"Leave, foul spirit!" Spar shouted, drawing his sword. He jumped off his steed. "Go on, get out of here, or I'll split you!"

"You get away," the captain's double yelled, with equal volume. He brandished his own sword, and set it ablaze. "You unnatural beast, you! I'll kill you, and then you can't kill me."

"Sir, stop them!" the Lums shouted, calling for Roan's attention. "Captains, don't!"

"Halt!" the Roans cried, rushing in between the Spars, reaching for their sword hands. "The legend is a lie! He can't harm you. Don't fight!"

But the Spars maneuvered around them like so many posts in a tilting yard, and ran at one another with an angry war cry. The princesses cringed and covered their eyes. The Spars raised their swords, and brought them down in a killing blow—

—On empty air. The blades passed straight through their bodies, and into the ground between their feet. The Spars were insubstantial to one another. They stared at the buried blades in disbelief, then began laughing loudly from relief.

"You!" Spar barked, gasping in breath with a big grin on his face. "Look at that! We couldn't've bashed each other if we'd tried!"

"Split each other! Good thing we couldn't do it!" the other howled. "There'd be four of us." Their knees collapsed under them, and they sat down on the ground, still laughing.

The second Roan looked up at the first, and put out a hand to touch his arm. The fingers disappeared into the dark-printed sleeve as if into shadow. Roan's double withdrew his hand with a worried look.

I'm the ghost, Roan thought, and just as surely knew that his double was thinking the same thing.

The two Colennas, friendly at once, sat down on the side of the road and compared the contents of their purses. Clearly, she, or they, didn't believe in the legend. The Felans stood nearby, arms crossed, talking in low tones, sharing a smug joke at the expense of others in the party.

"This is no time to be beside yourselves," Bergold said, blinking large orange eyes. There were two of the plump historian, both of them currently giant owls perched on horseback. The wise heads turned in almost full circles to catch everyone's attention. "We need to put our heads together and concentrate on our mission. It's convenient that there are twice as many of them. Heads, I mean."

"But what about our doubles?" Lum asked. "I mean, he's all right. I mean, he's me, but . . . are we a party of twenty instead of ten?"

"We're two whole parties now," Spar said. "Let's split up into two groups. We can cover more ground this way."

"Right," the second Spar said. "Brom can't stay hidden with two of us on the trail. Let's get moving."

"We can't really do that," the Bergold on the left said.

"We've been thinking about this matter quite a bit," the Bergold on the right added. "One or the other of us is a reflection caused by influence."

"That we could have guessed," the Felans said in unison. Their eyebrows were thickly shaggy on their foreheads. The right brows climbed up toward their hairlines in emphasis.

"That's also why we can't touch one another. We are the mirror as well as what is reflected in it. This has happened before. It's recorded in the royal archives. For example, I know that the duplicates, whichever you are," the owl nodded its beak at the two Roans and the two Mishas, "can touch both of anyone else, though not each other, so it will be difficult to decide who was originally with whom."

"Fascinating stories of mistaken identity," the other owl said, warming to his topic. "In one really interesting record—"

"Are they around here forever?" Felan shouted, interrupting Bergold.

"Certainly not," the owls told him sternly. "Don't shout.

Our hearing is excellent, even though we have no external ears."

"The doppelgänger effect is temporary," the righthand Bergold said. "That is why we can't act as two groups. Sooner or later the doubles will vanish, possibly stranding some of the "real" party who got mixed up with them. I beg your pardon," he said to the left-hand Bergold, who bobbed his feathered head to show no offense was taken. "We'd best go on all together."

Eighteen people and two owls set out again, each side by side with his or her double. At first, Roan thought the road seemed crowded, then he began to see advantages in redundance. The Lums rode ahead, watching for "weirdness." Both Roans looked for signs that had been left for him from ahead. Six guards, instead of three, kept watch for threats, with hands on sword belts. The others talked among themselves, some shyly, others with animation. An occasional traveler, passing by on foot or steed, stared openly at the long file of identical faces, and stepped up the pace, lest the effect be contagious. The other Roan must have caught his thought, because he gave him a sidelong grin. Should they pretend to menace the next person they saw, and curse him with twinness? It was really rather nice. Roan almost wished the effect would last. If Brom's power was growing stronger, they would need more help to defeat him when they caught up with him at last. On the other hand, there were two Leonoras and two Colennas they'd have to protect, dividing their attention unnecessarily.

The princesses were carrying on a lively discussion about fashion, upon which, not surprisingly, they agreed completely. Roan only listened with half an ear. He was still hoping to find clear indications of Brom's trail. The other Roan met his eyes occasionally to offer a silent shake of the head. He wasn't seeing anything, either.

". . . But I think the Nodite custom of printed headbands for babies is quite silly," Leonora said, drawing an armful of draperies across her own forehead in illustration. "When they can't even read them yet. . . . She's gone!"

"She merged with you," Misha said, hoarse with surprise. "Just now. When you had that cloth over your face. Horse and all, just moved toward you all of a sudden, and then there was only one of you."

"Oh," Leonora said in a small voice, her hands coming to rest on her saddle horn. "We were having such fun."

Roan looked up and down the line. All the duplicates were gone. Ten had seemed such a large number at first. After the crowd and the double effect, the party looked so small and lonely. He felt vulnerable, out in the middle of nowhere virtually alone. Leonora urged Schwinn forward to ride beside Cruiser, and offered her hand to him. He took it, and gave it a grateful squeeze. What a wonderful woman she was. How terrible it would be now if she left to go home. He still worried about putting her in danger, but how he would miss her!

"Am I the right me?" Lum asked, prodding his arms uncertainly. "Nothing like that's ever happened to me before."

"I feel the same way, Corporal," Roan said.

"It's a good sign when you can enjoy your own company," Colenna said, in a soothing manner.

Bergold said, scratching his feathered belly with a claw, "He knew everything I did. How very strange. I've never had such a meeting of minds with anyone before. I rather enjoyed it."

Spar was very worried. "Could this be a sign that we're about to ride into a Changeover?"

"No, it was a nuisance," Bergold said with a sigh. "A friendly one, but a supreme time-waster on the whole."

"It feels as if it was dragged here," the continuitor said, testing the air. "Or pushed. There's a strained sensation in the very fibers of the air."

"It's artificial, all right. Brom's picking away at our psyches," Colenna said.

"But how's he getting here and going away again without leaving a trace?" Lum asked. "We're not getting the constant thread of weirdness that we were getting before. I saw some distortion near where we ran into the nuisance, but that's all. They've got to ride on the road, right? And they aren't. Most things are normal, and they're not leaving tire tracks."

"If these distractions were pushed towards us, we don't have an idea of from how far away," Bergold said. "We'd have to search the whole wilderness, and we might never find the point of origin."

"It *could* be natural. This might be connected to a very active part of the Sleeper's mind," Felan said, staring up at the sky and squinting at an invisible document in his mental archives. "I've heard of as many as five simultaneous . . ."

"Unlikely," Colenna said, flatly.

"Well, it isn't like when we were following the trail before," Spar said, although visibly unwilling to contradict his beloved. "And we haven't seen tire tracks since we passed near that cliff face."

"I suppose it's too much to hope that that rockfall was on top of them," Felan said, sourly.

"Certainly not!" Colenna said. "These two nuisances so close together prove they're still alive and active, and we are behind them. Isn't that right, young Roan?"

Roan was grateful for her air of confidence. He felt very uncertain of himself. If they lost faith in him, they might turn back. Spar would insist that the princess accompany him back to Mnemosyne for safety. Roan would have the wish he had made a couple of days before of going on alone. He didn't want that wish any longer, and didn't care for the prospect of facing the gestalt on his own.

"We must have come too close to Brom," Bergold said, half-lidding his orange eyes. "But when? Why didn't we know he was nearby?"

"It doesn't matter," Leonora said, with absolute conviction and a confident look for Roan. "Now we're certain he's still ahead of us. That's what we needed to know."

"Hurry up, can't you?" Basil shouted.

"I'm moving as fast as I can," Taboret snapped, without looking at him. She dropped a block of nebulosity into place. "Think you can do it better?" She spurred her motorcycle smartly away from the front end of the road in a wide circle so she couldn't hear Basil's retort.

Short-handed because of Bolmer's injury and Mamovas's absence, the apprentices were having to work twice as hard as before. The Countingsheep brothers' obduracy had put them hours behind Brom's schedule. The chief was fretting, wondering if they would now make it to the road before Roan in spite of the traps laid to delay him. Because of the difficult terrain, the mercenaries had stayed away all afternoon. Brom had had no new message from his spy. He didn't like lacking information, and they all knew it.

Anger bounded up and back through the mental link until Taboret felt if anyone even looked at her cross-eyed, she would embed them in the pavement. They could not finish their road today, no matter how much the chief shouted. It was nearing twilight. Power, strength, and tempers were stretched to their utmost, and they were still miles from the main road.

At least six times during the afternoon they had felt the aching exhaustion that meant Mamovas had drawn upon them to create traps and distractions. The last one had been over an hour ago, and so strong that Taboret had to sit down and gasp for breath. There had been no theft of energy since. Surely that meant that Mamovas and the mercenaries were on their way back?

Yes, she felt an answering echo in her mind to the question. Within a few minutes, she heard three motorcycle engines approaching. Brom signaled them to a halt. It wasn't long until they could see the three riders. Mamovas just looked tired, and Acton vacant, but Maniune's face was grimmer than usual.

"Bad news, boss," he said. "We heard from our friend behind us. They've got a spy in our group."

Brom was so surprised the red spark in his eyes went out for a moment. "What? Impossible!"

"Not impossible," Maniune said shortly. Taboret guessed that Mamovas had been drawing on him, too, and he wasn't used to it. Weariness had even dulled *his* aggression. "They've been getting help from one of us. I don't know who, but I'll guarantee the message wasn't garbled."

"All right," Brom said, turning to the apprentices and clapping his hands. "Everyone! Stop what you are doing. I want your attention. Someone among us is sending information to our pursuers. That is not an approved-of activity. The spy will step forward at once. Now!"

Taboret felt Brom's superior force of will surge through the link, subduing her own. He bore down harder, grinding into her conscious thoughts like a drill. Confess! Taboret clutched her temples, trying to squeeze the headache out of her head. She wished she had something to confess, if only to make the pressure stop. And then she remembered that she had. Could they have found out about her aberration? It was only the one little time, one tiny little mark on one tree that could have been an accident. She tried hard not to think about it, and sought to suppress her feeling of guilt by concentrating on suspecting others. It could be Lurry who had blown the gaff, she thought. Or Gano. Now, there was a suspicious character!

Her efforts seemed to work. She saw Glinn looking at her with a curious expression in his eyes, and attempted to stare coldly back in her turn, but she was worried.

"No one will step forward? No one will spare his friends and comrades the pain of interrogation? Very well. I shall learn the truth of this later on," Brom said, raising his hand in the signal to move on. "Proceed."

Chapter 21

After an early breakfast at sunrise, Roan had the others out on the road. No one was sorry to leave the most uncomfortable campground in his memory. Everyone was groggy and fractious, like tired children.

Since the weather remained autumn-cold, Leonora had had to choose between her tent and her clothes. Roan and Misha helped fashion a new pavilion for her out of leaves and vines. It was very hard work to make anything using influence that worked together with something someone else made. The result wasn't nearly good enough for her, but she hadn't said a word. For a moment, Roan regretted that the gestalt would have to be destroyed when they caught up with Brom, because being able to combine strengths was a terrific idea.

It had been a hard night, full of random noises and creatures that, although strange in appearance, were ordinary Dreamish beasts, such as tangle-bats that always got tied up in one's hair, and young Monsters-In-The-Closet, who sought to make nests in the party's backpacks and panniers. Sleep had not come easily, despite their long day's ride, and when it did, it was full of broken dreams and nightmares. Then, they'd had to get up in the middle of the night to move camp from the top of the hill they had chosen, when it turned out to be an anthill, and nocturnal insects at that.

They still saw no reliable signs of Brom's trail. After twilight, Bergold the owl had flown several times over the general area, looking for Brom's group. The desert and savannah were crisscrossed with tire marks, but no concentrated pattern to suggest the Alarm Clock had ever come that way.

In the tentative light of morning, the party galloped down

the road hoping to run into another sign of artificial interference, a distortion or a nuisance. Roan hated that feeling of constant anticipation, as if someone was going to jump out from behind a tree at any moment and shout "boo!"

"There may be a problem ahead," Bergold said, poking his head out of a cocoon of map sheets. He was human again, after a good night's sleep, although he still had big round eyes and downy hair. "About three miles from here is a crossroads."

Roan noted three other routes intersecting their path. One turned west, but the other two, north and east by northeast, were possibilities. "And then again, we might find more indicators."

"Certainly we may," Bergold said, with an encouraging nod.

Automatically, he handed the map up the line until it came to Colenna, who folded it neatly, and stowed it in her handbag.

The older woman's mudcloth dress looked slightly different that day, as indeed did she. Her skin was darker, and her hair was piled high on her head. The effect was very fashionable. She was a remarkably good traveler, and Roan could tell that Leonora was learning a lot by observing her. When they reached the next town, he would have to make certain Leonora communicated with her family and let the king know where she was. It was odd that no message had caught up with them yet. He knew Felan had sent several communiqués back to Mnemosyne.

"Look, there's a man sitting at a desk," Leonora said, as the crossroads came into view.

"Hold!" Spar said, reining in before the man, who was dressed in a dinner jacket and black bow tie. He held a neat sheaf of paper in his hand. "Sir! Have you seen a large group of people pass through here? They would have been riding motorcycles. You know, bicycles with engines?" Spar mimed revving handlebars. "Which way did they go?"

The man looked up at them politely. "Good afternoon," he said. "In our directions today, north, that way, is the main road to the city of Reverie. South, in the opposite direction, leads to the towns of Hark and Lark, and eventually to the main road leading to the capital city of Mnemosyne. Northeast, a scenic road to the Dark Mysteries. West is the main road to the city of Barbandion, passing through numerous small towns. Updates as construction or Sleeper's whim occurs. Thank you for listening."

"Listen!" Spar shouted, swinging down from his horse and putting his face very close to the man's. "Did a large group of people ride through here with a covered litter? Which way should we go? Did they head for the Dark Mysteries?"

The man looked at them blankly. "Good afternoon," he began, shuffling his papers. "Your directions for today. To the north . . ."

"He's only a signpost," Roan said, disappointed.

"Of all the useless imbeciles . . ." Spar growled.

"He's not an imbecile," Bergold said. "He isn't even a person. He's a noninteractive, specific information source. It simply means we have to decide for ourselves where to go. Which way did they turn, do you think? Towards Barbandion?"

"Doesn't feel like it, sir," Lum said, squinting at the western turning. "I think it's this way." He looked at the signpost, who regarded him with a friendly expression but offered no more information. Spar pointed up the road.

"Look, sir, we want to know—"

"Good afternoon, said the signpost amiably. "To the north . . ."

"Never mind!" Spar shouted. "I heard you the first time!"

"No need to yell, dear," Colenna said.

"I can't help it. I feel as if I'm sleepwalking."

"I think everyone's is still groggy from dinner last night," Misha said, yawning widely. "Let's stop and have some lunch."

"You're always hungry, aren't you," Colenna said, fondly. "You're still a growing boy."

"Just taller," Misha said, patting the top of his head.

"Lunch is a good idea," Roan said. "I'm hungry, too. Felan, you've got our supplies."

They walked the horses to the northeast side of the crossroads where lush grass grew. As soon as Roan took out Cruiser's bit, the horse pulled up mouthfuls of fodder, and tossed his head eagerly. He welcomed the break. Roan found he was walking with a side-to-side roll as if he was still in the saddle. It was warmer here than it had been farther south, a relief to his aching muscles.

"I've got something special for lunch," Felan said, showing

the first signs of animation Roan had ever seen in him. He flipped out a cloth with a flourish and set it on the ground full of dishes, napkins, and flower vases. "You're going to love it."

The others all gathered around the picnic cloth. Bergold spread a napkin over his tidy shirt front and tucked the tip into his collar.

"Here we are! It's lamb stew." Felan produced the steaming dish proudly from a basket. "My mother's very best recipe. It took a while to turn the herbs into the ones she used, but there you are. Enjoy it!" Felan set down the casserole and lifted the lid. The steam that issued from the food was fragrant, but heavy.

"Lamb for lunch, too?" Bergold asked, surprised. "We had lamb chops last night. Surely you know from the Books of Concordance that mutton is a soporific. It makes you drowsy. We need our senses sharp, not dull, lad. You should have bought chicken. A good bit of rooster wakes you up nicely."

"Mutton was reasonable in Hark, and chicken was outrageous," Felan said grumpily, setting down the pot lid with a clatter. "If you don't like it, change it. Surely you can countenance altering your food," he said to Colenna, who opened her mouth and shut it, refusing to allow him to bait her into another argument. But this time Spar leaned in between them.

"Listen to me, you pup," he said, shaking a finger under Felan's nose. "I may only be an old soldier, but it seems you're pressing your luck to the point where not even a Divine Intervention will save you. You don't have a nice bed you can settle down on for a nap, so mind your tongue."

"What else did you buy?" Misha asked, politely. "Perhaps we can save the stew for later tonight when we are ready to sleep."

With ill grace, Felan offered his marketing basket. All the food he had bought was as boring as the mutton. There was a large container of egg salad, unornamented loaves of bread, mild cheese, and a tub of boiled celery salad.

"You could make a passable quiche out of all this," Colenna said. "It'll take some doing."

"Using up the energy this food is supposed to give us," Spar grumbled.

"Well, I got bargains," Felan said, defensively.

"Stupid," Spar said, throwing up his hands. "You don't know anything about traveling. Next time, we'll take our chances and make our own bargains."

Felan was insulted. "You ought to appreciate good cooking, instead of criticizing it. I went to a lot of trouble over this stew."

"All right," Roan said, holding up his hands. "Please don't argue. It isn't that bad."

"I don't want to fall asleep on the road," the captain of the guard said. "Have to be vigilant! We want something else."

They decided to use Colenna's idea, and make quiche. Roan was elected to try. He tasted the cheese, the bread, and the egg salad. After one taste he put the celery aside. He combined the rest as best he could. Roan had to admit that the resulting pie was not very appetizing, and it took a surprising effort to keep it from turning back into its component parts. The others looked a little disappointed. If they hadn't been so hungry, they might have turned it down and ridden on until they found another source of food. There was just enough to go around, without seconds. Lum and Hutchings tried not to look as if they were still hungry, but they scraped their plates clean of every crumb.

"Well, that was nice," Misha said, politely. "Did anyone else buy anything in Hark?"

"Hmmph!" Felan snorted.

"That won't be necessary," Roan assured the continuitor. "We will cope with what we have."

He picked up the casserole of mutton stew, and tasted it. It was very lamby, and exaggerated the tiredness he felt. He exercised his influence to transform the dish into a handsome chicken pot pie large enough to feed all of them, although not generously. He took another taste. It was now chickeny, perking him up nicely. He held out the dish to the others.

"It won't be perfect, but it's nourishing food."

Felan looked insulted and turned away.

"Smells delicious," Bergold said. "I think I sense one of *your* mother's recipes."

"Freak," Felan muttered sourly under his breath.

"And there's bread," Colenna said. "That looks very good,

Felan." The younger man wasn't appeased, and refused to face them.

"Felan, why don't you do that for yourself, too," Bergold said, "and have a nice sit down with the rest of us?" He patted the cloth beside him. The young historian ignored him.

"Your Highness, I have some very nice grapes I picked off the vines we passed earlier," Misha said, producing them from his knapsack. "May I offer you some?"

"Why, thank you," Leonora said. She started to reach for them, and Misha hesitated, to make sure the fruit was clean and perfect in appearance. Roan hid a smile. Leonora wanted to interact just a little more closely with her traveling companions, but they continued to treat her with infinite dignity and respect. She had already charmed them, Roan knew. Even Captain Spar, who was unhappy to have to be taking care of royalty in the midst of a dangerous enterprise, had thawed completely to her warmth and kindness. Everyone but Felan, whose behavior teetered just on the edge of cheekiness with her, as it did with everyone. He sat with his back to the rest of them. He'd accepted his portion of chicken pot pie, and turned it laboriously back into stew, and ate moodily, staring down at his plate.

"I'm sorry, Felan," Roan said, gently. "We have to be at our brightest. We need every edge. Brom is smart."

"Hmmph!" Felan snorted, and widened his back into a wall so none of them could see his face.

"Come along, come along," Spar said, tapping his fork on his plate. "We can't sit around here all day. Let's eat, and go on."

Roan turned to his own lunch. The transformation of the food wasn't perfect. They might be able fool their taste buds, but not their brains. The strong aroma might have been tempered, but it was still there. One bite was enough to tell Roan he couldn't change a thing's nature thoroughly enough. He was instantly drowsy. Lamb was lamb.

"What this wants is a little spicing up," Colenna said. She reached into her handbag and brought out a small wooden shaker. "Pepper to pep us up."

She cranked the top of the grinder and sifted plenty of gray, green, and red dust onto each person's portion of stew. It tasted very spicy, making all of them thirsty, but it helped dispel the residual grogginess. Roan felt much better. Everyone's eyes were brighter, and they moved with more energy. Colenna's pepper had done the trick. He sprang to his feet, eager to go on.

"Which way now, sir?" Lum asked, when they had cleaned up. He handed the folded picnic cloth back to Felan, who accepted it without a word and stuffed it into his saddlebag.

"I am not sure, Corporal," Roan said. He walked around the intersection again and again, looking for clues. None of the three roads had any characteristic that set one apart from the others. All were well paved and maintained. The signpost gave him a friendly look, but remained silent. What had Leonora said, that he had to buoy all of them with his hope, and his leadership?

"Wish we had more of a clue as to where they were," Misha said, squinting off in the distance.

"What, with all the influence they've been throwing at us? I'll bet we aren't an hour behind," Bergold said, bluffly. "Maybe two, with lunch."

"They have to stop to eat, too," Colenna reminded him. "An hour, that'd be all."

"We can't be a minute late to stop them," Roan said. "It would be as if we hadn't left the castle at all."

"We're lollygagging, sir," Spar said.

Colenna came over and took Spar's arm. "Don't rush him, dear."

Roan, too, was impatient to catch up with Brom before he got any farther ahead. Those tire tracks they had last seen proved that most of the scientists were on motorized transport. All things being equal, the party would fall behind more and more unless they had a great deal of good luck.

There was a chill wind blowing behind them. Every time Roan turned back towards the south he shivered. He moved away from the cold blast toward where it felt warmer, to the north side of the intersection. The crossroads must sit on a temperature isobar, he thought, because there were no trees or other windbreaks nearby. He looked up to search the sky, but didn't see any weather marks. The wind was cold to the west, too. How strange that there should be such a difference in similar places only yards apart. Deliberately, Roan walked across the intersection to the northeast road. Warmer here, too, but not as warm as the north road, where the air was almost hot. Think! He told himself. Cold, cold, warm, hot—what does that mean?

"This way," Roan said, excitedly. "I'm certain they're north northeast of us now. The best way would be to take the north route."

"What?" Felan asked, surprised out of his sulk. "There's no trail to follow."

"The Sleepers favor us, Master Felan," Roan said, with a feeling of sincere relief. "We have a clue." He explained his reasoning, and led the others around to each of the roads in turn, letting them feel the changes. Bergold nodded, and Colenna looked pleased. Leonora's eyes were shining.

"You're right!" she said. "Let's hurry!"

They set out for the north, buoyed on pepper and good spirits. But Roan's encouragement had little effect on their steeds. The beasts galloped their fastest, but still stubbornly refused to turn into sports cars, air ships or supersonic transport. The favor of the Sleepers toward their journey was reassuring, and for that, Roan gave silent thanks, but some way to attain more speed would have been welcome. The most the steeds would concede was to become racing bicycles, with narrow tires and curved handlebars that made the riders bend over forward.

The onward road continued to be good, and the air held that faint trace of warmth. Roan was troubled by the discontent that started to rise among the party. He expected Felan to complain about his competence, but Hutchings, too, began to mutter to himself about wild geese, and going home. He concentrated on pedaling his hardest, and ignoring the whispers.

"What in the devil is this?" Spar demanded, looking ahead where the road passed into thick woods. He braked to a halt, and pointed. From the side of a tall, rectangular hut, an orange-and-black-painted arm protruded across the road, blocking their way. "Tollbooth! This is the king's highway! It's free to all traffic!"

"Not if you want to go through," said a large, uniformed man at the gate. "Pay up, or you don't pass."

"On whose authority?" Spar asked.

"This is the king's highway, isn't it?" the man said. "The king!"

"How much?" Roan asked, feeling in his saddlebags for his purse.

"One chicken per horse, one loaf per person." The guard held out one huge hand, and waited.

"That's exorbitant!" Colenna said, shocked. "Do you know who this is? This is Her Highness, Princess Leonora!"

"Really?" the big man asked, peering at Leonora, who did her best to look regal in a tent dress. Like Colenna's, her costume had been much modified during the night, and now looked more stylish, if just as voluminous. She manifested a tiara, and the man nodded. "Royalty, three chickens. Payable in cash."

"Nonsense!" Bergold said.

"Make up your minds," the tollbooth guard said. "There's a lot of other people waiting who want to go through."

They looked behind them. On what only moments before had been an empty road, were lines of people in cars, carts, on horses, donkeys, bicycles, and several conveyances Roan could only describe as unique, such as a washtub containing three men with oars.

"C'mon, buddy!" shouted a man in sunglasses, leaning out the side window of his car. "Move it!"

"My kids are getting tired," yelled another man, in a cart pulled by a donkey. "Hurry it up!"

"Very well," Roan said, reaching for his pocket. As he touched the side of his tunic, he remembered that he had no pockets. These were not his original clothes. "Just a moment, please."

He opened his pack, and felt around in it for his purse. "That's odd," he said.

Bergold was watching him with wrinkled brow. "What is?"

"My wallet is gone. Do you have any money?"

"To be sure," the historian said. He dismounted, and reached into his pannier. "Why, mine is gone, too! How very singular."

"Not singular," Colenna said, stricken, looking up from her huge handbag. "Mine is missing." All of the others searched for their money pouches, but in vain.

"What about it?" the guard demanded, looming over them with crossed arms. Roan glanced up at him, continuing the search.

"We can't seem to find our money."

"Then we'll help you," he said. Several large guards descended upon the party, and began to turn out their knapsacks, panniers, packs, and Colenna's purse.

"No!" Misha shouted, as the men opened Leonora's pack, and began to unload her possessions onto the road. "You leave that alone!" he said, snatching a tiny vanity case out of one guard's hands.

"Misha, it's all right," Leonora said, her face red as she rescued a filmy blue brassiere from another's. "They're just doing their job. Oh, no, all my jewels are gone!"

"Please don't do that," Roan said, trying to take his pack away from a burly guard. "Sir, there's no need to go through all my luggage. I tell you, we haven't got the toll money. We'll go away and try another route."

"Are you trying to interfere with a legitimate inspection?" The guard holding Roan's pack continued to empty it out onto the ground. Roan couldn't believe the sheer quantity of things it held. He didn't remember having seen a yo-yo before. And what about that plaid cushion? Or the bowling trophy? Where had all these things come from?

"Hey, look at this, Charlie!" another guard exclaimed, holding up a whaleboned corset trimmed with purple lace. He dropped it on the pile of possessions, now growing to man height. Colenna, her face red, gathered it up and put it under her cloak.

"You're right, there's no money in here," the first guard said, tossing Roan's empty satchel on the ground at his feet. "You'd better move aside. And take all that stuff with you."

Roan picked up his bag and started to repack. The drivers behind them honked and yelled. The party tried to hurry, but the bags seemed now to be too small for everything to fit. Roan smiled and called apologies to the waiting drivers, but they swore and shook their fists at him. Colenna's handbag was overflowing, with an umbrella sticking out one side and a hot water bottle lying limply over an edge. Roan had his arms full of clothing and a set of pots and pans.

"We'll go around this damned thing into the woods," Spar said, picking up stacks of military hardware. A belt of machine-gun bullets slithered through his hands and he had to stoop over to retrieve it. "I will not pay an unjust and illegal toll."

"We'll have to," Roan said, resignedly. "Wait, look!"

Bells started ringing. Another booth sprouted up on the right edge of the road, with the neon words "You-Pass" glowing in red over the top. A yellow light in the frame of the booth lit up, the light overhead turned from red to green, and the orange-and-black arm swept from horizontal to vertical. From off the side of the road came a host of motorcycles. In their midst were the unmistakable forms of Brom and the covered litter. They went through the booth at full speed, and roared away down the highway. The arm ticked back into place, and the "You-Pass" booth sank back into the ground.

Roan dropped everything and ran after them, whistling for Cruiser. The tollbooth guards blocked his way at once.

"Where do you think you're going?" the chief guard demanded. He grabbed for the bicycle, which reared and squeaked.

"I must stop them!" Roan explained, trying to squeeze past and run under the wooden barrier. "They're enemies of the crown. You must help me stop them!"

"Was that them, sir?" Lum asked. The palace guards had thrown everything aside when Roan did, and were right behind him.

"Yes! They're getting away!"

"Listen, you," the tollbooth guard said, shaking a threatening finger under Roan's chin, "pick up your junk and get off the road. We don't have all day." The chorus of horns and shouts from the other drivers added to the uproar.

"Wait," Leonora said, running up. "Will you take an exchange?" She handed the man a little jeweled brooch. "What about this? Will this pay for our passage?"

"Your passage?" the guard asked, screwing a loupe into his eye. His eyebrows went up. "This'll pay for the whole road's worth!"

"Yay!" cried the driver immediately behind them.

"Then, take it," Leonora said, desperately. "Just let us through!"

"Right you are, lady," the guard said. He raised his hand, and the gate swung up.

Traffic streamed around them as the party picked up what goods they could and hastily pushed them back into the saddlebags. Roan fretted over every second's delay.

"We were ahead of them! No wonder there wasn't clean trace of them," he exclaimed, pulling the last strap tight on Cruiser's rack.

"Well, thank the Sleepers," Bergold said, gathering marbles and books into his pack. "There! Come on, let's go."

They sprang onto their steeds, and started pedaling through the press of traffic.

Roan gestured the guards into the lead. He wished with all his heart that they could make their steeds into swift motorcycles like Brom's, but hoped somehow that right would prevail, and the speed they required to catch up would be given to them before it was too late. He bent over the handlebars, and just thought about putting one foot after another and not running into anyone else. Hurry! They must hurry!

"Sir!" Lum called over the noise of the traffic. "There's no weirdness here. No distortion!" Roan looked up. The young guard was gesturing at the side of the road. Roan surged past a donkey cart and a pedal-driven wheelbarrow to catch up with him.

"Moondust, son!" Spar said, dropping back alongside. "They hit that booth at a hundred miles an hour. There just wasn't time to distort anything."

"I'll prove it, sir," Lum said. He nodded to Hutchings, who followed. They veered off the road into the woods, turning back toward the tollbooth. Roan watched them go, puzzled.

The guards rejoined them in a minute, coming from the woods on the right and merging through the mass of vehicles to their side.

"Like I thought, sir," Lum said. "No tire tracks. The ground should have been all churned up, and it's flat. Nothing but one patch of distortion at the side of the road near where that fake tollbooth was." Hutchings nodded solemn confirmation. "There should have been a dozen tire tracks all together, and there was only one line a hundred yards out. Could've been anybody."

"Pull over," Roan said, sadly, raising an arm to alert the rest of the party. He led them over to the shoulder. From there, Lum guided them back to the point where they had seen Brom come up onto the road. Roan studied the forest floor and the dusty waste around it. The young man was right.

"It shows all the earmarks of an artificial disturbance," Bergold agreed glumly. "We've been fooled."

"But we saw them!" Misha exclaimed. "Isn't that what they really look like?" he asked Roan, who nodded.

"It was an illusion. Maybe the Sleepers are dreaming about the disturbance, too, and it's echoing," Bergold said. "There might have been similar sightings all over the Dreamland. The disturbance is getting worse."

"Now we're back to square one," Misha said glumly, straddling his bike with his long legs on the ground. "We don't know what we've seen. We can't even believe our own eyes."

"What now, sir?" Lum asked.

"We go on," Roan said.

Chapter 22

The remainder of the passage across the desert wilderness had taken the apprentices all morning. The last yards of block had been laid, depositing them onto an expanse that was smooth and strong enough to sustain them all the way to the road, which she could see only a few hundred yards away. Brom sent the apprentices to ride ahead of the litter, using influence to smooth the sand and soft dirt into a path for the Alarm Clock, without ever getting off their motorbikes. Taboret was glad to say good riddance to the nebulosity, which had been falling apart and growing soft when changes were least welcome. She flung her last piece aside. It bounced several times and lay still. Let the nasty stuff go back to grass and pieces of statue, and rot!

Just as they were riding along the last yards parallel to the road, Taboret thought she spotted a woman through the trees who looked like the princess. Dressed in flowing white, Princess Leonora was surrounded by piles of junk and people waving their arms. By their expressions, Taboret could tell they were shouting, although she couldn't hear any voices or sound. She didn't look as if she was in danger, for which Taboret was thankful. But the princess would be able to see them when they broke cover. What would Brom do?

"Sir! Ahead of you!" Lurry shouted.

The narrow booth seemed to blossom from the forest floor. Brom saw it, and raised his hand. The lights reading "You-Pass" across the top turned from red to green, and the wooden arm lifted. They drove through the channel, litter and all.

A tall man that Taboret recognized as Roan ran after them, putting his fingers into the corners of his mouth. A bicycle broke free of the pack huddled by the left-hand booth and rolled to him, but a large man stepped in the way, preventing Roan from mounting. That was all Taboret had time to see before she was past and onto the pavement. The hard road under her tires was a blessing straight from the Sleepers.

She was relieved. At least the princess and the others were alive and well. They'd no need for another arrow to point the way from her. She glanced back again toward the tollbooth, to see if Roan had managed to get past the guards and the gate. The orange framework wasn't there. The road behind her lay empty for miles. Even the grove of trees was gone. She shook her head to clear it.

"What happened?" she shouted to the others.

"What in Nightmare's name was that?" Glinn asked. "Are they that close?"

"We're miles ahead of them," Mamovas called over the motorcycles' roar. She looked very pleased with herself. "That was the last trap. A double illusion with feedback capabilities. They could see us, but not touch us, even if they'd managed to get through. And we could see what they were doing. They should be stuck there a long time. They haven't got any money. I took it." She jingled a large purse and tucked it into her belt pouch. "That's part of the trap."

"You're a sneaky one," Carina said, admiringly.

"Artistic, too," Basil said. Taboret felt she couldn't help but agree with the others because of the link, but the private corner of her mind still harbored worries about what lay ahead.

"Hurry up!" Spar bellowed. "They've got to be up there somewhere."

"But they were never here, sir," Lum tried to explain, pedaling just behind his captain. "That was just an image. It could be imaginary—from the Sleepers."

"He put it there to taunt us," Spar said, dodging around two Holy Order sisters in an ancient carriage who were passing everyone else on the road. "Brom did. He was a sly boy, and he's become a nasty man. Wait until I bring him before the king."

"Captain, slow down!" Roan shouted. "Captain, even if they are ahead of us, we won't be able to keep up this pace for long. For the sake of the princess, hold!"

Spar glanced back. Leonora had fallen hundreds of yards behind them. Roan caught up to Spar and nodded at him until the senior guard braked.

"It's no use," Spar said, as the traffic whipped past them on both sides. "We're going to fail. They've got motors, and all we've got are foot-pedals. They're going to set off that infernal device, and there's not a damned thing we can do about it. Can we turn back, sir? Her Highness should be taken safely home before the end."

"Don't give up, Captain," Roan said, making his tone as positive as he could. We'll find help."

"Hooonnnk!"

A huge truck bore down on them from behind, honking and honking.

"Ignore it," Spar growled. "Let him go around us. It's another one of those traffic nuisances."

"No," Roan said, after one glance. "It's help. Pull over to the side!" Unlike all of the previous manifestations of highway traffic, this one vehicle looked real. The windshield was transparent, and through it Roan could see the driver's face. He swerved over to the right, turned in his seat and stood up on the pedals. With his fist clenched and thumb out, he flagged down the driver. The huge horn sounded again, sending the bicycles into fits and bucking, but the truck slowed down and rolled to a halt just ahead of them. The engine snorted deafeningly and fell silent. Roan pedaled up toward the driver's side door.

"Be careful!" Leonora cried. "It could crush you."

"It's all right!" Roan said.

"Goin' far?" the driver shouted down from the window.

"We've got to catch up with someone," Roan called up, "and it might be a long way."

"I'm goin' a long way," the man said, grinning to show gapped teeth. "Hop in. I like company."

"Thank you, sir!" Roan said. "We'd be most grateful for the ride."

The driver jerked a thumb back toward the rear of the truck. "Toss 'em up behind."

"Right you are!" Spar said, throwing a salute. "Guards!"

The captain ordered Lum and Hutchings to unfasten the

metal gate at the back of the flatbed. They whistled the bicycles into line and sent them up the extendible ramp, then slammed the gate firmly behind them.

The driver leaned over and clicked open the passenger door. Roan helped Leonora up the steps into the cabin, and scooted in beside her across the front seat toward the driver. To Roan's amazement, the upholstered bench expanded until it was wide enough to allow them all to sit side by side. The party clambered up one by one. Colenna, last in, yanked the door shut.

Swingy, whiny music came from grilles in both doors. It annoyed Roan at first, but once the driver turned on the engine, the music sounded pleasant, even homey over the baritone vibration.

"I'm Skorvald Nightcap," the driver said. He pulled back a heavy lever and put his foot down on one of the three sloped pedals on the floor.

"That's a good Dreamish name," Roan said, watching the operation with interest. "I'm Roan Faireven, Mr. Nightcap."

"Call me Skor," the driver shouted as the truck's transmission shrieked into gear. "Pleased to meet you."

"May I make you known to her Ephemeral Highness, Princess Leonora?" Roan said.

The driver looked at her with bright eyes in a nest of wrinkles. His weathered face creased a thousand more times and produced a smile as he touched the bill of his cap.

"Glad to make your acquaintance, Your Highness. Here," he reached over the wheel to a sheaf of folded papers on the dashboard shelf and handed her a map. "You navigate. I'd as soon take orders from you as anybody. We're on Route 2. Where do we want to go?"

Leonora unfolded the worn, battered pasteboards, and found the red line of the road that led over the bridge from Celestia. With her finger she followed it northward to an intersection with a green line, and glanced up at Roan with a tiny shrug. They peered down at the piece of paper together. The red line, which ran closely against the border of this province, was marked with tiny black dots indicating towns. A long blue line ran concurrently with the red line from the bridge, diverted widely to the east for a while, running through the desert, but rejoined it several miles south of the dot that marked the town of Reverie. Along the blue line were the words "They Went This Way."

Leonora looked up at Roan, lips parted in a smile and eyes sparkling.

"What is it?" Bergold asked. She handed him the map, and he let out a merry chuckle. Each of the others wanted to see, and grabbed the chart out of the hands of the last one holding it until it reached Colenna.

"This was fated," the older woman said, with a pleased nod. She leaned forward to twinkle down the line at Roan. Leonora held out her hand, and the map made its way back to her. "You were right, my boy. Well done for your perseverance."

"It may have been meant," Roan said, "but it doesn't mean we can take less care. This way, please, Skor. We're going toward Reverie."

"Right you are, laddie," Skorvald said. He slammed the shift lever forward.

Very deliberately, Leonora kept track of each turn of the road ahead with a finger placed on the blue line, nodding over landmarks as each appeared out of the broad windshield. The truck jostled and bumped along toward a Y-intersection.

"Turn right," Leonora said, seeing an arrow next to the right fork on her map. Skor obediently pushed up the signal lever on the steering wheel column, and the truck angled off in that direction. The princess shared a glance with Roan. If she hadn't told him to turn, he might not have gone the correct way.

They were in control of their destiny. No one was guiding them. Though the fate of the Dreamland rested on their shoulders, they still had to make the right decisions for themselves. The knowledge kept Roan silently thoughtful as the huge truck roared down the road.

"We're passing over the place where the blue line meets Route 2," Leonora said.

"Sir, the weirdness!" Lum exclaimed. And suddenly, they all felt it. Roan sensed it as a rubberiness in the air, similar to the waxy feel of his first encounter with the gestalt, but stronger than ever. He breathed out, an enormous sense of relief taking the place of the knot in his belly.

"There's a big black dot on the map just ahead," Leonora said, holding the chart up to Roan. "What is it? A town?"

Roan turned the ancient pasteboards over to find the legend. In a corner, the ink almost worn off, was a square showing a list of symbols and their meanings. Roan ran his finger down the list until he found a similar symbol, and flinched.

"Skor!" he cried. "It's a hole in reality!" He shoved the map at the driver, whose eyebrows rose into the bill of his cap.

"Oh, no!" the driver said, staring out the window. Suddenly, Roan saw it.

Ahead of them, a huge pit in the pavement yawned. Trees, houses, even birds were being dragged into the maelstrom at its center. Roan watched a full-sized lamppost disappear into it like a spaghetti noodle being slurped down into a subterranean maw.

Skor hit his brakes and veered off the side of the road to avoid it. The pull it exerted could be felt even through the sides of the truck.

Nearest the hole, the landscape was seemed to be divided into sections mounted on huge spools. It rolled down into the mass of chaos, leaving gaps of darkness where the scenery had been torn from its moorings below the sky. In between, Roan could see a few bright lights, shadowy figures, and skeins of wires and ropes.

Skor shoved his right foot hard down on the accelerator. The motor whined, but its roar gradually increased in volume until it had the power to break free.

"My, that's a big one," Bergold said, peering out the window as the landscape returned to normal. "It's affecting everything around it. Which nearly included us!"

"Lucky escape," Skor said, wiping his brow with a red-spotted handkerchief. "Lucky for me you're reading that map, Your Highness. That was a big one. I might'a gone right into that. Me and my rig are grateful to you."

They studied the map with care, but no other disasters were noted on it between that point and the next town.

The truck crested a high hill overlooking a large, neatly laid out town in a deep valley, and began to descend. According to the spot on the map where the princess's finger rested, this was Reverie. The blue line showing Brom's progress ran concurrently with the red route line all the way into town. The truck coasted downward until it came to a narrow stone bridge that led over a stream into the town, and came to a halt in a lay-by.

"This is as far as I go, lads and lasses, and Your Highness," Skorvald said, throwing the transmission into neutral with a flick of his wrist.

Leonora leaned up to hand back his map, and kissed his wrinkled cheek.

"I can't tell you how grateful we are for your help," she said. "Thank you so much."

He blushed redder than he'd been baked by the sun, and pulled the bill of his cap down over his face.

"Thank you very kindly, ma'am. It was a pleasure. We've helped each other. Hope you find what you're looking for."

Roan led Cruiser over the bridge into town, looking carefully for clues of Brom's passage. The smooth, hard-paved roads showed no tire prints, so they had to depend upon Lum's instinct for spotting the "weirdness." Odd little distortions, like postboxes with claw feet and pigeons feeding people, proved to them that they were on the trail. Bergold produced Romney's useful map, and opened it up to show the town's layout. They stopped beside a wrought-iron fence and unfolded the chart several times to see the street grid more clearly.

"Seems to head right along this street, and then into the heart of the city," Bergold said, pointing at the main road. He ran his finger down the line of the road past where they were standing and into the town square. Nearby, church bells rang the noon hour, and the church's image on the map quivered in sympathy with the bell tower they saw on the next corner. "Unfortunately, there it peters out. Where shall we try first?"

"This is a big place," Leonora said, scanning the street layout. "Brom could be anywhere."

"Are you sure he did come in?" Felan asked, peering at the map over Bergold's shoulder. "You'd think he'd avoid well-populated areas because he'd be afraid of being stopped. The king will have telegraphed every city and town in the land."

"They'll need supplies," Roan said.

"Then, they will want to leave without being noticed," Colenna said. "That won't be so easy."

Misha shook his head. "In a city this size, travelers come and go all the time."

"That big a group and that thing they're carrying will be hard to forget," Felan said. "And, there's the distortion it causes."

"Easier to hide in a town than in the countryside," Misha argued.

"I won't forget those daisies," Leonora said, with a shudder.

"It's a matter of distance," Bergold said, reasonably, closing the map down to show a larger scale of the area. He pointed out several routes with his fingernail. "If he does pass through Reverie instead of skirting it, he'll cut down his travel time. We'd have to go all around the perimeter and hope we find his trail. In town, his exits are finite. We stand a better chance of finding him."

"All we can do is ask," Roan said. "We can always backtrack if we are wrong."

They asked a woman wheeling a baby carriage, but she shook her head no, and kept walking without looking up. The baby shrugged and offered Roan a look of sympathy. The party reached the end of the street near the church without finding anyone who had seen Brom, the litter or a gang of motorcycles.

"Perhaps we should find out where the marketplace is," Colenna said. "If they're buying supplies, it's the most logical place to try."

"We're on the way to it," Bergold said, struggling with the map. Hutchings took it out of his hands and folded it to the correct plate. He handed it back, trying not to look triumphant. "Thank you. That's better. You can only go one way on this street. Do you see? There are no other outlets. Straight up this street, and first right."

"We should get valuable leads there," Spar said.

"And we can get some supplies for ourselves," Colenna said. Felan looked daggers at her. They fell short, clattering to the ground. Bergold stopped suddenly and put out his arms to halt the others.

"Uh-oh," the senior historian said, despair in his voice. "We're in trouble now."

"Do you see Brom?" Roan asked, squinting into the crowd.

"No, it's worse," Bergold said. "Look. It's a bookstore. A big one."

"Oh, no!"

Roan stared up at the brightly colored sign hanging over the sidewalk only twenty yards ahead. A bookstore! It was the biggest hazard of any town. What could they do? The route they needed to take to the market led directly past it. He made as if to turn the party back and lead them on a more circuitous route, when the expandable aura of pleasure and joyful anticipation the bookstore exuded engulfed him. The smell of coffee wafted past his nose. He rotated on his heel, facing the bright sign again, his mind clouding.

How nice it would be, he thought, just to browse for a while, perhaps sit and drink a cup of coffee and read . . . No! What was he thinking? He was on an important mission! He had to save the Dreamland! Perhaps there were how-to books on heroism in the sociology section. . . .

The others were falling under the spell, too. The pupils of Leonora's green eyes spread across the irises as she stared at the sign. Bergold was shifting his shoulder bag as if to judge whether there'd be some room in it for a volume or two. They all moved a step closer, and had the opposite foot raised to take the next step. Roan tugged them back, and the spell broke momentarily.

"This must be a very good store," Leonora said, clasping her hands around Roan's upper arm. "I can feel the urge from here. Hold on to me or I'll fall in."

"So will I," Bergold said. "We've got to help one another."

The urge to go inside was overwhelmingly powerful. The siren call of the books was such a loud howling in his ears that Roan put his hands up to stop them. Leonora put her head down against his shoulder, her eyes screwed shut. If they fell into the bookstore, they'd be trapped for hours, pulled along by sheer curiosity to scan every title, or draw an especially tempting book off a shelf and read, lulled by a hypnotic, lazy atmosphere to forget about the cares of the outside world. Their cause would be lost.

Roan felt himself inching forward again, his feet moving of their own volition on the pavement. Stop! he thought at them. Stop! They could not afford to lose the day. Brom was near, Roan could sense it. The Dreamland, he had to think of the Dreamland, and the threat of the Alarm Clock! But no, his feet refused to pass, started to turn in towards the doorway.

"We'll all join arms," Roan said, taking Colenna's elbow. She attached herself to Spar. Bergold took Leonora's other arm, and Misha held on to him. "We'll run across quickly. That way, we won't get sucked inside."

"Hold tight," Lum said, as the other guards linked arms. "Ready?"

"Ready!" Bergold said. They were within inches of the glass-and-green-paneled doors. The pull was so strong. "One, two, three, *go!*"

Roan launched himself forward. As the group hurled themselves past the doorway, they caught the full brunt of the attraction.

Succumb, the wordless song said. You know you want to. Everything else can wait. The smell of coffee tantalized, cushions beckoned, the bright colors danced, book blurbs whispered in their ears. Roan nearly hesitated in mid-dash. He could feel the others faltering.

"Help," Colenna moaned.

"Right, then," Spar said, stoutly. As usual, the guard captain seemed unaffected by the unseen forces that paralyzed everyone else. Spar marched firmly to the other side of the bookstore entrance, pulling his end of the line of people with him. He set his heels against a paving stone, and heaved. The others came flying toward him like corks out of a bottle. Roan stumbled to a halt, trying to cushion Leonora from running into the wall. He panted with the exertion, a bead of sweat running down into his eyes. Felan stood, gasping.

"There, now, you're safe," Spar said, putting an arm around Colenna. "Are you all right? My lady?"

Colenna leaned on his arm with a wordless smile, and Leonora nodded.

"My gratitude, Captain," Roan said. His throat felt dry from the cappuccino fumes.

"All part of the job," Spar said. He tucked Colenna's hand into his elbow, and marched forward, his spine proudly erect.

It was only a little easier to walk away from the entrance than it had been to resist walking toward it. All around them on the street were dozens of others without the captain's iron self-control. Roan feared for them. Some were clinging to lampposts, fire hydrants, and each other, in an attempt to resist. A woman, innocently walking a poodle on the other side of the street, was swept up by the seductive force and carried helplessly inside, the dog yelping behind her.

"It could have been us," Felan said, sadly, watching her sail past.

"Come on," Roan said, striding onward. "We shouldn't tarry. It could pull us back."

The outside wall of the bookstore was full of small glass display windows. In the case just ahead of him, Roan noticed a title out of the corner of his eye, and turned his head to see. "The Book of Love," the gaudy cover read. A good omen, Roan thought, squeezing the princess's hand in the crook of his arm. He continued to step purposefully forward, then had a sudden and irresistible urge to see the author's name. He stopped in front of the window. The title was perfectly clear, but the bottom of the book was fuzzy, as if someone had smeared soap across it. He started put his hand through the glass of the window to open the cover and read the title page, when a cry startled him, and the glass turned invincibly solid. He snatched back his hand.

"Come on," Bergold called. "The bookshop's just eaten another pedestrian!"

"Don't go back," Leonora pleaded, holding on to him.

Now I'll never know, he thought.

Chapter 23

"No, haven't seen any strangers but you," said a man on the street corner. The light changed, and the box on the opposite corner said DON'T WALK, so he ran across, and every car, carriage, and bicycle missed him, clearing the crosswalk just as he reached them.

"No one like that," said a flower woman, offering them each a daisy. Roan accepted his and handed it to Leonora. Spar looked sharply at the flower seller, and back at each of his guards to make sure they wouldn't do anything so nonmilitary as taking a flower from an unvetted civilian. The woman gave them a beautiful smile anyhow.

"Oh, yes, I saw them," said a seller of bread, changing a French loaf into breadsticks for a woman customer. "They asked me where to find a bicycle repair shop. I told them to go that way." He pointed a breadstick toward a street leading west.

"Thank you," Roan said, shooting an eager glance at his companions. The baker nodded and handed his customer a handful of breadcrumbs change.

"The weirdness, sir. It's fresh," said Lum, in great excitement. He indicated light-colored bricks full of holes in the wall at the opening of an alley. Roan examined them, and took a sniff. Yes, they were made of fresh Swiss cheese.

"The crucible must have passed by very recently," Bergold said, looking about, "since no one has yet noticed the damage and repaired it."

"Very recently," Roan exclaimed. He had caught movement out of the corner of his eye and turned to look at it. He pointed down the alley. "There!"

Several hundred yards ahead, but still unmistakable was

the humped silhouette he had been seeing in his nightmares: the Alarm Clock on its litter.

"Right! After them!" Spar said, drawing his sword. He whistled for the bicycles. "You ride straight that way, sir. Alette, with me to the left. Lum, you take Hutchings around the right. We split up, and we'll have 'em. Go!"

They swung into the saddle, and started pedaling. Roan, Misha, and Bergold were right behind them, pumping for all they were worth. Brom would not escape them this time.

"Hey, wait for me!" Felan shouted.

"We'll stay here!" Colenna called after them.

The guards peeled off in opposite directions at the first corner, leaving the four men riding along the narrow lane after the bobbing shape of the litter. Roan felt a moment of dread, remembering the last time he had faced the power of the gestalt. Did even eight brave souls have the strength to defeat Brom?

Reverie was a different proposition than Hark. The people who lived here had more influence, and therefore more command over their surroundings. Roan passed through sections of quiet where his tires and even his breathing made no noise on the brick street. Those passages were brief, however, and Roan feared that the noise they made would alert Brom that he was being followed. He kept the dread shape in sight. They would catch Brom now.

They came closer and closer to the litter. The lane opened up into a street, and Roan could see the group ahead of him more clearly. He counted between eight and a dozen people, all on motorcycles. Roan had seen motorcycles before, but never so many of them in one place at one time. The gestalt, again, altering the Dreamland's reality by concentrating too many modern things in one place. In a moment, dinosaurs would start walking the quiet streets of this town, to try and rebalance the proportions of nature. They must stop Brom and break the Alarm Clock up.

The silhouette of the litter veered to the right into a wide square full of neatly clipped grass and large buildings. Women in short uniforms and men in high-collared white tunics pushed invalids to and fro in Bath chairs. A sign on the side of the street advised, QUIET, HOSPITAL ZONE. The loud motors and wide tires disrupted the very air as Brom passed, shaking reality until some of the nurses were in the wheelchairs, and the patients, clad in short hospital gowns, were pushing them. Flowers were plowed up from the gardens in the square and flew in all directions.

By the time Roan and the others came through, the silence had reasserted itself aggressively. Even though the air was still filled with flying blossoms and dirt Roan thought had never been anywhere so quiet. Every sound they made was exaggerated. Their breathing was the rasping of saws on wood. Roan could swear he heard Bergold blink. When Misha raised a hand to bat away an airborne rose, it sounded like he'd hit a fly ball out of a park full of sports fans. The whine of their narrow racing tires roared as loudly as Skor's truck engine. Roan willed the air onto the outside of his tires so as to make them run silently, and gestured to the others to do the same.

Ahead of them, only three blocks ahead, the litter bearers rolled to a halt. The gaunt figure that was Brom stood up on his pedals to look both ways along the intersection.

Roan felt a thrill of anticipation. Riding on air, he knew he could catch them by surprise. He dodged a bunch of flying daisies. Where were Spar and the guards? Were they near enough to prevent the Alarm Clock from escaping? Two blocks. One block. Roan readied himself to jump off Cruiser's back onto Brom's motorbike. Catch the ringleader, and the others would be easily subdued. Could he get close enough to spring? Half a block. Six houses.

Only yards away from their quarry, Felan reached over and tapped Roan on the shoulder.

"I'm going to sneeze," he whispered, holding his nose.

"Don't!" Roan whispered back urgently. "Not a sound!"

"I can't help it," Felan hissed. "I'm allergic to flowers. I know I'm going to. I . . . uh . . . I . . ."

"Get out of this street," Roan said, looking for an alley or a doorway to push the man into, but there was nowhere to go where he couldn't be seen or heard. Felan's face wrinkled up, his nose twitched, and his mouth opened. "Don't do it!"

"Too la—" Felan sputtered. "*HACHOO!*"

The sneeze sounded like an explosion, even drowning out

the idling motorcycles. In unison, all of Brom's minions turned their heads to see what was behind them.

"That's done it," Roan said, abandoning stealth. No time to wait for the guards. "Charge!"

He and the others pumped their pedals to catch up with the bearers. Before Roan crossed the twenty yards separating them, a flash of white light flared, blinding them. He threw up his arm across his eyes. Cruiser squeaked alarm. When his eyes recovered, there was no one on the street but them. Roan pedaled to the intersection, but it was hopeless. The Alarm Clock was gone.

"Did you see them?" Glinn said, urging his steed up beside Brom's. Taboret was close enough behind him to see the glow in Brom's eyes turn to red flame.

"Yes, I saw them," Brom said, the calm in his voice belying the terrifying change in his eyes. "They are stalking us. The game has become more interesting now that they have caught up. We will have to take measures of our own. Follow me."

"Not a sign, sir," Alette said, coasting to a stop beside Roan in the foreyard of the big bicycle shop. She took off her uniform beret and ran a hand through her short red hair. "They're nowhere to be seen. We checked every turning between here and the edge of the city."

"They've vanished into air," Bergold said. "Not an unheard of phenomenon in this world."

"But temporary," Leonora said. "Otherwise they'd just have blinked themselves to the Hall of the Sleepers days ago, without bicycles."

"Should we stake out this place?" Spar asked, peering at the workshop. "They need a repair shop, and this is the best in the city." The yard was filled with steeds in every state and stage of disrepair or discombobulation. The mechanics, clad in dirty coveralls, regarded the party with uneasy glances, but kept on about their work, caring for skittish horses, hammering out bicycle frames, recaning balloon baskets. "There's plenty of places we could hide."

"No," said Roan, thinking hard. "Now that Brom knows we've spotted them, he won't come back this way. They'll find another shop. We'll have to blanket the city with observers, and hope we can catch them before they leave town."

"We don't have enough to make a pillowcase, let alone a blanket," Felan said, flippantly, although he still looked sheepish at having given them away with his sneeze. "Just where do you plan to get more observers?"

Roan pointed down the street at a familiar blue light. "The police," he said. "We'll ask for their help."

The large parking lot beside the building was full of official vehicles including blue bicycles, mopeds, one tall, boxlike car with a rack of lights on top, and horse-drawn carriages whose engine sections were munching on bags of oats. The party's bicycles crowded together at one end of the yard, as if the police vehicles made them nervous.

Roan led the way up the wide stone stairs. As he approached the glass doors, they opened out towards him, releasing waves of soft music and a sweet, flowery scent.

"Welcome," said a beaming policeman. He had bright pink cheeks and a jolly, round face crested with light brown hair that curled on his forehead. His uniform was a soft blue, and the double line of brass buttons were brightly polished enough for Roan to see his reflection. "Welcome to you all." He looked at the others over Roan's shoulder. "Welcome!"

"Thank you," Roan said. "We would like to see whoever is in charge."

"Well, of course," the policeman said, and called back over his shoulder, "Sergeant! These lovely people would like to see the super."

He pointed them toward a high desk and an equally rosy-faced man with the diamond insignia on his sleeve.

"I'll be happy to tell him you're here," the sergeant said pleasantly, lifting a black telephone receiver larger than his head. "What name shall I give?"

"Please tell him it's the King's Investigator and party."

"Of course. Just make yourselves at home."

The sergeant gestured them to chairs and spoke quietly into the mouthpiece.

The station was trim and spotless. The waiting room had been painted pale orange, and seemed light and airy. Soft music with a bouncy, gentle beat played over the public address system. It was all very relaxing. No one spoke above a murmur, not even the two masked men whose statements were being taken at small desks behind a glass partition. Roan and Leonora did not speak aloud to one another, but telegraphed messages to one another with their eyebrows.

"How odd this seems," Leonora's said.

"This isn't like any police station I've seen," Roan sent back.

"Do you think we'll have long to wait?" Bergold's eyebrows inquired.

"I hope not," Roan's replied.

"Sir?" The desk sergeant smiled at them. "I hate to interrupt a private conversation. I was delighted to tell the superintendent that you wanted to speak to him. He'll just be a moment. It won't bother you to wait, will it?"

Captain Spar gave him a sharp look, thinking the remark was sarcasm, but the officer's face remained friendly and open.

"Not too long, I hope."

"Not at all. There's coffee," the sergeant said, helpfully. "And doughnuts. Plenty of doughnuts in the squad room." He pointed to an open door to his left.

And so there were. The party helped themselves hungrily to the piles of still-warm rings and cups of very good coffee in a pink-painted room filled with easy chairs and footstools. Roan poured himself a large cup, thinking longingly of the bookstore and its coffee bar.

"Gosh, sir," Lum whispered, clutching half a dozen doughnuts and a steaming mug in his big hands. "Much better than our mess, huh?"

"Don't be too quick to praise 'em," Spar said, surveying the trays suspiciously. "Probably turn out tasting like book-paste and talcum powder, like that stuff in Hark."

But the pastries tasted as good as they smelled, and appeared to be in endless supply. When a platter was emptied, rosy-faced officers swept it away and brought another back full. After a snack of hot crullers and cappuccino, Leonora and Roan browsed through the break room, looking at the wanted posters pinned along the walls. According to the name in the bottom right corner of each, this seemed to be a series of aliases all of one man whose name was "Peter Max." The very stylized images had been drawn with heavy black outlines and deep, solid, unshaded colors. Behind each portrait, the background was filled with stars and rainbows and daisies.

"I think I'd recognize him," the princess said, examining one picture critically, "but I'm not sure. Strange style, isn't it? Not photographic at all. More impressionistic."

"Impressions are important in our business," the sergeant said, cheerfully, coming up behind them. "The super will see you now."

"Ah," Roan said, turning and offering an elbow to Leonora. "That would be super."

The friendly officer escorted them down a corridor painted with bright-colored daisies the size of Roan's outstretched hand. The effect was bewilderingly hypnotic. The faster he walked, the more the design put Roan in a state of near stupor.

"Easy, easy," the officer cautioned him, grabbing his arm to steady him. "Feeling the rush, are you? There's no hurry." He stopped before a door and tapped on it. Roan shook his head to clear it just in time for the introductions.

"It's so nice to meet all of you," the chief of the Reverie police said, as the sergeant showed them to chairs. "Please make yourselves at home. Now, how may I be of service?"

He waited courteously while the princess sank gracefully onto a cushion, and waited for her nod before seating himself in an overstuffed chair. Its tie-dyed upholstery against the flowered wallpaper was almost dazzling. Roan opened his mouth to speak.

"First," the superintendent said, interrupting Roan, "do let me say how thrilled I am that you are gracing our city, Your Highness. You are everyone's wanted poster of choice, if you will forgive a little professional joke."

"Gladly," Leonora said, patiently. But she tidied up her flowing white dress a little, giving the cloth a satinlike luster. "May we tell you our concerns?"

"That's what we are here for, to serve and protect and to be good listeners," the super said, leaning back comfortably in his chair. "Go ahead, ma'am."

"Here is our difficulty," Roan began again.

"I hope you have had a chance to see our beautiful city," the super said, sitting upright suddenly, as if a thought had struck him from behind.

"Not very much," Roan said. "Please!" He held up a hand to forestall another outburst by the police chief, who settled back in his chair with a disappointed expression. "Have you been notified by the Crown about a renegade band of scientists carrying a dangerous device across the Dreamland?"

"Why, we may have been," the super said. "Officer Toodle? Do go and see if we've had anything of that sort."

"Certainly, sir," the blond officer said, with a languid salute, and departed, in no hurry.

"Whose vision of the police is this?" Spar asked in a furious undertone to the others. "It's a joke!"

"There are pockets like this all through the Dreamland," Bergold explained in a quiet voice. "You can tell by the decor. Particularly the daisies on the wall, and the posters. It's a particular vision of a particular group of Sleepers. We've noticed that it appears to be characterized by a relaxed disposition among the inhabitants, and very often affects law enforcement or other officials."

"Well, I don't like it," Spar said firmly, looking with disapproval upon the flowered wallpaper and the rest of the oversized decor. "It's prissy."

"Super, here it is," the officer said, returning with a piece of neon-pink paper. "We had it on the 'To Be Read' pile. Awfully close to the top."

"Ah, good, right where it belonged." The superintendent put on a pair of gold-rimmed half-glasses and read through the notice.

"Uh hum. Uh hum. Uh hum. I see. I have all the details now." He put down the sheet of paper, and leaned toward them over his tented fingers. "What is it that you want me to do?"

"We want you to arrest Brom," Roan said. "He's here in the city now with the device. We saw him only a few minutes ago. He can't leave immediately. We have information that he is looking for a repair facility. That should give us enough time to raise the hue and cry. Arrest him and impound the Alarm Clock."

"That would be uncool," said the super. A frown creased his forehead, and then it relaxed again into a paternal smile. "Hue and cry? How very old-fashioned. Our job is to help troubled people so that they don't feel they must disrupt society. We can't just throw a cordon around the whole city and rope him in like a felon. What will that do to his self-esteem? You see, Mr. Roan, the way I see it our job is to help restore the self-esteem of the alleged felons with whom we come in contact. We are less concerned about the events that bring them into our little sphere and more about their mental state. We want to help those who commit crimes to understand that they are *loved*, and that they are *okay*. If we interfere in their behavior, it might forever scar them. We can't have that."

"But Brom seems very well-adjusted," Roan said. "We are not concerned with his self-esteem. It is his intentions that are malign."

"Well, then, you see, you don't need us at all," the super said, turning up his hands and smiling. "The problem is solved."

"Enough of this," Roan said, impatiently, slapping his hands on his thighs, to the evident disapproval of the superintendent. "We are losing valuable time. Captain Spar, I believe this is your department."

"Right," Spar said, standing up beside him. He squared up his shoulders and straightened his belt as he leaned over the desk toward the super, who flinched back into his puffy chair.

"Listen here, super. I am Captain Spar of the palace guard. Are you a loyal subject?"

"Of course I am," the super said patiently, drumming his fingertips together. "I am proud to be an imaginary denizen of the Dreamland."

"Well, then, listen here, friend," Spar said, with his finger within inches of the superintendent's nose. "When you treat an emergency like a chance to redeem wrongdoers you are not doing your job properly. You're the enforcement arm of the law." The finger stabbed down on the neon-colored paper again and again to punctuate his words. The super sat with his mouth hanging open. "You aren't here to make judgments about a perpetrator. And that's what you're doing. Your job is to catch him and let the courts decide what to do. Right?"

"Well, I suppose . . ."

"Right, or not right?" Spar demanded. "Make your decision!

Tell me!" He pounded his fist on the pink paper, which faded with every bang until it was plain white.

Spar's words, too, seemed to have an effect on the room itself. He may not have had much control of influence, but he knew how to command. The cheery orange paint faded to a dingy industrial yellow. The daisies vanished off the wallpaper, leaving it a plain, narrow stripe. Overhead, the speaker pouring out honeyed music started emitting short declarative sentences muffled by static. The room looked ready for business.

"By the Seven, you are right," the super said. He had changed, becoming less jovial-looking, and Roan was relieved to note, more competent. Although the buttons remained shiny, the police uniforms darkened to blue-black and acquired a businesslike cut. The superintendent picked up the document, read through it again, and gestured sharply for his assistant. The sergeant noted his superior's alterations, and though he remained apple-cheeked, his eyes hardened.

Still, he took a moment to wink at the princess.

"All right," the superintendent said, "then we'll arrest them. I'll need full descriptions." He picked up a pencil and a black notebook. The sergeant took an identical notepad out of his pocket, and waited, poised.

"There are between ten and fifteen of them," Roan said, watching them write down the numbers *10* and *15*. "Brom is of above average height. When I saw him closely, he was very thin, almost gaunt, with deep-set, hooded blue eyes with an expression I would almost describe is insane."

"Ah, insane," the super said, gesturing to his officer, who made an emphatic note. "Presumed dangerous. And how long ago was that? And where?"

"Four days ago, some fifteen miles north of the Nightmare Forest. We spotted them again here in Reverie and gave chase, but we never got close enough to get a good look before they disappeared."

"Any distinguishing marks?"

"Pocket protectors. They all wear them," Roan said. "Except for their two hired musclemen."

"Hmmph! Definite sign of psychosis," the superintendent said.

Roan gave quick descriptions of the others that he could remember, plus details of the litter containing the Alarm Clock. He mentioned the tread patterns of the bicycles they had been following, and Corporal Lum came forward to identify the specific patterns in a mug book. The genial officer jotted down the details.

"Right, then," the super said. The policeman snapped the notebook shut and buttoned it into his breast pocket. "We'll run all this through our computer and see how many changes he's likely to have made since then. This Brom's insanity will have lasted. That's a fact."

"Watch yourself, super," Roan said. "They are exceptionally tricky."

"They can't get around us," the superintendent said, curling his lip in scorn. "This is our turf. You leave it to us."

"That's more like it," Spar said. He saluted the police chief. "Pleasure to do business with you."

Chapter 24

The sound of sirens receding in the distance echoed in the street as they followed the superintendent down the steps into the parking lot. Roan whistled the bicycles over as the super himself issued orders to the remaining officers.

"Now, you lot spread out. Keep in touch at all times with control," he said. "Since they're the only ones who know what the 'distortion' is that this perpetrator causes, Captain Spar will lead his own contingent on a shrinking spiral around the main shopping district and point it out to the teams of officers patrolling each area. Murgatroyd, you go with him."

"Right, super," said a tough-looking officer sitting astride a battered blue steed.

"All right, on your bikes," the chief said. He climbed into the cab of the tall vehicle, which started up with a sputter. Men and women officers jumped onto the outside, and clung to it as it careened down the street, sirens blaring and lights rotating. Officers shot away in all directions.

"Now, officer," Spar said, climbing onto his own beast's saddle. "Show us the second-best repair shop in town."

"They've been here already," Lum said, disappointedly, braking to a halt.

Murgatroyd steered around a paving block made of red foam rubber, and came to a halt at the curb. He raised his radio to his ear.

"Found traces of distortion, but no sign of the suspects, sir," the policeman said into the mouthpiece. "We will continue to follow clues. Murgatroyd out."

He flipped a switch on the side of the black box. A hatch

on the top opened, and a little bird flew out. It circled once, then headed in the direction of the station house.

Roan listened hard. In a quiet residential area they should be able to hear the motorcycle engines. Yes, he heard a strange rumbling off to the left.

"Let's try this way," Roan said, pushing off in the direction of the sound.

He let Murgatroyd guide them through the twisting maze of streets, past houses and schools. Through the iron fences that surrounded a rainy park in one residential square, Roan spotted a handful of the apprentices making a left into an avenue lined with high hedges. He signed to the others, and they started pedaling harder in pursuit. Through turn after turn, they managed to keep the blue-and-white-clad riders in sight. The apprentices wheeled sharp right around a corner. Their pursuers fixed their eyes on the intersection and bore down upon it.

"That's a cul-de-sac," Murgatroyd said. "Or it was during patrol last night. We've got 'em!"

But when the cyclists followed, there was no one there but a man mowing his lawn with a goat held up by its back legs.

"Did they duck out past us?" Misha asked, looking around, bewildered. "They could have turned invisible."

"Another illusion?" asked Felan sourly.

"No, look," Roan said, pointing between two yards at three helmeted heads moving away. The cyclists had drawn themselves inward and upward until they were gigantic figures only two inches wide.

"Guards, with me!" Spar said. He shot around the corner of the cul-de-sac, his crew in formation behind him. In a few moments, he returned, shaking his head. The officers trailed dejectedly. "Gone."

"We're making no progress, and time is running short," Roan said. "Let's split up into pairs to continue the search. If any of us spot them, one of you keep following them wherever they go, and the other will report to the police station for reinforcements. Remember, we want Brom and the Alarm Clock most of all."

"Surround them, and conquer," Murgatroyd said, striking his palm with his fist. "We'll do it."

"Good," Roan said. He and Leonora elected to go with the policeman. Spar went with Colenna, Misha paired up with Felan, Lum with Bergold, and the two guards together. They moved out.

Roan and Leonora rode in silence, surveying both sides of the street for traces. Several times, they thought that they saw one or more of the apprentices disappearing into a cross street. They gave chase, but by the time they reached the same intersection, there would be no sign of the quarry.

"We simply are not having any luck," Leonora said, coasting to a halt after an hour of fruitless searching. "Maybe the others are." Murgatroyd listened to his radio.

"No, ma'am."

"We must keep looking," Roan said. "Wait a moment." The trees along the street were normal on the sidewalk side, but twisted and unhealthy looking on the street side. Some of the apples had not even stopped bouncing on the ground. They had turned to wood. Roan and Leonora exchanged triumphant glances.

"They must just have come this way," he said. "If we see them, I want you to ride straight for the police station. Don't hesitate. I don't want them to have an opportunity to use their force on you."

"Don't worry," Leonora said. "I'll *run* away if we come upon them."

"Sir!" Lum and Bergold came riding out through a passage between two buildings. The historian waved to them.

"We followed a pair of them coming this way," Bergold shouted.

"I know," Roan called back. "Look at the trees!"

"Do you see them?"

Lum stood up on his pedals and sighted down the street. He gestured excitedly. "There, sir! There they go!"

Roan spotted the Alarm Clock just as its riders slipped into an alley ahead of them. He pulled hard against Cruiser's handlebars, forcing the unwilling steed after it. The others came half a length behind him. Faster and faster Roan pedaled, until his legs felt as if they were part of his steed. Faster! The man riding at the rear of the litter turned to look behind, and his mouth dropped open. He shouted something to his companion, and the two motorcycles picked up speed.

In the narrow passage, Roan flew past doorways and ladders and trash receptacles, past slumped bodies and heaps of bricks, firewood and excrement, cats and dogs, bounced over stones and potholes. He saw light ahead. He must stop the Clock. If that infernal device reached the street too far ahead of him, its bearers would open throttle, and he would never catch them. Faster! His leg muscles felt as if they were burning. He had left the others far behind.

The litter emerged from the alley. Sunlight painted the back of the man behind with white. Roan followed the gleaming figure. He drew closer, almost close enough to grab him. Suddenly, the litter rolled to a halt. Roan slid to a stop, almost sliding into the rear cyclist. He jumped off his bike, and ran to pull the man off his steed. Then, before he could lay hands on the man, from underneath the canvas came a terrifying sound. The deep vibration almost shook him off his feet. Roan clapped his hands to his ears.

The soft, inexorable sound died away. He was so disoriented by the noise that it was a moment before he realized he was surrounded by flashing blue lights and uniformed officers, and a huge mob of civilians. He spotted the chief of police in the forefront of the crowd. Beside him was Brom. How strange, Roan thought. Brom looked exactly the same as he had the first time they had met in the desert outside of Mnemosyne. For some reason he was using the gestalt to remain in one form. Almost, Roan thought with a shock, like him.

Around their superior, the young men and women in blue and white huddled together, fingering their pocket protectors nervously. The two big men who had attacked Roan in the desert looked defiant.

"You've got him!" Roan said, exultantly. "Congratulations, superintendent. It looks as though you have captured the entire gang! That is the device I told you about. You must report to the Crown at once. You have stopped a terrible calamity from occurring. Well done!"

Brom raised a hand.

"Arrest him, superintendent," he said, magnificently. Instead of his gaunt traveling form, he had reasserted his court portliness. The long blue robe seemed a little travelworn, but the police and the people did not seem to notice. "I am fed up with his harassment of me and my staff. We have undertaken a difficult and secret experiment for His Majesty the king, and all that this man, this unchanging freak, has done has been to follow me, hounding me." He waggled a finger. Roan suddenly noticed that the rest of his party was present, too, surrounded by officers. "And them, too. They are accomplices!"

"What?" Roan could not believe what he was hearing, nor the expression on the chief's face. Two police officers stepped forward and clapped heavy irons onto his wrists. He pulled away, and they grabbed his arms, holding him in place. Brom continued to speak, letting the words roll with ponderous mellifluence off his tongue.

"You are all witnesses to one of the greatest malfeasances ever committed in the Dreamland!" The hooded eyes flashed red fire. "This evil man has corrupted the heir to the throne, the regal princess Leonora. Look!"

He held up his hands to frame the image of Leonora, dismounting from Golden Schwinn as gracefully as she could in the flowing white dress. Roan sensed that Brom used a wave of influence. Suddenly, the gown with which Leonora had taken so much trouble fell shapeless. There was no doubt at all that she was swathed in the folds of a tent, and one that was much too large for her. She grabbed at the yards of cloth as they fell about her, and pinned them hastily in place with splinters of influence.

Brom boomed on. "You see her before you, dressed in mean rags as if she was the merest commoner. A beggar. How *disgraceful* it is. I am ashamed to behold her in this sorry condition. It *disgraces* her. It *disgraces* us all."

The crowd took up the chant. "Disgraceful! Disgraceful!" Leonora turned scarlet with shame and anger. A couple of women came forward with armloads of clothing, which they pressed into the princess's arms. She dropped them and pushed the women aside, trying to get to Roan. The police, openly reluctant, blocked her way.

Brom raised his voice. "Aid your sovereign! Help restore his daughter to him! Look how even now he enchants her so that she is more concerned about him than her own modesty!"

"But I have come with Roan willingly," Leonora said, angrily. The lengths of tent material flowed into an ankle-length toga of classic design, and she added a diadem of gold leaves in her hair. The crowd murmured in awe. "No one forced me to come."

"That's worse," Brom said, shaking his head. He raised his voice. "He has deluded her. Of course it is unlawful for him to take her anywhere. Do you see a chaperone?"

"I'm with her," Colenna said stoutly.

"An official chaperone!" Brom said, dismissively. "This creature can't be, because this is not an official journey!"

"Why, you old goat!" Colenna began, dangerously.

"Jail them! Jail them!" the crowd shouted.

"Stop!" Roan called, holding out his arms as far as the chain links would let him. "It isn't like that at all. The princess is in no danger. He is misleading you! He is the wrongdoer, not us! Super, you have the bulletin from the palace about the Alarm Clock. Do your duty!"

The chief of police looked blank, then mulish. "We also had a document telling us to be on the lookout for Her Highness. I should have acted when you were in the office. I thought then she sounded like she was in her right mind, but this gentleman has convinced me otherwise. I'm making up for my mistake now. Roan Faireven, I arrest you in the name of the king for the unlawful detention of a royal personage."

Roan tried to shout over the angry crowd. "Sir, you've fallen under the influence of this evil man! He wields an enormous power, called the crucible. The device on that platform is capable of destroying the entire Dreamland."

"One matter at a time," the super said, his face set. "If it's true that Her Highness was removed unlawfully from the palace, it is our first duty to see to it that she is returned safely."

"Curse you, Brom," Roan said. They'd caught up with him, and the man had jumped two steps ahead of them again! He sprang for the chief scientist, and was pulled back by the shouting mob. The police officers had to yank him free. They formed a cordon around him. Roan could not believe the hate and anger on the faces of the people in the crowd. Brom looked at him with bland disappointment.

"And listen to that bad language," Brom said, raising his voice above the uproar. "Is that any kind of escort proper to the Royal Personage?"

"No! No!" the crowd howled. Brom swept Leonora a deep bow.

"Your Highness, I apologize to you that you should have had to hear such profanity."

Leonora looked baffled, and then angry. "How dare you behave as if nothing is wrong. You're the reason we're here in the first place!"

"He must have hypnotized the delicate lady," Brom said, to the crowd around him. "Madam, your father has been frantic, and your mother has taken to her bed."

"That doesn't mean anything," Leonora said, impatiently. "Mother takes to her bed at the drop of an eyelash. Father knows where I am. We've been sending him regular updates. Haven't we, Felan?"

"We certainly have," Felan insisted.

"I must stay with my friends," the princess said. "We are saving the world from *you*."

"Oh, Your Highness, how he has brainwashed you!" Brom leaned in, his lids drooping heavily over his burning eyes. Roan wasn't fooled, and he could see Leonora was terrified. "Don't you know me, Your Highness? I am Brom, assistant to Carodil, Minister of Science? Your *friend*. It was lucky I am here on an important experiment, otherwise this miscreant," he straightened up so that the crowd could hear him, "would have swept your princess away to the far ends of the world!"

"You can fool these people for a while, but we know the truth," Roan said. "Don't we, men?" He turned to his comrades.

"That's right, sir!" Lum shouted at the populace. "And I'm a corporal of the palace guard. We can't be corrupted!"

"But you take orders," Brom said, impassively, not having to raise his voice. "You don't give them. Certainly not to Her Highness."

"Well, no. . . ." Lum said, puzzled.

Brom met Roan's gaze with his glowing eyes. "You have

lost control here. You will never be in control where I am concerned."

"There's a trick here," Spar growled. "Keep an eye out."

"Yessir," Lum replied. Roan braced himself, wondering what Brom would do next.

"Enough of this affray!" the super said, stepping between them. "Now, then, when we notified the king, he informed us he is sending a messenger to escort his royal daughter home." He looked upward, and shaded his eyes against the sun. "Here he comes now."

A graceful white figure appeared between parted clouds, and circled in above them. Everyone gazed up at the man on the winged horse. The crowd made room on the cobblestones, and the Night's horse landed in their midst. He jumped lightly off his steed's back and bowed to the police chief. As soon as his feet touched the ground, the horse turned into a white convertible automobile, and the white hawk which circled in to land on the rear seat became a huge white hound with a noble face.

"Hail, Sir Osprey!" Roan called. "We need your help here!"

The messenger turned and recognized Roan, and frowned at the chains on his wrists. "You are in trouble, friend. I would aid you, but I have a mission to fulfill first. Where is the princess? My lady! Are you all right?"

Leonora fought free of her well-meaning hosts, and stood tall. "Help us, good Sir Night," she said. "I don't want to go home. They've arrested Roan, and he has done nothing wrong. This is the man who should be arrested." She pointed at Brom.

"I'm sorry," the Night said. His eyebrows drew together with concern. "My orders are clear, my lady. My commission is to bring you back to Mnemosyne at once. Nothing else. You can appeal when we return to the capital."

"I'm not going," Leonora said. She went to Roan, pushing past the police as if they were not there, and threw her arms around him. He clutched her, conscious of the heavy chains weighing down his hands.

"My lady, you must come home!" the messenger said, distressed. He touched her arm.

"If you were a true Night of the Dreamland, you wouldn't let such an injustice be done," Leonora said, shaking off his hand. Her eyes were full of tears. Roan embraced her more tightly. She must not be taken away from him, not now, or ever!

"I have no choice, Your Highness. Please come with me," Sir Osprey said, unhappily. He appealed to Roan. "Friend, do not make this difficult for all of us. Let her go."

"She stays with me," Roan said.

"Come on, boyo, we don't want to hurt you," a burly man said, pulling Roan's wrists outward. Gradually, the pair had to be separated by force, Leonora with gentle but inexorable pressure, Roan with no consideration at all. His hands were pinioned behind his back with another chain, heavier than the first.

"Leave him alone!" Leonora shouted.

"I am sorry," Sir Osprey said to Roan. "I will plead your case to the king when we return."

Leonora was bundled into Sir Osprey's car by the crowd. The Night shut the door behind her politely but firmly. Leonora sat in the front seat with her arms crossed, the gold wreath tilted over one ear. She wore a defiant expression that boded no good for the messenger, but she didn't move as he picked up Golden Schwinn and placed it in the back seat behind her. Roan thought she was biding her time to make a protest.

"Peregrine!" the Night said. "Guard!" The white dog on the top of the rear seat assumed a protective pose over Leonora's head, showing his teeth. "Superintendent, and Roan, I promise you she will be well protected until she is safely delivered back into her parents' hands. Farewell." He bounded over the door and took his place behind the wheel. The crowd parted, and the white car sped away.

"Very well," Roan said, turning away from her reluctantly to confront the police chief. "You have fulfilled that warrant. Now, what about Brom and his people? Now that the matter of Her Highness is settled, you do have a legitimate warrant for their detention."

"That's true," the super said, turning to Brom. "In the name of the king, I arrest you—" He reached out to take Brom's arm, but his hand passed straight through it. "What in the eye of Nightmare . . . ?"

"Hell's whirlwinds, he's done it again!" Spar shouted. He

went for the motorcycle litter, and ran through it into the crowd on the other side. The shrouded Alarm Clock, its bearers, and their steeds popped like a soap bubble. "Insubstantial!"

Brom turned and gave Roan one last leering grin, and the scientist was gone. Nothing was left but a glint hanging in the air where Brom's eyes had been. The superintendent and his officers looked baffled.

"They've escaped!" Roan said. "They've used an image to distract us and left the city. They did the same thing in Mnemosyne only a few days ago. Super, you must go after them! Help us. Release me!"

He held out his chains to the chief of police and started toward him, but his feet were held to the ground as if glued there. Spar and the others attempted to come to his aid, but they, too, were stuck in place. Colenna let out one squawk of surprise, then began to rummage in her purse. The Reveridians muttered to themselves. Roan did not like their mood. They were still angry, at him!

"We are not your foes," he tried to explain. "Brom is the villain. He will still try to destroy our homeland. This affair of the princess is a blind."

At the word "affair," there were more angry mutters.

"I mean, situation," Roan hastily amended. Unconvinced, the crowd took a pace closer, crowding the others about him. "Superintendent!"

"Those people were just an illusion," the super said, holding on to what he did understand. "Immaterial witnesses. I can't arrest them, because they aren't here. The warrant will remain in force. If they ever come back into Reverie, we'll see justice is done. As for these recreants," he pointed to Roan and his companions, "they shall stand trial here."

"Only me, superintendent," Roan said, standing forth bravely. "I am the only one responsible for Her Highness's presence, and the only one you must judge whether I put her in any danger. These soldiers are from the palace guard. They should go back to the capital now that she will no longer be with us."

"In a pig's eye," Spar muttered.

"Very well," the chief of police said, raising an eyebrow. "You can wait in this city until a pig's eye is available."

"I'll keep going on," Spar said. "So will my guards." The other three nodded vigorously. "That's what Her Highness would want us to do, right? She just didn't have time to put the orders in words, like. If anyone else wants to drop out, they're welcome." He glared at Felan.

"Not me," the historian said, quailing away from the captain, who was looking his largest and most official.

"Thank you, Spar," Roan said, warmed by their devotion though they were all still in danger. Who knew what other mischief Brom could have engineered while they were distracted by his illusion. "You'll be in charge, Bergold. Lum will help you track them. He's much better at it than I am."

"Aw, sir," the young soldier said, much gratified.

"It's true. I'll catch up when I can," Roan said. He rattled his chains in emphasis. "*Find them*. That's the most important thing of all. Find them."

"Right you are," said Bergold. With a frown of concentration, he mustered Roan's narrow features on his face, and made himself tall and thin. "I can't really take your place, but I'll do my best."

"I'm already on the scent, sir," Lum said.

"You'd better go," Roan said, as the angry townsfolk continued to close in on him. They seemed to grow taller and more fearsome. They brandished ropes, whips, and pitchforks. Some of them were slavering, like wild beasts. Fearing attack, Roan backed away from them. He lost sight of his friends. Bergold was the last to disappear amidst waving arms and swaying bodies, and Roan was alone within the mob. They shuffled towards him, blotting out his surroundings, forcing him to walk backwards.

"You'll probably have to wait until you get out of town to find their trail . . . !" he shouted to the companions he could no longer see. The wall of humanity engulfed him, shutting out all light and sound. Roan cried out, gasping for breath.

When the darkness passed, Roan stood by himself in a small enclosure facing a shadowy, tiered gallery of people. He could not see their faces well, but their brow ridges and the downturned corners of their mouths were full of darkness. Spotlights bloomed hotly from the ceiling, turning him into a glowing column of light. Under his hands was a wooden rail which he clutched for security. He was in the dock in a court of law.

"Order! The prisoner will face the bench!"

Roan turned slowly, scanning the chamber. Before him soared a wall of dark, carved wood twenty feet tall. Roan had to tilt his head right back on his shoulders to see. Yes, there was a judge seated at the bench, wearing a vast scarlet robe, half-glasses with gold frames, and the traditional white wig that lapped onto his shoulders.

"Order in the court!" the judge shouted, pounding his gavel. He pointed the hammer at the bailiff. "Read the charges!"

The bailiff stepped forward, and unwound a scroll. "Unlawful pursuit of court officials, restraint of a Royal Personage, harassment, malfeasance, misfeasance, nonfeasance, and unfeasance!" The legal gobbledygook puzzled Roan, but the most important thing on his mind was not himself. He felt bereft without Leonora.

Another bewigged man in a black gown, the prosecutor, walked back and forth before the dock, then spun hard on his heel to point at Roan.

"State your name!" he demanded.

"I am Roan Faireven." Roan clutched the rails. "Why am I being tried here instead of in Mnemosyne?"

"The prisoner will not ask questions," the prosecutor said, tilting his head so he could look haughtily down his nose. "The prisoner will answer them."

"I will be happy to answer any questions you have," Roan said.

"Very well," the judge said, banging down his gavel. "We will put you to the test. Begin!"

Chapter 25

The courtroom vanished. Roan found he was seated at a wooden desk in a very small room with stone walls. The desk was small, too. His long legs were hunched up underneath with his knees jammed up against the scarred top. In front of him was a sheaf of paper three inches thick. Printed on the sheet uppermost was "The Test."

Roan felt around the pile of paper. There was nothing to write with. He lifted the test paper and looked under it. He lifted the desk top, and found nothing in the metal interior but a few dried-up spitballs and a legend carved in the paint, "Jeff luvs Mim."

Roan looked around. There was only one door in the room, a blackened, iron-banded door so low he'd have to stoop to walk through it. Not that he could: it was closed with a heavy iron hasp and bolt with a padlock the size of his head.

Light came from a small window cut into the thick stone wall. He peered out and saw that the room was in a tower a hundred feet high. Down below, the tiny figures of Bergold and the others were just visible riding out of town on the main road leading towards the north. It was funny to see himself walking away. He squinted into the distance. Brom's party was nowhere in sight. They had given themselves a good head start with that illusion.

THWOCK! A wooden ruler slapped down onto his knuckles, and Roan snatched his hand away from the windowsill.

"Pay attention! Your time is limited!" said a thin-faced person in an black academic cap and gown, brandishing the ruler. Roan sat down at the desk. He felt in his pockets. They were empty of everything except his wallet and pocket knife, which did not have a pen attachment. He promised himself to update the knife when he next had the chance.

"May I have a pencil, please?" Roan asked the austere figure. It grew taller and taller until its mortarboard touched the ceiling.

"Unprepared?" the proctor demanded in an awful voice. "Ten points off!" Roan shrank back in his seat. The proctor reminded him of one of his earliest and most formidable schoolmasters. However, two unsharpened number 2 pencils were slapped down beside Roan's test paper.

"Thank you," he ventured, timidly. "Is there a pencil sharpener?"

"No talking!" The ruler waved threateningly. "If you do not finish this test correctly, you will be sent to the dean's office for the rest of your life!"

With a wary eye on the ruler, Roan got down to business. He whittled the pencil ends quickly into points, brushing the shavings neatly into an ink-stained depression at the top of the desk, and turned over the first sheet of the test paper.

In huge black letters above a blank page was the first question: WHAT IS THE PURPOSE OF YOUR JOURNEY? Roan stared in dismay. It was an essay test. He put the eraser end of his pencil in his mouth.

How to begin? he wondered. Best to phrase it simply, but would that be acceptable to the judge? With dread, he put the point down on the paper and began to write.

"We are attempting to stop a device being carried to the Hall of the Sleepers that when set off would wake them up," he wrote. "It is vital to the safety of the Dreamland that the perpetrators be found and brought back to the king."

There, that wasn't so bad. Now at least the page wasn't blank any more. But his answer was too short. The blank whiteness below chided him. There were dozens of pages left to fill. He had to say more.

"As a special investigator for the king, it was my duty to pursue the device. All of the people who accompanied me were volunteers, including Her Highness, Princess Leonora. They came to defend the Dreamland from the threat of discontinuation."

Roan kept writing, conscious all the time Brom was getting farther away. They'd been fooled, no doubt about it, and by one of the oldest tricks there was, deluding Roan into following a lure into a trap. And Brom had wriggled out of the snare himself with the same trick he had used before. How could they have forgotten?

The distortion the Alarm Clock created around it in Reverie was greater than it had ever been before. If Bergold and Lum were fortunate, they would be able to pick up the trail right away, but what if they weren't? He pressed down too hard on the page, and the pencil point snapped. Roan opened his knife to sharpen it again. The proctor rounded on him to glare in disapproval, smacking down the ruler on the desktop again and again. Roan moved his hand out of the way, but the ruler chased it. One swat caught him painfully on the wrist. He snatched it up and clutched it with the other hand.

"Let that be a lesson to you, then," the proctor said, turning away.

Not bothering to protest, Roan finished repairing his pencil and went back to his essay. Words came slowly but steadily. He framed his sentences with care, stressing a point here, erasing an embellishment there. With a flourish, he planted the final period on the page. There, that hadn't been so bad.

Thick black type appeared underneath his neat handwriting. EXPLAIN "DEVICE," it said.

Roan put down everything that he knew or speculated about the Alarm Clock, including his impression of the sound of its bells and the perversion to the land its passage caused. He mentioned the half-squirrel-half-cardinal they had seen.

EXPLAIN THE DANGER TO THE SLEEPERS, the paper demanded.

Impatiently, Roan wrote what he knew or thought he knew about Awakening, and Changeover, and the belief of the historians about what would happen if all seven provinces went through Changeover at once. He drove the pencil, filling page after blank page. When he finished with that question, there was another. And another.

DISCUSS IN DETAIL THE LEGEND OF THE HALL OF THE SLEEPERS. INCLUDE SPECIFIC EXAMPLES FROM HISTORICAL DOCUMENTATION.

Roan felt himself beginning to sweat. Why did they have to ask that? He hadn't made a formal study of the Sleepers, apart from the required reading in school, but that had been years ago. He had picked up much of what he knew from casual reading and listening to learned discussions among his father's colleagues. He had to concentrate. The fate of the Dreamland rested on his answers. If he was trapped here, Brom would carry out his nefarious experiment, and everything would disappear. How could he concentrate on philosophical questions? Don't panic, he thought. Think. Consider. He wrote down what he did know, or could remember with accuracy having heard. The question made him examine his own beliefs, leaving him to wonder if he knew anything at all, or if everything was imaginary, as some of the philosophers insisted. The answer ran four and a half pages. At the end he wasn't sure if anything he'd written made sense.

More questions followed, becoming more specific. WHAT IS THE PURPOSE OF THE DREAMLAND AS IT PERTAINS TO THE SLEEPERS? He found himself feeling anxious because he had to leave the space blank beneath several. As his nervousness grew, so did the pile of paper under his hand until it was more than five hundred pages thick. What would happen to him if he didn't know the answers? Would they keep him in this tower forever? Would he really serve detention for the rest of his life? He had to get out and join his friends in pursuit of Brom. He took a deep breath, and wrote more furiously.

WHY WAS THE PRINCESS LEONORA TRAVELING WITH YOU? WHAT ARE THE RESPONSIBILITIES OF THE PALACE GUARD IN SITUATIONS OUTSIDE THE PALACE? DISCUSS THE RELATIONSHIP OF A SOVEREIGN TO HIS/HER LIEGEMEN. DO YOU THINK A DEMOCRATIC GOVERNMENT WOULD BE MORE CONDUCIVE TO FREE INTELLECTUAL EXCHANGE?

Outside the window, the sun was going down. The city of Reverie went on about its business, seemingly unaware that a great wrong had been done the world, and that villainy was being allowed to be free. Roan worried about Leonora. He stopped to fidget with his pencil and stare up at the gaslamps on the wall. The Night was taking Leonora home to the palace. Would the king be very angry with her? With him? Would her having run away destroy Roan's chances of marrying her?

The test paper seemed to read his mind. ADMIT IT, it said when he looked down, YOU ONLY WANT TO MARRY THE PRINCESS SO THAT YOU MAY BECOME KING OF THE DREAMLAND.

"No, it isn't like that at all," Roan said, frustrated. The ruler smacked down on his hand, and his pencil went flying.

"No talking!" the proctor snapped.

Roan curled his hands into fists. How dare they question his love? What conceivable business was it of theirs? What an insult to the princess to have anyone think she was the means to an end, instead of the end in itself. Not even to mention the slight against his loyalty. He seized the second pencil and started writing, telling off his unseen inquisitors in no uncertain terms.

But writing down all the reasons why he loved Leonora helped to make them clear in his own mind. Why did he love her? Roan suddenly felt less anxiety, and his thoughts cleared. He *knew* how to answer this question. How simple. He only had to tell the truth. Leonora was unpredictable, intelligent, challenging, devoted, compassionate, and responsible. Those were only labels. How could he tell anyone that when he looked at her, his breath caught in his chest; if he exhaled too hard he would break the soap bubble of the moment, and she would vanish. To him, she was sunshine and the sweet scent of roses, and all other precious intangibles. It would have been illogical *not* to love her. The test papers melted away until there were fewer than ten.

Roan scratched away quickly. EXPLAIN, DISCUSS, the paper demanded. Roan explained his feelings, and discussed how he had grown from thinking of her as a childhood pal, albeit royal, to being her ardent admirer. How lucky he was that she cared for him in spite of his strange sameness, gave him hope that they might have a future together. She believed in him when he lost faith in himself. Leonora had grown up into a complex and wonderful woman. Look how well she had adapted to life on the road. He chuckled to himself about what it would take to get an "A" in romance. She'd be a straight-A student. And he? Ah, he did the best that he could. Warmed by thoughts of her, he filled page after page.

The test required him to write a love poem, at least eight lines in iambic pentameter. Not only could he remember what iambic pentameter was, but he tossed off the verses as if he was a bard.

The pile of paper melted away under his hand, until there was only one page left. EXPLAIN THE NATURE OF LOVE AS IT APPLIES TO YOU. Roan's thoughts were flowing now, and no more questions appeared. When he finished this one, they would have to let him go.

He scratched down his memory of the first time he knew he was in love with Leonora, how she had looked at him, and he had known suddenly that he was changed forever. He could recall it as if it had just happened. In that moment he had been exalted and humbled—

The pencil hissed on the page, and Roan examined it. The point had run down to the wood. He took up his penknife to sharpen it, and shaved away scrap after scrap of wood. Though it was still three inches long, there was no lead left inside. He put it aside, retrieved the other from the floor, and continued writing. Only two paragraphs to go.

The second pencil turned into a feather pen. Roan sought about for an inkwell, but could find none. The top of the desk was black with the spilled and dried ink of dozens of schoolboys in the past. He tried using influence to gather it and wet it, but it refused to pool. He dabbed at it several times, but couldn't get more than a dot's worth. Time was running away. Brom was marching toward the northeast with the Alarm Clock. When it went off, it wouldn't matter how many of these questions he got right. He needed ink. What could he use?

In desperation, he plunged the point of the feather pen into a vein on the back of his hand. Roan winced as the blood welled up, but he filled the nib from the flow, and kept writing. Hurry, he thought. Hurry.

". . . And because I know that she loves me, too, I hope some day to ask for her hand in marriage."

Triumphantly, he jotted the final period.

The proctor appeared at his side and gathered up the sheaf of paper.

"Your time is up," the austere voice said.

"I am finished," Roan said, leaning back in his chair and clamping his handkerchief down on his bleeding hand.

"Don't be impertinent," the proctor said, turning away and vanishing into thin air.

Roan rose from his desk to stretch. His backside, knees, and wrist were all stiff, but he felt good. His mind had been stretched, too. What a load of old history he was carrying around in his memory. He was surprised at all that he had been able to remember. Even better, he had been able to tell someone exactly what it was he loved about Leonora. He only wished it was she he had been able to tell. It was almost certainly for the best that she had been sent back to

Mnemosyne. She would be safer at home, but he would miss her terribly. When this mission was over, and the Dreamland was safe, he wanted to take her aside to somewhere private, and explain and discuss all the things he had learned about himself and her, with maybe just a little bit of sweet clarification.

Roan paced to the window and looked out over the city of Reverie. To his astonishment, the sun was rising. The test had taken him all night. How far had Bergold gone in that time? And Brom? Where were they? Had the battle been fought without him?

How much longer until they graded the exam and let him out? He paced the small room for a while, feeling as if he would go crazy with impatience. He made himself sit down at the little desk and stretched his long legs out in front of him. He would wait patiently. Fingers of light crept to the edge of the stone sill. Roan watched them until they reached all the way to the inner edge.

WHACK! The noise of the ruler smacking down on the desktop roused Roan from a sound sleep. It was full daylight now, and dust motes danced in the bright sunlight coming in through the window. He looked up into the disapproving face of the proctor.

"You are acquitted," the thin voice said, although the mouth was drawn down at the corners. "Your answers were satisfactory. Not highly satisfactory, but satisfactory. You may go."

So the world would have to be saved by an average to good student, not a perfect scholar. Roan wasted no time finding and arguing with whoever had graded his essay. He collected his belongings, and left the city by the north road.

"Sir!" A voice hailed him as he passed over the north bridge, identical to the bridge at the south side of the city. Roan looked in the direction of the voice. A young man with a fresh, pink face and light brown hair and wearing camouflage fatigues stood out from the tree where he had been resting. "Private Hutchings, sir. I waited for you. Corporal Lum said you'd need an escort. Was it very bad?"

"Bad enough," Roan said. "But now I'm eager to be on the way."

"Right you are, sir," Hutchings said.

He put forefinger and thumb in his mouth, and whistled. Roan heard the jingle of harnesses. Cruiser and Hutchings's regulation steed trotted out of the brush.

"He was waiting for you outside the courthouse," Hutchings explained, as Roan patted his white beast's soft nose, and felt in his pocket for a sugar lump. Cruiser nickered and crunched the offering happily. "Didn't want him locked in the local pound as abandoned."

"Thank you," Roan said, swinging up into the saddle. Cruiser whiffled at him softly, and twitched his tall ears. "How many of the others stayed with us?"

"Everybody, sir," Hutchings said, with pride. "We're a team, we are. They've all sent you their good wishes. Are you ready to ride? I've got breakfast we can eat while we travel. Corporal Lum said he was going to leave a trail for us. Do you think Master Brom left behind any spies or traps for us?"

"Count on it," Roan said, spurring Cruiser into a trot. "Keep thinking he'll be two steps ahead of us, because he is."

Chapter 26

Taboret felt the undercurrent of worry as they shot out of Reverie. Brom had had them make their escape as silently as possible. They had muffled the sound of the motorbike engines as far as the city limits, when the pent-up noise escaped in a mighty roar. By the time anyone had realized they were gone, all there'd been left to catch was dust. Oh, why hadn't Roan outsmarted them? They'd be nicely arrested now, and sent back to Mnemosyne all safe and sound.

She knew she wasn't the only one who was afraid. Brom was insane. She stifled the thought as soon as it appeared in her brain, but felt it echoed faintly through the link. Who else had thought so when she did? Taboret let her eyes slew around. Basil must have. Riding at the fore of the Alarm Clock with his shoulders bent under the weight, his head was tilted down just a little more than necessary, to keep anyone from looking directly into his eyes. Who else? Carina? Gano?

But it was a dangerous guessing game to play. Taboret felt an unmistakable chill, and knew the chief scientist himself was looking at her. She didn't even have to turn around to see. She put rebellious notions straight out of her head, and concentrated on riding five feet—no more, no less—behind Gano's green steed. Conformity, obedience, and speed were all that was required of her.

Carina's mount gathered itself to jump a pothole in the road, and landed heavily on the other side, its tires flattening. Bolmer's, behind her, balked at the gap, and went around it, pushing Glinn's steed out of line. Taboret was surprised, because it was an easy jump. Instantly, she felt disapproval surge through the link.

"Halt!" Brom shouted. "Bolmer, what is wrong with your motorbike?"

"It's getting tired, sir," Bolmer said, revving the handlebars of his bike. It let out a low rumble. "I noticed it hasn't been keeping up with the others so well. It could be metal fatigue."

"I've noticed a similar weakness," Glinn said. "Should we be concentrating on incubating new steeds? We have more paperclips."

"Only if we can breed them straight into motorcycles," Mamovas, the specialist in inanimate biology, said. "New bikes would go too slowly. Now that the Crown knows where we are, we need to keep moving fast."

"Knew where we were," Brom said, firmly. "Besides, that dolt of a police chief did not want to get involved. By the time word comes back to him from the Crown with definite orders to follow us, we will have finished our experiment."

"Well, the steeds are doing all they can," Glinn said. "They may have reached the limits of their ability."

"Then it is time for the next stage," Brom said. "Plan Sixteen. We will combine them into a single unit, capable of carrying all of us and the Alarm Clock, thereby putting less stress on any single unit. Let us get off the road and prepare the crucible."

They bumped off the road into the heavy, sweet-scented brush, rumbling over reeds and marshy patches. Surprised frogs jumped in every direction to get out of their way. As they rolled into a relatively dry clearing, Glinn raised his hand for them to halt.

"Everyone but Maniune and Acton," Brom said. "We will need them to remain mobile to guard our passage."

The mercenaries withdrew to a dry patch to watch, while the others dismounted and stood in a circle around the motorcycles. Taboret took the hands of the people on either side of her. Basil was very short today, standing only waist high to her, and Carina was very tall and bulky, like an oak tree made human. Taboret felt as if she might teeter over leftwards at any moment, but Carina's strong arm held her upright.

"Plan Sixteen," Glinn announced, giving them time to call up the memory of its specifications in their minds. No cribbing from notes now. "Mass transportation."

A haze rose from the swampy ground to envelop the motorcycles, and quickly turned into a whirlwind. In Taboret's mind's eye, she saw a buslike vehicle, a horseless carriage with big wheels and padded seats. No, she had overstepped the specs. Someone else's thoughts corrected hers. Plan Sixteen called for the very minimum of comfort and the maximum of efficiency. The seats had a thin layer of rubber on them to keep passengers from bouncing out. The spinning wind whipped at her cheeks, dragged at her clothes. Inside, the curved forms melded into one large, dark blob that shrunk, melded, then grew outward, acquiring protuberances and angles.

The power ceased to flow. Taboret sensed that someone had broken the circle. She let go of her companions and turned to look. The whirlwind died down at once, revealing a vehicle.

That was the only name she could give it. It wasn't like anything else she had ever seen. Nor did it match the diagrams that Brom had had them learn before they left Mnemosyne. This was *similar*, in a perverse way.

On a bed of multiple wheels was a roofless platform on which were arranged leather seats. One would not sit down on them; rather, they would have to be straddled like the backs of rocking horses. In front of each was a kind of metal crossbar to hang onto—all that was left of the motorcycle handlebars. The seats were arranged with three pairs on either side of an empty aisle large enough for their luggage and the Alarm Clock. From a quick glance around, she knew she wasn't the only one dismayed by its appearance.

"It will have to do. Load up, and we'll be on our way," Brom said, outwardly unaware of their disapproval. He hopped up on the platform. Hiking the skirts of his robe out of the way, he swung his trousered leg over the saddle at the front of the vehicle. "There is no time to lose. Our pursuers will be delayed only so long in Reverie."

Taboret could tell at once that the vehicle wasn't a success. It didn't have the completed feel of any of their camps or even their artificial nuisances. She hated the way it looked as if it was constructed of spare parts. Instead of riding with dignity past other travelers, she'd be afraid they'd laugh at her.

She felt the faint discomfiture of the others as they took their places. Glinn sat down beside her on his hobby-horse seat, and grasped the metal handlebars. Taboret glanced up at him, and he smiled at her. She was glad he was nearby. He always seemed so confident. On Taboret's other side, the Alarm Clock hunkered under its canvas covering, a malign lump.

Brom set his foot down on a large floor pedal. The combined engines below the platform jerked into a loud roar, and the vehicle lurched forward. It was so large it had to be turned in a wide circle, mowing down the marsh reeds. Taboret observed as the vehicle crossed its own path that it had four rows of tires underneath, suiting it for heavy duty, though not grace.

Sprays of murky water rose around the edge of the platform to either side. Brom had difficulty at first in steering the makeshift transport. Like the dozen bikes it comprised, it seemed to want to go in several directions at once. When he was finally able to direct it in a straight line, he aimed it back toward the road.

There was now no question that they would have to stay on the main highways all the way to the mountains, Taboret thought. Lucky there were only small habitations between here and there. They'd be easy to follow, and hard to forget. She hoped to the Sleepers, if they existed, that the King's Investigator would get free and catch up with them in time. But how would that be? When the scientists had pulled out of Reverie, the mob was howling for his blood for the supposed abduction of the princess. He might be lynched, or imprisoned forever. She had heard the legends about Roan, how he had escaped from some terrifying adventures in his time. She hoped he'd pull through this one, too, and quickly.

The platform lurched to the left, and Glinn was nearly thrown into her lap. Brom was still driving as if he was alone, taking sharp curves too fast, and braking hard around obstructions.

She wished she was riding her own bike, and imagined that she felt it calling to her to free it from the connection with the others. There shouldn't be any residual possessiveness, she thought, chiding herself. This bike wasn't a long-treasured possession. It had been bred up from a paperclip only days before. Why did she feel so uncomfortable about riding a multiple-passenger transport? She slept in camps that they used the crucible to construct for them all. It was because the bike had been made for her particular use, and conscripting it for the party was like taking away part of her individuality. She was more attached to the bike than to any section of a camp, like a stove, or a latrine.

She could tell from the *sub rosa* murmur that everyone else was thinking the same thing. They could all feel their identities leaching away into the gestalt, combining like this mass monstrosity under their feet, and they didn't like it. It made them edgy.

Private thoughts were at a premium. The group would go through periods where each could hear everything the others were thinking, then a kind of reaction when everyone rebelled against the "togetherness," blocking all other minds. Taboret used one of those precious moments to think that perhaps she should leave another sign for Roan to follow.

It worried her that it had seemed too easy to subvert those police officers back in Reverie. This journey no longer bore any semblance to a legitimate experiment. It was becoming . . . unlawful. She had felt truly upset by Roan's accusations. Maybe Roan should be allowed to stop them until everyone could think things through. She was beginning, to her horror, to doubt what Brom said. She disliked having a role in a criminal action. The only way the King's Investigator would find them was if she left another clue to mark their trail.

The appalling transport drew up to a crossroads, and Brom paused to allow a file of feathered honkers to cross. Taboret seized the moment of privacy in her own mind. Should she?

Brom caught the edge of her insecurity, and turned to look fully at her. His glowing eyes burned with suspicion. Taboret felt her heart pounding. She tried to look down, but her gaze was held firmly. Taboret felt as if she would faint with terror.

Fear was as catching as a yawn. Someone else in the link was touched by the edge of her fear, and sent out an emotional icicle of his own. Taboret gasped as an unfamiliar sense of fright came back to her, and swiveled her head to look. Was there something else threatening them? Everyone's insecurities came out in a rush, adding to the emotional soup. What were they doing there? Who were these strangers they'd been traveling with? The experiment couldn't really work, could it? The feedback of fear cycled through faster. If bicycles could be turned into one single vehicle by the crucible, couldn't that happen to people? Them?

Brom sensed the buildup, and rose to his feet with his hands raised.

"Calm! I demand calm!" he shouted. But it was too late. The platform began to heave and shake under his feet.

Taboret was bucked out of her saddle-seat at the extreme left edge of the vehicle, and landed painfully in the low ditch next to the road. There was a loud crash behind her, and the unmistakable hum of an Alarm Clock bell. She covered her head with both her arms and lay there until the noise stopped. Taboret rolled up to her hands and knees, and rested there, shaking her head. The hair dangling around her face was red, not blonde, the way it had been since that morning. They must have run into another cloud of influence.

But, no. When she looked up, the vehicle had turned back into a clattering herd of single motorcycles, with the litter at a crazy angle in the middle of it, its cover askew. Acton and Maniune were on the scene in moments, helping to pull Brom and the others free. Some of them had been thrown clear, as she was, but the ones on the inside, near the Alarm Clock, were unlucky. They were stuck in the road, where the chiming of the bells had changed it to syrup.

The damage didn't stop there. The plants around them had mutated from gum trees to . . . gum trees, complete with colored paper bark and foil leaves, and small animals fled through the brush, changed into who knew what.

Glinn put a hand out for help, and she and two of the others hurried to help him, turning over motorcycles, and carefully avoiding the litter. Everyone was bruised, and the motorcycles were all dented and scratched.

Brom sprang up and pulled the cover off the Alarm Clock. It seemed intact, apart from a slight scratch on the brass casing, but that small mark seemed to drive the chief scientist into a frenzy.

"You fools!" he exclaimed, steam spouting out of his ears.

"Do you realize what your emotional outburst could have done? Look at that!"

"We can buff that out, sir," Glinn said, waiting patiently while Basil and Carina lifted a motorcycle off his leg. "We have the metal polish and cloths with us in the repair kit." His calm voice seemed to placate Brom momentarily, but not before the chief had turned and glared at Taboret. She quailed, knowing she had been responsible for the collapse. Glinn must have sensed her fear, because he reached out and put a hand on her arm, keeping her from withdrawing any farther. "There are no broken bones or cogs. It is only a temporary setback, sir. We can be ready to proceed in just a few minutes."

"All right," Brom said, unappeased, his eyes half-lidded. "But we will have to start over. And this time, everyone will concentrate fully. There must be no more dissension." His eyes met Taboret's, but Glinn's warm grasp kept her from panicking.

"No, sir," Taboret said, evenly. In fact, she didn't even feel frightened by Brom. The moment Glinn touched her, she experienced that near-telepathic sharing that followed the gestalt link, and she knew that he liked her and thought she was intelligent and attractive. He felt-thought that sitting next to her on the short-lived bus was more than pleasant. He yearned to have that experience repeated, if possible. Taboret tried to conceal her feelings of pleasure from the others, and admitted that she liked him, too. She enjoyed his presence and support, and knew in that moment he had picked up on her thought-feelings to that effect. When Brom turned away to scold someone else, Glinn caught her eye, and smiled warmly. The deep brown eyes he had today were good for soul-searching. Taboret felt a little tingle of pleasure as she bent to work again.

Once the motorcycles were all upright, the Alarm Clock yanked out of the syrup, and the apprentices' bruises seen to, Brom had them form the gestalt.

"Plan Sixteen," he said. "This time, get it right. You know the specifications."

But the plans didn't work this time, either. Taboret watched in dismay as the motorcycles huddled together, looking weary. The more the gestalt tried to force them to meld and change shape, the more they wilted.

"We will have to carry on on individual steeds as before, sir," Glinn said, breaking the circle. Taboret felt the white haze fade with relief, echoed by the others through the link. "They can't change again so drastically so soon. They're only matter, after all. They have only minimal energy of their own to bind them. If we overstress them, we may lose them entirely."

Brom checked the motorcycles for himself, and assumed a bored expression that masked his irritation, still palpable in the air. "Oh, very well. We shall try again later."

Everyone pulled his or her growling bike out of the mass of steeds, and mounted up. Almost everyone had a bruise or two. Every bike had a dent. Basil had been almost behind the Alarm Clock. He was moving very slowly, favoring his right leg. Bolmer clutched his left forearm with his right hand. This was his second big accident, and he was snappish.

"If the rest of you had really been concentrating," he snarled, massaging the swelling down, "that would have held together, and none of us would have gotten hurt."

"As if you're the tower of strength," Carina said, with a sneer.

"It was her fault," Lurry said, pointing at Taboret. "She started it."

"Friends, please!" Glinn said, distracting them. "Is anyone seriously injured? No? Then, shall we go on? We want to cover more ground before dark."

"Yes," Gano said, with a sympathetic look for Taboret. "It's not like anyone has to pedal. Come on."

Taboret was grateful, but she pulled back toward the end of the line, hoping to ride by herself, as far away from everyone's tempers as she could get. Her bruises were mostly on her left side. A good thing indeed that they did not have to pedal. To her dismay, Bolmer elected to limp along beside her on his dented bike.

The engines started up, not without some protesting sputters, and the party rolled on. At the front of the line, flanked by the pair of mercenaries, Brom sat on his steed with his back straight and his head craned forward. Taboret knew he wasn't thinking about them any more. His mind was far away, probably solving the mass-transportation problem. Bolmer began some carping complaint, which Taboret immediately allowed to enter one ear and leave by the other. Quick, her brain said, feeling the weight of the chief's regard leave her, what about that clue?

The smooth, newly paved roadway didn't suggest any means for her to leave a message behind for their pursuers. There was no convenient scree of stones to twist a tire in, causing a handy fall. The trees flanking the road in clusters were young and narrow. There was hardly room to daub *Look Out* on any of them with a finger, and what would she say if one of those bruisers doubled back and saw her message? No, it had to be a distinctive item that wouldn't be on this road for any other reason, and it had to be something she could pass off as having fallen by accident.

They passed through a tiny town. Brom ordered them to disguise the Alarm Clock as a haywain, to avoid commentary. Taboret had no privacy of thought until they were past the last house.

Her opportunity came almost immediately thereafter, at the next crossroads. On the map in her mind's eye that she shared with everyone else in the gestalt, she knew it led toward the border of Wocabaht and Rem. Brom was so busy seeing the Alarm Clock safely negotiate the left turn that the riders at the back of the queue were very much on their own.

"Halt!" Brom called. "Lurry, you and Basil apply your wits. We require a deterrent to be left here at this point. Just in case."

"But Roan and his people are in Reverie, under arrest," Glinn protested.

"Arrest is temporary," Brom warned him. He turned to Basil. "Remain here until you have completed the assignment, then catch up."

Taboret could feel Basil's reluctance, but he rolled his bike to the side of the road. Quickly, she wrenched off the top button of her tunic. As she came around the corner, she dropped it on the new road very close to the bushes so the followers would understand which way they had gone, and be warned something was ahead. There. It was done.

If Roan or his friends got this far, they'd see it.

The rest of the afternoon was uneventful. Everyone began

to relax again, and the link began to fill with smatterings of thought. Taboret damped down the fear she felt that the chief might have seen her treasonous act. She tried to avoid getting sucked into the mass database of thought, but she had to cooperate and be part of the gestalt, or explain to Brom why not. Fortunately, Gano, Basil, and Carina were beginning to be upset by the invasion of their private mind-places, too. And no one was happy to know personally the intimate thoughts of the Countingsheep brothers, who were as offensive inside as out. Thank the Seven—if they existed, and Taboret fervently hoped they did—for Glinn. Was that warm, fuzzy feeling just the link talking? Was she now permanently joined to the whole group, in the laboratory and out? Would they contract a mass-marriage or some similar bond when this was all over? The idea repulsed her thoroughly.

No, she thought, examining her feelings carefully, she still didn't feel any attraction to Brom or Doolin and Dowkin. She supposed that it could happen later on, and sincerely hoped it wouldn't. The feelings she had were all for Glinn. Occasionally, she felt a return spark from him through the link. More than anything, she wanted the day's ride to be over, so she could take him aside in private, and find out if she had made up the tantalizing pictures she was getting in her mind.

With the delightful prospect to occupy her, she forgot all about the button until they reached Brom's appointed stopping place for that night.

"Taboret, your tunic's torn. Look, the top button is missing," Gano said, helpfully, on the way past to park her motorbike in the makeshift corral. Taboret couldn't help blushing.

"Is it?" she asked, trying to look innocent. She felt the loose threads, and every thought she'd had that afternoon came flooding back to her.

"She must have lost it in the scrum when the transport fell apart," Glinn said, coming to her rescue. "It's a wonder no one was hurt." She shot him a grateful look.

"Slovenliness," Brom snapped, appearing beside them like an unwelcome burst of lightning. Taboret jumped. He eyed her tunic and gave her a look of utter disgust. "Repair it. It detracts from your appearance."

"Um, er," she stuttered, clutching at her throat. She wished Glinn would help out again, then wondered at her difficulty in framing a simple reply. She had never needed anyone to speak for her before. What was the matter with her? The strain was beginning to fog her brain. "I haven't got a sewing kit, sir."

"Improvise," Brom said, tersely. He willed a small round stone to hop up to his hand from the ground. He pinched it flat between his thumb and forefinger, and two small holes appeared in it. He flung it at her.

Stung, Taboret caught the stone before it hit her in the face. With a burst of personal influence, she finished flattening it out and smoothed off the excess matter. Using just a little more, she lengthened the broken threads under her collar and tied the stone button in place. She had always hated sewing. Brom became bored with watching her fumbling with the threads, and went away to see to the safety of the Alarm Clock. At least he hadn't questioned the circumstances under which she'd lost the button. Tying off the last knot, Taboret thanked her lucky stars, or whomever was looking after foolish young scientists, and hurried to assume her duties in helping set up the camp.

Chapter 27

Roan and his party rode on. It had taken him and Hutchings hours riding at a full gallop to catch up with Bergold. The moment he'd appeared, Bergold let his form go back to a version of his preferred shape, shorter, rounder, and more relaxed. He rode along beside his friend on his red gelding.

"Whew! It's a strain being you," Bergold said, with a broad smile for his friend. "I never properly appreciated how hard it is to stay the same."

"It's easier when you've done it for a long time," Roan said, lightly.

"Did you see Her Highness before you left Reverie?"

"No," Roan said. "Sir Osprey departed before you did." He sighed, staring ahead forlornly at the far horizon. A few of the pogo-stick-hopping rats leaped across the scenery, black silhouettes against the yellow sky. The sun was going down. "They'll be home by now."

"She'll be fine, lad," Bergold said, reassuringly. Roan nodded.

"Well, I shall miss her," Colenna said, turning around in her saddle and leaning her elbow on her handbag. "She was a gallant little girl."

"I'll miss her, too," Roan said. The words were so inadequate, they felt like the cork in a bottle of emotion boiling up behind it. Any moment, all of it would burst out in a stream of eloquent speech about true love and the pain of separation. But, no. He couldn't find anything to say. All the words he had were back in Reverie on reams and reams of paper. Instead, he was left with worry and frustration roiling inside him, knotting his heart and belly into one unhappy mass. At least she was safe from the danger that lay ahead.

"She'll want news of our progress. I'd be happy to lend

you some stamps, if you wanted to send her a message yourself," Felan offered politely.

"I would be obliged," Roan said, surprised. The younger historian seemed more subdued than before. He wondered what kind of pressure the others had put on him after they'd left Reverie. Captain Spar was looking smug. Surely there hadn't been any violence, but Felan spoke civilly and calmly, where he had been cheeky before. The others had noticed, too.

"Are you all right, dear?" Colenna asked. "Are you feverish?"

"I'm fine," Felan said, without his customary rancor. "Maybe I'm tired. I'm not used to travel."

"It was good of you to continue on with the group," Roan said. "In spite of Captain Spar's gentle persuasive techniques."

"Hey?" the guard captain called from the front of the line, pretending to look innocent.

Felan laughed. "Not so bad, really. What did they do to you in Reverie?"

"Essay test," Roan said, more shortly than he had intended, but he'd used up much of his vocabulary on the exam.

Felan shuddered. "You have my sympathy."

"It's starting to get dark," Corporal Lum announced. "We ought to think about stopping soon. We could run flat into one of Master Brom's pet monstrosities without seeing it."

"I'd dearly love to see how he controls nuisances," Bergold said thoughtfully. "What a help that would be."

"Brom probably thinks we're still back in Reverie," Felan said. "He left before us."

"Do not underestimate Brom," Roan said, raising an eyebrow. "He's intelligent, and he's tricky." He borrowed the map from Bergold, and held Colenna's multipurpose lamp over it. "Not too far ahead is a low hilltop that overlooks a bend in the road. Providing it hasn't flattened out in the meantime, that should make a fairly defensible and dry camp."

"Speaking of dry camps," Bergold said, poking Roan in the ribs as he retrieved the map, "do you remember staying in that wadi town in the desert near Bukara?"

Roan laughed, jostled out of his present misery. "I certainly do! I thought it was the nicest place I'd ever been, until we found out the whole thing was a mirage." He turned to explain to the others. "We were there to meet a fleet of ships of the desert that had sighted a living sphinx and get their report. We'd been drinking sherbets and lying about the pool in a luxury hotel, when everything vanished, and we were flat on the sand by ourselves. The real wadi was miles away."

"You'd nothing to worry about, but I was taking a bath when the illusion collapsed. Sand, sand, sand, and more sand," Bergold chuckled, folding and refolding the map. Suddenly, he bundled it into Colenna's hands. "Here, will you do it, dear lady? It just doesn't like me. Ah, those were the days."

Roan smiled. Those had been happier days than these. He and Bergold had shared many good times. Reminiscing about them just reminded him how much he liked and respected the historian. It was a relief to have him along on this journey. When he thought he would give up hope, Bergold kept their spirits going. He was a man of surprising resources.

It seemed unbelievable that it had only been a few days since the party had set out from the capital city. Roan felt he had changed since then, albeit all inside. He'd become both more confident, and less. More, because he'd been made to lead, and had surprised himself with the cooperation the party had given to him. Less, because he had never appreciated before what it took to be responsible for so many other lives. Bergold, bless him, seemed exactly the same, affable and unflappable, whatever his external appearance.

Roan eased his sore bottom to find a place that hadn't been battered to a bruised pulp on the hard ride. He was looking forward to using the salve in his pack when they stopped.

Twilight on the plain brought with it an icy chill. Winter was coming on quickly in Wocabaht. The Sleeper's will evoked animals and sights strange to those who'd been brought up in Celestia. Little gray bears with double thumbs and big sad eyes hugging tree boles stared at them as they passed. Night birds swooped down over their heads. Exclaiming sharply, Spar ducked one that came within a hair's breadth of his cap.

Shadows deepened among the scanty trees and bushes, casting odd, unexpected shapes on their path. The horses trod warily. Roan thought that this thicket was what the Nightmare Forest looked like millennia or billennia ago.

"Did you hear something go *'bzzp'*?" Lum asked, into the sudden silence.

"Ray gun noise, bug zapper noise, or possibly an animal noise?" Bergold asked, fumbling in his pack for his useful book.

"Couldn't say, sir," Lum asked, swallowing deeply. "I don't know all those technical terms."

But a noise that needed no explanation came from behind them on the trail: a constant rhythmic thudding.

"Horses!" Misha exclaimed.

They stopped to listen. Roan strained his ears, picking out the sounds.

"It could be them," Felan said, pulling his steed safely behind Hutchings and Alette.

"I think it's only one horse," Lum said.

Captain Spar drew his sword. "Could be a trap. Soldiers, on guard! Show a light, Colenna. Let's see what it is we're facing."

Roan gripped his quarterstaff, and bent low over his horse's neck, trying to get a glimpse of their pursuer. Cruiser, between his knees, let out a low nicker. What did the steed sense?

Colenna hoisted her lantern high. The strong beam burned away the shadows, and lit up the figure of a golden horse with a golden-haired girl on its back. She threw up her arm to shield her eyes. Roan knew her at once.

"Leonora!" he shouted.

"Turn that thing down!" Leonora snapped. "You're blinding me." Colenna cranked down the intensity until the torch was a simple flaming brand.

"Your Highness!" Spar yelled. "What are you doing here?"

Roan didn't wait for the answer. He spurred Cruiser to her side and swept her up in his arms across his saddlebow, kissing her with all the intensity of ten essay tests behind him. She looked tired, disheveled, in an obvious temper, but beautiful as always—and there.

Her eyes, luminous and dark in the flickering light, twinkled as she sat back against his arm to see his face.

"That's a marvelous greeting," she said, touching his cheek playfully. "Oh, don't put me down yet. I am so sore on the bottom I can hardly sit."

"Where did you spring from?" Bergold asked. "I thought the Night was driving you home."

"I couldn't leave all of you to go on without me," Leonora said, cuddled comfortably against Roan's chest. Golden Schwinn rubbed noses with Cruiser, and nibbled at his bridle as if glad to see him. "I waited until we stopped to ask directions. When Sir Osprey was asking directions from that signpost, and not paying any attention to me, I sneaked my steed out of the car, made him a simulacrum out of some sticks, and made off through the woods. Now, Sir Osprey will get home with what he thinks is me, and by that time, I hope we've caught up with Brom. I had to chain the dog to the seat and mix up my scent. I was sorry to do that," she said, with evident regret, "but he might have been able to track me, otherwise. After that, I just followed the roads north."

"Well done, my love," Roan said. "A heroic job of orienteering."

"Thank you," Leonora said.

"You could have missed us completely," Bergold said, worriedly, although he was as glad to see her as Roan. "You could have been set upon by vandals, or—or swallowed up by a pothole, or disappeared into an anomaly."

"You must be exhausted, my dear," said Colenna.

"Oh, I am," Leonora said. The arm she had wrapped around Roan's ribs tightened for a moment in a quiet hug. Then she nestled in more closely. "I'm also a bit sorry to have missed the inn he said we were to have stayed at this evening, with real baths! But I had to get back. I'm part of the group, am I not?"

"Of course!" Roan exclaimed, holding her to his pounding heart with a mixture of delight and dismay. The regret he'd felt at having her depart had changed to guilt. She was at risk again. Should he try to persuade her to turn back on her own? He sought Captain Spar's eye. The chief guard shook his head no, slowly but sadly. It was no use.

"But you wait until I see Brom again," Leonora said, and the tone of her voice boded no good for the renegade scientist. "Just wait."

"How far to this hill?" Felan asked, a few miles down the road. It was growing darker by the moment. "I haven't galloped at double time all the way from Reverie, but I'm sore, too."

"Not too far ahead," Bergold said. "It says it's just the other side of a small town. Ah! And there's the town."

Felan peered at the few little cottages with warm, flickering lights showing in the windows and tiny curls of smoke winding up from the chimneys.

"That's the minimum definition of a town, as far as I'm concerned," he said.

"I came from a place like this," Misha said, defensively. "It functions in every way as a community. You can't say fairer than that."

"Ah, well, that's all that counts," Bergold said. "It's as well to live simply, since one never knows what the Sleepers will give or take away next."

Almost as he said it, the little huts swelled suddenly into huge mansions with gleaming carriage lights and paved areas in front of them, and crowded the small road. Roan caught a glimpse of a big black disk of metal with a skinny metal arm sticking out of it, mounted on a pole in the back yard of one establishment, and a swimming pool in back of another.

"Good heavens," Leonora said. She was back on her own steed, restored after an application of Roan's healing salve. "Is this modern, or old-fashioned?"

"Modern, dear," Colenna replied. "No ornamentation to speak of, you see."

A man and a woman heard the sound of their passage, and came out to see what was going on. In spite of their grand homes, they were dressed in simple, loose clothes, carefully patched, suitable for working in the field. The man had a peaked cap and a beard. The woman wore a kirtled gown and a cotton scarf on her hair. They stood on the stoop of their great house and watched the party go by as if it were a parade.

"Evening," Roan called to them.

"Evening, sir," they called back.

"Brom came this way, sir," Lum said, scanning the ground. "But we'd better stop soon. I can hardly see the signs."

"We're not far away," Bergold said. "There's a crossroads, and then the hilltop is along a little way after that."

"What's that up ahead?" Colenna said, peering ahead. She

lifted her lantern to see, but hardly needed its help. The orange object on the road gleamed brightly, and it had a round barrel light on top that flashed on and off.

"Why, it's a sawhorse," Bergold said, as they approached it. "What's it doing here? There's no road repairs beyond it. Look."

"Warning us that there will be some soon?" Felan asked. But the road appeared to be perfectly smooth and in good repair.

"Wait a moment," Roan said. He spotted something else on the side of the road just short of the barricade, and spurred Cruiser to the front of the line and urged them to halt. Swinging out of his saddle, he went to retrieve the object.

"It looks like a button, dear," Colenna said over his shoulder.

"It is," he said, fingering it. There was a strand of thread still caught in the holes. "I wonder how it got here."

Roan pondered it for a moment longer. He started to put it in his pocket, when a body landed heavily on his back.

"Down, sir!" Lum shouted in his ear, pushing his head down against the pavement. "Everyone, down!"

The others scrambled to the ground, and pulled their beasts with them as a noise like a hundred thunderstorms roared overhead. Roan glanced back to make certain that the other guards were protecting the princess, then buried his head under his arms. Something impacted against the ground not six feet from him with a sucking, devouring sound. He squinted out from under his arm. Where there had been bushes and grass, there was a huge, jagged hole in the ground.

"There it goes!" Misha cried. Roan and Lum sprang up to see.

Roan had seen visible waves of influence before. He'd been inconvenienced by nuisances, and skirted holes in reality, but this was the first time he'd seen one that looked like a hole turned inside out. Against the darkness of oncoming night, it was a greasy mess of glowing color: green, orange, sickly brown and gray, all tied together by a swirling mass of black. It skittered along the ground like a tornado, picking up trees, rocks, grass, and anything else it touched.

"It's heading toward those houses," Bergold said.

"Great Sleepers, you're right!" Roan leaped onto Cruiser,

and spurred the steed toward them. "We have to warn those people!"

Cruiser leaped over the trench carved in the road, with only the backward twist of his ears betraying his fear. Roan was too concerned for the fate of the villagers to be worried about himself or his beast. They could always dodge the dancing hunger. The villagers were on foot, and unaware.

"Get out!" Roan shouted, trying to make himself heard over the roar of the wind. "Danger! Get out of your houses! Run away!"

"What?" The man who had come outside to wave at them appeared at the door of his house with a lantern, and leaned out to look. His mouth dropped open. "What in Nightmare's name is that?"

"Run!" Roan shouted at him, as the hole veered sharply right and made straight for the house. "No, not that way!" he cried, as the man, frightened and disoriented, dropped his lantern and started toward the hole itself. "Stop! Turn away!"

The whirling vacuum split a tree and swallowed half, leaving the torn remainder standing at a cockeyed angle. It carelessly wrenched the corner off a nearby house. Then, it bore down upon the man, who stood looking up at it helplessly as it picked him up. With a wild cry, he disappeared in the swirl of angry color.

"Damon!" His wife ran out of the door to where he had last been standing. She stood on the spot, wringing her hands and crying. "Damon, no! No!"

The hole in reality passed her as if she had been a stranger on the street, and tore through her house. The building shuddered, then exploded outward in a hail of splinters and shards. Roan reached the woman, pulled her up onto Cruiser's back, and turned the steed out of the path of the debris.

Pieces of house rained down upon them, but the woman didn't seem to notice. She muttered to herself when Roan set her down in the midst of the group, not looking up at any of them.

"Are you all right?" Leonora asked, coming up to put an arm around the woman's shoulders.

"He's gone," the woman said, staring back over her shoulder

at the ruin of her house. Her face was pale with shock. "He's gone."

"You couldn't stop it," Leonora said, in a soothing voice. "There's nothing you can do about influence."

"Sleeper's will," the woman said, blankly.

"That's right. Someone, find her something to drink," Leonora said, leading her toward Golden Schwinn. The steed obediently became a bench, and the two of them sat down on it. "How long were you together?"

"All our lives," the woman said. Then she burst into tears. "Oh, I can't believe he's gone!"

"There, there," Leonora said. She reached into the air for a handkerchief. The woman sobbed into the square of cloth. The princess patted her shoulder and murmured kind words. Colenna filled a tiny silver cup with brandy from her bag, and Leonora urged the woman to drink. She choked down the liquor, and color returned to her face. She had looked forty before. Now she looked eighty.

Roan stood by, speechless in the face of such a tragedy. What could he say to someone who has just lost the most important person in her life? He knew how he would feel. He had had a taste of desolation when Leonora had been taken away from him in Reverie, and never wanted to feel worse than that in his life.

"Let's find your neighbors, dear," Colenna said, always ready to cope in a crisis.

"I'll go," Spar said, wanting to take any kind of action to help.

"No, send Alette," Leonora said, appearing plump and motherly. She rocked the grieving woman against her shoulder, letting her cry. The guard sped off in the darkness. "The rest of you, will you find her things?"

Roan hurried off at once. Other villagers started to come out of the other big houses, lanterns and torches in hand. Roan explained the situation to them.

"We'll take Jennet in, of course," one woman said. She seemed to be about the same age.

"Better," said a tall, thin man. "We'll build her a new house, nicer than the one she had. It's the least we can do. I've got wood I was going to build an addition on with."

"I've got a raft of extra shingles," another said.

"We have paint," a woman put in. Suddenly, they were bubbling over with plans as they bustled around picking up Jennet's scattered possessions. Roan listened to them with admiration. He knew that even if the donations were insufficient, they would burgeon into the right amount for the job to match their donors' generosity.

When he returned to the others, a couple of neighbor women had taken Leonora's place, and were comforting their friend.

"That *thing* cannot have been an accident," Leonora whispered to Roan. "It was waiting for us, wasn't it? It was Brom's doing."

"Almost certainly," Roan said. "These traps are getting more dangerous each time. I think he's going mad."

"It's full dark, Your Highness," one of the neighbor women said, coming up and bobbing a curtsey to her. "You ought to come and stay with us. It'd be an honor."

"Thank you, but we have to go on," Leonora said, exchanging glances in the torchlight with Roan. He knew the same thought was in her mind as in his. If any more traps had been set for them, she didn't want them sprung on innocent bystanders, not with such grievous results. She leaned over, took Jennet's hand and kissed her.

"You have good neighbors," she said. "They'll have a new house for you in no time. You'll be able to pick up and keep going with your life."

"What's life without him?" the woman asked, not really caring. "My son has always nagged at us to come and live on the border, where it's safe. We can get away from Changeover, he said. It's too late. If Changeover comes, I'll let it take me."

"You can't think that way," Leonora said, firmly, shifting back to her girlish figure for travel. She squeezed Jennet's hands. "Please. Don't let your negative thoughts affect your life. What about your influence? You have some, too. Everyone does."

"There's that," the woman said, drying her eyes. She stood up. "Don't want to make the crops fail by being negative. My husband would never have stood for that. He always worked so hard." Her eyes started to well up again, but she dried them, and set her chin, firmly. "Thank you, Your Highness. You're as good as you are beautiful."

She kissed the girl on the cheek. The neighbor women led her into another house, where inviting amber lights burned in the ornate glass windows.

"Will that be enough to help her?" Misha asked, watching her shut the door.

"No," the princess said, sadly, "but it's all we can do."

Chapter 28

The action of setting up camp was beginning to settle into a routine, almost pleasant because one knew exactly what was expected of one. Taboret took her assignment from Basil, who was the officer of the day, and began tying together branches for torches to put around the perimeter. Crucible power would soon make them into beautiful iron sconces. The neat and orderly parts of her mind that Taboret knew were indeed her own took pleasure in creating something from raw materials in ways that had been hitherto unknown in the Dreamland. In spite of her misgivings, she was enjoying the use of great power.

The site Brom had chosen for that night's camp was very comfortable. It was a rounded gully that had been the oxbow joint of a river long ago in some Sleeper's deep dream. Now the riverbed was dry and full of saplings as narrow as her finger. The ways in and out were very close together, easy to watch and guard.

The fact that they needed to be on guard reminded her that she had once again betrayed the cause. That button she had left behind—who knew what it might have become by way of warning. She hoped someone would see it. Would the police in Reverie have put Roan in jail? Or worse? She'd heard of Durance Vile. Although she didn't know where it was, the pictures the name had always summoned up in her mind were horrible. Taboret forced the memory of the lost button to the back of her mind, and made herself think harder about her job. Blend with the others, and no one would notice any discrepancy in her thoughts. It was hard, though. Every time Brom turned her way, she expected to hear an accusation. He'd had his eye on her for some time, now. No, she admonished herself, think *sconce*.

She spotted Glinn in the kitchen area. He was piling stones together to make the refectory table and benches. Taboret watched him fondly. They'd been working together for almost a year, and she had never seen him as more than a colleague. How blind she'd been.

He must have sensed her regard even all the way across the camp, because he looked up and smiled directly at her. She felt that little, warm tingle run up and down her skin. Then she felt a surge of panic. What would Glinn do if he knew she was a traitor?

Glinn straightened up and beckoned to her. She shook her head, pretending to have trouble tying up some of the twigs. This was the last torch. When she finished with it, she'd have no excuse not to go and help him. He gave her that silly sideways grin that she had always liked. All right, she'd go, but she promised herself she'd keep a tight rein on her thoughts.

"You're finished," he said, as she joined him. "Would you like to help me?"

"Of course," Taboret said. "What do you need me to do?"

Glinn looked around at the others. Everyone else seemed to be very busy, or deliberately not looking their way. Even Basil had his back to them, choosing bottled herbs from his pack.

"Come on back here," he said, escorting her behind the cobblestone stove. "We can shore up the insulation and help save fuel."

Taboret recognized the excuse as a thin pretext. Basil always saw to the stove and the utensils himself, jealously guarding the privilege, and he never asked for help. Something savory was simmering in a big pot on one of the two burners. Taboret took a good sniff as she went by. Pepper, she thought. It could use another pinch. She realized she had acquired at least a small portion of Basil's gourmet cooking mentality. Who knew what else, or who else, was in there now. The twinge of guilt returned, and she tamped it down hard.

"Come on," Glinn said. "I'd like to have a quiet talk with you."

He took her hand, and pulled her into a kind of alcove consisting of the back of the stove and a jutting wall of rock that almost met it. Between them, she saw Carina go by. Carina shot her a friendly leer and a wink. Taboret realized suddenly that she couldn't understand what the other woman was thinking. She gaped up at Glinn.

"What did you do?" she asked.

"I've given us a little privacy," he said. He took her in his arms, making her tingle in all kinds of places. A little nervously, she put her arms around him, too. His present form was very thin. She could almost feel his ribs, but there was a good layer of muscle over them, and that was reassuring. Glinn lowered his face so it gently touched her hair and moved down next to her ear. His light exhalation made her tingle again.

"I know what you did," he said, very quietly. "Back there on the trail." She jumped, almost feeling her bones pop out of her skin. He folded her tighter against him. "Don't panic. It's all right."

"I didn't do anything," she protested, putting her hands on his chest to push him away.

"That's what happened to the button, isn't it?" he asked, keeping his grip on her. She could feel his mind pressing against hers, but no one else's. Was he trying to get her to confess? To report her to Brom?

"No, it was an accident," she said. "That's what happened."

"It's not," Glinn said, quietly. "I know you dropped it on purpose so someone following us would not miss that turning. Please, tell me the truth. We're shielded from the others, but it can only last for a short time. Brom will get suspicious if we're out of the loop for too long. Quickly!"

"Yes, I did," Taboret blurted out before she could stop herself. "I did it once before, too." She stopped and put both hands over her mouth. But instead of having her stomach turn somersaults of guilt, she was relieved. It helped to have someone to share her secret with, someone she could trust. But, oh, could she trust him? Then she realized it wasn't only her relief she felt. She could feel the muscles in Glinn's neck and back relaxing, in sympathy with her own.

"I'm glad," he said, looking around to make certain no one was watching them too carefully. Everyone was still walking by with smirks on their faces. He put her arms down around his waist again, and enfolded her in his arms. "So have I. I've been leaving signs all along for the King's Investigator."

"*You?*"

"Yes. Do you really want to help?"

"Oh, yes," Taboret gasped. "But how?"

"Help me," Glinn said. "I can't stop Brom by myself. Neither can the two of us alone. Roan has to catch up with us and join his strength to ours. With help we can use the gestalt itself against Brom."

"But you're the one that he trusts, his second-in-command," Taboret said, bewildered. "How can you be the one trying to stop him?"

Glinn grimaced. "Because he's not making sense any more. I thought the experiment was interesting in the beginning. I also thought he had permission to fulfill it. I should have known the king would never give his leave to rouse the Sleepers. It's too late. Partly my fault, for being too fascinated with the concept to think about the outcome. Will you help me?"

His plan was so daring it was exciting. Her mood rose at once, now that she knew she was no longer alone in her fear or her feelings.

"Of course I will," Taboret said, shifting a little bit so his upper arm was comfortably settled in the curve of her neck and the other one was around her waist. "I would keep leaving a trail anyway. I've been so afraid one of the traps would kill . . . someone. . . . Is that the only reason we're back here alone?"

Glinn smiled at her, his soft brown eyes crinkling at the corners. He glanced down at her mouth and back to her eyes. "You know it's not. You can hear what I'm thinking."

With pleased satisfaction, Taboret knew that he wanted to kiss her, and he felt shy about it. So did she. He understood that, and his gaze was tender. Very slowly, he dipped his head, his lips reaching for hers. She tilted her face up, waiting. The moment they touched, she felt skyrockets of joy exploding inside her. She locked her arms around him and hugged him close. The meeting of bodies was as nice as the meeting of minds.

"I said, come and get it!" Basil's voice shouted over their heads. "Come on, you two, everyone's waiting." Sheepishly, they broke apart.

"Remember," Glinn said, in so low a whisper that she had to put her ear right next to his mouth to hear him. "One mistake, and Brom will know what we're doing. He needs us for the gestalt, but not so badly he'll keep overt traitors around. Shield your thoughts. The safety of the Dreamland depends upon it."

"I will remember," she said. But it was too tempting, standing there close to him in the shadow of the trees. She turned her face up for another kiss, and Glinn was only too happy to respond.

When they came around at last to join the others at the table, Dowkin and Doolin jeered at them.

"Doing a few biology experiments of your own, are you?" Doolin asked.

Taboret felt so wonderful she didn't care. She gave each brother a friendly smile and sat down at her place.

"What's wrong with extracurricular activity?" she asked, and realized she was smirking.

"As long as it does not interfere with our work!" Brom boomed from the head of the table.

"Of course not, sir," Glinn said, concerned, facing their employer. "I wanted to mention to you, sir, that I had some ideas for increasing our speed without endangering the steeds. . . ."

In daylight, the distortion to the landscape was almost an unbroken ribbon ahead of them. Lum shook his head and walked his bike back to join the others.

"You don't need my skills any more, sir," he said to Roan. "You could follow this with a glow worm in a snowstorm."

"Are you certain that there is no residual effect on passersby?" Misha asked, surveying half-melted rocks, and birds with whiskers perched in the trees.

"There shouldn't be," Bergold said, uncertainly. Today he had a curly blond beard, which he scratched thoughtfully. "But I really don't know. I've never seen anything like the gestalt before. Brom certainly isn't trying to hide his passage any longer."

"I'm not sure he can," Roan said. The paving stones formed a crazy-quilt under his steed's tires, almost too soft to ride over. "This is worse than it has ever been. There's one small comfort, though. If the Alarm Clock is causing this much ill-effect, he'll have to travel through as few habitations as possible, but because it's so cumbersome, he must stay on major roads. We won't have to follow him cross-country."

"There will be towns on every road at the edge of the province," Leonora said, in a worried voice.

"Surely we'll have caught up with him by then," Roan said, and hoped he sounded more certain than he felt.

"But just where in the mountains is he going?" Felan asked.

Bergold opened the map.

"Brom took us on a merry chase when we first set out in pursuit," the historian said, "but I don't think he can afford to waste any more time. Since we are now going northeast, my assumption would be he is heading toward the Dark Mysteries, although to what part I cannot guess."

"He must be miles ahead," Spar said. "We need motor transport like theirs."

"We don't need physical transport if we have the luck," Bergold said. "Keep working hard to attain our goal, and we'll earn that luck. We've been going about this the wrong way. Our steeds are old-fashioned, and we can't make them into jet engines or motor cars or airplanes. Only the Sleepers can do that, and only on a whim. We can't count on it."

Misha nodded. "This is also doctrine according to Continuity. So what can we do?"

"We all have influence, to a certain extent," Bergold said. "Use it. Keep striving honestly forward, and hope for good luck. The Sleepers created us to be their problem-solvers, and that's what they'll favor. I've always found that the more focused I am, the luckier I am."

"No, no," Colenna protested. "We're supposed to be contented with what the Sleepers send, not change it."

"You don't believe that," Leonora said. "Otherwise you would never have left Mnemosyne."

"I have come along to stop someone who is interfering with the Sleepers' will, not to change things myself!"

"This is where Brom and his crucible have their advantage over us," Roan said. "They have been concentrating on a single goal, and it has kept them ahead of us. We need to catch up. Therefore, we need to cooperate."

"Goblins and closet monsters, what do you think we've been doing?" Felan demanded.

"We have to go still further than we have," Roan said. "Colenna, it does no harm to hope for luck. Our ultimate goal is the same: to stop Brom. We'll argue dogma when it's all over."

"All right," the older woman said, with a half-admiring sideways grin at him. "Truce."

"Very well," Roan said, and he held out his right hand. "Brom's method seems sound. Let's put our hands together as a sign of unity of purpose." Bergold and Leonora put in their hands at once. The others followed suit a little more reluctantly. Spar and Felan looked as though they felt silly, but reached out to touch the others. Roan found the contact reassuring and strengthening.

"To one purpose," he said. "For good luck."

"To one purpose," they echoed.

"Good. Let's go on, then," Roan said.

"This is amazing," Felan said, as they rode through a field of four-leafed clovers. "I've traveled before. Why has this never happened to me? All of these symbols of good fortune?"

"A combination of circumstances," Bergold said. "Most of us do have significant influence of our own. I would also cite Sleepers' whim. And perhaps it is true what has been said in the past, that effects are magnified or multiplied as one approaches the Seven's presence." Roan thought he believed in the latter, since Bergold had been changing shape more frequently than ever. His beard had brightened to red, and he was smoking a long, thin pipe.

"That would make Brom's messes worse as we go," Leonora said.

"Well, aren't they?" Misha said.

"Yes, but look behind us," Bergold said, pointing back with the stem of his pipe. "Our own passage has erased some of the effects of the Alarm Clock. We're already having a beneficent influence on the land itself."

Roan felt more optimistic. They were making excellent time. The sponginess of the road had become an advantage, instead of a liability, as the steeds turned from bicycles into horses again, and bounded along happily.

"Look what I've found," Hutchings said. He showed them a brimming double handful of shining, ruddy coins. "Pennies!"

"Lucky man," Felan said. Pennies had no monetary value in the Dreamland, but they were much prized as amulets of good fortune. Hutchings's brows went up in surprise.

"Yes, that's it! Take one, sir. You, too," he said to Roan. "Everybody should have a lucky penny. It'll give us an extra push."

"Everything helps," Bergold said, accepting his lucky piece with pleasure. "This is a strange manifestation of Sleepers' will. Look at that." He nodded toward a soft-looking hill in the middle of the green field to their left. It appeared to be made of hand-sized patches of multicolored cloth.

"Alette!" Spar commanded. "Go and see what it is."

The guard trotted over, and came back with an armload of cloth.

"It's socks, sir. Stockings and leggings and socks. All one of a kind." She started to sort through them. Felan reached over and grabbed a royal blue sock with a diamond embroidered on the calf.

"That's mine!"

Roan stared at him. "You're joking."

"No, I'm not," Felan said, sulkily. "My mother gave those to me years ago. She said they were unique. . . ."

"Well, they are unmistakable," Colenna said, her lips twisting in a grin. Felan ignored her.

"Then, one of them disappeared in the wash. I never found it again. I'm sure this is it." He tucked it carefully away in his saddlebag, and turned his nose up at the snickers.

"This is a lucky place," Bergold said, looking very pleased. "All kinds of things that have been lost are here. We may find items we've lost all the way back to childhood. I often wondered where things vanish to." As they rounded a bend in the road, more heaps of clothes came into sight. Roan spotted the gleam of shiny black leather, and let out a whoop of joy.

"You see a sock?" Leonora asked.

"No, my boots!" He handed her Cruiser's reins and slid off to go get them. And next to them, he found the suit that had been stripped off his back by the nuisance, and his underwear and socks and his silk top hat. Close by was a small heap of scanty, periwinkle blue underthings that could belong only to Leonora. He stood up and beckoned the party over.

"This is a good omen," Bergold said, shaking out his clothes. They were slightly too long for his current frame, but he stowed them away anyhow. "An excellent one."

They turned their backs on one another, and changed into their real clothes. With pleasure, Roan tied his silk cravat, and settled the knot comfortably under his chin. In the pockets of his suit, he found all kinds of little things he had lost over the years, including a baseball card, a coin with a buffalo on it, and a plastic decoder ring that was a family heirloom.

The road led out of the broad glen and into a narrow passage between high walls of gray stone that squeezed them from both sides until they were riding single file. Gradually, the file slowed to a stop. Roan stood up in his stirrups to see what was happening, but all he saw was the back of Spar's head. The way was too constricted for the steeds to pass.

"What's the holdup up there?" Felan shouted from the back. His voice echoed up the stone passage.

"I can't get through!" Spar called back. "There's a bar across the road. We might have to back out of here."

"What's around you?" Roan asked.

"Well, nothing!" the captain said, feeling the walls with both hands. "The sides are flat stone—no, wait a moment. There's a metal slot here on the side, about as wide as my thumbnail." Roan looked at his own thumbnail.

"The pennies," he shouted. "Try the penny Hutchings gave you, Spar."

"Yes, sir," the guard captain said dubiously, putting his hand into his saddlebag with difficulty in the tight space. But there was a grinding sound, followed by a rusty screech. "It's lifting!"

He moved forward. There was a heavy *THUNK!* and Colenna stopped next. "My turn," she said. Roan watched her elbow shift to the left, and heard the mechanical whirring. "That's it," she said. "Like an entry gate."

"I knew those pennies'd be lucky for something," Hutchings said happily, as they rode out of the narrow passage and into another valley.

The sky had changed from sunny on one side of the gate,

to breezy and damp. The ground around them was wet, as if it had just been raining. A mountain with a forked top lay immediately to the west, and Roan saw a distant line of mountains just over the horizon to the north. The land they had just left was no more than rolling hills.

"Where are we?" Lum asked.

Bergold produced the map, and surveyed the surroundings. "I would say that we're here," the historian said, pointing to a spot not far from the border of the next province.

"How'd we do that?" Spar demanded. "We should still be clear back here." He put his thumb on the map on a spot farther to the south.

"We wanted transportation," Bergold said. "We have been transported."

"So the Sleepers still favor us," Misha said, his boyish face in a grin. "This is better than the Déjà Vu."

"None of their favor is free," Bergold reminded them. "We still have to strive onward. If we grow lazy, they could change our luck to the worse just like that." He snapped his fingers, and a flower fell out of the sky. He looked up. "Ah, it's a tree shedding blossoms."

"Another hole in reality," Colenna said, with satisfaction. "All according to the Sleepers' will. This time it was a good one for us. Brom can't cause them to destroy, unless the Sleepers will it. He can only steer us into them, or if that evil power of theirs is so great, push them our way."

"So that man who fell through the hole . . . ?" Leonora asked, tentatively, recalling the horror of the night before.

"Might still be alive, my dear," Roan said, as positively as he could. "He might even be able to get home again." Leonora looked relieved.

"If the dreamers dreaming him don't wake up," Felan said, always ready with the negative alternative. The princess frowned, starting to worry all over again. Roan turned to glare at him. "Or if he doesn't get killed where he landed. . . ."

"Shut up, you!" Spar snarled. "All happy and positive, remember?"

"There's hope," Bergold said, reassuringly, patting Leonora's hand. "There's always hope."

Roan nodded solemnly, and rode beside them in silence.

For him, the most difficult part of keeping a positive attitude was that small, nagging doubt that still remained in his heart. It was hard to focus on saving the world when a part of him didn't really believe that Brom could put an end to the world. No matter what grandiose plans he had, he was still a creation of the Sleepers, and they had power over him. And yet, Roan had to believe in the threat. He had to force himself to believe that Brom's success could mean the end of everything he knew and loved. To his surprise, he didn't fear the coming catastrophe, but he was angry about it, angry that Brom and his minions would dare to terrify those people Roan loved for the sake of a question. It wasn't that there were things Man was not meant to know, but there were some with such a high price that Man was not meant to test them. Brom should have taken into account the potential for danger that would befall others.

If he admitted the truth to himself, Roan did not know what he would do when he finally caught up with Brom. He worried what he would do to him. He was so angry . . . could he kill? But he must control himself. He couldn't break the law just because Brom had. He was Roan, the King's Investigator, a representative of the crown and people of the Dreamland. If he did something as evil as that, the king would be disappointed, and he would no longer deserve Leonora's love. But he honestly wouldn't know how he would behave until the situation was in front of him. He had learned a lot about himself so far on this journey, but not that, not yet.

Chapter 29

Taboret didn't feel her saddle bruises, sunburn, or any of the verbal barbs that the Countingsheep brothers kept shooting her way. She was happy. Every time Glinn looked her way or even thought about her, she felt warm inside. She knew at once what he was thinking, and knew he did the same. The landscape looked more colorful. The trees were taller. Birdsong was sweeter, and all because he was with her. She knew she was being terribly subjective, and didn't care.

Their romance was the subject of much amusement among the other apprentices.

"Think it's a side effect of the gestalt?" Carina asked, playfully, as they rode northeast into the worsening weather. "Who's next?" Taboret turned back her parka hood to make a face at the older woman.

"You are," she said, lightly. "You'll fall in love with both of the Countingsheeps at once."

"I hardly think so!" Carina called back, and laughed. The brothers glared at them, and Taboret felt dark thoughts from them.

Taboret was glad she and Glinn were helping to raise the company's mood. Brom had been sour since the morning, when he had tried for the third time to change the motorcycles into an efficient truck. He had not been able to make the gestalt raise enough power to complete a lasting structure. Even with Glinn's input, the transformation into a single unit was not working as Brom had planned. He didn't know why, and that upset him. His feelings permeated the link, making everyone else uneasy. He kept muttering about controlling the individual will, which worried Taboret. They were scientists, not mindless, long-haul transport workers. The steeds were protesting the harsh treatment, and she was afraid they would reach the end of their strength before they reached their destination. She tried hard not to think that having to stop short would be a good thing.

However, Brom had succeeded in having the gestalt upgrade the motorcycles to a higher technological level than before. Their engines ran more quietly and smoothly, reducing the number of times the Alarm Clock bells chimed by accident. Taboret found that to be a minor comfort.

"This is the step before complete integration," Brom said, half to himself, half to Lurry, who was riding beside him. Lurry was a good conduit. Taboret could hear the conversation as perfectly as if she was inside him. "It is only a matter of time. I will fine-tune the parameters still further. We will end up with not only a supertransport, but a superhuman to drive it! One being! One unit!"

The gestalt energy changed almost from hour to hour. Taboret was aware of a growing oneness in behavior among the apprentices. At lunch, all of them reached for the same plate of food. They all stood up when one of them drove over a bump in the road. At first they did it in sequence, but now they did it each time in unison. The increasing physical coordination worried Taboret.

Glinn, riding beside her, must have sensed her concern. He put out a gloved hand to squeeze hers. She mimed a surreptitious kiss in his direction, and he tilted his head, as if catching the kiss on his cheek. Gano caught sight of the interplay, and teased them. Taboret felt her cheeks turn hot, but she knew Glinn didn't really mind.

She'd never had much patience before with lovers who constantly mooned about their "one and only," but she'd never left herself vulnerable to affection before. She had thought married life and families, like those of the villagers whose small town they were riding through, were ordinary and dull, never something she wanted for herself. Now, a little of the ordinary would be a nice, new experience if only she lived to have it. When the Sleepers woke up, everything would change or die or go away. It hadn't mattered to her before.

Why had she valued her own life so little? Now that it was almost over, there was someone else to care about. She wanted to see what happened over time when two lives joined. The experiment would prevent it, not only for her, but for all the couples in the Dreamland. And families, she thought with a blush and a growing curiosity to see what it would be like to have her own.

A child's shout made her and all the other apprentices look to the right in unison. A little girl was running through a cottage garden, laughing. Taboret felt her heart sink at the sight. She wanted desperately to stop the experiment, but she feared it was too late. Glinn gave her hope. He thought he knew what to do. She clung to that. Someday, the two of them might have a little lab of their own, maybe in a place like this. A junior scientist or two, blowing up retorts on the kitchen table. . . .

She stopped staring at the little town and turned her attention forward. To her shock, Brom was looking back at her, his red eyes ablaze. She realized she had been thinking without filtering her thoughts through the usual haze of obedience and optimism. Oh, no! What had he heard? Had anyone else been listening? But Brom turned around again and kept riding, without his usual sour comment. Perhaps he'd just caught the edge of her discontent, and was saving a lecture for her later. She hunched over her handlebars, and tried to review her thoughts.

She was still feeling distracted when they came over the headland and saw the bronze bridge leading to Rem. It was very handsome, with ornamented arches and spans, standing on granite pilings stained green with algae around the water line. The road ran past it, rather than to it, and two pairs of shiny rails spanned its length. It was a railway bridge.

"That has to be half as old as the Dreamland," Bolmer said. "Metalwork like that hasn't been common for ages."

"You have the soul of an architect," Basil said. But Taboret knew they all saw the image in their minds and admired it with Bolmer's interest and expert knowledge. She hoped that if she survived the experiment, she would retain some of what the others' minds had put in her memory.

To either side along the bank overlooking the gap, she could see numerous small villages, each with its own little footbridge spanning to the other side. Some of them were as uncomplicated as a few ropes and some planks, some more elaborate. Did they indeed help as escape routes in times of Changeover? She also wondered, guiltily, if they would serve any function at all when she and the Alarm Clock reached the Sleepers. It was funny to see palm trees on the far side and icicles on the near one.

Brom signaled them to the left.

"We will cross here!" he said. He rolled forward, and the tires of his motorbike widened and became ridged to fit over the left rail. Lurry hastily caused the same alteration to his steed, and rode the right rail.

As she and Glinn passed side by side over the bridge, Taboret took a brief look down into the deep gorge, and experienced a surge of vertigo. That was one of the facets of shared intelligence that she didn't like, since she was not normally this afraid of heights.

Halfway across, the weather changed from winter to summer. It was a hot day in Rem. All of the apprentices began to shed layers of clothing. And, as usual, when passing from one Sleeper's influence into another, their bodies changed, too. Once she had shed the sweaters, thick pants, parka, and boots, Taboret was pleased to see that she'd acquired a more shapely form than her usual practical body type. Had it been wishful thinking on her part? Was this a subconscious, nonintellectual attempt to attract Glinn's attention? It worked. Glinn's warm thoughts were more ardent than before. If they stopped in a while for a meal, she'd make sure they found themselves a little privacy.

They rolled down the gravel bed of the railway cut until they found another road, and bumped up onto it. Brom directed them to the right, so they were heading north again.

A few miles later, a broad, sharp-edged shadow veered in over their heads. Taboret was just in time to see the huge, white-headed bird zoom in for a landing on the ground beside Brom before it turned into a small square envelope with an eagle stamp in the corner. Lurry jumped off his bike to retrieve it for their master.

Brom tore open the envelope and read the single page within.

"They are close behind us," he said, and no one had to ask whom he meant. "We need another deterrent set." He glanced up and down the line, and his glowing gaze lit on her. "You." His head swiveled until he found Glinn. "And you. Go with Acton and Maniune. Roan has not yet crossed the bridge. We can use that to our advantage. Men, here are your instructions."

He turned to the pair of mercenaries and started to talk to them in a low voice. Taboret, through Lurry, tried hard to eavesdrop. What kind of nefarious trap did Brom want them to set? She found that the chief had thrown up a privacy barrier, in exactly the same way she and Glinn had the night before. Drat. She wondered why he was blocking them out, then decided he must have been doing it all along, but the link hadn't been strong enough before for her to have detected it.

Brom looked up at last. "Glinn, hand Basil your nuisance detector. We do not want to encounter any snags while you're gone."

"Yes, sir." Glinn undid the gold chain and handed over the watch-sized object. Taboret found Brom's expression puzzling. He looked disappointed. Could it be that he felt Basil was not as adept at Glinn at reading the little indicator? True, the philosophical device was a complex piece of machinery, but it was as easy to use as a compass. She felt a surge of pride, to think that in the eyes of their employer Glinn was not considered to be easily replaceable.

"Go immediately," Brom instructed them. "We will continue on until we reach our optimum stopping point. This distraction must be enough to dissuade Roan once and for all. You will use the gestalt power. Draw whatever you need, but it must be effective. We are trusting you with the entire bank of power."

Taboret nodded solemnly. She'd have been flattered if it wasn't so wrong. She turned her motorbike to follow Acton. Glinn fell in behind, and Maniune brought up the rear.

As the sounds of Brom's motorcade receded behind them, Taboret felt a sudden urge to rev up her steed and speed away home. She glanced back at Glinn, who shook his head. He had something in mind, she felt it. They would set the trap, just as Brom had directed them to, and then find some way to prevent anyone from falling into it. That wouldn't be easy with the two bruisers breathing down their neck.

The road widened out, and Glinn sped up to ride side by side with her.

"I'm glad he sent both of us," she said in a voice low enough she hoped neither of the others could hear.

"It's nice to be able to ride alone with you for a while," Glinn agreed, with a smile. Taboret tossed her head. Her hair, not usually her best feature, waved and curled around her face beguilingly.

"Hey, lovebirds!" Acton called over his shoulder, in a sneering voice. "When you smooch, do the rest of them get it on vicarious-like? Huh?" He laughed loudly at his own wit. "Huh? You touch her, and those others get a handful, too? It's better than those feelaramas they talk about in the Waking World, huh? Hey, too bad we're not part of your intimate little circle, huh? I wouldn't mind having a piece of that!"

Acton could use a solid scientific explanation and a few spare IQ points, since he had none of his own. Taboret looked daggers at him. With a quick swipe of his hand, Glinn brought them down out of the air. The knives clattered to the ground and vanished. She glanced at him in surprise. Then she realized that making enemies of the mercenaries would ensure they would keep a close eye on both of them the whole time. Taboret felt ashamed of herself. Glinn was by far the better strategist. He always thought farther ahead.

"Our personal lives are really none of your business, gentlemen," Glinn said, evenly. "Why don't you give us details of the mission we are on?"

"You'll see when we get there, huh?" Acton said. "Right, Manny?"

The temperature was almost oppressively hot, and their clothes thinned out further. Taboret found she was watching Glinn. This form was a nice body, slim, with big, capable hands. But then, he'd been sort of attractive through most of his changes. He must simply have a handsome base shape. She wondered what he thought of her, and got a quick burst of sensation through the link of satisfaction with her beauty. She felt herself blush, and hoped Acton had not noticed. He did, however, continue his lewd comments, only semi-audible over the rumble of his motorbike.

Maniune shouted them to a stop near a cluster of nebulous boulders on the road where it passed over the rails. He swung one muscular leg off his bike, and leaned against the saddle with his arms crossed.

"Himself noticed these when we came up this way," he announced to the apprentices. "He wants you to plant a hole out there," he nodded toward the way they had just come, "using this stuff for anchors. Leave it wide open, so things can come out of it from the other side. That's what he said. Make it a good one, right?"

"Right," Glinn said, striding down the road. "Come along, Taboret. We'll make this the best way we know how."

Taboret understood. They'd set their trap, but they'd make it so obvious that no one who could see would fall into it. She gathered handfuls of the nebulosity and followed him.

She formed the pseudorock into tent stakes and sky hooks while Glinn surveyed the spot where the hole was to go. He directed her where to place the stakes and helped hang the sky hooks in the air on either side of the road.

"It won't hold long if someone rides into it," he said, stroking his chin thoughtfully, a gesture that he must have caught from Brom, "so we won't worry about that. It isn't meant to hold, just to scare Roan and the others off. He'll see it in time."

Glinn put out his hand, and waited for her to lay hers on top of it.

Acting as a conduit for the entire crucible made Taboret feel like the business end of a fire hose. Power surged into her from nowhere and everywhere, and all but sprayed upward into a gleaming net. It was too much at once. She couldn't control it. She felt panic, and mentally stamped down on the flow. But Glinn was prepared. His mind-touch was gentle as he helped her open up again, guiding the burst of energy.

She felt more than saw the breach open up in the fabric of reality between them. The hole began as a tiny, bright gleam that quickly burned away the edges of nature until Taboret could see through into that other sphere beyond everyday existence. Madness lay there, she had been told as a child. Madness and formlessness.

Glinn let go of her hand and stepped backward, stretching the hole between them. Taboret feared at first that breaking contact would end the gestalt, but its form had advanced far beyond the primitive structure of the first day. The link held. She took hold of the near edge of the tear, and drew it outward.

The broad oblong was like an elaborate, silver-gray spider web, spiraling down into an endless center. If one stared at it too long, the whirling took hold of one's mind. Taboret turned her eyes away and listened to the faint roar. She thought it sounded like a cry of pain. As if he was hanging curtains, Glinn tacked up his side of the hole, and came around to fasten the edges on her side. Taboret felt like bursting into hysterical laughter. Chaos, neatly pinned and tucked.

"And if he doesn't see it in time?" Taboret whispered to him. Glinn didn't answer. She knew. He put his arm around her and held her. She was grateful. He felt so real.

"Good job," Maniune said. He and Acton came over to inspect. The two burly men looked the web up and down, approving the stakes of nebulosity holding it in place. "All done, then?"

"All done," Glinn said, dusting his hands. "It's as deadly a trap as we can make it. I think Master Brom would be pleased."

"Good," Maniune said. "We'll just test it." Each of them grabbed one of Glinn's arms, and rushed him backwards toward the web. Glinn scrabbled for a handhold, but they were prepared for a struggle. Grinning ferally, Acton threw a punch at Glinn's narrow middle, and Glinn doubled up on himself with a grunt. Taboret screamed, and jumped on Maniune's back, pounding his head with her fists. The bruiser brushed her off without effort, picked Glinn up bodily, and tossed him into the hole. Shouting, Glinn was swept down and out of sight.

Taboret ran to the edge.

"Glinn!"

The infernal winds battered at her face. All she could see was swirling nonexistence, defying her senses. She reached into the hole, hoping to find him. There was no sign, none at all. Had he been reduced to a singularity? Her eyes danced with the gray dazzle. She felt for him with her mind, but the link had been broken.

She felt a shove from behind. The mercenaries were trying to push her in, too! Taboret twisted and clutched the arms and hands coming at her, refusing to let go.

"Don't!" she cried, refusing to let them peel her off them. She found a face: Maniune's. "Please! Help me get him out."

"He's done for," Maniune said, carelessly, but his face was pale with terror. He hadn't known what chaos was like until that moment. "The boss doesn't like traitors. He wants you both finished. We're going to do the job."

"Please don't," Taboret begged. She clung to them both, gripping with an unnatural strength enhanced with gestalt power. "Please! Look what happened to him. He was torn to pieces. Don't kill me."

"All right," Maniune said. "All right, you can live for now. But that'll be you next if you don't cooperate. It'd be easy to throw you right in after him." He jerked a thumb toward the swirling mass.

Taboret felt her heart wrench in her chest as if it was tearing itself in two. Maybe that would be the best thing that could happen. If Glinn was dead, there was nothing left in life she wanted to do. She felt dead inside, too. Taboret let the men put her down, and she brushed at her clothes and hair, which felt as lifeless as her soul. She couldn't even cry.

"I'll behave," she said.

"Good," Maniune said, relieved. "That'll do. The boss will settle for that."

"Hey, she bruised me," Acton complained, rubbing his skinny neck.

"Tough," Maniune said, glaring at his comrade. "Take it. You're getting paid to take what happens."

"What does Master Brom want us to do now?" Taboret asked.

"He wants us to make sure this trap of yours works. He didn't trust you not to put a monkey wrench into it. Well, it won't, because you know what'll happen if it does." Maniune mimed giving something the heave-ho. Taboret had no trouble understanding him. She glanced behind her at the hole, and saw a pair of unearthly lights like eyes.

She shuddered. Maniune whistled the bikes to him, and they headed down the railway cut toward the river.

✧ ✧ ✧

"That way, sir," Lum said, pointing at the bridge. Roan looked at the slagged grass and jumbled cobblestones leading to the shining silver rails. Parts of the golden-brown bridge bulged and buckled, the result of the Alarm Clock's passage.

"Why would they go over a railroad bridge?" Misha asked.

"Anything else might pass too close to habitations," Bergold said, casting a look in either direction along the gap. The nearest spans were a good quarter-hour's ride each way. By then, Brom would have regained the advantage in distance. Roan was unwilling to let him take another inch.

"We'll have to walk the steeds across," Roan said. "The beams look weaker than they ought to be."

"Hmph!" Colenna snorted. "Considering what's been this way, it's no wonder."

Waving her back to a safe distance, Spar and Lum took the lead onto the near edge of the bridge. Misha and Felan came next. The others fell into line, and Roan brought up the rear, ready to pull anyone back if the footing became unsound. As Spar moved forward, the old bridge let out a loud and piteous groan. The captain flinched once, but kept marching.

"Don't crowd up too close," Felan called back to those behind him. "This thing could give at any moment."

Roan looked down. The gorge was deep, and the river at its bottom flowed as fast as any train that had passed over these tracks. He pulled back a pace from Leonora, giving her a moment to get a few yards ahead of him. Curious that the bridge had been so badly damaged, but the rails themselves remained in perfect shape. There was a permanence about the railroad that ran deep in the fabric of the Dreamland. Brom might be able to pervert it, but he could not destroy it. When it was his turn, Roan picked his way carefully. Every beam of the bridge seemed to have been transformed into a different material along its five hundred feet: cork, chalk, cheese, leather, rubber, diamond.

Spar gave a wordless shout, and Roan raised his head. The noise that had alerted the guard captain reached him, too. A train was coming along these tracks!

Roan scanned the bridge. The first wave was already past the middle of the long center span. Could they and their steeds huddle at the sides, and let the train pass them? No. It was impossible for these spans to support the weight of a train and the party, too. The train would plummet into the river far below, probably killing everyone on board.

"Turn around!" Roan shouted at them. He turned Cruiser and gave him a swat on the rump to send him off toward the bank. "Come back! I'm going to warn the engineer!"

The chug-chug-chug sound grew louder. Leonora's long dress suddenly wrapped itself around her legs and split into trousers, freeing them for action. She wheeled Golden Schwinn in a circle. The others turned, too. Roan beckoned them past him so he could run ahead and stop the train, if he could.

"Don't crowd," Bergold warned, stretching his short legs out to reach from beam to beam. Colenna trailed him by one pace, watching his feet before placing hers. "It'll collapse under us."

"Hurry!" Felan called from the end of the line. "That train's getting closer."

"Hurry," Roan said.

"Hurry!" Spar shouted.

The clattering and clicking began to echo into the canyon. The train was still concealed by the overgrowth of brush at the top of the bluffs. Roan sprang from beam to beam as fast as he dared. Thank the Sleepers, the length of his legs made the distance between the spans no difficult jump. What if the engine came onto the spans? If they braked hard, would the rest of the weight behind keep the front from falling in? He glanced behind him. The others were passing the tower and moving onto the far span. The train was coming on faster now. He didn't think he could save it. Could he save himself?

Two gleaming white lights appeared through the brush, and shot towards him on the rails. The clattering became deafening. Roan stared at the lights. That didn't look like any train engine he had ever seen. The tan and gold scale pattern of the boiler front looked like an animal head, almost reptilian. Those lights were like slitted eyes.

Roan gaped. They were eyes. In fact, it wasn't a train at all. It was a rattlesnake the size of a train.

"Run!" Roan shouted at his friends.

The snake slithered forward. Its long tail shook, producing

the noise that had fooled them into believing in an oncoming train. But this was worse. Opening its huge, pink mouth, the snake displayed man-height fangs dripping with venom. Faster and faster it came, seeking to engulf the tiny humans. And the bridge began to buckle under its weight.

"We'll have to jump for it!" Roan called.

There was no more time. He vaulted the guard rail, and the bridge crashed into pieces above him as he fell.

Chapter 30

Taboret let out a little shriek as the bridge collapsed into the gorge. The giant snake, people, steeds, and all tumbled down the steep banks into the river. She ran to the edge, and parted the brush with her hands. She searched the water for bodies. Was anyone still alive?

The snake surfaced briefly. Its eyes dimmed, and it broke into sections, each about the size of a train car, as the current carried it off. Once it was out of the way, Taboret could see heads bobbing up above the surface. She blew a gusty sigh of relief.

"Hide yourself, nitwit," Maniune snarled behind her. She drew up a cloak of invisibility from the crucible, and continued scanning the silver expanse for other survivors.

Brom's intelligence pushed at her mind, wanting to know more, to see more. She poked her head farther out of the brush. The pursuers' steeds reverted to horses. They swam to the far bank and scrambled up onto the sand, where they shook themselves dry. Their human riders were less efficient at self-rescue. The current shot them in every which way against the banks, so they were widely separated. She couldn't really tell how many there were.

"Hello?" asked a small voice, choked with water. "Is anyone there?"

Taboret looked down. A slender figure dressed in white clung dripping to the rocks almost immediately below them.

"Someone? If you are up there, please help me."

Taboret gawked. It was Princess Leonora.

"Your Highness!" she shouted.

Taboret was appalled. She thought the princess was safely back on her way to Mnemosyne. She must not fall back into the river. She would drown.

"The princess?" Maniune hissed. "Grab her!"

Taboret pushed him out of the way and flattened herself on the muddy bluff. She held on with one hand to the branches while she extended the other arm down toward the princess. The twigs scratched her face. She spat out leaves.

"Your Highness, can you reach me?" she called. Her voice was distorted by an echo, but the young woman seemed to have understood. A hand appeared from amidst the wet draperies, and lengthened, stretching upward.

"Where are you?" Leonora's voice cried. "I can't see you."

Taboret dropped her invisible shield. She wrapped her strong fingers around the princess's wrist, and pulled.

"I'm making myself as light as I can," Leonora's voice said plaintively.

"Help me," Taboret gasped over her shoulders at the mercenaries. "Pull us back."

Maniune and Acton took hold of her legs, and dragged her along the ground. Taboret tucked her free arm under the princess's shoulders as soon as she could, and held her tight around the ribs as the two men hauled them to safety. Leonora crawled a couple of paces on her knees, and stopped, rubbing her elbows, which were battered and scraped. She sealed the wounds, and looked up at her rescuers.

"Thank the Sleepers for you," she said, pushing back her wet black hair and wringing the water out of her clothes. "I wouldn't have made it without help. Do you live nearby? I suppose most people live on the border. It is safer, isn't it? My friends will be looking for me. Have you seen any of them?" Leonora looked up with a friendly expression, which abruptly turned to horror when she noticed Taboret's blue-and-white summer tunic and pocket protector.

In a twinkling, she was on her feet and running away like a doe. Just as swiftly, Maniune and Acton had separated, headed her off and pushed her backwards into the bushes where she couldn't escape.

"Not so fast, madam," Maniune said, with a leer, leaning over her. "We're happy to have you drop in for a visit."

The girl stared at both of them, then took a deep breath, but before she could scream, Acton had clamped a hand over her mouth.

"Hah! This is even better than a trap," Maniune said. "She'll make a good hostage." At that, Leonora started to change, becoming bigger and stronger. She intended to be no one's hostage. Her clothes turned to leather armor, and a sword appeared in her hand. Taboret stared in admiration. Leonora had an astonishing amount of influence. In a moment, she would break free, and probably slay them all. Maniune rounded on Taboret, who ran up to help her.

"Control her, damn you! Shut her up!" the mercenary growled. "Take that blasted sword away. Now! Or you know what's coming to you."

Or into the hole, Taboret knew. Much against her will, she sent a wave of gestalt power at Leonora. The sword melted away into air, and the fist holding it dwindled into a small, ladylike hand once more. Leonora stood struggling in the hands of her captors, looking tiny, ethereal, beautiful, and delicate in the huge surcote, and furiously angry. The men seized her wrists. With a snap of her head, she changed her clothes back to the regal white robes, and glared at Taboret. She opened her mouth, but no sound came out.

"I'm sorry," Taboret said, wishing she could explain. "I can't let you yell. I have to do what they say, or else. They won't hurt you, I promise." Leonora turned up her nose and looked away. Taboret felt like a traitor.

"Come on," Maniune said. Leonora didn't move, so he dug in his heels, stooped, and hoisted her over his shoulder. The princess kicked and punched at him as best she could upside down. He ignored the attacks. Thanks to Taboret she wasn't strong enough to hurt him. "Master Brom will be very pleased with us."

Behind her, Taboret could still hear voices calling to one another, and shouting out the princess's name. With a heavy heart, she followed the two men up the bank.

Roan stood on the top of the bluff above the empty pilings of the ruined bridge with his hands cupped around his mouth. "Leonora!" He bent his head to listen, but heard only the echo of his own cry. There was no answer.

It had been hours since they had climbed out of the river. Within a short time, everybody else had been found safe, if bruised and shaken. Golden Schwinn had turned up, saddle empty, but Leonora had not followed her horse. Devastated, Roan had run from village to village on the footpath along both sides along the gap, asking if anyone had seen her. No one had. Worried people from every town had come out to help in the search. They roamed both banks, calling.

"Leonora!" he shouted, huskily. He was growing hoarse. The worst of it was that he blamed himself. Why hadn't he made her go home to Mnemosyne as soon as she turned up in the desert with the steeds? Why had he allowed her to come along on what he knew would be a dangerous journey? It was all his fault. He had no idea if the snake had eaten her, or if she had drowned in the river current, or if she had come out ahead of them, and was waiting somewhere, wondering where they were. He hoped it was the latter. Roan had no idea how he would break the news to the king of his daughter's disappearance. He'd probably be ordered to discontinue. If he was responsible for Leonora's death, he'd do that anyhow.

She had come back to him after Reverie, only to be lost again. This was *precisely* what he had feared from the beginning.

When Bergold had fallen from the bridge fleeing from the snake, he'd become a seal. In that form he had spent the last hours diving and swimming, searching the water for traces. Roan hadn't seen him in some time, and wondered if he had found anything. He scanned the river again.

"Leonora!" he shouted. The echo of his call skipped across the water.

"She's not down there," Bergold's voice said. Roan turned to look into the seal's sympathetic brown eyes. "I saw no traces of blood or fabric. There's no evidence at all of anything ill having occurred, lad. She'll undoubtedly turn up farther down river, and somebody will see to it that she gets home. She's more resilient than you think." His black whiskers lifted in a ghost of his usual cheery grin, and Roan knew Bergold was as worried as he. "You'll see. We'll get back to Mnemosyne, and she will meet us at the very gates, demanding all the details before we're even off our bikes." He blew out his cheeks, and shook his sleek head, spraying water in a broad arc.

"She's spirited, I've always said it," Spar put in gruffly. His eyes were red, and the lines framing his mouth were engraved deep. "Never give up."

Colenna laid a kindly hand on his shoulder. "You can't kill an ideal, Roan."

"We'd better go on," Roan said, at last. "We must complete our mission to save the Dreamland, no matter what. Leonora would want us to. But I want to leave someone behind, in case she finds her way back to this point. If she does return . . . here," he added, a little less certainly, "then take her back to the palace immediately. I won't risk her again."

"Alette, Hutchings," Spar ordered. "Your assignment. Keep the search going. One of you remains on duty here at all times."

"Yes, sir," the guards said in unison, standing at attention.

Golden Schwinn squeaked piteously, and Cruiser leaned against her and rubbed front tires. Everyone was upset. They all wanted to say something to Roan, but when they met his eyes, they fell silent. Too devastated to speak, Roan mounted, and led the way up the headland. They rode along the rails several hundred yards downhill until they came to the point where the main road crossed overhead. Lum spurred his bike upward and scanned their surroundings as the others walked their steeds up the sharp incline and came level with him. The young corporal's brows drew down as his gaze fixed on something to the right, and he jumped forward to pick it up.

"Look at this," he said, holding out a handful of dried flowers. Roan took it from him. It was the daisy chain Leonora kept in her locket. There was no mistaking it.

"That's hers," he said, definitely. He tucked it very carefully into his watch pocket. It was one of her treasures. She'd want it back.

"She had to be out of the water to drop it here," Bergold cheered. "She's alive! I told you so, my boy."

Roan smiled. The ton weight on his heart fell away. He looked around. "But where did she go? She ought to be waiting here for us."

"Probably started walking," Felan said. "We've got her steed. We'll catch up with her in no time."

"Which way?" Colenna asked.

"There's no prints on this road to show," Lum said.

"But she had to come up here from somewhere," Roan said. "Help me find the place. We'll trace her steps back. There must be a clue."

Spar called his guards back. With renewed hope, everyone began to search the edge of the road. It was Misha who found the torn clump of grass at the edge of the bluff, and Hutchings a patch of gravel that showed signs of having been disturbed.

"Here!" he shouted. Lum came running to investigate.

"This is it, sir," he said. "I see footprints. Right there!"

"Are they Leonora's?" Roan asked.

The corporal sprang off his steed and knelt on the ground in the tangle of weeds. He looked up and his face was shining. "It looks like the shoes she was wearing today, sir. Flat bottoms and just a short heel. They were very wet, sir, but they're pretty clear. She came up out of the water there." Lum pointed at a spot at the edge of the bluff where the weeds were tangled and torn.

Colenna clutched her hands to her heart. "She's all right, then? Where is she?"

"Those aren't a woman's prints," Spar growled, pointing at other marks in the rough, sandy soil.

"No, sir," Lum said. "They're riding boots. A big man's. It looks like he helped pull her up. There's signs of some active movement, then the woman's prints stop. Must be carrying her."

"Heavens," Colenna said, alarmed. "I hope she's all right."

"There's a lot of footprints. Might be more than one other person, but it's hard to tell." Lum walked along hunched over, reading the signs. Roan followed him, his heart full of hope. "The prints end at the surfaced road, of course, sir."

Bergold smacked one flipper into another. "That messenger, Osprey. He must have caught up with us. Depend upon it, he discovered her prank and came after her to complete his assignment. He must have carried her to his vehicle. There you are, lad. She's been carried off to the capital, just as we hoped."

Roan was still troubled. "Why didn't she leave us a message?" he asked. "Why throw out the daisy chain? If the Night has taken her, she would have had time to write a proper note and pin it to a tree."

Bergold rolled an amused eye. "She gave him the slip the last time he let her have a moment alone, didn't she? He probably took off at once so she wouldn't do it again. That beast of his can fly, can't it?"

"Yes, it can," Roan said, relieved. His sense of purpose came flooding back. "So, she's going home. Thank the Sleepers. I will borrow some of your writing materials later, Felan, so we can send her reassurances that the rest of us are all right."

"Of course," Felan said. He had a thoughtful look on his face as they helped boost Bergold into his saddle. The steed had obligingly become a broad-backed donkey, wide enough to carry the seal comfortably. "Roan, I'm happy for you."

"Thank you, my friend," Roan said, touched. "Now, let's get back on the trail of the Alarm Clock."

Lum swung onto his steed. "That way, sir," he said.

The distortion had fused the road into a shiny, curved, glass ribbon that made it difficult for the steeds to keep their balance. They went single file slowly along the center with Lum at the lead. Within a few hundred yards, the young corporal let out a wordless exclamation, and held up his hand to signal the others to halt.

He jumped off his steed, and tottered unsteadily to pick something off the road. He brought it back to Roan.

"Is this hers, too?" he asked. It was the miniature portrait of the King and Queen. Roan frowned over it.

"Yes, it is. She keeps it in her locket."

"Well, well," Bergold honked. "It's another sign she came this way. She's leaving us breadcrumbs to help us follow the trail."

"But she would never throw this away so casually," Roan said, growing more worried. A little farther along, Lum picked up a blue silk scarf that Roan had also seen in Leonora's possession. And a bottle of perfume, her favorite scent. The conclusion that she had gone along willingly with her rescuer diminished in likeliness with every new discovery.

"She's in danger," Roan said, touching the pocket where he had stowed the small treasures as if he could feel her thoughts through them. "She's dropping these things to let us know she's in trouble. She doesn't dare to do anything more open, such as making these into SOS messages."

"Nonsense," Felan said. "She's left that locket open, that's all. It probably broke when she climbed up the riverbank, and she's spilling things out without knowing."

"No," Roan said, positively. "She loves these things. If they fell, she would notice. I know she's in trouble. Those male footprints—they must belong to one of Brom's people. They watched us fall into the water, and they took Leonora when she came ashore."

Bergold's whiskers turned downward. "Then we have a double purpose in catching up with Brom."

Roan nodded, his lips set. His confused feelings jelled into fierce determination. They would catch up with Brom, and they would put an end to him and his monstrous machine.

More of Leonora's treasures turned up farther down the road, and Roan put them in his pocket with the others. But the folding knife he had given her was not among them. Had he missed it? No, he was certain he had not. She must have kept it. It was a powerful symbol of her fellowship in the company of those going to save the Dreamland, and a most useful tool which Brom would not suspect she had. Even under duress, she kept her wits about her. Roan was more determined than ever to find her and make her safe.

"Your Ephemeral Highness," Brom said, ballooning into his portly court self just for a moment as he bowed before Leonora. He deflated at once into his gaunt traveling form. "This is a pleasure." When Leonora mouthed a furious comment at him, he turned to Taboret.

"You may release her voice," he said. "She can do no harm here."

"Yes, sir," Taboret said, with a heavy heart.

". . . Dare you, sir!" Leonora said, erupting into sound with the intensity of a steam valve. "My father will have you imprisoned in a rote dream for three eternities for your treason!"

"Treason?" Brom affected an innocent face, but his eyes flared with red fire. Leonora saw that and backed up a pace, bumping into Maniune, who put a restraining hand on her shoulder. Taboret didn't blame her a bit for recoiling. "Not at all, dear madam. As I saw it through the eyes of my subordinate here," he indicated Taboret, "we rescued you from certain doom. Isn't that so?"

"Yeah," Acton said.

"And now," Brom continued, his eyelids half-closing, "we offer you our hospitality and care. You are so obviously in shock after your ordeal. You will travel with us until . . ."

"Until what?" Leonora demanded. She sounded brave, but she was trembling.

"Until the end," Brom said, simply.

"This plan of yours is monstrous," Leonora said, her own eyes shooting sparks of fury. "You take a half-baked theory that endangers the lives of millions, and sneak away like thieves, when my royal father tells you not to do it. . . ."

Brom snapped his fingers, and Leonora's voice stopped. She continued to glare at him. If she'd been capable of telepathy, Brom would have gotten a mindful, Taboret was certain.

"Enough!" Brom announced, looking bored. "Carina! Come and help Her Highness into some dry clothes. Keep an eye on her. As for you," he turned to Taboret, and opened his eyes until the ruby fire filled her with quaking fear, "you and I will talk about your disobedience."

Chapter 31

Brom's lecture had been a thorough one, and not at all private. He had been watching Taboret for several days, it seemed, and catalogued instances that she had completely forgotten when she thought about going home, or did something else that failed to promote the greater good of the gestalt. He knew all about her minor treasons, even the button incident. Taboret was so completely demoralized that she was ready to give in completely to the crucible.

She heard the others snickering at her. Taboret felt her last personal memories penetrated, shared, and dealt out like a pack of cards to all nine of the others. They laughed over embarrassing moments as they were dragged out and replayed again and again. The final indignity, a coat of tar and feathers had been dumped on her. It didn't hurt, but it was humiliating and smelly in the hot sun. The others weren't talking to her, but she could hear their thoughts and they hers. She knew Gano and Carina, and even Basil, were sympathetic but they didn't dare to be tarred with the same brush.

Reeking of pitch, Taboret rode by herself at the tail end of the group, behind Carina and the princess, who had been given Glinn's motorbike. She no longer cared if her individual identity was taken away. She would do whatever Brom wanted her to. If she went back to Mnemosyne, her career was over, anyhow, for taking part in the great experiment. Glinn, who could have explained that the two of them had made it possible for the King's Investigator to stay on their trail, was gone forever. She reached out through the link, seeking for any vestige of his mind, and felt a gaping, Glinn-shaped hole where he ought to be. Part of her heart was gone, too.

The other apprentices tended to shrink from her mind-touch,

offended to find out that she didn't believe in the experiment. Privately, with what was left of her private mind, she thought some of them agreed with her and were afraid even to think it, for fear of guilt by association. The mind-link was a damned nuisance now. Whenever she heard one of the others thinking about her, it was always disapproving and scornful. She felt very lonely. To her dismay, she was still riding in time with the others, rising and sitting, revving the engine, even scratching when they did, which was a great nuisance with tar on her hands.

Leonora had some trouble managing the motorcycle, even though they were going slowly and the road was smooth. Taboret felt sorry for her, but there was nothing she could do to help. Her access to the gestalt power was scrutinized every moment, and her personal influence wasn't enough to take the vocal gag off the princess, let alone help her escape. The forest was thickening here, in full summer leaf. They could run off into the woods, but the cover that would conceal them would also hamper their movement.

"Strong cloud of influence," Basil said, reading the dial of the gold-cased detector. "Not a nuisance, but very powerful. They're coming more often now that we're over the bridge."

"Where?" Brom asked.

"Very close," Basil said, braking to a halt. "It's going to cross the road. In six seconds. Five, four, three . . ."

Gano and Bolmer, strapped to the Alarm Clock, angled to the roadside, and stopped. Taboret came to rest beside them. Bolmer turned away at once from her face, but Gano gave her a puzzled, hurt look. Dowkin and Doolin rolled past, talking in angry monotones under their breath. Enveloped in their own protective shell, they sailed straight by Basil and Brom, and into the shifting orange light tumbling over the lane.

"Stop, don't go that way!" Basil shouted in alarm, holding up his detector. The brothers' motorbikes squealed. "There's an . . ."

". . . Influence," Doolin said, standing up on all four trotters. "I know, I felt it. Shut up." His voice was a juicy, breathy snort, and his tiny eyes glared at them all with malice. He'd become a pig.

"Why didn't you warn him sooner?" Dowkin said, surveying

his brother from his pink ears to his curly tail with horror.

"I said it as soon as I knew," Basil said, peevishly. "Why didn't you hear the alarm through the link? The rest did."

"Look at him!" Dowkin said, and knelt beside the pig, who stood astride his fallen motorbike.

"Do something," Doolin snorted, nosing the ground with his snout.

"Together, now," Dowkin said. He put his forehead to his brother's, and they closed their eyes. Their outlines blurred slightly, but when the influence cleared, one was still a pig. Taboret looked at them, and couldn't help giggling. There wasn't much difference between their usual surly expression and the pig's jowly disapproval.

Princess Leonora, sidesaddle on Glinn's bike, let out an amused sniff. The brothers favored her and their companions with a hateful grimace, then tried again. This time, they shimmered together, drawing on the gestalt itself. Taboret was frightened, feeling as if she might be drawn into it any moment and become a pitch-covered pig. Thank fate, that attempt failed, too. Dowkin looked up with despair in his homely face.

"Chief, we need your help. Let's make the crucible and make him identical again!"

"Nonsense," Brom scolded them. "You're wasting time. He'll turn back eventually. The force of the influence was dispelled on him, but it is temporary, as are all changes in the Dreamland. Get back on your transport, and let us go on. We are nearly at our destination."

"No," Dowkin said. "Wc want to be identical." He sat down on the ground next to his brother, and gave himself a pig face and ears, which was all he could do with his measure of personal influence.

"In ordinary circumstances we always look alike," Doolin oinked. "This is serious power we're playing with here. Leaves us without our normal defenses."

"That's right," Dowkin said, flinging his arm over his brother's round neck. "Our identity. We're not going anywhere until you fix us."

Brom glared from one to the other, and got double his ire back from the brothers.

"Oh, all right," he said, disgustedly, stepping off his transport. "Stupid, petty, emotional people, hooked on minutiae, when I have so much to think about. Form the crucible!"

"What about Her Highness?" Carina asked, hooking a thumb over her shoulder.

"Easily done," Brom said. With a wave of his hand, the motorbike Leonora was sitting on became a metal cage. Her support yanked from beneath her, Leonora fell on her bottom on the grass verge. She gasped. Taboret winced and started toward the princess, but the gestalt power dragged her back toward the place where the apprentices were gathering. Brom was keeping her on a very short lead. She gave Leonora a sympathetic look, but all she got in return was another glare. What the princess was saying couldn't be heard, but the meaning was evident.

It took very little of the gestalt's power to bring the Countingsheep brothers back to normal. Taboret was annoyed for having to spend time and energy on them, but that part of her that now contained the brothers' consciousness, was irritated with everyone else for not hurrying up. And the Brom feeling, overall, filled her with repression, impatience—and fear. Taboret was surprised, and hoped she hid it in time. She could also feel the other apprentices' enthusiasm for the unity, and wished she truly shared it, instead of getting a wisp of contact euphoria from the link. Didn't they realize they could all die? She hoped she was concealing her own fear, but decided it didn't matter. She blocked out as much of the link as she could, and the others were happy to let her be alone with her thoughts when it was over.

Doolin produced a mirror to admire his newly restored countenance. Dowkin almost pranced around his brother in delight.

"That's better," he said. "It's not right when we don't look alike."

Taboret heard a screech overhead. The great post-eagle winged in and landed on a tree branch next to Brom. As soon as the chief scientist reached for it, it flattened into an envelope and fluttered into his hand.

"Ah, an update," Brom said, tearing it open, and reading the message. "They made it out of the river."

"Too bad," Maniune said, revving his motorbike engine. "We left 'em to drown. They must be good swimmers."

"Yes," Brom said, absently, running his eyes down the note, which appeared to have been scrawled in haste. "Yes, they've concluded that we have Her Ephemeral Highness in our custody, but they are not turning back. Tenacious, aren't they?"

"Stupid," Acton said.

"Send a message," Brom said, turning to Gano. "Addressed to Master Roan. Tell him that if they cease their annoying pursuit, the Princess Leonora will be returned safely when our experiment is concluded. Leave it vague as to what will happen if he does not. In the meantime, we must hurry. We are almost there. We shall know from our friend's next report whether or not they have taken us up on our offer."

Taboret heard another gasp, and glanced behind her at Leonora, whose eyes were wide and eyebrows raised high on her forehead. She had the look of someone who had just had a startling revelation.

Chapter 32

The huge, white-headed bird sailed down and fluttered its wings to land lightly on the road in front of the file of bicycles, and converted into an air mail delivery envelope. Spar's beast was surprised into bucking, and the guard captain had to backpedal energetically to make it stop. Roan jumped off Cruiser to pick up the envelope, and read the insert. Angrily, he crushed the paper in his fist.

"What is it?" Bergold asked, his whiskers erect.

"Read it," Roan said grimly, thrusting the note at his old friend. He didn't trust his own voice.

Bergold unfolded the crumpled paper and spread it out on his handlebars. "Yes, this confirms our guesses. How can he think we'll withdraw? His possession of the princess only doubles our need to catch up with him."

"He must have some means of seeing our movements," Colenna said, digging in her handbag for her handkerchief. "Does that power collective of his have a kind of clairvoyance?"

"They must," Felan said. "How else could they know what they do?"

"It's a bluff," Spar said. "They won't dare hurt her. Does that self-important bully say so?"

"No," Bergold said. He rolled the note back into a ball and balanced it on his nose, then flipped it to Roan.

"Then we go on," Spar said. "Right, sir?"

"We do," Roan said, swinging back aboard Cruiser, who stood with his handlebars quivering, echoing his master's intensity. "Brom just gave up his last hope of mercy."

"We'll tear him to pieces," Spar said, spurring his beast onward. "And what's left, we'll scoop into a little bag to bring back for trial. I'll personally give him a grand tour to his insides.

And," he looked over his shoulder at Roan, "I'll . . ."

But Roan was staring past the guard captain in alarm.

"Spar, halt!" he cried. He reached for the rear bumper of Spar's bike, and Colenna leaned against him just in time. Spar stopped short, almost turning his bicycle over in his haste.

In the middle of the main road was an irregular rectangle of gray film, or so it seemed. But as Roan looked at it, a pattern emerged in it, like a gigantic spider web, compelling them forward like helpless flies. The grayness tore at his mind, thirsting for his life. Roan shuddered, and turned his eyes away, breaking the spell. It was the largest hole in reality he had ever seen.

"Nightmares!" Misha breathed.

"Nightmares, indeed," said Bergold.

"You nearly went into that, Spar," Felan said, the blood drawn out of his face.

"I saw it," Spar said, peevishly. "Almost as obvious as the nose on your face. Some subtlety Brom's showing, hanging this thing in the road like the day's washing. Ride around it!" he shouted to the others, a little more forcefully than necessary. "Lum, Hutchings, Alette, on guard! Move it! Keep clear!"

Roan steered Cruiser and Golden Schwinn to the left, guiding them past the pegs of rock obviously securing the web of influence in place. He felt the pull of the vortex. It was strong. Brom and his minions were playing with dangerous levels of power. Left unchecked, a hole this big could devastate a large city.

"Hurry up," Spar said. "If we linger too long it might yank us in any which way."

"Who's that?" Misha cried, pointing. Roan gasped as one hand, then another, appeared from inside the hole, clutching the bottom edge for dear life. The fingers were bleeding and burned. They rushed towards it. "Could it be the princess?"

"Stay back!" Spar barked. "It's a trap."

"No," Colenna said, holding onto Misha as an anchor. She bent down to peer over the edge. "There's a man in there. He's just barely holding on." She put her arm into the vortex, and Misha braced himself to take her weight. "Can you hear me, sir?" she called. "Take my hand!"

"Can't," came a feeble voice over the roar. "Help me!"

Colenna looked impatiently at the circle of men. "Well, do something!"

Roan took a rope out of his saddlebag, and opened the piton attachment of his pocket knife. He tied the rope to it and plunged it into the ground. He unreeled the rope into the hole. It immediately went taut as the vortex took it, and started to whirl in a circle. Holding the rope, Roan inched himself close enough to look in. His hair whipped at his ears and eyes, but he got an impression of a figure with dark hair clinging to a wisp of solidity that was part of the barrier between reality and chaos.

"Can you take the rope?" Roan shouted to the man. The man's face turned up toward him, eyes squeezed nearly shut. His body was flat out, feet toward the vortex. He shook his head at Roan.

"Don't dare."

"I'd better go in for him," Roan said, over his shoulder. He reached for the rope, and looped it around his arm. The spinning length chafed at his wrist, whipping his skin again and again. He played the rope out a foot or two, preparing to climb into the hole.

"Not you, sir," Lum said, holding on to his shoulder. "Can't risk you. I'll do it."

"I'll do it, sir," Alette said, turning to Spar. "I'm good at rappeling."

"Well, *someone* do it," Colenna said, impatiently, wringing her hands. The man's fingers tightened in agreement.

Roan and Misha felt over the edge until they found the man's wrists, and hauled at him. Felan and the guards held tight to their belts and legs. Bergold stood by and honked raucous encouragement.

The vacuum pulling at them from the hole was tremendous. Several times Roan felt his feet leave the ground. It was only the determination of Spar and Alette hanging onto him that kept him from being whisked into the next world. He could hardly see a thing in the swirling blankness. The stranger let go one hand and grasped Roan's sleeve.

"Ready?" Roan shouted. "One big pull! One . . . two . . . three!"

"Three!" Misha yelled, throwing his weight back. The man

came shooting out of the hole like a greased cork, and landed on top of them. He lay still for a moment, then feebly raised his head.

"Thank you," he gasped. They helped him to sit up.

He was young, perhaps in his mid-twenties, with a shock of dark hair and tan skin that was just beginning to regain its color. On one side of his face there was a colossal bruise, and his hands were bloody. Colenna had a wad of cotton and a bottle of disinfectant out of her purse before Roan could even ask for it, and was treating the lacerated palms.

"Just a minute," Spar said, looming over them. "Look at his clothes! He's one of Brom's people! Corporal, arrest him!"

Roan glanced at the young man's attire. He was indeed clad in the blue-and-white tunic of the Ministry of Science, but he had lost all the pencils out of his pocket protector. The man shook his head, open-mouthed, in protest.

"Left here as a decoy," Lum said, staring at him fiercely.

"No, I'm not a decoy," the man said, swallowing hard. "They threw me in, tried to kill me. Roan, you know me. My name's Glinn."

"They'll say anything," Spar growled, thrusting his face into the young man's. "Don't trust him!"

"But I do know him," Roan said, pushing the captain away. He squatted down beside the apprentice. "Glinn, why did they throw you into that hole?"

Glinn groaned, and gingerly put the icebag Colenna offered him on the side of his face. "I've been leaving clues for you to follow. Brom must have found out."

"You're the one?" Roan asked. Glinn struggled to his feet, and Roan supported him. They were almost the same height. "I cannot tell you how grateful we are. We'd have lost the way a dozen times without your help."

"Well, we don't need it now," Spar said, dubiously. "That cursed Clock's leaving a swath of distortion as wide as the great outdoors."

"What?" the apprentice demanded, swaying unsteadily at his feet. He politely refused Colenna's offer of brandy. "What distortion?"

"Your master's device has been perverting reality," Bergold said, pointing up and down the road with a flipper. "It's grown worse as you've gone along. Look at the road. See that glassing effect? Look at that squirrel, er, raven, er, whatever." Glinn looked up and down at the shiny expanse of the road and the bird-animal perching on a nearby park bench.

"I never saw any of this," he said, pale and shocked. "We hardly ever backtracked, and I was preoccupied. How unaware I've been. What horrors!"

"Well, that's one bird in the bag," Spar said to Roan. "We'll catch the others, too. Do we have to tie him up?"

"I won't run away," Glinn said eagerly. "I want to help. Ever since we left Mnemosyne I've been trying to get Brom to go back."

"It's another trap," Hutchings said, putting his hand on the hilt of his sword.

"No, truly," Glinn protested. "I mean no harm. I want the experiment ended as much as you! When Carodil and the king said no to the plan, I did try to persuade Brom to stay and study further, but he was convinced, and talked my colleagues into going along with him. I was outnumbered as well as outranked. It was impossible to reason with him. When Brom told me you were chasing us, I welcomed it. I thought when you caught up we could persuade Brom to return."

"Didn't work, did it?" Felan said, unimpressed.

"Not very well," Glinn admitted, hanging his head. "I stayed with the group to act as the voice of sanity. I was doing fairly well, too."

"What happened?" Bergold asked.

Glinn shrugged simply. "I fell in love," he said. "She's been helping me, but she started leaving by markers behind on her own. She's a good scientist. Even she was appalled by the reality when she understood it. I think she let a thought slip accidentally, and Brom found us out. She's still in their hands. Brom is . . . not kind to dissenters."

"We'll save her, but we must get Leonora back," Roan said. "He took her from near this spot. Is she all right?"

Glinn closed his eyes. "I think so. All I am seeing right now is a pig. But I can tell you where they're going."

"Good," Spar said. "That'll take the guesswork out of things. Where?"

Glinn started to speak, but Roan stopped him. "Do you have some kind of telepathy with Brom?"

"The link is a function of the gestalt," Glinn said. "I'll explain it all later, but you are right. They can see through my eyes, even hear what I say." He turned around and put his hands behind him. The hands pantomimed wiggling.

"Snakes?" Bergold guessed. "A river?"

Glinn's hand made an "ok" sign.

"Follow the Lullay?" Roan asked. No, the hand waved back and forth, then the first two fingers made an arcing gesture. Glinn shook his head. "Ah, over."

"Toward the Dark Mysteries?" Felan asked.

The hand waved no, and Glinn edged so his backside was pointing more toward the north, then he clapped his hands over his ears as the others exclaimed aloud.

"Ah! In the *Deep* Mysteries," Bergold said, enlightened, clapping his flippers together. He tapped Glinn on the knee. The scientist uncovered his ears.

"Where among them?" Bergold asked. "It's a big place."

The hand wiggled again.

"On the river?" The hand made an "ok" sign, then bent upward to pat Glinn on the back over his heart. The apprentice certainly had flexible wrists. "To its heart?"

"The source," Bergold said, eagerly. He and Roan spread out the great map between them. "But there's nothing here but the waterfall, and upriver, the Dreamland ends."

No, the hand twitched. It arced again, this time angling down. Roan nodded. Underneath. Glinn covered his ears again.

"To its source," he said. "The Hall is underneath the waterfall." He tapped the apprentice on the shoulder.

"How very interesting," Colenna said. "Do you know, there are theories to that end, although no one has ever been able to penetrate the waterfall. According to my studies . . ."

"Don't," Glinn said, concerned. "Please. Anything I hear, they hear."

"But we've only been guessing," Colenna said. She whipped a large slate and chalk out of her bag. She turned the board toward Roan and the others and began to write. She must have taught school, Roan thought, as she wrote upside down and backwards in perfectly legible script.

"What he says makes sense," she wrote. "The Lullay has always been a symbol of the Collective Unconscious. The Sleepers, if they are anywhere, could well be there." Roan nodded agreement. They would go in that direction.

"But I must warn you," Glinn said, when they had finished, "there's a spy in this camp, telling Brom your every move."

"Who?" Roan asked, shocked. "Who is it?"

"I couldn't tell you," Glinn said, staring carefully at the trees, and not at them. "I don't know. Brom never let us know his or her name. He or she's been misleading you at Brom's orders. But I am a worse spy. As part of the gestalt, what I know is open to the others. It's still intermittent as yet, but they can see through my eyes, hear my thoughts. They can even use my strength at a remove. I can do it, too, but I am only one of a great and powerful whole. They outnumber me, so they could pull back all influence I try to use. You must not tell me anything or say anything in my presence you don't want Brom to know. He might already know I am with you. Be very careful."

"We should tie you up and leave you here," Spar said, impatiently. "You're just planning to lull us into believing you, and then, kerblam!" Some of the others muttered agreement. Roan couldn't blame them, but he remembered Glinn as a truthful and honorable man.

"No, truly, I am willing to help," Glinn insisted. "How can I make you trust me?"

"Where's the princess Leonora?" Roan asked.

Glinn shut his eyes again. "I can see her now, but only weakly. That means only one or two of them are looking at her. She's alive and well."

"Thank the Sleepers for that!" Roan exclaimed. Poor Leonora, in the hands of those unscrupulous villains.

"We were sent back on the road with Brom's two mercenaries to set up a trap. They must have kidnapped her when you had your backs turned. She makes a good hostage. Her safety is important to you, and Brom knows it. I can feel that in his mind."

"You'll have to come with us. We'll blindfold you," Roan said. He felt in his pocket for a handkerchief, and came out with Leonora's blue silk scarf. "Stay with us. We have a good map. Will he return?"

"I doubt it. He'll know I said this to you, but he can't afford to waste time turning around to get me. He'll go on. I would. It is logical to continue." He held still as Roan bound the scarf around his eyes.

"Don't believe this man," Felan said, astonished. "He's a traitor! He betrayed one confidence, he can betray another."

Glinn shook his head. "Think what you will. My job as a scientist is to discover truth, and I would be less than a man if I didn't stick to that."

With care, they put him on Golden Schwinn, who consented to carry him only because he bore a token that smelled like the princess. Roan spoke to the steed very gently until Glinn was in the saddle.

"Hurry," Glinn said. "This is the last push."

Spar directed his guards to ride flanking the scientist, as an added security measure, then led the party onward, up the plain toward the gentle rise in the land that hid the Lullay from view. Roan stayed beside Golden Schwinn to reassure her.

He wished someone would reassure him. A spy in the camp. Who could it be? He liked and trusted all of his companions. They had stuck by him throughout the arduous journey, in the face of personal danger and hardship. Could it be that they had missed catching up with Brom because of some traitor's machinations? Had he been led astray by design?

". . . What do you think?" Glinn asked.

"I beg your pardon?" Roan asked. The scientist had been talking, and Roan hadn't heard a word. Glinn turned his blindfolded face toward him.

"We can go directly to where Brom is taking the Alarm Clock, or you can continue to follow his trail," he said. "Under most circumstances I'd recommend the former alternative, because we memorized no fewer than eight separate plans with variations in the route indicated, but you are concerned about Her Highness."

That put Roan on the horns of an uncomfortable dilemma.

"Will he do anything to Leonora?" he asked.

"Nothing before he reaches the Hall of the Sleepers," Glinn said, tilting his head toward the sound of Roan's voice. "He won't dare. She's the only real weapon he has against you. That, and distance."

"We have to stop him before he gets there," Roan said, and gathered the group under his eye. "To whichever of you has been sending Brom messages, you can tell him that we will catch him, and I will see that he's punished for his deeds."

"Can we speed up at all?" Lum asked.

"I can tap the gestalt," Glinn offered, "but bear in mind that Brom might snatch the power back at any time. He might even try to control us through me. We are all so near to becoming one entity that I have to fight all the time to keep my mind clear. If he does try, you might have to kill me to break the connection."

"No fear, my lad," Spar said, tapping the hilt of his sword. "Go on, then, give us a boost."

"To the river," Roan said.

Subtly at first, the bikes began to speed up. Their tires narrowed by half, then half again, humming on the road. At the next turn of influence, they changed back into horses. Bergold went from seal to man in the space of one pace, and clutched the back of his plump steed, which streamlined into a long-legged racer, speeding as smoothly as an express train. Faster and faster the hooves thundered on the slick roadbed. The landscape whipped by, and Roan concentrated on only what was ahead of him: Leonora, Brom, and the Alarm Clock.

Chapter 33

"The time has come," Brom said. He stood with his hands raised beside his motorbike at the side of the road. "Maniune, Acton, to your guard posts. We must not be disturbed."

Taboret raised her head. Over the headlands before them, she saw the majestic panorama of the Deep Mysteries, broad, purple-black peaks against the sky, wreathed with ruffs of white cloud. There, on the other side of the broad Lullay River, lay the answer to the question Brom posed, and there would be the end of everything as she knew it. Surely her next existence wouldn't include a coat of tar. She hated her own smell, and she stuck to everything, including the bicycle seat and handlebars. Brom's voice boomed out again, distracting her from her misery.

"It is time for the gestalt to fulfill its final promise!" he announced. "The failure to achieve unity the last time was because I did not evince sufficient leadership in our conjoining, and control the emotional feedback. Now, it will last. I will guide the transformation, and we will become that single, powerful entity that we have worked to become! We can take the last steps to our destination as if we were wearing a pair of seven-league boots! We will be one!"

Yes, came the mind-voices through the link.

Taboret felt the excitement from her fellow apprentices, and looked at them with despair. *No!* she thought, but her thoughts were no longer under her control. Nine other minds pulled at her. Against her will, the diagram appeared before her mind's eye, of a giant composite being, and the wonderful wheeled transportation device that it would ride, carrying the Alarm Clock as easily as one of them now carried a pencil.

The princess, who had become an ice-pale beauty with

translucent blue-white skin, refusing to speak to any of them even after the silence spell had been removed from her, dismounted haughtily, and turned her back on Brom. The green motorbike's frame arched up and outward like a spider capturing its prey, and reformed as a cage around her. She spun, almost saying something, then put her nose in the air in disdain.

"Apprentices, move your motorcycles together," Brom ordered. "Then, come here to me."

As one, the apprentices dismounted. Taboret resisted, but she was dragged by sheer influence toward the place the crucible would be formed. An impulse not her own pulled her hand to the center of the circle.

"Do we have to touch *that*?" Lurry asked, drawing back from the tar smeared on her skin. Most of the feathers had sunk into the resin or had fallen off.

"Certainly not," Brom said. "I think the point has been made." He drew his hand downward from his head to his feet, and Taboret felt the fresh air rush over her skin. She looked down, and found she was clean.

"Thank you, Master Brom," she said, sincerely. He ignored her, staring off into space to visualize the parameters of the final transformation. Taboret put her hand lightly on top of Gano's, and waited for Dowkin to cover hers.

When it came through her, the wave of power did have a different feeling than before. This time it was more coherent, more all-encompassing. Brom's mind penetrated through it all, controlling, guiding, so that she had no conscious impact on the shape things were taking.

The motorcycles changed first. The white haze roiled around them, surrounding, concealing them. When the mist cleared, there was one single vehicle there, a giant cycle with six sets of handlebars.

"Concentrate on combining yourselves," Brom said.

"Yes," Doolin said. He stepped a pace closer to Dowkin, and the two of them moved toward, and into one another.

"Look at us!" Dowkin shouted. "We're each other! Fantastic!" Then they started to lose their shape, broadening and flattening out into a single mass that flowed into the apprentices next to them.

Taboret felt the transformation begin on her. She cried out one final protest before her tongue became a tendon, and her teeth became sinews. Her limbs stretched out taut and grew stiff. It hurt. Her skull became a knee-bone, and her legs stretched out and bent forward, shaping into a single great foot. She felt the foot rise and come down on a bicycle pedal as large as a bed. She'd have screamed if she had any physical equipment left to scream with.

Brom's great voice boomed through them.

"Together, now!" it cried. Taboret could no longer see through her own eyes, only through Brom's eyes, who was the head of the giant body they had become. They stood taller than the treetops. To the north was the river, and the enormous waterfall that concealed their destination, the Hall of the Sleepers. To the south, she/they saw a cloud of dust, and the tiny figures riding toward them up the slope of the land. The great mouth smiled. Too late. With its left hand, the giant gestalt-being scooped up the Alarm Clock, then reached for Leonora with its right.

Taboret felt a shock run through the entire being, as she/they realized that there was no right hand at the end of its arm. Glinn! she thought. That should have been his position, and he was gone. The monster roared out its frustration, making the ground shake.

"Those peaks are the Deep Mysteries," Bergold said, peering at the massif, having consulted his map. He handed the map over to Misha for folding. "The oldest dreams of all the Collective Unconscious have been seen near the mountains everywhere in the Dreamland, but the deepest archetypes occur the most here at the source of the Lullay: dinosaurs, volcanoes, spirits, cavemen, angels, all things left over from when the world of the Sleepers was young."

Roan caught a glimpse of movement among the undergrowth. He sat upright with a feeling of deep satisfaction. "There goes my caveman," he said.

"Look!" Misha shouted, in great excitement. "A dragon! A big green dragon!" The huge, scaled beast zoomed overhead, seeming to skim the clouds with the tips of its wings. "Uh-oh, it's coming back!"

"Duck!" Felan yelled. The party scrambled into the undergrowth, pulling the protesting steeds in behind them. The dragon made another pass, then went on in search of easier prey.

Bergold took out his notebook and made several notes in great excitement. "This will be worth *at least* one paper," he said. "My hat!"

"No!" Glinn cried out in a terrible voice. Roan reached out to help him. The apprentice scientist was tearing at his face, dislodging the blindfold. His eyes were wild beneath it.

"What's wrong?" Roan asked. Glinn looked at him as if trying to say something, then his face went blank. It did not merely lose its expression, but its features as well. His head rounded and widened, joining to his shoulders and arms in one nearly featureless cylinder of flesh, like—like a wrist.

His legs went through the most fearsome transformation. They shrank and fused together, then separated from two into five extensions of flesh and bone, even growing nails on his altered feet.

"My soul," Bergold said, staring. "He's becoming a hand. A right hand."

The forearm that was Glinn tottered and fell over in the saddle, sending Golden Schwinn crazy with fear as the enormous fingers dropped over her eyes. The mare galloped away, Glinn flopping helplessly. Roan leaped onto Cruiser's back and kicked him into a canter. He pursued Schwinn down the slippery road until he could force her against the trees and grab for her reins. Cruiser was chary of the giant limb, too, but he stayed calm enough while Roan arranged the arm over Schwinn's saddle.

The others caught up with him. Bergold met his eyes with a question in his own.

"If something so horrible is happening to this young man," he asked, "what will become of Leonora?"

There's no other hand, the mass-intelligence thought at Brom, looking at the arm that ended at the elbow. I/we can seize the princess or the Alarm Clock, but not both.

"We can have both!" the overarching Brom intelligence cried out. "Take her, mount the cycle, and begin pedaling!"

Obediently, the body bent down toward the tiny girl in white. She cowered away from it, feeling for the bars of her cage. Taboret saw it the moment she realized that there was no cage there any longer. The material comprising it had gone to make part of the singularity cycle.

Brom/they reached out for her with the stump of its right arm, but missed her by six feet, the length of the missing limb. Leonora scrambled to her feet, and started to back away. Brom/they swiped at her again. It must capture her, it must use her. She wasn't going to come quietly. She opened something between her hands and struck out at the stump of the arm with a jet of fire from a flamethrower. The Brom-being recoiled.

"Fools! You left her with a weapon!" Brom boomed. "Concentrate on the gestalt. Grow us a new right arm, now! Raise the power!"

But Taboret knew he had made a mistake in his calculations. The gestalt had no power and no concentration left. All its strength was taken up in maintaining the giant it had become. They began to sway. Leonora stared at them in horror.

"No, concentrate!" Brom cried. "We are one!"

And in one astonishing moment, they were one single being. Suddenly, the being began to grow smaller and weaker. Taboret knew now why such a thing had never been tried successfully in all the history of the Dreamland. Now that they were all one, they had only the strength of a single person. The crucible could not exist with only one part. In that moment, the gestalt began to collapse.

The Dowkin-Doolin part of the union was openly scornful at the failure of yet another attempt. The Taboret-Gano-Basil-Lurry-Bolmer-Carina-Mamovas part was terrified. The Brom part tried to cope with the loss of power and control, but realized that without Glinn, it had no good right hand. Taboret felt it all, heard it, was part of it, and knew that part of her was mourning Glinn's loss, but also gloating. Roaring, the gestalt being rose up and reached to the sky. It needed more power, but this was all they were. It tried to reach out for Leonora again with the stump of its right arm, thinking to capture her, thinking to use her, and jarred the Alarm Clock, still held in its left hand. The bells echoed from tree to rock, through Taboret's teeth-now-sinews.

Leonora waited no longer. She turned and ran off into the woods. Good, Taboret thought. Run. *Run*.

The bells rang on, clanging through her head. The gestalt-being heaved together painfully. Then it collapsed in a heap of people, coat hangers, and bicycles, with the litter containing the Alarm Clock on top of everything.

As they came to the edge of the river, the arm that was Glinn slung across Roan's saddle started to fuss and kick. Roan reined in Cruiser as the huge limb began to take on detail, parts separating into legs and arms and a head, and finally a face. A restored Glinn lay over the saddle on his belly. His mouth opened, gasping.

"Something is happening," Glinn panted. "I'm weak. All my influence has been drained away by the gestalt. There's been a catastrophe."

"Leonora!" Roan exclaimed, helping the scientist to sit up. "Is she all right? Where is she?"

"I . . . don't . . . know," Glinn said, drawing his brows down. He shook his head, as if trying to clear his mind. "Brom must have started the final plan, but I don't think it went well. I can't see anything, I mean, through anyone else's eyes. *Something* has happened."

Golden Schwinn and Cruiser set up an excited whinny. Roan looked at them in surprise.

"Leonora must be around somewhere," he said. With all the influence he could muster, he molded the two horses into bloodhounds on leashes. At once, the dogs began to run, noses to the ground, raising their heads to bay.

From near the bottom of the heap of people and things, Taboret looked up, grateful to see with her own eyes once more, and saw a chain of paper clips dangling across the bridge of Brom's nose.

"Touch hands!" Brom said, hoarsely. "Touch hands!"

Taboret found her hands. She thought she had absolutely no strength left, but she stretched one out, and helped form the crucible. It was a shock as Brom's fingers clasped hers, because there was so little of the force of his personality behind it. To her secret delight, she could no longer hear Brom's or anyone else's thoughts. She was actually able to concentrate on his hands, the dry fingertips, slightly clammy skin, and the palm which widened even as she grasped it. He was changing in a burst of influence, in spite of his efforts not to, just like the rest of them.

The mist rose weakly above them. There wasn't much, but it was enough to get the Alarm Clock off their backs. It was heavy as a boulder. When they were all on their feet once more, Brom took stock of the situation.

"We haven't enough bicycles left for everyone, and there is no time to wait for more to mature," he said. Taboret looked twice to realize that almost all the motorcycles had reverted to simple bicycles.

Maniune and Acton came racing back, standing up on the pedals of their steeds.

"What happened?" Maniune demanded, screeching to a halt before the ruin of the singularity cycle. "We heard the bells ringing, then this thing lost all its power!"

"The gestalt overloaded," Brom said, already onto the next problem. He indicated armloads of the bicycle parts. "Put those together. And those."

The apprentices bent to pick up the pieces and set them where their chief indicated. Taboret's muscles were stiff, but she was entirely herself once again. She set to work willingly, blessing the privacy of her own thoughts, which could be as rebellious as she wanted. Sadly, it meant that she wouldn't have been able to read Glinn's mind any more, but that didn't matter since he was dead. Now and then, she seemed to feel his presence as if he was still alive, but put that down to imagination, something with which she was not extraordinarily gifted, but love did funny things to a person. Typical of the Dreamland, where illusions were the stuff life was made of.

"Come on, Master Brom, we've got to get moving," Acton said, impatiently, shoving a heap of gears and wheels into the piles. He didn't look nearly as menacing as he had before. Taboret wondered if he, too, had been enhanced by the power of the crucible. They moved around him, dumping bicycle parts in heaps. "They're coming up fast behind us."

"We are working on the situation," Brom snapped. "Assist, or get out of the way."

Dowkin and Doolin Countingsheep sat side by side on the ground next to the pile of broken parts. They had long, thin faces with heavy foreheads and eyebrows, all drooping mournfully.

"It was almost perfect," Doolin said. Taboret was surprised that she could still tell them apart, even without the help of the link. "We're separate beings again. It's no good."

"Have to find a way back to that state, brother," Dowkin said. "I can start the calculations."

"It's been a conspiracy all along," Doolin said, with a dark look for the others. "We had a perfect bond. They copied it, then they broke it."

"Dowkin! Doolin!" Brom shouted, throwing a set of handlebars at them. "Enough! Put these together!" Sullenly, the brothers got up and set to work, muttering under their breath to one another.

The remaining bicycles were jury-rigged into tandems and trandems, and a makeshift yoke was concocted to carry the Alarm Clock to the banks of the Lullay. Taboret hung back, hoping to be ignored until she could escape into the woods, but Brom's personal radar found her even at the back of the crowd.

"You, and you," he pointed at Lurry. "Take the litter. The rest of you we will need for the final construction. We haven't much time. Hurry!"

The silver-and-gold bloodhounds veered off the road, dragging Roan behind them. They rushed into the woods, vacuuming scents off trees, lolloped over piles of bracken, and splashed through brooks. The trees dodged this way and that. Roan got tied up in the leashes more than once avoiding running into the landscape.

There was a rustle in the undergrowth ahead of Roan. The two dogs lifted their heads toward the heavens, and set up a loud howl of joy, and scrambled forth into the brush.

"Who's there?" a voice asked tentatively, over the excited baying. "Oh, Schwinn!"

"Leonora!" Roan shouted, running toward the voice. He pushed through a brake of flowering lilacs. The princess stood there, high on her pedestal for safety, looking exactly like an exotic blossom herself. The dogs frolicked and danced around her, jumping up to lick her feet, tying the plinth up in their leashes. Roan felt as if he could dance, too. His heart was overflowing with delight and love. He rushed to her, and she jumped down and threw her arms around him. The music he'd heard that night on the hilltop filled the air.

"My darling, I thought you were dead, and then I was so angry and worried," Roan said, in between eager kisses, as all his thoughts tumbled together. "We've been coming to rescue you."

"Wait until I tell you what happened," Leonora said. "If I could only have gotten that wretched steed loose from their influence, I could have been back with you ages ago. They'd never have caught up with me. I have so much to tell you."

The others came crashing over the fallen brush, and gathered around them to welcome the princess back.

"Dear lady, I am so glad," Bergold said. "It's nearly been the death of my poor young friend here."

"We're happy you're safe," Felan said, smiling at her with relief.

"I found your treasures," Roan said, pulling the daisy chain out of his waistcoat pocket. He folded them into her hand. "I knew you didn't throw them away idly."

Leonora kissed Roan soundly once more, then pulled away.

"Oh, thank you, my darling," she said, with a sweet smile. "Just one moment?"

She spun on her heel, and slapped Felan across the face hard enough to make him stagger backward.

Without conscious impulse, Roan and the other men responded as all gentlemen of the Dreamland did when a lady demonstrated that she had been offended. They picked Felan up, marched him to the nearest river, which happened to be the Lullay, and threw him in.

"Wait! Hey! Blub!" Felan shouted, spitting out a mouthful of water. Not waiting for him to climb out on the bank, Roan went back to Leonora.

"Now, please tell us why we did that," Roan said. The princess stood with her hands on her hips, tapping her foot impatiently. She was angry.

"Felan betrayed us," she said, her eyes flashing. "He's Brom's spy!"

"Felan?" Roan asked, watching the historian crawl up the bank somewhat downstream from where he went in, sputtering, his clothes streaming.

"He's been sending Brom air-mail reports all along," she said. "One of them came while I was with them. He has been telling them all our moves from the time we left home!"

"He must be the one," Glinn said. "You know, you'd have caught up with us days ago if it hadn't been for him."

"What?" Spar asked.

"What?" Bergold asked, his usually mild face turning purple.

"Who is this?" Leonora asked, spinning to study the scientist. Her eyes widened when she saw the blue-and-white tunic and the pocket protector. She clenched her fists.

"This is a brave man, and a true friend of the Dreamland," Roan explained, putting his hands on her shoulders to reassure her. "He was the one leaving trail markers for us."

"*You're* the spy?" Spar demanded as Felan squelched back to the group, shaking water out of his shoes. "You never sent any reports home to Mnemosyne? You dragged us through the Nightmare Forest on purpose?" The historian changed his sheepish look for an arrogant one.

"Ha!" he said. "I thought you'd forgotten about that."

"Forgotten!" Spar shouted.

"Is it true?" Roan demanded.

"Of course it is," Felan said, impatiently. "I'm not surprised that a one-faced freak like you was never able to figure it out on your own. Not one of you understand what Brom is trying to do. All our life is a lie unless we find out the truth about the Sleepers."

"But I *do* understand," Glinn said. "I was one of the apprentices who drew up the design parameters for the project. Ringing the Alarm Clock could mean utter destruction. If not that, then certainly upheaval, terror, and danger for countless Dreamlanders."

Felan pretended not to care, but Roan could tell he was upset by Glinn's speech. Leonora was angrier than ever, but Roan never anticipated how furious Felan's betrayal would make Bergold. He had never seen his dear friend so angry.

"You young fool." The senior historian grew to a giant, eight feet tall with hands the size of watermelons. He picked Felan up, and threw him overhand back in the river. Felan sank with a splash.

"I for one don't care if he never comes up," Spar said, scanning the surface of the Lullay. A dark head broke water. "Oh, too bad. He can swim." The figure that climbed out was a changed man. Felan was smaller and humbler-looking, almost wormlike. But this time he didn't come back to them when he waded ashore. Keeping well away from them, he started walking south, and slunk in among the trees. The leaves closed behind him, and he was gone.

"Good riddance," Spar said.

In as much detail as she could, Leonora told them about the rise and collapse of the gestalt-being. Roan listened, horrified.

"Thank the Sleepers he failed," he said.

"It won't stop them," Glinn said. "But they'll be moving much slower. This is our chance to catch up with them at last."

"What about you?" Bergold said, holding up the blindfold. Glinn shook his head.

"I won't need that now. The gestalt is broken. I'm free. Besides, it won't matter if he can see through my eyes now. He is nearly there."

The party took to horse again, and rode west along the banks until they came to a place where the shore was churned into mud.

"There's weirdness everywhere," Lum said.

"This is where they took to the water," Roan said. "But on what?"

"Brom is endlessly inventive," Glinn replied. "He can make a sailing ship out of a brick and a bedsheet. He might truly have had to do something of the kind. He has a way of using opposing forces to his benefit."

"Which way do we go?" Roan asked.

"Upstream," Glinn said. "To the source."

"Follow me," Roan said. He backed Cruiser up a dozen paces, and spurred him straight at the shining water.

Chapter 34

Taboret hung on to the bow of the speedboat. It wasn't a pretty craft, but it worked. Brom had transformed the remaining steeds into a single water vehicle that skipped along the river. He had hooked the remaining bicycles together with paperclip chain and coathangers, and the craft looked as if it had been constructed out of odd bits. The chief scientist held onto the tiller at the stern, staring straight ahead with his glowing eyes.

The gestalt was nearly burned out. It would never again be able to raise enough power to make them into a single entity, but it was just enough to impel their engines. That was all that mattered. Brom was fixed upon a single goal, and was pushing them to succeed. To keep the crucible power going, they had to maintain physical contact with one another. Brom had taken one of the remaining coat hangers and made handcuffs out of it to hold them all together until they got to the waterfall, which Taboret could see ahead of her. It reached all the way to the sky.

Every time the boat hit the waves, the bells would chime, transforming things. Taboret was tired of changing form every time it happened. She clutched at the side of the boat with fingernails grown into talons and longed for the journey to be over at last.

They must reach the Hall of Sleepers before Roan did. He wasn't far behind them. The King's Investigator wasn't the only peril facing them. Sharks large enough to swallow them whole had been pacing the vessel since it took to the water. Giant lizards with strange eyes stared at them through the trees. Titans the size of trees threw rocks at one another and laughed with deep, earth-shaking voices. And Taboret was certain she had seen at least one dragon. If they didn't win through to the Hall soon, their noisy engines would attract more unwanted attention.

"Hold tight!" Brom shouted at them, as they entered the waterfall's great pool. The spray soaked them, and the thunder of the falls drove the little boat out and away again and again, threatening to capsize it. Water serpents circled the hull, looking for little tidbits, like humans, to fall over the side. Taboret drew back into the shell and found herself flattened against the Alarm Clock's draped side. "We must pass under the curtain," the chief scientist said. "Pay attention, all of you! Open the way for us. Focus on driving straight through! Use all the influence you have! Join it all in the gestalt! Now!"

Taboret thought there was nothing left inside her, but slowly, the pillars of the thundering, gray torrent parted. A narrow, dark slot opened in the great cataract. She stared at it, blinking water off her eyelashes. That couldn't be large enough to let their boat pass! Brom leaned over, and turned the throttle up to full. The sound of the bells was drowned out by the deafening boom of the falls. Terrified, Taboret huddled in the bow and helped will the boat through the opening in the cascade and into the cave she knew was beyond. The water hammered down against the invisible substance of their barrier. Taboret was afraid it wouldn't hold. She prayed Roan was close behind them.

Cruiser splashed his great splayed hooves on the surface of the water, kicking up little sprays like clouds of dust. The others rode strung out in a long file behind him, leaping waves and dashing over whitecaps. Roan glanced back at Leonora, who was clinging to Golden Schwinn's mane with a grim expression on her face.

Because every vehicle is appropriate to its circumstances, the steeds had become water horses when Roan rode them at the river and turned them upstream. The hippocampi had two great finlike forefeet, a long back, and fishlike tails. Roan thought that they were very beautiful, but their looks were not as important as their speed. It was as hard as galloping uphill to ride upstream, but the steeds were willing, and their riders' influence was oddly strong. Roan was sure it was because they were so close to the Sleepers.

The current of the mighty river was as powerful here at its point of origin as it was one and a half turns of the world away where it flowed into Nightlily Lake at the heart of the continent. This was the origin of all life in the Dreamland, the symbol of the Collective Unconscious. All along the shore, things were climbing or flying out of it, some things Roan had never seen before. Most of them were beautiful, true reflections of the Sleepers' minds. Many were terrifying, living nightmares, manifestations of the troubles they sought to solve. This happened at other places along the banks of the Lullay, but much more frequently here. He wished the errand was less urgent, so he could study some of the emergent life forms, and bring back a report to the king. But there would be no reports if they didn't succeed.

The sound of the great waterfall filled their ears. It seemed to be falling from the very top of the Mystery massif, falling from heaven itself. though they were still miles away from the cataract itself, the spray of it filled the air. Roan blinked away the wet mist, and kept his eyes on the falls, arched over by rainbows, roofed by clouds, and streaming over many-colored rocks the size of palaces. They were glorious, terrifying, and huge.

"There they go!" Lum cried over the roar of the water. He leaned over to point. Roan sighted down his arm until he saw the tiny gray craft in the heart of the basin. A dark hole seemed to open up in the wall of water, and the craft vanished.

"Did they go down?" Leonora shrieked.

"No, they went through!" Roan shouted.

"Through!" yelled Misha. "Impossible!"

"Not for the gestalt!" Glinn shouted at him. "It still has power!"

"We need to go faster!" Bergold yelled. "We must fly if we are to catch them!"

Fly? Roan wondered. Could they? They hadn't been able to achieve flight before. But this close to the Sleepers, even the smallest thought should be enough to precipitate change. Keep thinking of the job at hand, Roan thought. Concentrate. All things depend upon this. He pulled back on Cruiser's reins, pulling the water horse's head higher and higher. Cruiser lifted up. He grew wings, finned feet became hoofed and with a mighty leap, he was airborne!

"Follow me!" Roan shouted.

Roan heard cries behind him as the others pulled their steeds up and into the air. He heard Leonora scream. Roan turned, worried that she was frightened, but her face was filled with wild delight. Bergold added his whoop of joy as his beast spread pink wings beside Schwinn's gold. They were airborne. Spar and the other guards flew by in bubble-shaped craft with a big gold star on each side, a spinning propeller on the top, and a flashing blue light on the tail.

It was a glorious feeling to fly again. The exhilarating wind whipped his cheeks and hair. If only it hadn't been such an urgent errand, Roan would have enjoyed the experience more. The sky here seemed more blue, and the clouds whiter and higher than anywhere else he'd ever been.

The face of the cataract was just ahead, a pillar of sapphire stretching upward to the very edge of the sky. The spray soaked them all, and the wind caused the flying horses to dip and flutter their great wings. No one in recorded history had ever passed into the great cataract and lived to bring the story home to the Historians. But Brom had gone in. Roan must repeat the feat he had just witnessed, and bring them all safely through or all existence was forfeit. Would the force of the water dash them down into the pool? Could their mission end in watery failure? It must not, Roan thought. They had to catch Brom. If the scientists could pass through, so could they. Onward!

"Have no fear," Roan shouted, steeling himself. "Believe you can do it, and we will!" He aimed Cruiser straight at the moving wall of water. Pumping his great wings, Cruiser shrilled a war cry. Roan bent over his neck and held tight to the steed's feathery mane, willing the cataract to open, willing them through.

He was so full of determined force that the thundering flood felt no stronger than a shower on his back as he passed under the curtain, and into a giant cavern. He was alive. He pinched his arm just to make sure. He steered Cruiser toward a shelf of stone. The pegasus spread his wings and soared lightly in a descending spiral.

"Please don't let me crash this time," he prayed the Sleepers. "Too much is at stake. No falling dreams! Not here!"

The Sleepers must have heard his plea. The winged horse touched down onto solid footing, trotted a few paces, and shook himself dry. Roan swung off Cruiser's back and looked around him, filled with wonder.

What a place this was! He had never seen such a huge cave. It felt older than time itself. The waterfall seemed to be both above and below this place, but the sound was oddly muffled. The river also ran underneath the floor of the cavern. The second flow joined the first behind the curtain of the falls, as if adding a secret ingredient that the cook didn't want anyone else to see. Lit by the azure light that filtered through the waterfall, the cavern's walls and floor were a rich, amber-colored stone. Glittering chunks of bright gemstone glowing from within were inlaid in patterns too complex for simple human minds to comprehend. At the back of the cavern, on the peak of a smooth stone ramp, stood the arch of a vast doorway through which came the softest light Roan had ever seen. There was no sign of the scientists or the Alarm Clock. They had to have gone through the door already. Doom could come at any moment. He started running toward the threshold. The others would follow.

"Hyahhhh!" came a wild cry. A body landed on him from behind, driving him down to his knees.

The bigger of Brom's two mercenaries dragged Roan up, and the smaller aimed a fist for his stomach. Quickly, Roan drew on his influence to wiggle free. He tried to drop down into the stone shelf, his old trick, but it resisted him. The material of the Sleepers' own home threw off ordinary influence. Instead, he made himself too slippery to hold. The big man grabbed for him as he squeezed free. Roan ducked, and came up directly into the way of the small man's punch. The blow stung, but squirted off, doing little damage. Roan hit back, dodging blows as best he could. The mercenary struck doggedly, driving him back against the wall of the cave, where the other thug was waiting. Roan glanced at the high doorway, and his heart pounded. Brom must be nearly ready to set off his device. He must get free!

A stuttering splash and a cry made them all look up. Bergold had won through the cascade. His winged steed lost altitude for a moment, its waterlogged wings and the battering of the water pounding it down. In a heartbeat, it recovered, flying toward the ledge. Bergold's eyes were wide with alarm. He was followed swiftly by the others, popping through the translucent wall one at a time.

"Help," Roan shouted to them. Seven combatants against two, they should be able to take care of their foes in no time.

Leonora and Colenna remained on their steeds fluttering in the air above the stone shelf. Misha, Bergold, Glinn, and the guards' air choppers arrowed in towards Roan. But as soon as his friends touched down, two more mercenaries popped up and rushed toward them. Those two split into more and more, until Roan lost count of the throng. The two holding him started hitting him again, heading him off each time he tried to change direction. Roan realized they were trying to push him toward the edge of the shelf. If he fell into the falls, he would be sucked under. He couldn't save himself from drowning in that current. He had to use his wits. With a snap of his wrist, he opened the staff attachment of his pocket knife, and went on guard.

Captain Spar climbed out of his helicopter, and took immediate assessment of the situation.

"Don't you worry, sir!" he shouted. "His Majesty's royal guards are prepared for any eventuality! You, Lum, over there! You, Alette, that way! You, Hutchings, up the middle. The rest of you," he cried, swinging his arm forward over his head, "follow me!"

And dozens of Spars clambered down the helicopter steps after the original. The other three guards multiplied until they, too, were legion. With a cry of "The Dreamland!" the army of guards joined battle.

Roan ducked under the arm of the larger ruffian attacking him, and jabbed the smaller one in the kidneys with the end of his staff. The latter fell flat, but the originals were joined by plenty of reinforcements, all roaring obscene war cries. Roan threw himself back against the wall, striking and striking with the staff. Its length was slowly whittled away by the endless blows of swords and clubs. Every time he knocked down one foe, another took his place. The enemy never seemed to grow any fewer.

Suddenly, dozens of Hutchingses, side by side with as many Alettes, broke through the line of identical ruffians. Three Lums formed a defensive barrier, and pulled Roan to a stone ramp where they were defending Bergold and the women.

Down below, Roan watched a hundred Spars form a flanking maneuver against a sea of mercenaries, who began to recede. A host of Alettes in formation marched Glinn up to join them. Then, Misha tumbled through the crowd to land at their feet, his long limbs splaying like a spider's.

Behind him, one of the smaller mercenaries broke through the cordon, sword out, lunging for Roan's heart. Roan fumbled with his folding knife. There wasn't room in such tight quarters to open out his quarterstaff. Instead, he leaped back, and the enemy charged again. Bergold flipped open the map, dropped it on the mercenary's head, then bonked him on the head with his condensed archive. The villain swayed on his feet and dropped to the floor, unconscious.

"There," Bergold said, shaking the map. "It's the most good it's done all this journey." Miraculously, he was able to fold it up and put it away in his knapsack. "Wonderful! That's the last time I'll use *that* until I see Romney."

All of the Spars lifted up their heads and shouted at Roan. "Get, get going, going, lad, lad. This is your, your chance!" Without waiting for a reply, they waded back into battle.

"How do you suppose they multiplied like that?" Roan asked, as he, Leonora, Bergold, Misha, and Glinn ran up the ramp toward the inner chamber.

"I seem to remember a slip of poetry from the Waking World," Bergold said. " 'My strength is as the strength of ten . . .' I can't remember the rest. It seems to have hit a multiple chord with the Sleepers."

Chapter 35

They stopped upon the huge stone threshold, and paused, staring into the chamber beyond. The first thing that struck Roan was the silence. They could no longer hear the fighting or the waterfall behind them. On the far side of the portal, all was quiet. It felt as though it had been silent since the beginning of time.

The inner room was far larger than its antechamber. The Hall of the Seven Sleepers looked as Roan had always imagined it would, with a vast, vaulted stone ceiling supported by jeweled bosses. The lighting, coming from hooded sconces along the walls, was muted, so that it did not disturb those who reposed there. This was a place of rest.

The Sleepers themselves were giants. Each of the Seven lay on his or her high platform-like bed, surrounded by dressers and tables laden with precious things like photographs and stuffed animals and piles of books. Roan looked at them in awe. These were the Creators who had made his world. He removed his hat and shaped it and his suit into their most formal state. The others were as awestruck as he.

"It's the Waking World," Misha said, in a hushed voice. "If we step forward into it, we'll cease to exist!"

"No. This room does not exist in any real, physical sense," Bergold said, in the quietest of whispers. "It's an echo of the Sleepers as they are in the far corners of the Waking World, gathered here on the edge of the Dreamland." His mouth curled up in a wry smile. "You might say it's the end of the world as we know it, and the beginning of theirs. We exist only in their postulata, but here we may interface. From here, this place, all things flow, and to here the answers to their questions return."

"Why isn't it better defended?" Misha asked. "There's no door."

"That waterfall is guardian enough," Bergold said. "I don't know how we got through it in one piece ourselves."

"But someone must have tried before!"

"Would you dare the Sleepers?" Roan asked.

"We're only here because we're fated to be," Colenna said with a raised eyebrow.

"Oh," Leonora whispered, gazing at the vaulted ceiling and the distant walls. "It's huge!"

Her voice died away into a susurrus that seemed to travel throughout the vast room, causing a disturbance. The Sleepers muttered and twitched in their sleep. One of the giants, a man with gleaming golden hair, muttered to himself and kicked at his pale blue silk coverlets with a foot. Another, a woman with teak-brown skin and a snub nose, breathed out a musical sigh under her intricately woven blankets. Another Sleeper turned over on his vast bed so he was facing them. He wore rust-colored pajamas, and his two blankets were red and blue. His eyes were closed, but one of the corners of his mouth turned up in a smile. His dark hair was tousled on his pillow. Roan stared at the face, feeling his own mouth drop open. Suddenly, the odd dreams he'd been having all his life made sense. The Sleeper looked like *him*. He goggled, appealing to the others to reassure him that he was seeing what he was seeing. They were all staring at the Sleeper. Blindly, Leonora put out a hand to make certain he was still standing beside her. She looked from him to the giant and back again. Her lips were parted in amazement.

"So you are dreaming one of the provinces of the Dreamland," Bergold said, in a thoughtful whisper. "I wonder which one."

"It isn't me," Roan said, his voice rising. The Sleepers stirred at the sound. The noise died away in the heavy air.

"Shh!" Bergold whispered, clapping his hand over his friend's mouth. "It *is*."

"We'll argue that later," Glinn hissed. "We must deal with Brom! There they are!"

Dwarfed by the huge beds, the scientists were in the center of the floor, setting up the Alarm Clock, which looked like a toy compared with the huge Sleepers. A plump figure, Brom himself, stood a little apart from the others, supervising the construction. In his hand he held a brass key as long as his arm. The apprentices were working silently, making adjustments to the device with padded tools. Their shoes were covered in cloth bags to prevent accidental noises. The precaution seemed ironic, when Roan considered that in a few moments the chief scientist intended to set off the din to end the world. A few of the others were setting up monitoring devices, standing by with pads of paper, and big movie cameras complete with hooded lenses and side cranks, preparing to record the event.

The Alarm Clock, unveiled, looked thoroughly menacing. The perverted sun at the top of its glass-covered dial gleamed with an evil light. Roan was even more terrified now of having the Sleepers awakened. If he vanished in this world, would he—or rather, his dreamer—die in the other? He didn't want to give up his life here. He wanted to go home and marry his true love.

Better not wait any longer. They did not know how long it would take until Brom was ready to proceed. The scientists could not retreat from here, or risk giving up their experiment. Roan's most pressing and immediate goal was to disable the Alarm Clock before it could go off. Roan gestured to the others to spread out, and they began to move in.

Taboret worked with deep concentration on her task. Her long-standing final order was to oil the gears of the clock so they would run smoothly and silently. Brom told them he would give no verbal orders once they breached the hall. But they all knew what to do.

According to the diagram, there were exactly ten thousand gears and wheels inside the clock mechanism. One hundred to the power of two. Though the gestalt was broken, there was still a vestigial trace of overlap and synchronicity of movement with the other apprentices. She found herself looking up occasionally when the others did. The Countingsheep brothers were the only ones who truly mourned the loss of concord. The atmosphere was brisk, but not unfriendly. She concentrated on her job to avoid thinking about what was going to happen in a few moments. Brom would wind up the clock with the key in his hands. The bells would ring, and the Sleepers would all wake up.

If only Glinn could have been there with her, there at the end of the world, she could discontinue happily. A thought intruded into her mind.

But I am, said a voice in her mind.

She looked up. Glinn was walking toward her, healthy, handsome and whole. He had to be an illusion. He was dead.

No, said the silent voice. *I'm here*. He smiled.

"Glinn," she said out loud. And all calamity broke loose.

The single spoken word caused another ripple of movement among the Sleepers. A scatter rug the size of an island rolled itself up, and would have taken Roan with it if he hadn't thrown himself onto the stone floor. Bats came down from the ceiling in swift, silent clouds and blanketed all the humans, stifling them in huge, flannel wings to stop the intrusive sound. Roan pushed them away, trying not to make any noise, but it was almost impossible. The impact of a shoe on the floor, a gasp, or a cry of pain set off more reaction from the Sleepers, which gave rise to further clusters of illusion. Each sound was swallowed up in silence almost as soon as it was made, but they all disturbed the Sleepers' repose and created more illusions to defend them. Roan had to muster all his sanity to keep from being driven mad.

Luckily, the scientists were as beset as themselves. Roan fought free of the enveloping folds of bat-cloth, and kicked off his boots. Running lightly on the balls of his bare feet toward Brom, he opened out his quarterstaff and padded it with the fabric of his cloak.

Brom clawed the last of the bats off his face, and threw it away from him. He turned and saw Roan coming toward him. His red eyes glaring, he thrust out his hand, palm outward to halt Roan.

A burst of power rushed toward Roan and struck him in the chest. Roan staggered but did not stop. He stalked Brom, and held out his open hand, silently demanding the key. The red eyes flashed fire, and Brom whirled the key around in a circle, making it into a huge brass staff.

I'll give you the key, a voice said in Roan's head. *In your insides!*

Brom feinted with the wards toward Roan's head, then quickly twisted the looped end upward, aiming for Roan's crotch.

Roan had nearly forgotten what a dirty in-fighter Brom was. He jumped backward, just saving himself from disabling pain. He brought the padded staff around and connected with Brom's shoulder. Brom glared at him, his face red, but he had his teeth gritted together to keep from crying out loud. Clearly, he did not want to trigger the Sleepers' defenses before his experiment was ready. He waved to his assistants, who, with nervous looks over their shoulders at the giant forms of the Sleepers, rushed to join the fray.

Brom swung the key at Roan's head again. Just in time, Roan brought up the staff to stop the blow, and pushed the brass rod down toward the ground. He swung his foot over it, intending to trap the key on the floor so Brom couldn't use it as a weapon, but the chief scientist was too quick for him. He snatched it away, and shot it forward into Roan's stomach.

Gasping, Roan staggered backward, and Brom slammed the key down on his bare foot. Tears flooded Roan's eyes, but he swallowed the yell that came bubbling up his throat. *Must not scream. Must not scream.* It was hard to fight someone without making any noise.

Brom swung again. Roan ducked, and ducked again, trying to time the swings so he could reach up and disarm his opponent. The other apprentices surrounded Roan, reaching for his arms and legs. Luckily, they were more suited to scientific tasks, not strategic ones. They got in one another's way more often than they impeded the King's Investigator. Roan threw handfuls of influence in every direction, padding them well so they would cause an impact but no noise. Scientists went flying in every direction, much farther than Roan was normally capable of making them go. The proximity of the Sleepers seemed to cause an overload of reaction. He tightened his control, and threw only pinches of power instead. Unfortunately, making his enemies land softly enabled them to get up and attack again, almost at once.

Bergold appeared beside Roan in the shape of a fat-bellied python. He flicked his forked tongue playfully before lashing out his long tail to trip one of the two identical apprentices about to leap upon Roan. Misha pushed the other twin, who fell into Bergold's coils. The historian-snake snapped around him and squeezed. The twin exhaled and turned red.

The apprentices seemed to beset the king's party from every side. Misha used a measure of influence to form a rope. The young man vanished in the center of a coil the size of a well. The identical twins scaled the sides of the heap and jumped on him. Roan lost sight of them when a couple more of the apprentices tried to jump him from behind with the tarpaulin from the Alarm Clock. He wrapped them in their own rug, and turned just in time to avoid a blow from Brom. He countered, trying to knock the key from Brom's hands. Without it, the Clock was useless.

A man in blue and white sought to capture Colenna in a lacy potpourri puff the size of a barrel. She produced a scissors and cut it into tiny segments of net and herbs. Roan worried the *snick* of the scissors would cause a further backlash from the Sleepers, and he was right. The pieces of net fluttered up, instead of down, and grew into strands that tied Colenna up with her attacker. Roan heard the *snick-snick-snick* of her scissors, but didn't watch the results.

Two women chased Leonora around the sleeping chamber, trying to corner her. Roan was torn whether to abandon Brom to defend her, but he did not have to. Where influence reigned, she was self-sufficient. She ran to the shelter of a tremendous plush teddy bear, which she animated and sent after them. The last time Roan saw the women, they were fleeing from the amiable-looking stuffed toy, lurching glassy-eyed after them. Leonora was getting the hang of the enhancement to her normal gifts. In fact, it looked as if she was enjoying herself. Roan admired her. When they had first set out after Brom, he had thought Leonora to be a helpless court lady, skilled in coping with domestic and diplomatic crises, but unfit to handle danger. She had proved herself the equal of any of her experienced companions.

Roan had no time to appreciate the irony. Three of the male apprentices separated and began to move in on him.

Roan swung his staff around, making them jump backward. He caught the third one solidly in the temple, and the young man collapsed with a gasp. He wouldn't get up for a while. Before Roan could turn around, another of them rushed up behind him, swung out a leg, and tripped him to the ground. All three sat upon him, striking him with their fists, reason and caution forgotten. Gritting his teeth, Roan heaved upward with a burst of influence, sending the men hurtling toward the ceiling. So they wouldn't make any noise when they landed, he formed a huge net to catch them and tie them up. No more soft landings. He had to keep them from coming back at him. The price of failure was too great.

As soon as he regained his feet, he saw Brom. The chief scientist had taken advantage of the melee to run back to the Alarm Clock. Nothing seemed to deter him from his evil purpose. Brom inserted the long brass key into the back, and began to wind it. Roan ran at him, knocking him backwards, away from the device. He must not activate the Clock. Roan would die rather than let him set it off.

Brom still maintained a hold on the key. He used it as a bludgeon to batter Roan over the head and shoulders. Roan tried to shield himself, but Brom was as powerful as he. The scientist pushed away Roan's protective shell of influence, leaving him vulnerable to the attack. Blood running into his eyes, Roan fell to his hands and knees, and Brom raised the key over his head for the coup de grace.

Suddenly, a huge shadow passed silently overhead. Bergold, in the shape of an immense red owl, flew over them. He extended his talons, and snatched the key out of Brom's hands, and winged upward, leaving him unarmed. Roan staggered to his feet. He leaped at Brom, clasping him around the arms, and formed a glass bubble about them both. The glass around them was thick, and acted as a magnifying lens. Everything around them looked bigger than before. Roan felt like a dust mote in the presence of the universe, and only he stood between it and destruction.

"Stop, you fool, " he said to Brom, in an urgent hiss. "If you waken them it will be the end of all of us." He grabbed Brom by the hair and tilted his head back toward the nearest bed, where his avatar slept. "You must not awaken *him*."

Brom glared at Roan, then looked up over Roan's shoulder, then back to Roan, and his face slackened into a mask of astonishment.

"No!" he breathed. "Impossible!" Then he broke free of Roan's grip. The bubble shattered into fragments and he began to fight like a dozen insane giants, battering and kicking with all the force that was left in him. "No!" he screamed. The Sleepers' defenses flooded in upon the noise, stifling and smothering. Monsters and nuisances attacked Roan from all sides. Telephone solicitors implored him to buy siding. Girl scouts in green skirts offered him cookies. Men in long saffron robes stuck flowers in his face. All the while, Brom belabored him with his fists and feet.

Roan defended himself as best he could, raising the staff to deflect blows, trying to avoid using any but the barest touches of influence to dispel the nuisances. He must stay focused upon his opponent, and not allow any distractions to claim his attention. He had a new advantage. Brom's sanity had fled, and with it his superior control of influence. In fact, Brom ought to be vulnerable to control of influence, now. Roan dodged Brom's fists, striking out with his staff, attempting to concentrate on a safe transformation for the chief scientist, but he slipped in a patch of his own blood as a miniature fury created by the sounds of the melee swooped down on him and clutched his hair. Roan tripped, hit the ground, and lost hold of his multiple-bladed weapon. The staff flipped out of its enveloping cloak and clattered to the floor, causing more disruption among the Sleepers. Roan crawled for it on hands and knees, but Brom grabbed it first, quick as a snake, and smashed him over the back with it. Roan fell flat.

"Roan!" Leonora's voice cried out and was swallowed up in stifling silence. Roan glanced about for the princess, letting his attention wander for only a second from Brom. The chief scientist took the opportunity to slam the staff down on his shoulder. Roan gasped and fell. Brom raised the staff again. Roan used influence to help him to his feet. He was whisked almost into the air, remembering too late to damp down on how much power he used. Brom swung for him. Roan reached delicately into the stuff of matter, and draped him in ropes and chains to hold him still until his fury passed. Brom dismissed it all with a sneer, and rushed toward him, weapon high. Roan was taken by surprise. Brom leaped on him and began to choke him against the floor with his own quarterstaff.

Leonora started to run to Roan's rescue, then thought better of it. Instead, she picked up one of the metal rods on the floor, and struck the alarm bells as hard as she could.

The ringing echoed throughout the hall. One of the Sleepers yawned in her sleep and began to rouse. Then, another twitched and felt out at the side of his bed for the gigantic, steaming mug that sat on his bedside table. Then, another moved, until they were all stirring. Everyone, scientists and defenders alike, stopped fighting for a moment, and stared at the huge beds. Leonora stood beside the device and saw what she had done. The Sleepers were waking up.

"Yes!" Brom shouted, exultant. He stood up and threw away the staff. He raised his arms in joyful triumph. "Yes, my precious experiment! We will see the outcome at last! Wake up, everyone! Wake up!"

"No!" Roan cried. He threw himself on the bell of the Alarm Clock, grasping the edge with his hands, to stop the noise. With a snarl, Brom pulled at his legs, trying to drag him off.

The vibration of the bells drove right into Roan's head. He gritted his teeth, ignoring the pain. The bells were trying to change him, but he, the unchangeable, resisted it. He used all his influence to stop the chiming.

"Shush," Roan whispered, willing it to be true. "Quiet. Silence!" The racket of the bell deadened slowly into silence. Roan let out a sigh of relief. The Sleepers slowly settled back into their dreams, but reality had been shaken. The room was full of illusions, nuisances, and influence—but not enough to destroy the world.

Brom's red eyes nearly popped out of his head.

"You fool," he said, snarling. He leaped for Roan, his hands out for the man's throat.

Roan slid down from the Alarm Clock, careful not to disturb it again. He backed away from it, drawing Brom into the midst of the chaos. Quickly, before the chief scientist could look back, he threw up a fountain of influence that enclosed the Alarm Clock in a ring of fire. That should keep the apprentices from trying to complete their master's work.

The room had filled with manifestations of dreams, to protect the Sleepers from the unexpected disturbance. Rugs whirled like falling leaves, knocking people apart and pushing them over. Monsters crawled out from under the beds and threatened to disembowel the humans. A crowd of little gray-haired ladies interrupted the individual battles that were going on around the vast chamber.

"Now, now, what would your mother say?" a granny asked a short, sour-faced apprentice who was attacking the Bergold-owl. "Play nice!" He ignored her, striking out at Bergold. The owl fluttered up out of reach, but the granny took hold of the apprentice by one ear, and marched him toward the door of the chamber. "You're going to your room, young man!"

One by one, the apprentices were carried off by nuisances. The twin brothers, stripped stark naked and painted blue, were carried off on horseback by the Seventh Cavalry. The two older women joined a mob of happy people dressed in loud, flowered shirts and short pants doing a dance that involved rhythmically touching their arms and heads, and shimmied off into the shadows. In a short time, the scientists were all gone except one young woman who was wrapped in Glinn's arms and staring up rapturously into his eyes.

Roan had no time to congratulate himself. Suddenly, he was blindfolded and spun around in a circle by a bunch of little girls in party dresses with bows in their hair. When the blindfold was taken off, he was left alone facing Brom.

"It is only the two of us now," said the chief scientist, his broad face a mask of hate. He brushed away a Sleeper-sent shower of pillows as if it was confetti. His madness might have robbed him of control, but it gave him strength.

Roan steeled himself. All right, he thought at the Sleeper with his face. If I am any connection to you at all, aid me now!

Brom raised his hands, and they were full of fire. Rounding them together, he made a ball, and flung it two-handed at Roan. Roan threw himself to one side. The fireball whizzed past him with a crackle. Brom formed another, and another. Roan countered with handfuls of anti-air that snuffed out the fireballs as if they were matches. Brom clapped his hands together. The fireballs vanished, but invisible walls full of spikes began to press in on Roan from all sides, crushing him.

Don't scream, he told himself, though he was gasping with pain. *Think!* With a surge of his own influence Roan blunted the spikes, but Brom's mad power crushed the walls inward. Roan felt his bones grind against one another. He called upon his reserves to save himself from being mashed flat. The flames around the Alarm Clock abruptly went out. Roan looked at Brom. The chief scientist smiled.

With a burst of influence, Roan destroyed one wall, but the other three formed a triangle, tighter than the square. Mustering his strength, he knocked out another, and was sandwiched between the two remaining. Roan pushed out at them, drawing painful breaths sideways. He was getting tired, but he must not flag. All existence depended upon him. Brom closed in on him, grinning, enjoying the sight of his enemy in torment.

Roan managed to dissolve one of the two walls, but the last and strongest wall shifted until it was in front of him, and pressed him back against the bedstead belonging to his enormous avatar. Roan put all the strength he had left into a single thrust. The wall shattered loudly into invisible shards.

Brom howled with anger as the recoil of power hit him. The last vestige of humanity vanished from his face. A change came over him. He sprouted coarse, black fur, and his teeth became twisted, razorlike spikes. He was truly dangerous now, but also more vulnerable. Roan looked around for Bergold, or Misha, or any of the others to help him. He saw no one. He knew his friends were there in the Hall somewhere, but the Sleepers had chosen him to make this final battle. He must succeed alone.

Brom advanced upon him, his eyes glowing red slits. Roan knew Brom was truly vulnerable to change now. His heart still insisted upon mercy, regardless of his anger. *Render him harmless*, his mind said, even as the beast raised its talons to tear out his throat. Defensively, Roan reached out with all his influence. He dragged the coarse hair out into long ropes that wound themselves around and around the Brom-monster, pinioning his arms. Roan made the beast's clawlike toenails lengthen and penetrate into the honey-brown stone floor, stopping him in his tracks. Perhaps when the chief scientist calmed down, he'd be more manageable.

The beast struggled in his bonds, growling and snorting his fury. Roan backed away, preparing another change if it should be needed. With a roar that was swallowed up in the vastness of the Hall, Brom thrust out his huge arms and tore the ropes of hair asunder. As Roan watched in astonishment, Brom picked his feet out of the stone a toe at a time, and moved in on Roan. Brom could only just manipulate reality, yet he could break down the barriers he made like a scythe cutting grass. The beast grew in size, until he was nearly as high as one of the Sleepers' beds. Roan tried to control it, but influence behaved so strangely that it outstripped his control.

The pupils of Brom's eyes slitted. Smoke poured out of nostrils grown huge in a long face. He tore at his chest with his claws, revealing scaly skin of poison green. His arms lengthened and flattened out into translucent green sails that spread, blotting out the rest of the chamber. Roan recognized the dragon Brom and the gestalt had brought into being in the royal court of Mnemosyne. He threw more influence, hoping to control the beast, but all his thrusts went wild, adding to the stuff of the dragon. Brom's eyes glowed with glee. The dragon was a manifestation of himself, but it was also a true part of the Collective Unconscious. Because it was a natural creature, a mere Dreamlander couldn't destroy it, and Roan had less effect upon it than he would on an ordinary nightmare beast such as Brom had just been. Roan scooted backwards, scrabbling for control over those parts of the dragon which were Brom, but they were indistinguishable from the rest.

The Brom-dragon drew in a wheezing hiss, preparing to incinerate him with its fiery breath. Roan made a shield of all his remaining strength, and dropped to his knees behind it on the floor. Brom exhaled. Roan braced himself against the flood of fire that smashed against his shield. He cringed from the heat, mentally begging the Sleepers for help. Send something, he pleaded. *Anything!*

"Sell IBM! No, buy! Buy IBM!"

Suddenly, he was enveloped in a crowd of men and women, all in white shirts and ties, chattering into their cellular telephones. They pulled Roan to his feet, and took the dragon by its paws. They twirled Brom around, chanting arcane invocations.

"Microsoft at 130! AT&T at 45! P&G at 80!"

"No!" Brom shouted in a terrible roar. "I must not be robbed of my revenge! I must kill him! Let me go!"

Still shouting bids, the investment brokers formed a conga line, sweeping Roan and Brom up with them, hustling them toward the door. The Brom-dragon struggled to get loose, but they kept a tight hold on him, walking and talking and dancing. As he was pushed along, the dragon became a human again, and slowly, his white-and-blue robes turned into a charcoal gray suit. A cellular phone suddenly appeared in his hand, and his face assumed an expression of the utmost horror. He, too, was becoming an investment broker.

They cha-cha'ed toward the threshold. On it, a tunnel opened up, full of whirling green numbers and flowing rows of strange acronyms. Roan fought against the arms that held him around the waist, but this nuisance had been sent by the Sleepers, and was far stronger than his influence. The conga line moved inexorably towards the tunnel. Brom screamed in terror. Roan fought with every ounce of strength he had.

Just before they reached the threshold, the man behind Roan gave him a hard shove that sent him sprawling on the tiled floor, and tipped him a merry salute as he disappeared through the round portal. The investment brokers vanished down the glowing tunnel, taking Brom with them. He had the phone to his ear, and he was talking to it as if he'd done it all his life. Appropriately, Roan thought, the chief scientist had become part of the nuisance. The tunnel shrank out of sight, and the great room fell quiet again.

Roan clambered to his feet, and ran to see where the other scientists had gone. He dashed out into the antechamber, searching for signs of life. No one was outside except Spar and his guards, four lanky, mustachioed soldiers in wool uniforms with gaiters and flattened tin helmets, sitting at their ease on the stone shelf around a small campfire. Spar pinched out a cigarette between his fingertip and thumb, and nudged the others. They rose respectfully to their feet. Roan scanned the room. The two mercenaries were lying on the floor beside them, neatly trussed up with standard military knots. Brom was nowhere to be seen.

"Is it all over?" the captain asked, looking up at Roan.

"Yes," Roan said, hardly daring to believe it himself. "It's all over."

On tiptoe, Roan led them back into the Hall of the Sleepers and looked around. The chamber was serenely quiet. All illusions were gone. His boots stood neatly beside the threshold with the others where he had left them. They'd been cleaned and polished.

In the middle of the floor stood the Alarm Clock. It was sealed into a block of amber, probably by the last vestige of the Sleepers' attention before they settled back into their slumbers. Roan walked over and tested the integrity of the matter with all his strength, and found he couldn't budge it at all. It was solid, on every level. Perhaps his friends were right that he and the avatar had a lot in common: they, too, preferred to render harmless without destroying. He was satisfied. The Alarm Clock could never be used again to disturb their repose. The Dreamland would never have to fear it. The Sleepers would sleep on soundly, as they had from the beginning of the world.

Beside the block someone had made a transparent dome like half a soap bubble. Underneath, Bergold, Misha, Colenna, Glinn with his ladylove, and the princess Leonora were standing together, staring up at the Sleeper that was and was not Roan. Roan and the guards passed through the pliant wall and joined them inside. Leonora looked up at Roan lovingly, and he put his arm around her. She was safe, and so was her realm. They had succeeded.

"It's a silence bubble," she explained, pointing up at the clear dome. "We can talk in here. They haven't budged an inch since we put it up."

"Good thinking," Roan said. Leonora smiled.

"I had the example of a good leader before me."

"It's a wonder in here, sir," Lum said, looking around with his eyes popped halfway out of their sockets. He caught a glimpse of the Sleeper above them. "Great night!"

"It's not me, Corporal," Roan said, but it was no good. The young soldier regarded him with delighted awe.

"Think of the benefit to historians everywhere," Bergold said, happily making notes in the blank pages of his pocket archive. "Being able to observe the Sleepers themselves at close range. Every single one will want to take a turn."

Roan chuckled.

Glinn presented his young woman to Roan. "This is Taboret. I could not have succeeded as well as I did without her."

"I did try to help," the young woman said, shyly. "I was careless, but I'm glad it all worked out. I did what I could. Princess, I'm sorry I had to . . . do those things to you."

"I understand," Leonora said, patting her hand. "No hard feelings." Taboret looked relieved and awed. Glinn hugged her closely.

"We owe you our thanks," Roan said to them. "Both of you. It will be in my report to the king."

"I hope you'll speak to Carodil on our behalf," Glinn said. "Someone will have to answer for Brom's actions and we're the only ones left."

"That will not be a problem," Leonora said, definitely. "I will explain everything to my father. Everything that I can explain, that is." She looked significantly at Roan.

"How strange," he said, staring up at the great face. "So all along, there was a reason why I never changed. I was an image dreamed by another who looked like me."

"Incredible," Colenna said. "You, or rather, he must have a very stable personality. There've been a thousand Sleepers since the world began, and I have never before heard of a man who stayed the same all his life. Someone should have guessed the connection."

"How could they know?" Leonora asked. "No one has ever found their way here before."

"Do you know," Bergold said, with a chuckle, "I never checked the dates." He pulled the little archive out of his pouch and thumbed through it. "Yes," he said, pointing to an entry. "You were born at the time of a Changeover, you know."

"Yes, I know. My mother told me," Roan said.

"Which province was it?" Leonora asked.

"Celestia," Bergold said, with a broad smile. The others let out wordless exclamations. "Yes, that's right. It looks as if you're dreaming the center of the Dreamland. And I can't think of anyone in whose hands we would be better off."

"Bergold!" Roan protested. "He's not me!"

"It's a fact, my boy," Bergold said, slapping him on the back. "You can't get away from facts, any more than you can change the face you were born with. And now we see what a noble countenance that is, eh? It would explain why you never have changed. You were born to the job. You're dreaming us all."

"I am not a Sleeper!" Roan protested. "He is. He's dreaming me, too!"

"Shh!" Bergold said, a finger to his lips, as the Roan-giant stirred and nudged his blue and red blankets with his foot. "Calm down. He feels your agitation, even if he can't hear you."

"This puts you far above us poor mortals," Leonora whispered, solemnly. Her eyes were huge and luminous, and she looked very lovely. "What does it mean when you are dreaming me?"

Roan swept her into his arms and kissed her.

"It proves that you truly are the woman of my dreams," he said. "I couldn't imagine a more perfect love than you, or I suppose I—He—would have. Why are you smiling?"

"I was just thinking," she said, twirling the locket at her throat with a dreamy look. "Now my father can't possibly have any objection at all to me marrying you."